WYOMING WEDDINGS

THREE-IN-ONE COLLECTION

DIANA LESIRE BRANDMEYER
SUSAN PAGE DAVIS
VICKIE MCDONOUGH

BARBOUR
PUBLISHING

Trail to Justice © 2009 by Susan Page Davis
Hearts on the Road © 2009 by Diana Lesire Brandmeyer
A Wagonload of Trouble © 2009 by Vickie McDonough

ISBN 978-1-61626-124-5

All scripture quotations are taken from the King James Version of the Bible.

This book is a work of fiction. Names, characters, places, and incidents are either products of the author's imagination or used fictitiously. Any similarity to actual people, organizations, and/or events is purely coincidental.

Cover Design: Kirk DouPonce, DogEared Design

Published by Barbour Publishing, Inc., P.O. Box 719, Uhrichsville, Ohio 44683, www.barbourbooks.com

Our mission is to publish and distribute inspirational products offering exceptional value and biblical encouragement to the masses.

ecpa Member of the
Evangelical Christian
Publishers Association

Printed in the United States of America.

TRAIL TO JUSTICE

Susan Page Davis

Dedication

To Vickie McDonough and Diane Brandmeyer.
Working with you two on this series was a joy. I wish you
great success in your writing careers and joy in the Lord.

Acknowledgment

Thank you, Carl Wiggin, for advice on the airplane-related
sections of this book. Any mistakes are totally my fault.

Chapter 1

Ruby Dale let her palomino gelding, Lancelot, canter across the prairie toward home. They'd had a good workout—twenty miles plus—but Lancelot was still ready to go. In two weeks he'd demonstrate his mettle at the Wyoming 100 competitive trail ride, but she didn't need that proof to know he was at the peak of condition. Both were more than ready for the hundred-mile ride.

This was what she loved—getting out away from the claustrophobic atmosphere at home and her stressful job at the police station, alone with her horse. The burnished gold palomino had given her many hours of comfort in the last few years. If only Julie were riding beside her.

She was about to pull Lancelot down to a walk to cool him off when he missed his footing. He stumbled, lurching to the side. Ruby flew forward onto his neck, clutching desperately at his mane. She slid down his shoulder but tried to push herself upright as the horse recovered and found his footing again. Too late. Her center of gravity had shifted too far. She wouldn't be able to get back up into the saddle.

"Whoa, boy!" she called as she slipped down his side. For a moment she hung helpless, clinging to his mane. Her foot inched over the saddle. This was always the worst instant of a fall, not knowing how you'd land. She tucked her head and pushed off, falling hard on her left shoulder, and rolled quickly away from the horse's hooves. For a long moment she lay panting in the dry grass assessing her pains. Nothing major. Good thing, or her parents would have fits and forbid her to ride alone, even though she was twenty-four and well into adulthood.

Slowly she raised her head. Lancelot had halted and stood shivering a few yards away. She rose stiffly and stretched out her limbs. Nothing broken, but she'd have some colorful bruises by morning. She hobbled to the palomino's side and stroked his withers. "Are you all right?"

She grasped his reins and urged him to walk forward. Lancelot gave a decided hop to avoid putting weight on his off front hoof. Ruby ducked under his neck to his right side.

"Let me look, fella." She bent to lift his front foot, and Lancelot raised it for her. "Oh, man. Lost a shoe." She surveyed the chipped horn around the edge of his hoof. "I was going to have the blacksmith come next week, but I guess we need to get him over here sooner." She sighed. "I hope you're all right." She unbuttoned the pocket on her denim shirt and pulled out her cell phone. Her father insisted she always carry it on her long rides, and though she sometimes felt a bit smothered, this time she was grateful.

"Hey, Dad? It's me. Lancelot threw a shoe."

"What? Are you okay?"

"Yeah, I'm fine. I don't think he's hurt either, but I'm going to walk him home. We're only about a mile out."

"Let me come get you."

"No, really. We're okay. We'll just take our time." She glanced down at the palomino's feet. He was holding his right front foot off the ground.

"Where are you?" her father asked. "I can hitch up the trailer and come after you."

"Well. . .okay. Maybe that would be best. We're near the Danbridge Road." She looked around. "Maybe a half mile past Simpsons'."

"Okay, I'll be there in ten minutes."

"Thanks. We'll get up to the edge of the road." She put the phone away and patted Lancelot's neck. "Okay, boy. Let's go."

She led him slowly through the grass, and Lancelot kept pace with only a slight limp. Still, it was enough to worry her. Would it keep him from entering the ride two weeks from today? She opened her phone again and keyed in the number for the veterinary clinic. Dr. John Hogan, the senior doctor in the practice, answered.

"Hi, Dr. Hogan. This is Ruby Dale. My horse threw a shoe, and I wondered if you or Dr. Sullivan could look at him. We're training for a competitive ride, and I don't want to keep exercising him if it's going to hurt him."

"Sure, Ruby. Let's see. Chuck is off today, but I'll give him a buzz and see if he's able to stop by. If he can't, I'll come over in about an hour. Is that all right?"

"It's perfect. Thank you."

She pocketed the phone and resumed the walk up to the roadbed. By the time she and Lancelot climbed up the grassy bank, a cloud of dust in the distance told her that her father was on his way.

❧

The veterinarian's pickup rolled into the driveway a half hour later. Ruby hurried out to meet him, surprised after what Dr. Hogan had told her it was Dr. Chuck Sullivan responding. Not only that, but his truck was pulling a horse trailer. Lancelot seemed to have recovered his animation, and he trotted back and forth in his paddock and whinnied. An answering neigh erupted from the trailer.

"Hi! Thanks for coming on a Saturday," Ruby called as Chuck got out of the truck. She'd managed to skirt the issue of her own fall, and her parents were satisfied she was all right. If they'd thought she was injured, Mom and Dad would be out there watching her like a couple of hypervigilant hawks.

"No problem," Chuck said. "This actually worked out well for me. I was just on my way home from a long ride. I took Rascal up to the hills this morning."

Ruby glanced toward the trailer. "Rascal is your horse? I didn't know you had one."

Chuck grinned, clearly pleased with his mount. "Yeah, I got him last spring. He's an Appaloosa. I've been riding him a lot, and we're starting to get comfortable with each other. Want to see him?"

"Sure." Ruby followed him to the rear of the trailer.

Chuck lowered the back door that made a loading ramp. The horse's well-muscled haunches were a snowy white, flecked with dark spots in a flamboyant blanket pattern. Chuck climbed the ramp into the empty side of the trailer, and Ruby followed. Her pulse accelerated as the horse whinnied again and tossed his head.

"Easy now." Chuck stroked the gelding's cheek.

"He's beautiful." Ruby reached out to pat the warm, dark withers. "How old?"

"Seven."

"Perfect."

"Yeah," Chuck said. "I figure he's the prime age for endurance riding."

"You're getting into distance riding?" Ruby looked up eagerly into his blue eyes.

"I sure am. You know I've volunteered for a couple of years at the Wyoming 100, and I've been jealous of the riders. I decided to let someone else man the checkpoint this year and compete myself."

"That's great." More than great, Ruby thought. "I'm riding, too."

"Terrific. Lancelot and Rascal will get to know each other." Chuck gave Rascal a soft slap on the neck and turned away.

Ruby swallowed hard and looked out toward the paddock. "That is, I'm riding if Lancelot's foot is okay."

"We'd better take a look. Dr. Hogan said you had a little mishap?"

She nodded. "Yeah, we were loping across a field, and Lancelot threw a shoe and stumbled. He limped a little at first, but now that he's had a short rest he's putting weight on it again. I probably got you out here for nothing."

"Let's hope you're right."

Ruby hated to end the moment of camaraderie, but she edged over to the ramp and walked down it. Chuck stopped at his truck to retrieve his on-the-road medical case. "Okay, do you want to hold him while I examine him?"

"I'll put him in the cross ties." Ruby went to the paddock fence where Lancelot waited eagerly, his muzzle over the top of the gate. She grabbed his halter and swung the gate open with her other hand. The palomino walked meekly beside her into the barn and let her hitch him in the alley between the stalls, with a rope clipped to the rings on each side of his halter.

"Looking good so far. I can't even tell which leg."

"Oh, it's the right front."

Chuck ran a hand down Lancelot's off foreleg and lifted his hoof. "I always know I'll see a healthy horse when I come here, Ruby."

"Thank you." She stood by Lancelot's head and scratched beneath his forelock.

"How's your training for the ride going?" Chuck asked.

"Good until today. We've been doing ten miles or so mornings and one longer ride on the weekends." *Calm down,* she told herself. She sounded like an eager twelve-year-old. She shrugged with a little laugh. "I'm starting to believe we'll be able to finish."

"Sure you will."

"I don't know," she said. "We did two fifty-milers last year, but this will be our first one-hundred."

"Well, it's my first long ride, too. But the woman who owned Rascal had been training him for a while before I bought him, and I think he's ready." Chuck turned to his medical case and pulled out a file. "I don't feel any swelling or hot spots on his leg. I'm going to smooth this hoof up a little so he doesn't chip it any worse before the blacksmith comes."

"Thanks," Ruby said. "Dad called him, and he said he'll come Monday. I won't ride Lancelot tomorrow."

"That's wise." Chuck bent over the horse's hoof again. "Still working at the police station?"

"Yes."

"How's that going?"

"I love it," Ruby said, "but I've been putting in a lot of hours lately. They need to hire one more dispatcher to fill out the schedule."

"Cutting into your riding time?"

She nodded. "Some. I've had to pull a few double shifts lately while the officers were out chasing cocaine dealers. That doesn't happen often, though."

"I hope not. I imagine they want their dispatchers to stay alert."

She'd liked Chuck since she'd first met him three years ago. Okay, more than liked him. But she'd tried not to make it too obvious. Perhaps as a result she'd never had a chance to get to know him well. The older veterinarian, Dr. Hogan, had brought Chuck on board in his practice to handle the large animal part of the business. Chuck had quickly become a favorite with ranchers and horse enthusiasts. Whenever he came to tend to Lancelot—which was only a couple of times a year—she got to spend a few minutes chatting with him and then spent weeks going over the conversation in her mind.

He set Lancelot's hoof down gently and patted his shoulder. "I really don't see anything wrong. Why don't we wrap this overnight? You can call me if he's limping tomorrow."

"Okay." She held the halter firmly while Chuck got out a bandage and wound it around the horse's pastern and cannon. Lancelot nickered, and Ruby stroked his long, smooth cheek.

"All set." Chuck stood and smiled at her over Lancelot's withers.

Right there. That smile. That was what put her in a dither. Last year they'd both attended a picnic for the volunteers working at the Wyoming 100. That was when she'd first begun to imagine Chuck liked her, too. But she'd been so busy all winter, and her horse was so annoyingly healthy, that their paths had only crossed a few times since. He'd given Lancelot a complete checkup in the spring before she began intense training for the hundred-mile ride, and she'd seen him twice over the summer—once at a horse show and again in the foreign foods section of the grocery store, of all places, where they'd discovered they both loved Chinese food. She'd wondered at the time if he thought he was too old for her—there must be six or seven years' difference in their ages. But neither of them was a kid anymore, and the older they got, the less that would matter.

"I guess we're done." Chuck was still smiling at her, as though he almost wished he had more to do at the Dales' house today.

"Great. That's a gorgeous Appaloosa you've got, Chuck. I hope you have a good time at the ride."

"I expect I'll see you there."

"Yeah, I guess you will." Brainless comment. Why couldn't she come up with something better? She unsnapped the cross ties and led Lancelot out to the paddock. When she had let him go and closed the gate, she turned and saw Chuck standing by his pickup. She walked over, her pulse fluttering at the thought that he was waiting to speak to her again.

"Hey, I was thinking." He looked off toward the hills and laughed. "Something I do now and then."

"Really?" She couldn't help laughing, too.

"Yeah. And I was wondering why we couldn't do a training ride together sometime. Assuming Lancelot's none the worse for his little incident today, I mean. I want to take Rascal for a nice long ramble in the hills—say thirty or forty miles."

"That would be a great warm-up for the 100." She bit her bottom lip. He'd just asked her to spend a day with him. She felt the heat climbing her cheekbones. "It would be fun."

"That's what I thought. We did twenty this morning, but Rascal needs a few lengthier practice rides." He eyed her for a long moment, and she waited. "Could you do it next weekend if your horse is all right?"

"Yeah, I think so."

"Great." There was the dazzling smile again. Ruby had to look away. "I could come by with the double trailer, and we could drive up toward Powder

River and start our ride there. What do you think?"

"Fantastic. It would give Lancelot and me some new scenery to look at. How about if I pack a lunch?"

"Sounds good. But be sure to tell me if there's any problem with Lancelot. We don't want to take any chances with him."

"I will." She hoped desperately Lancelot wouldn't show any signs of pain tomorrow.

Chuck nodded and opened his truck door, smiling.

Ruby watched him drive out and waved as he pulled onto the road. Chuck waved back. She exhaled and looked over toward the paddock. Lancelot was rolling, all four feet thrashing, as he flopped back and forth on the turf. Ruby went over and leaned on the fence. "Did you hear that? We've got a date next weekend."

Lancelot rolled to his stomach and pushed himself up, front end first, then his hindquarters. He shook his head and shuddered all over, sending dust and bits of grass flying from his coat then pranced over to the fence and whinnied.

"You big baby." Ruby scratched his forehead, beneath his white forelock, and looked down the road in the direction Chuck had driven. She turned back to the horse. "I can't believe he finally asked me out. And for a trail ride. Does it get any better than this?"

❧

Chuck pulled into the yard at the Dale home early the next Saturday, anticipating an enjoyable outing but at the same time a little nervous. He hadn't dated anyone seriously since moving to the area, although several women had tried to snare his attention.

Seeing Martin Dale sitting in a rocker on the front porch didn't help. It struck Chuck that Ruby's father was watchdogging his daughter's social life—and Chuck was cast as the suspicious intruder.

"Good morning, Mr. Dale," he called as he exited the truck.

Ruby's father stood and came to the top of the porch steps, holding a white china mug. "Morning, Dr. Sullivan."

Chuck smiled as he walked toward him. "Please, call me Chuck."

"All right then. Ruby says you're going riding up in the hills today."

"Yes, sir. We're both training for the Wyoming 100, so I thought we could give the horses a workout together."

Mr. Dale nodded, his eyes slightly narrowed. "I suppose you know the trails up there."

"Not very well, but they're clearly marked."

"Well, Ruby's a good rider."

"I'm sure she is, sir."

Mr. Dale grunted and sipped his coffee.

"I assume Lancelot is all right," Chuck said. "Ruby said on Monday he seemed fine."

"Yes, she babied him for a couple of days, but she was saying last night he seemed right as rain."

"Great. Uh. . .is Ruby ready to go?"

"She's in the barn. You had breakfast?"

"Yes, I have. Thank you."

Her father nodded again and jerked his head toward the barn. "She's been out there for an hour. That palomino must be shiny enough so's you can see your face in his hide."

Chuck laughed. "She takes good care of him. Every time I see Lancelot, he looks like a pampered and contented horse."

"You'll watch out for her?"

"Of course."

"I suppose I sound like a meddling old nanny, but we don't know you very well, Doc."

Chuck gulped and tried not to let his smile slip as he took a step closer to him. "Sir, you don't have to worry about Ruby with me."

Their gazes locked for a moment, and her father pursed his lips. "All right then. Call me Martin." He shifted his coffee mug and extended his right hand. Chuck shook it solemnly, determined to live up to the implied promise.

Measured hoofbeats behind him told him Ruby and Lancelot had emerged from the barn. He turned just as Rascal let out a piercing whinny from inside the trailer.

"Hi," Ruby called, holding the lead rope firmly as Lancelot tossed his head and nickered, his ears pricked toward Chuck's rig. The palomino's rounded flanks really did gleam in the sunlight. Ruby looked ready to hit the trail in faded jeans and a blue-and-white striped T-shirt, topped by a denim jacket. Her glossy hair was caught back in a braid.

"Good morning. How's he doing?"

"He's fine," Ruby said. "Eager to go."

As Chuck walked around to lower the ramp on the trailer, Ruby's mother pushed open the screen door and came out of the house to stand beside Martin.

"Hello, Dr. Sullivan. I thought I heard you drive in. You two are getting an early start. Or should I say, 'you four'?"

Chuck laughed. "You're up early yourself, Mrs. Dale." It wasn't quite seven, the time he and Ruby had agreed on.

"It's hard to sleep in on Saturday when you're up early all week." She smiled at her daughter. "Want me to bring out your lunch cooler, honey?"

"That would be great, Mom."

Chuck reached for the lead rope. "I'll load him, unless you want to."

11

Ruby surrendered the lead, and Lancelot whickered, spewing a few drops of saliva on Chuck's shirt. Chuck spoke to him and patted his neck, and the horse went calmly up the ramp with him. A moment later Lancelot was secure beside Rascal, who pulled his head around as far as his tie-up would allow to inspect the newcomer.

Chuck left the trailer and found Martin ready to help him swing up the ramp. Ruby and her mother were settling a soft pack in the back of his pickup.

"I'll get your tack," Martin said and hurried to the barn. He returned with Ruby's saddle, blanket, and bridle, which Chuck stowed next to his own gear in the truck bed. They all said good-bye, and Chuck rounded the front of the truck with Ruby to open the passenger door for her. He realized how short she was—not quite to his shoulder. He offered his hand for a boost. She glanced at him with a quick smile, took his hand, and pushed against it for leverage as she swung up into the cab.

On the way to their destination Ruby was very quiet at first. As soon as he'd checked in his mirrors to be sure the trailer was rolling smoothly, Chuck looked over at her. "Thanks for coming. Sometimes I get kind of lonesome on the trail with nobody but Rascal to talk to."

A dainty dimple appeared at the corner of her smile. "Thanks for asking me. I usually ride alone now, and my folks worry about me."

"No kidding."

She laughed at his "could have fooled me" tone. "Yeah, they're afraid Lancelot will dump me somewhere and come back with an empty saddle."

"Well, some parents are a little overprotective." He glanced at her again. Her expression had gone sober.

"I guess they're allowed," she said. "I keep telling myself I need to move away from home and get a life, but I love Mom and Dad. And I know they'd miss me."

"Are you an only child?"

She hesitated. "I am now."

So. That explained a lot of things. The Dales kept their surviving child close. "I'm sorry," he said softly. They rode along in silence for a few minutes, and he was sure he'd put his foot in it.

As they passed a horse ranch, Ruby caught her breath. "Oh, look!" Several yearling colts raced each other across the broad pasture, heads held high and tails flying.

"I was out there a couple of weeks ago," Chuck said. "One of the mares was lame."

"I envy you." Her eyes were gentle brown, almost golden.

He looked away, straight ahead, but he could still picture them. "Why is that?"

"You get to work with animals, and you must be outside a lot on the job."

"Yeah, sometimes when I wish I could stay home. Rain, sleet, or snow I'm out there."

She chuckled, and his heart lurched. Her momentary sadness had passed, and she was ready to embark on a lighter thread of conversation.

"At least you have an interesting job." He hoped she would continue to talk. He liked the quiet flow of her voice.

"Yes, I admit it's not dull. But I sit there for hours with headphones on, taking calls. Fender benders, domestic disputes, prowlers, shoplifters. We get to take breaks, but sometimes it's so busy I forget. I usually go out of the police station on my supper break, though, just for a change of scenery and to stretch my legs."

"That's a good idea for people with sedentary jobs."

She nodded. "Yeah. But since I work from four in the afternoon until 2:00 a.m., it's dark out at suppertime after we turn the clocks back."

"You get off at two o'clock in the morning? That's a long shift."

"Yeah. I do four 'tens' a week. The officers are good about escorting us to our cars when we change shifts, so the security part of it doesn't bother me. Sometimes I get sleepy toward the end, though, and then I have to drive home late. But I do like having most of my days free. I can ride for an hour or two just about every day and more on my off days."

"I hear you. It's been hard for me to carve out the time, but I love riding."

They'd reached the foothills. He pulled in to a grassy place off the road. Two other vehicles were parked there, one with an empty ATV trailer behind it.

"I'll bet the horses will be glad to get out and have a look at each other," Ruby said.

Chuck smiled at that and tried to imagine being tied up in a trailer beside a stranger and having to ride next to him. He got out of the pickup. Ruby met him at the back of the rig, and he lowered the ramp. When their owners unhitched them, both horses backed down to solid ground, whinnying to each other. Chuck showed Ruby where to tie Lancelot securely. He hooked Rascal to a rope on the other side of the trailer, and they both saddled up.

"Did you want to take the lunch along or come back here for it?" Ruby asked when the horses were ready. "I put everything in a small insulated pack to keep the drinks and things cold, but Lancelot can carry it behind his saddle if you want."

"Okay, let's do that." Chuck brought it from the truck. It was fairly heavy, but the horse didn't flinch when he set it gently behind the cantle of the saddle.

"You use an English saddle," he said in surprise. "I'm sure I saw a Western saddle in your barn last week."

Ruby shrugged. "This is lighter. When we're going on a long ride, I like to keep the weight down, for Lancelot's sake." She strapped on the pack. "I take my lunch with me in this cooler sometimes. It's great not to have to hurry back and to have a cold drink and something to eat when you get ten miles from home and realize you're starving." She walked forward to unhitch Lancelot and reached down to grab her baseball cap from the trailer's fender. After settling it over her rich brown hair, she gathered the reins and lifted her left foot to the stirrup. In an instant she was sitting astride, smiling down at him. "All set?"

Chuck was still looking at her scuffed white running shoes and calculating how much lighter his gear would be if he switched to an English saddle and left his boots home. But the week before his first hundred-miler wasn't the time to change equipment.

"Yeah, sure." He unclipped Rascal from the trailer and mounted. The trail they chose rose gradually at first, and they trotted along together then slowed as the incline increased. The sprinkling of trees on the rolling hills became denser as they progressed along the trail. The foliage was turning color on the hardwoods. Chuck inhaled deeply. He loved this time of year.

Ruby reached out and plucked a golden leaf from an aspen as she passed, rolled the stem back and forth between her fingers a few times, then let the leaf flutter to the earth. When the track narrowed, Chuck let her lead the way. Her palomino had a nice rhythm, and Ruby sat easily in the saddle, obviously comfortable.

A steep grade slowed their pace, and after a while Ruby hopped down.

She turned and walked backward beside her horse for a moment, holding his reins. "I'm going to walk up this one."

Chuck climbed down, too, and Rascal lowered his head with a snuffle, plodding up the slope behind Lancelot.

They came out on a rounded knob above the tree line. Ruby led Lancelot to a fairly flat spot and stood looking out over the plain below. Chuck eased Rascal over beside them.

"Terrific view."

She turned toward him. "Isn't it great? I've never been up here before. You can see clear out across the plains."

"You ride very well."

"Thanks." She looked down and fiddled with the reins she held.

"How long have you had Lancelot?"

"About five years. I bought him while I was still in college. I stayed home and commuted."

He nodded, thinking it must have been nice to be able to afford college *and* a good horse.

Her rueful chuckle squelched the thought. "It's probably why I can't afford my own apartment."

"Horsemanship is an expensive sport." He let Rascal put his head down and crop the drying grass.

"Well, it's been a sort of compensation for me."

"Oh?"

She looked up at him, and that sober, faraway look returned to her eyes. "My twin sister and I went to Cornell University together our first year. Pre-med. But. . .there was an accident. A car crash. It wasn't her fault, but. . .after Julie died, my parents wanted me to stay close."

He nodded, trying to put the pieces together.

"Anyway, Dad said it would mean a lot to them, especially to Mom, to have me nearby. But they figured I'd be giving up a lot. They offered to help me buy a good horse." She sucked her upper lip into her mouth for a moment. "But living here and going to the community college was a lot cheaper than the university, so I guess we've all saved money in the long run. Probably for the best." Her frown belied her words.

"It's been rough for your family."

"Yeah." She puffed out a breath and smiled. "But God knows what He's doing. I believe that."

Her gaze met his, and Chuck nodded. "I do, too. Are things getting better now?"

"Some. The pain never goes away, you know?"

"Yeah, I do." A memory of his father's gentle face flitted across his mind.

After a moment she looked over the knoll. "Do you want to keep going? This trail seems to go down a ways, but I think it goes up that ridge over there." She pointed to the next hill.

"Sure, if you're game."

"Let's go." She positioned her reins and put her foot in the stirrup to mount.

Chuck pulled Rascal's head up and swung into the saddle. He liked Ruby. So far she'd lived up to his expectations. Frank, no-nonsense, direct. Cute. Great horsewoman. Very cute. Her golden brown braid bounced against the back of her denim jacket. In spite of her delicate frame she had a toughness. She would fall into the featherweight class for certain at the ride while Chuck figured he'd hit middleweight with all his gear at the weigh-in. But despite her small stature Ruby would never be one to shirk her own stable chores. Chuck liked that. He liked the fact that she trusted God with her future, too, no matter how bleak things must have seemed for a while.

The horses wended downward then entered a cool stretch of conifer forest. A magpie flew across the trail from a low-hanging spruce branch, and Lancelot shied but settled down under Ruby's firm hand. When they emerged from the woods fifteen minutes later, the path widened. Chuck trotted his Appaloosa up beside Ruby and Lancelot. She looked over at him.

Without giving much thought to his words, Chuck said, "Yeah, this is a lot better than riding alone."

His momentary fear that he'd been too forward was erased in the glow of Ruby's smile.

Chapter 2

The day with Chuck was as close to a perfect day as Ruby could remember. They ate their sandwiches, vegetable sticks, and cookies at a camp spot near the trail and let the horses graze while they talked. By the end of that half hour she'd lost a little of her shyness with him, though she still felt under-qualified in his presence.

She'd aspired to medical school once—for people, not animals, but she knew vet school was as difficult and perhaps more competitive. Chuck had made it through. She hadn't. She'd had to switch majors when she left the university. Instead of pre-med she took a bachelor's degree in humanities. She wished now she'd taken a vocational course, but at the time she'd been too numb to concentrate on the future.

Not that she minded her job at the police station. She helped stop crime indirectly and had even received credit for helping save the life of a young woman who called in a medical emergency. But it was a job, not a career. Ruby couldn't see herself sitting before the communications console at the station for another forty years. Sometimes she wished she'd taken criminal justice and become a police officer. In the five years since Julie's death she'd avoided making long-term decisions. But maybe it was time.

"I'm not too old to go back to school," she told Chuck as they rode slowly back down the trail toward the truck.

His eyebrows shot up as he looked over at her. "Well, sure. Even medical school, if you still want to."

His quick affirmation brought a smidgen of comfort. Spending an entire day with Chuck Sullivan had given her much to mull over. She'd learned more about him, and all of it was good—his family in Laramie, his struggle to put himself through college and graduate school, his great relationship with his mom and siblings. The only bad part was his father's death from a heart attack fifteen years ago.

He was a good enough rider to compete in the Wyoming 100, and he took excellent care of his mount. No need to worry about his pushing Rascal too hard. Some riders new to the sport asked more than their horses could give, but Chuck wouldn't.

As he turned his pickup in at her family's driveway, she watched his sturdy hands on the wheel and the way he automatically checked the trailer in the side view mirror. Detail oriented. . .steady. . .diligent. . .handsome. He pulled up in front of the barn.

"Thanks, Chuck. I had a really good time today."

"Me, too. I think getting a horse has been good for me. And riding with you was good for me, too."

She ducked her head, feeling a blush warm her cheeks.

"Are you planning to help set up for the 100 next Friday?" he asked. "I think you said you don't work Friday."

"Right. I'm planning to be there."

"I'm going to try to go, too. If I'm not swamped with patients, I'll see you there. But I'll be there for sure at the riders' meeting and campfire that night."

She couldn't hold in her smile, but she didn't want to try. "That's great." He opened his truck door, and she pulled the latch on hers and hopped down. Too late she realized he was going around the front of the truck to help her down, not heading directly to the trailer.

"Uh, thanks." She glanced up at him then away.

He laughed. "I guess that's a good sign."

"What?"

"You're not used to having a gentleman do things for you."

"Not very often."

He nodded. "Like I said, that's good. . .for me."

She wondered suddenly how many women he'd squired around. Not many since he came to live here, she was sure. In a small town like this she'd have heard rumors.

They walked to the trailer, and he lowered the ramp.

"I can get Lancelot," she said.

"Okay, I'll get your tack."

When she'd backed her horse down the ramp, Chuck was waiting near the barn door, carrying her saddle. Rascal pawed inside the trailer and whinnied. Lancelot answered him and pulled at the lead line.

"Settle down." Ruby walked him to the barn door and into the dim interior. The familiar smells of hay, sweet feed, leather, and manure greeted her. She walked him into his box stall and released him. Lancelot whinnied again and shook his white mane.

"Relax, would ya? I'll get your supper in a minute." She put her hand to his throat to get a quick count of his pulse. Slow and steady.

Chuck was waiting for her just outside the stall, grinning. "I think he and Rascal bonded."

"For sure."

"I put your tack away."

"Thanks."

They walked to the truck, and he hefted the lunch pack out.

"Are you camping at the ride site next Friday?"

"I don't think so. I know most of the riders do, but I live so close I figured

I'd go over early Saturday morning. Lancelot will sleep better in his own stall that night."

Chuck nodded. "That's what I decided to do. They said we could do the preliminary vet check-in Saturday morning if we got there early."

The house door opened, and her mother came onto the porch.

"Hi. Did you have a good time?"

"Yeah, it was great," Ruby called. She glanced at Chuck in apology, but it didn't seem to bother him that her folks hovered. They walked over to the steps.

"Did you have a good day, Mrs. Dale?" Chuck asked.

"Yes, I made applesauce and cleaned the hall closet."

Ruby smiled at her mother's idea of fun. "We had a good workout."

"The horses did, too," Chuck added with a grin.

Her mother laughed. "Would you like to stay for supper?"

Chuck glanced at Ruby. "Well, I ought to get over to the office for a while and see if Dr. Hogan had any emergencies. He told me he wouldn't call me today, but I should check in with him."

"Another time," Ruby's mother said.

Ruby didn't look at him, so Chuck nodded and murmured, "Thank you. Ruby, if all goes well I'll see you next week at the setup."

"Right. Thanks again for today."

Chuck smiled at them both and turned toward his truck. Ruby could feel a barrage of questions coming on from her mother.

"I need to feed and water Lancelot." She hurried toward the barn.

❧

On Wednesday afternoon Ruby took her place in the police station's communications center, a few feet away from the other evening dispatcher, Nadine Carter. They shared most of their overlapping shifts, but Nadine had been on duty an hour when Ruby checked in. This system prevented them from losing track of situations in progress when the dispatchers changed.

Nadine finished a call and turned to face Ruby. "Pretty quiet today. I'm monitoring a traffic stop on Antelope Street and a domestic call in town."

Ruby nodded and reached for her headphones. "Thanks." She settled into her padded chair. The next few hours were moderately busy, with routine calls. She answered questions and directed officers to respond to requests. In the slower moments she let her thoughts stray to Chuck. He'd called her last night, "just because," and she was still smiling over that. He'd confessed he'd rescheduled a few routine procedures for bovine patients in order to increase his chances of seeing her on Friday. Not "helping set up for the ride," she'd noted. "Seeing you." That was enough to keep her head in the clouds.

The patrol sergeant's sudden intrusion brought her swiftly to earth.

"Dispatch, we have a high-risk situation," called Sergeant Harrison's voice in her headphones. "I need you to track detectives Austin and Wheeler." He gave the numerical code for a drug-related incident. Ruby's mind clicked into focus, and all thoughts of Chuck and the ride fled.

"Got it." Ruby tapped the officers' badge numbers into her computer. The system would give her an electronic tone every five minutes to remind her to check on them.

Over the next hour the incident evolved into a major surveillance operation. The two detectives and three uniformed officers took up positions where they could observe an isolated private airstrip, hoping to catch drug runners when they landed their plane.

The officers performed their status checks on schedule, giving her a "status quo" report each time. Austin's voice sounded more and more sleepy as time passed. It was a fairly boring exercise for Ruby as well, but she knew if the plane landed things would get busy in a hurry.

As the hour grew later she felt her energy droop and went for a cup of coffee. At one o'clock Nadine's relief came in. Ruby told the graveyard shift dispatcher, Larry Tivoli, about the case she was tracking, and he took over Nadine's console and her ongoing incidents.

Just before 2:00 a.m. Ruby's relief dispatcher arrived. The detectives were still checking in faithfully, but the plane they were waiting for hadn't arrived. Ruby turned her headphones over and headed home, eager for some sleep. She considered grabbing another cup of coffee, but if she did that she'd be wired and unable to sleep for hours. She was glad the drive home was only four miles.

2a.

"I think I can give you Friday off again," Dr. Hogan said genially as he lifted a Scottish terrier out of his kennel in the veterinary office. "You covered for me all day yesterday. And the whole town knows the office will be closed Saturday because we'll both be at the ride. Everyone needs a day off sometime to have fun, right?"

Chuck grinned. "Right. Everybody will know where to find us the day of the 100. Thanks, John."

The older man smiled and set the small dog carefully on the examining table. "There, Hamish, are you feeling better this morning?" He put his stethoscope to the dog's rib cage.

Chuck glanced over his schedule for the day. Two house calls at ranches this morning and office hours after lunch. Not bad.

He drove to the first appointment, a ranch where he was scheduled to vaccinate a small herd of Angus cattle. After an hour with the rancher he headed to the Riley home. Fifteen-year-old Rebecca Riley's barrel-racing horse had pulled up lame during practice two days earlier. Chuck had treated the mare, Shasta, and advised Rebecca to keep the horse in a box stall so she would rest, dose the leg with liniment, and rewrap it daily.

A young blond woman he recognized as Rebecca's older sister, Claire, met him in the yard as soon as he pulled in. Chuck grabbed his veterinary bag and climbed out of the truck. "Good morning, Claire. How's Shasta doing?"

"Becky says she's better. She wanted to stay home from school so she'd be here when you came, but our mom made her go. I told Becky I'd make sure Shasta got the best treatment."

Chuck smiled, but he wished Becky, or even her mother, were present. Claire made him nervous. She'd deluged him with cookies and invitations to community events when he'd first arrived in town. She was pretty, but her aggressive manner put him off.

Claire led him into the barn and leaned on the bottom half of the stall's Dutch door while he examined Shasta's leg.

"Oh, that feels much better," he said. "No heat in it today. Would you mind walking her out for me so I can watch her stride?"

"Sure." Claire clipped a lead rope to Shasta's halter and led her into the alleyway and out toward the driveway. Chuck tried not to notice how tight Claire's leggings were. He concentrated on the horse's steps and the way Shasta placed her weight evenly on each foot as she walked.

"Great," he called. "She's bearing weight on it. Turn her around."

Claire walked the horse back toward him. "Tell Becky I said to give her another day of rest before she rides her, okay? And no barrel racing for another week. That's too stressful. I'll come back next week to check Shasta over, and if she's okay then, I'll give Becky the green light for practice again."

"She'll miss the competition in Casper next weekend." Claire led Shasta back into the box stall and removed the lead rope.

"I'm sorry about that, but it's better than doing permanent damage to her horse's leg."

"Right. I'll remind her of that." Claire smiled at him as she emerged from the stall. "How about a cup of coffee, Chuck? I've got a fresh pot in the kitchen, and I made some brownies."

Uneasy prickles skittered over Chuck's arms. Why did Claire make him feel so. . .stalked? Ruby never gave him that sensation.

"Thanks, but I have office hours coming up. I need to get back to town."

She raised her chin. "Maybe another time."

He almost said, "Sure," but caught himself. Even that generic response might cause her to claim later he'd made a promise. "Uh. . .maybe. Thanks for the offer." He climbed in his truck and drove away feeling as though he'd escaped an unpleasant experience. He supposed Claire wasn't so bad, but she'd come on so strong ever since he'd met her that she'd killed any natural inclination on his part to get to know her better.

Now Ruby was another story. She was quiet, perhaps even a bit reserved, but she had substance. Yes, she cared about animals, but she cared about people, too. The ease he felt in her presence was worlds away from the fidgets Claire gave him. He flipped the radio on and hummed as he drove, thinking of Ruby in her sneakers and baseball cap. Not a glamour girl, but perhaps something better. He wanted to find out.

When she arrived at work Thursday afternoon Ruby felt better. She'd slept until noon, and then she'd taken Lancelot out for an hour-long workout, riding around a large ranch that belonged to the Dales' easterly neighbors. The ride energized her and increased her anticipation for the upcoming hundred-mile contest. Lancelot was at his peak, and the ride was only two days away.

She sank into her padded swivel chair behind the console unable to stop envisioning what tomorrow would bring. She planned to arrive early at the ride start, ready to post markers, set up checkpoints, or anything else the committee needed. And Chuck would be there. Well, probably. She sent up a quick prayer that he would have no emergencies and be able to take part in the setup fun. She refused to consider the letdown that awaited her if he couldn't make it.

Nadine signed off on a call and turned her chair. "Hi."

"How's it going?" Ruby asked.

"A little busy."

"Did that plane ever come in last night?"

"No, the detectives stayed out until 5:00 a.m., and it never showed. Oops." She swiveled quickly back to the console and answered another call.

Ruby went to the duty room to stow her purse in the locker she'd been assigned. Officer Nelson Flagg was working at one of the computer stations but glanced up at her.

"Howdy, Ruby."

"Hello, Nels. How's the baby?"

"Good."

She closed her locker door and pushed her hair back. "Everything going okay today?"

"Yeah, except the detectives are moaning about those cocaine runners they thought they were going to nab last night. Seems their reliable tipster isn't so reliable after all."

Ruby grimaced at him. "That's too bad. I know Detective Austin was counting on making some arrests."

Flagg nodded. "We all want to stop the drugs from coming into the county. But they've been trying for months and haven't succeeded in catching the dealers."

"I know. Maybe they'll find out what went wrong and get another chance."

"Let's hope so."

Chapter 3

Ruby's Jeep spun dust clouds behind her as she drove the dirt road to the ranch where the ride would begin. The owner allowed the sponsoring horsemen's club to use one of his back fields as the start area every year. It was only a mile from a campground many of the contestants used. The club had built a wood-framed booth for the ride officials and a small storage shed on the edge of the field. Riders, their vehicles, the veterinary check-in post, and spectators would fill the area tomorrow, but now there were only a few SUVs and pickups. She parked and climbed out, pulling on her baseball cap.

"Good morning, Ruby!"

She smiled and joined Hester Marden, an energetic woman who was a mainstay of the club. Hester and her husband, Tom, both in their fifties, raised Paso Finos.

"Looks like we're early birds," Ruby said.

"Yes, but they're trickling in. I think we'll have a good group to put up the markers today." Hester nodded toward the gray pickup entering the field. "There's Jeffrey Tavish."

"Last year's winner," Ruby noted. She'd never actually met him but had watched him win the trophy.

"Mm. Second time in a row," Hester said.

"He's a good rider."

"Oh, yes, and a good trainer. He deserves all the ribbons he wins. And he rode in the 100 for five years before he worked his way up to first place. I'd say he's earned his laurels." Hester nudged her as Jeff got out of his truck. "Not bad looking either."

Ruby smiled. "Come on, Hester. What if Tom hears you talking like that?"

Hester laughed. "Oh, he can take it. Say, there's Sandy Larkin. I need to see her. The check for my club dues hasn't cleared the bank yet." Hester strode off to buttonhole the club treasurer.

Ruby looked around and spotted a few more people she knew from the club and from helping with the ride in previous years. As she chatted with the ride secretary, Jeff Tavish joined them.

"Looks like we've got a good crew today," Jeff said.

"Yes." The secretary, Allison Bowie, surveyed the gathering. "I expect we'll get everything done before suppertime."

Jeff gazed at Ruby with twinkling gray eyes. "You look familiar. Have we met?"

"I've helped out the last few years," Ruby said.

"She's one of our best workers," Allison told him. "You must have met Ruby."

"No, I think I'd remember. Suppose you introduce us."

Ruby felt her color rise as Jeff continued to watch her. She didn't know much about him, except that he'd mastered the art of endurance riding and took excellent care of his horses.

"Ruby Dale, meet Jeff Tavish," Allison said with a bit of a drawl.

Jeff lifted his Stetson and extended his other hand. "Very pleased to meet you, Ruby."

She shook his hand briefly. "Thanks. Are you going to defend your title?"

"I'm surely going to try." He definitely wasn't bad looking—dark blond hair that fluttered in the breeze, a long face set in a solemn expression belied by his laughing eyes. "Will you be helping at one of the checkpoints tomorrow?"

Allison laughed and swatted at his arm. "No, she won't. She's competing this year, and I've seen her horse. She'll give you a run for your money, Jeff."

He nodded, surveying Ruby with new respect. "I look forward to it."

From the corner of her eye Ruby saw a black pickup pulling into the field. She didn't want Chuck's first glimpse of her to also be one of Jeff Tavish.

"Have you made up the assignments for today, Allison?" she asked.

"Tom Marden's taking care of that."

"Well then, if you'll excuse me, I think I'll go see where I'm needed." She nodded at Jeff and Allison and walked quickly to the knot of people near the officials' booth. As she had hoped, Chuck was also approaching the group.

He smiled when he spotted her and diverted his steps in her direction.

"You made it!" She couldn't help the cheerleader smile that sprang to her lips. The answering glint in his eyes set her pulse thudding.

"Yes, I'm free for the day. Do we know what we're doing yet?"

"Tom Marden is starting to give assignments, but I think a lot of people went to the campground first to leave their gear." She and Chuck edged up to the back of the small crowd and listened as Tom described each chore and wrote down the names of those who volunteered to see the job done.

"For those of you who want to stay close to base camp today, we need volunteers to set up for the barbecue," Tom called. "Dick and Loreta Halstead will be in charge of the food, but I'm sure they could use an assistant or two, and we need to set up tables and so on. The riders' meeting and campfire will be held over at the campground, immediately after the barbecue."

Several people stepped forward to volunteer.

"Now, folks," Tom said after a few minutes, "this year we're changing the route a little bit. We got permission to follow the old stagecoach road in the hills for a few miles."

"Yes, and it's a beautiful section of trail," Allison said, and Ruby realized the secretary and Jeff were standing near her and Chuck.

Tom nodded. "We'll pick it up at Mile 56, after the second bridge. It's pretty good footing."

"Wasn't that road abandoned back when they built the new highway?" one of the men asked.

"That's right," Tom said. "It's as crooked as a snake, but it should be safe enough for horses. Since we haven't used that stretch before we need all new markings for several miles, but it's not a terribly difficult section. It will loop around and hit our regular route at the old Mile 59, which will now be Mile 63. We're moving the sixty-mile checkpoint down there to even things out a little, but that stretch between checks will still be a long one. And after that, of course, all the mile markers need to be adjusted. We're taking out the loop around Pikes' ranch, and the finish line will be about a mile east of where it was last year."

Chuck looked down at Ruby. "Want to do the new part?"

"Sure."

Chuck raised his hand. "Tom, we'll take the new section. Me and Ruby."

Ruby could feel Jeff's intent gaze on her. She glanced over, and sure enough he was watching her. It was flattering to think he was interested in her, but her heart had room only for Chuck these days. She flashed Jeff a quick smile and turned her attention back to what Tom was saying.

"Right, Chuck. You can drive up to the bridge and start there. It's only about twenty-five miles from here by the road, even though it's at Mile 56 on the trail. Our route for the 100 loops around and switches back through the hills."

Chuck accepted a sheet of paper and a roll of orange surveyor's tape from Hester, who was assisting her husband at assigning the jobs. Hester handed Ruby a sheaf of laminated arrow signs and showed them on the printed map where to post the arrows and ribbon markers.

"Want to take my Jeep?" Ruby asked, looking up into Chuck's blue eyes.

"Sure, if you want."

As they walked toward the parked vehicle, Ruby spotted Jeff in the center of a group of laughing people. She was glad he'd found some congenial companions.

With Chuck sitting beside her in the Jeep she found it difficult to concentrate on the winding trail. He held their supplies on his lap and watched eagerly out the window as she drove.

"I love riding in this area," he said, "but it's a little far from home. I've only managed to bring Rascal up here once, and we did the first six miles of the ride route, up and back."

"That's a start," Ruby said. "At least he'll recognize the beginning. That will probably help him feel at ease."

"I hope so. He loved being out on the trail with you and Lancelot last week, but he'll have more than fifty other horses around him when we come here tomorrow."

"True. Amazing how this ride has grown over the last few years." Ruby slowed the Jeep as she maneuvered a sharp turn. "I'm glad we can drive some parts of the trail. It makes the setup easier. But I know I'll love the remote parts best. It's great getting out away from civilization on a horse, where you know you won't meet any cars."

"I agree. But I hope we don't have to walk the whole seven miles of our section and back."

Ruby grinned and jerked her head toward the backseat. "I did pack a few sandwiches. I figured we'd need something between now and supper."

Chuck's jaw dropped. "You mean we *are* going to walk fourteen miles today?"

"No, but probably five or six."

He bobbed his head back and forth as though weighing that. "I guess I can handle it. I got a little smarter and wore my running shoes today."

After a half-hour drive she parked the Jeep at the side of the trail before the log bridge at Mile 56. When the competitors reached this point they would have to cross the narrow span to continue the ride.

"We'll have to walk in from here and flag the next mile or so," she told him, "but then we can come back and take the Jeep around the mountain. There's an access road off the highway. I volunteered at the checkpoint up there last year."

Chuck studied the crude map Tom had given him. "I think I see it. This dotted line?"

"Yeah. It's not a great road, but we can get the job done. This loop here, though—from about Mile 61 to the end of our section..." She pointed on the map. "We'll have to walk that part, too. But the scenery should be spectacular."

"Right." He smiled at her. "I guess we can drive around to the other end of the stagecoach road and walk in for that part."

"That's what I figure. We'll do that section last."

Chuck picked up his pile of signs, tape, and a hammer. "Ready anytime you are, Dr. Livingstone."

Her stomach fluttered as she folded the map and tucked it in her pocket. She had definitely drawn the best chore today.

The task took longer than Ruby had anticipated, and she realized they would be riding over some very rugged terrain during the race.

"What's the record time for this ride?" Chuck asked as he cut several strips of orange tape with his pocketknife.

"Fifteen hours and twenty-nine minutes, held by Jeff Tavish. Do you know him?"

"He's not one of Doc Hogan's and my clients, but I met him last year at the ride. He had a fantastic Arabian–quarter horse cross. He didn't get the best conditioned award, but he came close, if I remember correctly."

"You probably do. Jeff lives in Casper. He's the defending champion, and he's here today." She hesitated. "Well, not right here now. I mean he came for the setup. I saw him for a minute this morning."

They finished the first part of their assignment and drove by little-used trails up to the spot where the Mile 63 checkpoint would be. From there they drove as far as they could, posting arrows and hanging ribbons on branches.

"Getting hungry?" she asked.

Chuck looked at his watch. "Yeah. It's after one. Why don't we eat before we do the last part where we have to walk in?"

They found a spot on a ridge where they could sit to eat their sandwiches looking out over the valley. "That's the Medicine Bow River." Ruby pointed to the stream far in the distance. Between them and the river the land sloped down, with abrupt falls from cliffs and rock outcroppings. Deep ravines cut between the summits, and spruce trees stood stiff and spiky, with little underbrush beneath them.

"I hope I get through this part before dark tomorrow," Chuck said. "They really should have railings on some of the curves up here."

Movement between the trees beneath their high perch caught Ruby's eye. "Look. Someone's riding down there."

"Where?" Chuck leaned over behind her and sighted along her arm as she pointed.

Ruby felt his breath move her hair, and a prickle slid down her spine. "Down there, to the left of that boulder."

"I see them." He straightened and squinted down at the figures. "Looks like two horses."

"I thought at first they were elk," Ruby said, "but the riders are leading them."

"It's great weather for it. Cool, but not too chilly."

"Don't remind me about what's coming in a couple of months." Ruby ate the last of her sandwich. "Want a brownie?"

"Sure. I didn't know I was getting a two-course meal."

She laughed and reached into her day pack. "Just light refreshments. The real feed is later." She glanced up at him. "You're staying for the barbecue, right?"

"Wouldn't miss it." He accepted one of the fudge brownies and looked down into the ravine again. "Hey, look. They've tied up their horses."

Ruby frowned and focused on the tiny figures below them again. "There's a rockslide or something over there."

"Probably too rough for the horses," Chuck agreed. "I wonder if they're just out hiking, or if they have something to do with the ride."

"That area looks too rugged for the ride. Even though they make it tough, riding in terrain like that would be dangerous." Ruby looked at her watch. "Guess we'd better get moving."

Chuck stood and offered her a hand up. "Okay, we can't drive any farther."

"Right," Ruby said. "We'll have to do this last part of the stagecoach road on foot. At the rate we're going, it will probably take us at least a couple of hours to finish." She stooped to brush off her jeans.

"We've got plenty of time."

Two hours later Ruby scrambled down a sharp incline clutching the few remaining arrow signs.

"This is really steep, Chuck. Are you sure we took the right fork back there?"

"Well. . .I was thinking we should have hit the main trail again by now. This looks dangerous, doesn't it?" He eyed the drop-off at the edge of the narrow path. "Let's make sure." He fished the map out of his shirt pocket and smoothed it out.

Ruby climbed back up to stand beside him. They both bent over the map, and she was aware once again of his nearness as his masculine scent tickled her nose. She made herself think about the trail, not her charming companion.

"See? Right here." She pointed on the map to the last place where they'd posted an arrow. "I assumed we'd keep going around the side of the hill, but it almost looks like we were supposed to go over the top on this one."

"You're right. Let's hope the grade is more gradual on the other side." He looked back up the trail with a frown. "Guess we'd better start taking down markers. It's after three o'clock, and we need to finish before dark."

"Before the barbecue, you mean."

He laughed. "Right. And we sure don't want to lead any riders down here. Come on. We'd better hang extra ribbons up there to make sure." He held out his hand. Ruby took it, and they struggled back up the slope together.

When they finally got back to the Jeep, certain all the markers were placed correctly, it was almost 4:30.

"I don't suppose you'd want to drive back?" Ruby asked, wiping the sleeve of her sweatshirt across her forehead.

"Sure. Are you okay?"

"Yeah, just a little tired."

Chuck put the tools and leftover ribbon in the back of the Jeep. "Well, pile in and let's go get some supper."

Ruby hesitated. "Just a sec."

She walked a few yards to the spot from which they had seen the riders in the ravine. Chuck came to stand beside her. She squinted down into the shadows below and caught her breath.

"Chuck, they're still down there."

"You're right. I can still see the horses. I hope everything's okay. The riders have been gone more than three hours."

"Odd they left those horses tied up that long."

"Oh, wait. It's okay." Chuck pointed off to the left. Just coming into view on the scree from the rockslide were two dark-clad figures.

"That's them," Ruby agreed. "Wonder what they were doing."

"At least we know they're not in trouble," Chuck said. "Probably just exploring. Well, we'd better get going if we don't want to be late for the barbecue."

One of the tiny figures below stopped walking. Ruby caught her breath. The man—she was sure it was a man—was looking up toward where they stood on the ledge. A moment later his companion stopped, too, and turned around. The first person pointed up toward them.

"I think they see us." Ruby raised her arm and waved. There was no response from the hikers. They turned and scrambled over the rest of the rocks to where the horses waited. Within moments the mounted riders disappeared among the spruce trees.

Chapter 4

Chuck loaded his plate with barbecued ribs, baked beans, and biscuits but made a concession to nutrition by adding a scoop of salad around the edge. He and Ruby found places to sit at one of the tables the crew had set up during their absence along the trail. "What do you want to drink?" he asked. "I'll get it."

"Oh, thanks. Bottled water is fine."

Chuck walked over to the ice-filled coolers that held the drinks and chose spring water for Ruby and a can of cola for himself. He shook the bits of crushed ice from the plastic bottle.

"Hey, Doc," said a voice next to him. He turned and recognized Marcia Bennett, a client whose horse he had treated a few days earlier.

"Hi, Marcia. How's Lady doing?"

"Just fine. She seems to be over that colicky spell."

"Glad to hear it. I'll try to drop by Monday and take a quick look."

"Thanks."

"Are you going to ride tomorrow?" he asked.

"No, I don't do more than five or ten miles at a time. I'm going to help log in riders at checkpoint 3."

"Great. I'm bringing my Appy. It will be our first competitive ride."

"You start out big, Doc."

He grinned. "I just hope I'm not being too ambitious. We've been training for several months, and the previous owner had him in top condition, so I hope we can last to the finish line."

"Good luck," Marcia said and stooped to pull a can of soda from the cooler.

Chuck hurried back toward the tables. He broke stride for a moment when he spotted Ruby. Seated beside her was a handsome young man about thirty years old and wearing a black Stetson, white shirt, and leather vest. The champ had his eye on Ruby. What was more, Jeff Tavish didn't look as though he'd been working all day. Chuck suddenly felt grubby.

He ambled over and set the water bottle on the table between his plate and Ruby's.

She looked up at him. "Oh, thanks, Chuck. You said you've met Jeff before, right?"

Chuck nodded at the champion. "Hi. Chuck Sullivan." He set down his cola and reached to shake Jeff's outstretched hand.

"Howdy," Jeff said. "I was just giving Ruby some pointers on pacing herself for the 100." He turned his gaze back to Ruby, whose soft brown eyes seemed mesmerized by him. "I'm sure you won't have any trouble finishing, with all the practice rides you tell me you've had, but that first official competition can be stressful. Just relax and enjoy it. That's the main thing."

Ruby's musical chuckle reached Chuck, although she was turned mostly away from him. His view of her glossy brown hair would ordinarily have pleased him, but not when she was chitchatting with another man, especially one who had topnotch horses and had walked away with the trophy two years in a row. Chuck sat down on the bench beside her and brushed away a fly that buzzed around his barbecued ribs. He didn't like the way his appetite had fled because of Jeff's proximity. Last year he'd cheered him on and congratulated him on his win. What right did he have to treat him differently now?

"So you've entered the ride? What kind of horse have you got?"

Chuck realized Jeff was addressing him. He leaned forward to look past Ruby. "Oh, uh, Appaloosa gelding."

"Yeah?"

Ruby said, "Rascal's a terrific horse. I know he'll do well tomorrow. We had a forty-mile trail ride last weekend, and he came through it like a pro."

Jeff nodded and looked from her to Chuck and back. The brim of the Stetson shaded Jeff's eyes, but Chuck thought he detected a bit of speculation going on.

"So what did you all do today?" Jeff asked.

Chuck let Ruby tell him about their trek along the old stagecoach road while he dove into his cooling food.

"It's gorgeous up there. Panoramic views at every turn."

"I can't wait to see that part of the trail." Jeff's eyes glistened. "I love riding new ground, although it probably means I won't shorten my time any, having to go over terrain I don't know. But it's fun."

"Yes, it's a beautiful area," Ruby said. "There are some places where you have to be careful, though. Sheer drop-offs and steep grades."

"On the stagecoach route?" Jeff popped the top on a can of root beer.

"Well, the worst part we saw wasn't actually on the route for tomorrow's ride," Ruby admitted, "but there are a couple of spots where you don't want to get too close to the edge."

Jeff tipped up his can and took a deep swallow.

"I was surprised to learn they took coaches through these mountains," Chuck said.

"Well, back in the mining heyday they cut some pretty precarious roads." Jeff picked up his fork and looked at them eagerly. "Hey, did you hear about the payroll robbery?"

Ruby shook her head. "I usually hear about all the crime in these parts."

"Oh, this was a long time ago," Jeff said. "Back in the 1880s, I think. They say a stagecoach carrying a payroll was robbed somewhere in these parts. The robbers drove off in the coach, leaving the driver dead and the passengers tied up. The marshal got up a posse to chase the thieves, but the stagecoach was never found."

"I think I've heard something about that before," Ruby said.

Jeff nodded and picked up a biscuit. "Some people think the coach wrecked in these mountains and the money is still out there somewhere."

"Doubt it," Chuck said. "That's a long, long time ago. Somebody would have found it by now." He thought of the hikers they'd seen that day, poking around in the ravine. There probably wasn't a square foot of land in Wyoming nobody had walked over in the last 120 years.

"Not necessarily." Jeff lowered his voice to a spectral tone. "Some folks say the coach still roams these hills, with a ghostly driver holding the reins."

Ruby shivered. "I don't believe in ghosts."

Jeff laughed. "Me either, but it makes a good story."

They continued to talk, with Jeff carrying most of the conversation. Allison and Marcia sat down across the table from them.

"We've got a record number of entries for the ride tomorrow," Allison told them with a proud smile.

"How many?" Ruby asked.

"Sixty-eight."

"Wow! That's a lot."

"It will take us longer to check everyone in. I hope folks get over to the registration booth early," Allison said. "Of course most of them did their preliminary vet checks this afternoon."

"We're planning to get ours done in the morning," Chuck said, sliding a glance at Ruby.

"Well, be here by five," Allison said. "I doubt we can get another vet here any earlier to check you in."

They continued to talk about the competition. The sun sank behind the trees, and Tom Marden put a match to the pile of wood the volunteers had prepared for a bonfire. Chuck noticed Ruby rubbed her arms as if to warm them.

"I don't want to rush your eating, folks," Tom called, "but gather round the fire when you're done. We'll go over the particulars for the ride. You should have picked up a packet with your maps and other information, but we'll review a few things. And for afterward Dick and Rory brought their guitars. Let's sing a few cowboy songs. What do you say?"

The crowd began to drift toward the fireside.

"Last call on beans and barbecue," Loreta Halstead called.

"Oops, that's my cue," Jeff said, rising. "I've been gabbing so much I almost missed out on seconds."

Chuck wasn't sorry to see him go. He leaned closer to Ruby. "Are you finished?"

"Yes, I'm stuffed. But you get some dessert if you want it."

"No, I'm fine."

"Well, I'm getting some," Allison said. She and Marcia went in search of the dessert table.

"You sure?" Chuck asked. He saw Jeff heading back toward them carrying his newly heaped plate. "We can go over to the fire if you want."

Ruby stood and gathered up their plastic silverware, paper plates, and napkins. Chuck took the drink containers, and they made a stop at the cleanup area. People were opening canvas chairs or spreading throws on the ground near the fire.

"We should have brought something to sit on," Chuck noted.

"Oh, I've got Lancelot's old blanket in the back of the Jeep," Ruby said.

They were soon settled cozily among the laughing horsemen. For the next half hour Tom Marden and Allison Bowie reviewed safety concerns, unique features of the trail, and procedures at checkpoints. Jeff Tavish stood at the edge of the crowd with a couple of other men. When all questions had been answered, Tom called on the two musicians.

Dick Halstead strummed his guitar and started singing "Riding Home." Those who knew the old song joined in. As the shadows deepened, Chuck found himself watching the firelight play on Ruby's face. He was sitting next to the prettiest woman at the gathering. Her hair glistened a deep chestnut in the firelight. She glanced over at him and smiled, and Chuck's heart flipped.

"Excuse me. Got room for one more?" Jeff sank down on Ruby's other side and crossed his long legs, his cowboy boots sticking out between two other people toward the fire.

"Sure, Jeff." Ruby edged over a little closer to Chuck, and he told himself this wasn't a bad thing. Ruby's shoulder touched his sleeve now. He didn't mind a bit. He tried not to think about Jeff. They were all adults, and he had no reason to be jealous. Ruby had chosen to spend the day with him. She could have invited Jeff to help them hang trail markers, but she didn't. And Jeff had inserted himself into their suppertime, he was sure, just as he did now at the campfire.

After a few more songs Tom told how the Medicine Bow Mountains acquired their name.

"The Indians used to cut the cedars to make their bows. The wood was tough and springy, and it made such great bows they thought it was good medicine to use that wood."

"That's a great story, Tom," Hester said.

"Hey, I've got a story," Jeff called. "It's about the haunted stagecoach. Ever hear it?"

Ruby leaned close to Chuck. "Not again."

"Oh, well," Chuck said. Ruby smiled at him, and that made listening to Jeff's tale again tolerable.

Jeff's voice rose and fell, and he leaned forward with a sweep of his hand as he told of the stagecoach robbery. The crowd listened intently, and Jeff's story sprouted new details. "And those people swore afterward they could see right through the robbers."

Ruby scrunched up her face and shot Chuck an inquiring look as she listened to the latest embellishments.

"And those robbers stole all the people's jewelry and money, and they climbed up on the stagecoach and drove off with it and the payroll. A coach with a six-horse hitch and two transparent robbers. It drove off up the trail where we're going to ride tomorrow, and the folks hereabouts never saw that coach again."

"That's quite a story, Jeff," Allison said. "I've never heard it told quite that way."

"Kinda spooky," Dick said.

"That's not all," Jeff shot back. "Folks say if you're up there on the mountain at midnight on a full moon evening, you might see the coach roll by with those two robbers on the seat, and if you look just right you'll see the moonlight shine right through 'em."

"Folks *say*." Hester Marden's tone was laced with sarcasm.

"Well, *Jeff* says, anyway," her husband, Tom, retorted. The crowd laughed, and Tom said, "Hey, Rory, Dick, how about another tune?"

Jeff called out, "Yeah, how about 'Ghost Riders in the Sky'?"

Chuck knew it was all in fun, but as the eerie melody echoed around them he noticed Ruby's face was sober. He leaned over and whispered, "You all right?"

She nodded. "I'm tired, though. Guess I should head home soon."

"We can leave anytime," Chuck told her.

She seemed to consider, and as the song ended she nodded and stirred. "Excuse me, Jeff. I hate to take your sitting place away, but I'll need the blanket."

"What—you're leaving?"

Ruby nodded. "Yeah, it's time for me to hit the road."

"You're not scared, are you?" Jeff stood and scooped up the blanket for her. "I can give you a lift home if you don't want to drive alone."

She chuckled. "That's okay. I'm fine. But we have a long day ahead of us tomorrow."

Chuck reached out and took the wadded blanket from Jeff's hands. "Thanks, Jeff. We'll see you in the morning."

He was rewarded by a chagrined look from the champ. Chuck wished he'd arranged to pick Ruby up that morning and drive her home. He walked beside her to the Jeep and stowed the blanket for her.

"You sure you'll be okay?" he asked.

"Absolutely. Are you heading out now, too, or are you going to stay awhile longer?"

Chuck didn't even glance back toward the fire. "I'm going. I can follow you as far as the turnoff for your road."

She smiled. "Thanks. Hey, isn't that a full moon up there? I wonder if the old stagecoach will ride tonight."

Chuck laughed. "You're a good sport."

"Well, I've got to admit that when Jeff told that story I was thinking of the riders we saw today."

"Oh? I wondered about them, too."

"It was probably nothing," Ruby said.

Chuck opened the Jeep door for her. "Well, drive safely. I'll see you in about ten hours." He reached out and gave her hand a squeeze. Ruby's smile caught the moonlight with a dazzling gleam. Chuck's social life was definitely on the upswing. He left her and went to his pickup, already thinking about seeing her again tomorrow. But as soon as he arrived home he pulled out his detailed topographical maps of the ride area and searched them for a trail in the location where they had seen the horses.

Chapter 5

Ruby paced her room in her pajamas, too keyed up to sleep. Memories of the day played over and over in her mind—her time with Chuck, Jeff's attention to her, the mysterious riders in the ravine. She knew she needed to rest so she would be at her best tomorrow. She owed it to Lancelot.

She paced to the window, her bare toes scooting across the carpet. Pushing the curtain aside, she peered out toward the barn. Everything lay still and peaceful, but she couldn't help imagining the ghostly stagecoach tearing up her parents' driveway.

With a sigh she scuffed back to the bed and sat down. The clock on her night table told her it was nearly eleven o'clock.

Would Chuck want to ride with her tomorrow? In these competitions it was every man for himself if that man wanted to win; she knew that. You couldn't loll around waiting for your friends and hope to make the top ten.

Rascal was a good horse, and Chuck rode well enough to place in the ride, even though he was inexperienced in the sport. Chances were they wouldn't have consecutive numbers, in which case they wouldn't start near each other. The race had a staggered start, with riders leaving the holding area two minutes apart. She might not see Chuck and Rascal all day. And if they did start close together she would tell him to go on without her. Especially if Lancelot wasn't keeping up with Rascal, though they were both in top condition and had seemed evenly matched on their practice ride.

She picked up the pewter frame she kept beside her bed. She and her sister, Julie, peered out at her, laughing and carefree. *I miss you so much!* What wouldn't she give to have Julie at the ride with her tomorrow?

Ruby closed her eyes in prayer. *Lord, thank You for this opportunity. I just want a fun, safe day, that's all. I don't want to get all caught up in thinking about Chuck. Let me concentrate on the ride. I don't ask You to let me finish in the top ten. I just want to make it through in the twenty-four-hour time limit, with Lancelot in good condition. And as for Chuck. . .well, yeah, I like him. A lot. But if he's not the one You have in mind for me, then help me not to get too carried away in thinking about him.*

She replaced the frame on the nightstand and climbed into bed. After reading a psalm she turned off the lamp and went over the ride route in her mind. Maybe she should have camped at the tenting area down the road from the ride start like the others. She could have trailered Lancelot over today and taken care of the pre-ride veterinary exam. She hoped her palomino was getting more rest than she was. The moonlight streamed in between her eyelet curtains. Ruby rolled over and closed her eyes.

When she woke again, her luminous clock said 3:30. The ride was scheduled to start at six, and Allison had suggested arriving an hour early. Probably most of the riders would arrive at the starting area around five. Ruby slipped out of bed and pulled on her clothes. Tiptoeing down the stairs with her shoes in her hand so she wouldn't wake her parents, she determined to force down breakfast, even though she didn't feel like it. While her bagel toasted she checked over her pile of gear on the table. Canteen, water bottle, hat, sweatshirt, hoof pick, granola bars.

"Figured you'd be up early."

She jumped and turned to face her father, who leaned against the kitchen doorjamb.

"Hi, Dad. I hope I didn't wake you up."

"I don't know if you did or not, but how about a cup of coffee?"

She grinned. "Sure. I'll put some on. Want a bagel with it?"

"Why not?" He opened the refrigerator while she measured the coffee. By the time the coffee began brewing and the first bagels had toasted, he'd lined up margarine, jam, cream cheese, and honey.

"Wow. Quite a spread," she said dubiously.

"Nothing like a pre-dawn bagel party." He opened a drawer and selected knives and spoons.

Ruby checked the sugar bowl to make sure it wasn't empty. Her father took a teaspoon in each cup of coffee. They sat down together, and Dad asked a blessing, seeking special care and safety for all the riders.

The coffee was only half brewed. Ruby held a mug next to the machine and quickly yanked the carafe out, slipping the mug beneath the flowing stream of coffee. Although she was quick, a couple of drops splashed on the hot base and sizzled.

She slid the carafe back in place and carried the full mug to the table. "Here you go, Dad."

"Thanks. Are you nervous?"

"A little."

"Well, we'll be there with the lunch basket, waiting for you at Eight-Mile Creek."

"Thanks. I wish you could see the race, but there's no good place where you can watch much of it."

"Don't worry about it. What's the earliest you could get to the checkpoint?" Her father sipped his coffee and set the mug down.

"I hope to be there by noon, but it could be one or later if things don't go well."

"We'll be there at eleven in case you're early. But don't worry if you're late.

We'll enjoy the scenery and cheer on the riders that come in ahead of you. We'll be praying for you, too."

"Thanks. The first part of the ride is the easiest, so I have hopes of getting to the lunch stop by noon. It's forty miles on the trail."

"Really? I think it's less than twenty miles from here. You know, Grandma said she and Elsie will come. I told her they can't take their semitruck on the mountain road, so they're coming to the house and will ride up there with us."

"Oh, that will be neat." Ruby smiled just thinking about the pink semi with gold lettering that her grandmother and her sister-in-law, Elsie Daniels, roamed the roads in. The two widows hauled limited amounts of freight for businesses their husbands worked with in the old days and loved their adventures on the road. "When are they going to retire, anyway?"

"When they're good and ready, I guess. Believe me, I've tried to talk them into it. Your cousin Dylan may be coming, too, and maybe Holly." Dad spread cream cheese on his half of the first bagel and topped it with a squirt of honey.

Ruby poured orange juice for herself and put a little cream cheese and strawberry jam on her half of the bagel. Behind her on the counter, the second one popped up in the toaster.

"I'll get it." Dad jumped up and grabbed the hot bagel halves, dropping them onto his plate. "Ouch. Hey, where did you get cranberry bagels?"

"Not me. Mom must have found them somewhere." Ruby accepted one and decided to eat it plain while it was hot. "Yum. You were right, Dad. This is fun. Thanks. Like I said, I'm a little nervous."

"You'll do great." He took a bite of the cranberry bagel, slathered in cream cheese, and closed his eyes. "Mm. That's even better than the cheese and tomato bagels." He chewed another bite and swallowed. "So, honey, we'll all be over at the finish line to see you come in at the end of the ride tonight."

"That's fantastic, Dad. Thank you." She wiped her hands, stood, and reached for her sweatshirt.

"Want me to help you load Lancelot?" he asked.

"No, I'll be fine. I packed his tack in the trailer last night."

"Well, I already hitched the trailer to the truck for you."

"Great. I'll see you later, Dad." She stooped to kiss his cheek and went out into the dark, damp morning. When she opened the stable door, Lancelot nickered softly.

"Good morning, fella."

She walked to his stall door and stroked his nose then scratched around his ears. Lancelot whuffed in response and rubbed his head against her shoulder. Ruby brought him a short ration of oats and a bucket of water. As he ate, she went over his glistening golden coat with a soft brush.

"We're going to have fun today," she told him. His soft whicker made her smile.

At 4:15 a.m. she led Lancelot out to the horse trailer, and he stepped eagerly up the ramp. Ruby hooked the cross ties to his halter and gave his withers a final pat. The drive to the starting area was only a few miles, and she knew she'd be very early, but she didn't mind. She and Lancelot could enjoy the dawn and watch the other competitors arrive.

She passed the road to the campground but didn't see any vehicles coming out. When she came to the gravel road leading to the field where the race would start, she flipped on her turn signal. Just as she was about to swing onto the road, a light-colored pickup truck emerged. Ruby eyed it in surprise. She wasn't the earliest of the early birds, after all. The driver pulled out onto the paved road without making eye contact. He seemed to be in a hurry. She didn't recognize him, but stocky men in Stetsons were a dime a dozen in Wyoming.

She eased her rig carefully onto the smaller road and drove slowly toward the field. A whiff of smoke caught her attention. Last night's bonfire was held at the campground. Surely she wouldn't be able to smell any lingering hints of it from here. The field used as a parking area opened before her. The unnatural glow in the early dawn pulled her gaze toward the registration booth, and she almost jammed on the brakes but squeezed the pedal down slowly out of deference to Lancelot. The wooden booth was engulfed in flames.

Chapter 6

Ruby pulled out her cell phone with trembling hands and keyed 911.

"This is Ruby Dale. There's a structure fire off the Howard Road at the field where the endurance ride is supposed to start this morning. It's on the Landry ranch." She gave the dispatcher her cell phone number and more precise directions.

The fire crackled, and inside the trailer Lancelot pawed and whinnied. As the wooden booth crumpled and collapsed, embers fell to the ground. The dry grass surrounding it flared up in several spots. Ruby was torn by the desire to run over and try to stamp out the smaller fires, but Lancelot's safety came first. She threw the truck into gear and drove out to the paved road. She pulled to the side and opened her door. In a matter of minutes a siren greeted her ears. The small town fire department's obsessive drilling had paid off with a quick response time.

The first fire truck roared down the road but slowed as it neared her. The driver brought it to a stop beside her and killed the siren. Ruby squinted against the flashing red lights and pointed up the gravel road.

"Up there in the field," she called, pointing.

The ladder truck swung onto the side road, and a stream of cars and pickup trucks followed, some pulling horse trailers. Ruby drove slowly down the road to a place where she could safely turn her rig around and then went back to the field. A second fire truck—a pumper with a large tank body—swooped past her.

By the time she returned to the starting area, dawn had broken over the plains. The fire was out. Competitors, volunteers, and ride officials gathered in clusters to stare at the firemen as they rolled their hoses.

As she climbed down from the truck, Chuck approached and called out to her.

"Ruby! You missed the excitement."

She gave him a shaky smile. "Hi, Chuck. Actually I think I was here at the start of it." She told him what she had found on her arrival, and he whistled.

"You should talk to the fire chief. He was asking if anyone knew who called 911."

One crew of firefighters was still soaking the grass in a wide swath around where the blaze had been. Chuck pointed toward them.

"The chief's over there."

Ruby nodded and swallowed. Her throat felt scratchy. "Okay."

Chuck took her hand. "Come on. I'll go with you."

She smiled up at him. "Thanks. This wasn't exactly how I envisioned the start of this day."

Chief Ripton greeted her soberly then stepped aside with her and Chuck and listened to her explanation.

"It's a good thing you came along early, Miss Dale, and that you had a cell phone. If the grass fire had spread, this whole area could have gone up in flames."

Ruby gulped. "In that case I'm glad I was too nervous to sleep late."

"How far advanced was the fire when you first saw it?" Ripton asked.

She shuddered, recalling that first moment of realization. "It was. . .the booth was already burning. Flames were all over the counter area and running up the roof supports."

The chief nodded. "What else did you see?"

"I. . ." She glanced toward Chuck. For the first time she realized he was still holding her hand. "I saw a truck pull out of here when I came. A pickup. A. . .maybe a Dodge, I'm not sure. But it was a full-sized pickup, and it was light. Gray or tan maybe. I don't think it was white, but the sun wasn't up then."

The chief produced a notebook from somewhere within his turnout gear. "I want to take your name and contact information, in case the fire marshal wants to talk to you later."

"Sure," Ruby said.

Chuck squeezed her hand. "She's entered in the ride," he told the chief. "She'll be on the trail all day."

"I wish you success," Ripton said. Ruby gave him the data he requested, and he wrote it down. "Miss Dale, did you get a look at the driver of that truck?"

She squeezed her eyes shut. Her knees felt a little wobbly, and she was glad Chuck was beside her. She clung to his hand shamelessly and opened her eyes to face the chief.

"He was wearing a cowboy hat, low over his eyes, but I had the impression of a big man. Stocky. He was white. No beard or glasses. His. . .his chin. . ." She thought hard about what she had seen. "His jaw was kind of square. He didn't really look at me, and he peeled out onto the road as though he was in a big hurry."

"No doubt," Ripton said dryly. "Anything else?"

She hesitated, trying to recall every detail. "He had something hanging from the rearview mirror. Not those stupid dice, but something. Maybe an air freshener." She shrugged. "I'm sorry. That's about all I can remember."

"You're doing great," Chuck murmured, and a pleasant warmth slid through her.

The chief tucked his notebook away. "Thank you very much, Miss Dale. I hope you do well in the ride, and we'll be in touch later. This was definitely arson."

⠀⠀⠀⠀⠀⠀⠀⠀⠀⠀⠀⠀⠀⠀⠀⠀⠀⠀⠀⠀⠀⠀⠀⠀⠀≈

Chuck led Ruby back toward her rig. She staggered suddenly, and he slid his arm around her waist.

"Are you okay?"

"Yes. Sorry. My legs are a little rubbery."

He tightened his grip on her. "Let's just take it easy then. This was a bit of a shock, wasn't it?"

They approached her pickup, and he could hear Lancelot pawing inside the horse trailer. The smell of smoke still hung in the air.

"How about if you sit down for a minute and I get Lancelot out of the trailer?" Chuck asked.

"Yes, the poor thing." She glanced up at him with wide eyes. "Thank you. They will hold the ride, won't they? I mean, this won't stop it?"

"Oh, I don't think so." He glanced at his watch and noted it was already the starting time and he'd done no preparation beyond getting Rascal out of his trailer. He looked around the field for signs of activity among the ride officials. "Look over there." He pointed to where Tom Marden and Allison Bowie were setting up a folding table. "I think they're going to make do and keep things rolling."

"That's good." Ruby's voice held only a slight tremor now. "I haven't done my vet check."

"Me either. Just sit for a minute, and as soon as I get your horse on the ground we'll find out what they're planning."

Ruby opened the driver's door of her dad's truck and climbed in, leaving the door open. Chuck went to the back of her trailer and lowered the ramp. Lancelot whinnied. Chuck walked up the ramp, speaking softly to the palomino. As soon as he'd unsnapped the cross ties, Lancelot backed up and found his footing on the ramp. His steps thudded loudly as they edged to the ground. Chuck hitched the horse to the bracket on the side of the trailer and stroked his glossy neck, speaking gently to him. Other riders and spectators had arrived by the scheduled start time, crowding the parking area. People walked by leading horses and carrying buckets and tack. Chuck nodded to those who called greetings as he walked over to where Ruby sat. He leaned down, bracing against the doorframe.

"How are you doing?"

"Good," she said. "Thanks again."

"You're welcome. You know, I've been thinking about the fire and all."

"And?"

He watched her sober face. "God must have a reason for allowing this to happen."

Ruby managed a shaky smile. "That's just what I was thinking. The arson seems meaningless and cruel, but we don't know what God has planned. I was sitting here thanking Him for bringing me out early and helping the firefighters stop it so quickly. God is in control here, for sure."

Chuck reached out and squeezed her shoulder. "I'm glad you're thinking that way."

"Hey, Doc!"

Chuck looked up to see Jeff Tavish walking toward them. He straightened. "Morning, Jeff."

Jeff wore a bright red Western shirt trimmed in black and a cream-colored Stetson with soft, worn jeans. Chuck looked closely at his footwear and noted that, though they gleamed, Jeff's black cowboy boots had seen a lot of wear. No doubt the champion would be comfortable today, but he would still cut a dashing figure for cameras at the finish line.

"I got here after the excitement," Jeff said, "but Tom Marden told me Ruby's the heroine of the day."

Chuck smiled, but a glance at Ruby told him she was uneasy with the designation. She climbed out of the truck cab and stood beside him.

"I just got here before anyone else, that's all. One of the blessings of insomnia."

"You're too modest," Jeff said. "They told me your quick action kept the fire from spreading. This could have been a disaster if it got away and started burning range land."

Tom Marden's booming voice, made even louder with a bullhorn, called out, "Attention, everyone! The ride officials have decided the ride will go forward, but the start will be delayed sixty minutes. The first riders will leave the gate at seven o'clock, which is just over a half hour from now."

All over the field, riders let out a cheer.

"Of course the maximum finish time will also be adjusted to 7:00 a.m. tomorrow," Tom went on. "Our ride secretary is now set up to register the competitors, and the judges have a special request. They would like Miss Ruby Dale to come to the registration table where the ride secretary will present her with bib number 1, in recognition of her role in stopping the fire this morning."

Ruby's face went scarlet, and she looked up at Chuck. He smiled, thinking how attractive her modesty made her. He grinned at her and jerked his head toward the registration table. "Come on. Let's get you over there so we don't hold things up any longer."

He and Jeff walked on either side of Ruby as she crossed the parking area to resounding cheers and applause. She raised her hand in a shy wave and lowered her gaze as soon as she reached the table. Allison Bowie handed her a numbered bib.

"Let's see, Ruby. You haven't had your vet check yet."

"I know. Is there time? Chuck's horse hasn't been vetted either."

Allison pointed across the field. "Dr. Hogan and Dr. Sawtelle are over there right now. Better hustle."

"Thanks." Ruby looked at Chuck.

"Go ahead," he said. "I'll be right behind you."

"Okay, thanks." She threw a smile in Jeff's general direction and hurried toward her rig.

Jeff stood back and gestured for Chuck to go next. Chuck nodded and smiled at him and quickly gave Allison his information. She handed him bib number 2. Hester Marden had begun registering more riders at the other end of the table, and he saw Jeff had number 3. Chuck would just as soon Jeff was farther down the line of riders. *Oh well, if he passes us first thing, we won't have to worry about him for the rest of the day.*

He realized he was jealous of the champion, and not because of Jeff's riding ability or his flashy good looks. Chuck sent up a quick prayer for calmness and God's guidance as he saddled Rascal.

When both their horses had passed the veterinarians' inspection, Ruby walked over to his truck, leading Lancelot. The palomino tossed his head and nickered. Rascal pulled his head around, stretching the tie rope taut, to look at his friend and whinny in response.

"I think these two are buddies for life," Ruby said with a chuckle.

"That's good. Horses need social interaction just like people."

"Is someone meeting you at the noon stop?" She hitched Lancelot to the side of the trailer.

"Just Dr. Hogan. As soon as all the riders have started, he'll drive up there. He's manning the vet check at the lunch stop today, and he has a ration and a water bucket for Rascal in his car."

"My folks are coming."

"Great."

Ruby had braided her hair, he noted. Although she seemed calm now, her face was still pale.

"I've got some cold drinks in my cooler," he said. "Would you like some juice?"

"That sounds good. But you need to finish getting Rascal ready. Anything I can do to help?"

"No, I'm all set except for putting this bib on. Why don't you help yourself and bring me a bottle of apple juice?"

"Okay." Her dark braid hung down below her hat against the back of her blue gingham-checked shirt as she leaned over the side of his truck's bed and opened the cooler.

Chuck tore his gaze away and pulled the marked bib over his head. *I'm riding in back of the prettiest cowgirl in Wyoming,* he thought. *If I have to eat Ruby's dust all day, at least I'll have a terrific view.*

As he tied the strings to anchor his bib, Ruby returned with two bottles. Chuck stowed Rascal's halter and lead rope in his saddlebag and took the bottle of juice she held out.

"Hey, how you folks doing?" Jeff Tavish led his horse over close to them. Chuck looked over the compact bay mare with appreciation. Close coupled with a deep chest, she looked wiry and tough. No doubt she had the stamina to complete the rugged ride.

"Is this the horse you won on last year?" Chuck asked.

"Sure is. Her name is Annabelle." Jeff beamed with pride and stroked his mare's shoulder.

"She has to be the best endurance horse ever." Ruby's eyes practically glowed as she gazed at Annabelle.

"Thanks. What's you all's strategy?" Jeff might be addressing them both, but he looked only at Ruby.

"I'm not sure I have one," Chuck said. "I just want to finish safely."

Ruby smiled at him. "Me, too, but I was figuring to start out with a canter across the fields. We'll have plenty of slow places when we get up in the hills."

Jeff nodded. "Yeah, that's good. But you want to keep your time down if you can. Remember—it's not the horse that crosses the finish line first; it's the one with the shortest overall ride time. So you can leave first and finish first, but if Chuck finishes a minute after you do he's the winner, since he's starting two minutes later."

She nodded and shot a glance at Chuck. "Well, I'll keep an eye on this hombre if he starts creeping up on me."

They all chuckled, and Jeff asked, "Do you want to stick together for the first leg?"

Chuck eyed him in surprise. He'd figured the champ would breeze past them and lead the entire race. "Is that what you usually do?"

Jeff shrugged. "Sometimes. It's good to have a buddy or two at the start. It's not like a short race. Pacing is critical. These horses need some energy left for the second half, so I like to start out at a moderate pace and enjoy it."

Ruby smiled at Chuck. "It might be fun to ride together for a while. But if you guys find I'm slowing you down you need to go on ahead and not worry about Lancelot and me."

"You'll probably do better than me," Chuck said with a shrug.

"We'll stay together if it works for us then," Jeff said. "If it's holding any-one back, then it's every man for himself. Or woman."

Ruby grinned. "Got it. Do you want me to start out slower—just trot along?"

"No need," Jeff said. "We'll catch up. Right, Chuck?"

"Sure." Chuck wondered if he'd just agreed to an alliance that would cost him Ruby's attentions as well as a chance to lead the pack for a while. Once Jeff caught up to him and Ruby, there would be no question of who the ultimate winner would be. And as far as Ruby's heart was concerned. . .he eyed her as she chatted with Jeff. Her smile for the champ was as bright as the one she'd bestowed on Chuck earlier.

"Attention," came Tom's unignorable voice. "The ride will begin in five minutes. Will the first riders please report to the starting line? Number one is Ruby Dale, riding Lancelot. On deck is Dr. Chuck Sullivan on Rascal."

Ruby took a quick sip from her bottle. Her hands quivered a little as she replaced the cover. "Guess we need to look sharp."

"I'll put that away for you." Chuck took the bottle and placed it with his in the cooler. When he turned around again, Ruby had mounted and was gathering her reins.

"So we'll stick together at least until the checkpoint at Mile 10," Jeff said, grinning up at her.

"Got it." Ruby took a deep breath and looked over at Chuck. "Are you ready?"

"Yep, I'm right behind you." Chuck reached for Rascal's reins.

As Ruby trotted Lancelot toward the starting box, Jeff stepped closer to Chuck and extended his right hand. "Well, Doc, I wish you luck."

Chuck smiled and shook his hand. "May the best man and horse win."

Jeff grinned. "Oh, I think you've already won."

Chuck stared after him as Jeff turned and led Annabelle away.

Chapter 7

Ruby waited just outside the starting box. Chuck had mounted and was riding her way. He and Rascal reached her just as Tom Marden called, "Two minutes to start."

"Time for you and Lancelot to get into the starting box." Chuck nodded toward the area marked out on the grass with lines of flour.

Ruby glanced toward the officials' table. "I was wondering if we had time to pray."

Chuck's smile melted away any lingering nervousness.

"Sure." He sidled Rascal up next to Lancelot, and the Appaloosa snuffled Lancelot's face. "We'll have to keep it short." Chuck bowed his head, and Ruby followed suit. "Lord, we thank You for bringing us here for this exciting day in such a beautiful setting. We ask that You'd give us a good time today and, above all, safety. Amen."

"Amen," Ruby said and opened her eyes. Chuck's blue eyes regarded her soberly.

"Better get in the box," he said. "I'll see you soon, if you don't decide to gallop off in a cloud of dust."

She smiled. "You don't have to worry about that."

"One minute to go," said Tom Marden.

Lancelot seemed reluctant to leave Rascal but obeyed when Ruby pressed his side with her leg. He pivoted and entered the rectangle marked on the dry grass. She fingered her bib to make sure it lay flat against her shirt and pushed her hat back a bit. She'd considered wearing a more fashionable Stetson today but had opted for her comfortable old baseball cap. The sun had risen above the horizon and promised them a clear, warm day. She patted the pack behind her saddle's cantle. Canteen, sweatshirt, granola bars, trail map. Check. She could almost feel the stares of the spectators and the sixty-seven other contestants. When she glanced back at Chuck he raised his hand to his hat brim in salute, and she felt a surge of adrenaline.

"Rider number 1, go," came Tom's voice. He continued talking as she urged Lancelot forward. "Folks, the Wyoming 100 has officially opened, with Ruby Dale and Lancelot riding out first. Rider number 2 will enter the starting box. That's Dr. Chuck Sullivan on Rascal. On deck is number 3, Jeff Tavish, our current champion, riding Annabelle."

Tom's voice faded as Ruby set off along the edge of the field to where the trail skirted a fenced pasture, crossed a creek, and continued fairly flat for a half mile along a Jeep road. Her slight trepidation kept her on edge. *This is it,* she told herself. She leaned forward and patted Lancelot's withers. "Okay, fella, this is what we've trained for. Let's go."

She squeezed him with her legs and gave him plenty of rein. Lancelot slipped into his easy canter. Ruby grinned as they flew along the verge of the field. For two glorious minutes they were alone on the course, setting the pace for all those behind. She was glad she knew the route well.

To her right the wire fence bounded the trail, and a herd of Hereford cattle grazed in the pasture. For the most part they ignored her, but a steer near the edge of the enclosure lifted its head and watched her and Lancelot fly past. It let out a mournful lowing, and Ruby laughed as they approached a rustic wooden bridge. The rancher maintained the span over a small stream that flowed through his property. The sturdy structure was held up by stone abutments on each end. They slowed to a trot, and Lancelot's shod hooves struck the decking made of two-by-eight boards. His hoofbeats echoed, but he reacted only with a twitch of his ears.

"Good boy," Ruby said as he stepped evenly forward over the bridge. She was now on a gravel road the rancher used to access the back acres of his land. Looking over her shoulder, she realized they were out of sight of the starting area. It felt a little strange to be out here in front, all alone. Again she thought of Julie. They'd done everything together, it seemed, until they were separated by death. Julie would have loved this ride. "I love you, Jules," she whispered. Could her sister see her now?

Lancelot lowered his head and quickened his steps. Ruby let him slip back into a canter. They approached a stand of rather spindly spruce trees. She looked back toward the bridge again. No sign of Chuck yet. As Lancelot loped along, she wondered if she should slow down. No, the two men had told her to set her own pace. Lancelot was fresh. She couldn't see any sense in wasting time on this easy stretch. Plenty of time for a slower gait later on.

The sun filtered through the tree branches as she followed the trail through the sparse woods. A sudden flash of movement ahead startled her, and Lancelot flinched as a deer bounded across the trail, but he continued steadily onward. She came to a spot where three ribbon markers indicated a turn onto a narrower path that eased upward into the foothills. As she turned Lancelot onto it, she heard hoofbeats behind her.

A glance over her shoulder told her Chuck and Rascal were fast closing the gap between them. She fought the instinct to stop and wait for them but let Lancelot trot up the slight incline. The smell of the evergreens and the sounds of creaking leather and hooves on the trail engulfed her.

She looked back again. Chuck waved. He might have been riding a solid brown horse from what she could see of Rascal. The gelding's dark head, shoulders, and legs, with only a strip of white on his nose, gave no hint of his glorious white markings behind the saddle.

"The trail widens out ahead," Ruby called as Chuck brought his mount up closer. "Want to canter awhile longer?"

"Sure," he replied. "Let's make all the time we can without tiring them out."

She turned forward, urging Lancelot to resume his canter. He snorted and picked up the pace, running easily along the gently undulating trail. A short distance later they emerged onto an almost flat meadow owned by the Bureau of Land Management. Most of the grassy area was fenced by an abutting rancher, but there was plenty of space along the edge for the two horses to run side by side. As Rascal overtook Lancelot, Ruby looked at Chuck. His grin of sheer delight made her laugh. Something about racing across country on an eager horse inspired a confident joy deep inside her.

At the far side of the meadow the grassy trail again wove through a scanty copse. Chuck slowed Rascal to allow Ruby to move her horse ahead of his.

"Jeff's coming up," he said, and Ruby looked back.

The bay Arabian mare tore along the trail at the edge of the meadow, her black mane floating in the breeze of her speed. Ruby could spot Jeff a mile away with his light-colored hat and blazing red shirt.

"Think she's going flat out?" she asked.

Chuck shook his head. "Naw, she's just stretching her legs. I'll bet she could do a lot faster on a racetrack."

Ruby realized they'd slowed to a walk. She clucked to Lancelot, squeezing his sides. Might as well let Jeff work a little to catch up to them.

⌘

Jeff's bay mare galloped up fast behind Chuck. Rascal snorted and flicked his ears back and forth. The rhythm of Annabelle's hoofbeats changed, and the mare whinnied.

Chuck looked back and waved at Jeff. The path was too narrow for them to ride abreast, so Annabelle fell in behind them.

Ruby slowed her mount as they approached a downward sloping bank, and Chuck pulled Rascal down to a trot. Ruby pushed Lancelot forward. The palomino bounded down the bank and picked up a gravel road around the edge of a large hayfield.

Chuck gave Rascal an encouraging nudge, and the Appaloosa followed Lancelot without hesitation. Almost as soon as they hit the gravel road, Annabelle galloped past and fell into stride with Ruby's horse.

"Ready to move out?" Jeff yelled.

Ruby threw a questioning look over her shoulder at Chuck. Part of him wanted to say, "No, you go on ahead." Wouldn't a leisurely ride with Ruby be better than maintaining their lead on the pack that would follow? The other part of him wanted to behave like a serious contender and give himself every advantage he could. What sense did it make to enter a competitive ride and not act like a competitor?

Was the alliance a mistake? Jeff had agreed that if he felt they held him back he'd move out alone, but he'd also agreed to keep the threesome intact until the first checkpoint. Chuck had thought Rascal moved quickly, but compared to Annabelle his mount was a plodder. Maybe the defending champion would tire of waiting for them and leave them well before Mile 10.

They went on steadily, trotting most of the time, cantering on open stretches and walking on steeper grades, but Chuck knew they were still in the easy part. Just after Mile 5 they picked their way downhill to a swift-flowing stream. When Ruby and Chuck caught up to Jeff, he had dismounted and led Annabelle down to the water so she could drink.

"How you folks doing?" Jeff called.

"Fine," Ruby said. "We're going a little faster than I usually do."

"We'll have to slow down now. The trail gets a lot more rugged after this." Annabelle raised her head and shook it, splattering Jeff with water droplets. He led her up the bank and out of the way.

Ruby led Lancelot down to the edge of the stream.

Jeff turned his horse in a circle so that he stood near Chuck. "Do we need to take it easier?"

Chuck shrugged. "You're the pro, Jeff. Ruby and I probably aren't used to pushing hard at the start, but if you think we're okay. . ."

Jeff frowned at his watch and pushed a button on the side of it. "We're making pretty good time." He eyed Rascal critically. "Your horse seems to be taking it all right. Let him get a drink, and we'll head out. But if you think you need to slow down give a whistle. That goes for you, too," he said to Ruby as she led Lancelot up from the water.

"Well, we are in a race." Ruby moved her palomino back up to the trail. "I don't want Lancelot to be exhausted by the halfway point. He's doing pretty well, actually. He's not even sweating yet."

"You're right about not overdoing it. The horses' condition is what matters. But sometimes our expectations of what a horse can do are too low."

"True," she said. "I don't want to hold you and Chuck back, though. So far we're okay."

When Rascal had finished his drink, Chuck took him back up to the trail. Ruby was mounting, and Jeff had already begun to trot off toward the hills. Chuck hopped into the saddle and smiled at Ruby.

"Ready?"

She nodded. "I was thinking how crazy I was to agree to stay with Jeff. Lancelot and I could be ambling along at our leisure instead of pushing to keep up with the champ. But Lancelot seems to be doing fine."

"If you want to drop back and let Jeff go on ahead. . ." As he spoke, Chuck realized he was beginning to feel like a frontrunner. He didn't want to give up the lead they'd maintained so far.

"You know I'm not in this to win. I just want to finish the course with Lancelot in good condition. But. . ." She looked his Appaloosa over. "How's Rascal doing?"

"He seems to be enjoying himself so far. Hey, wouldn't it be great to finish your first hundred-miler in the top ten?"

She grinned and gathered her reins. "Let's go!"

Chapter 8

At the first checkpoint they trotted in together. Chuck was pleased with the way Rascal still pranced and tossed his head at the waiting officials after having gone ten miles. Jeff reined Annabelle in at the last second and gestured for Ruby to precede him across the line.

"Going to keep the one-two-three order?" the ride secretary's assistant asked with a grin as Ruby dismounted.

"Why not?" Jeff hopped down and stood aside, holding Annabelle's reins and watching the back trail.

Ruby held Lancelot's head while the secretary took his pulse. "You're good." She jotted the precise time down on Ruby's vet card. "Just take your horse over there, and the vet will do the exam." On duty was Dr. Philip Nickerson, whom Chuck had met on several occasions.

The secretary checked Rascal's pulse next, then Annabelle's. All were within the acceptable range, and they proceeded to the square where the veterinarian evaluated each horse.

"I only caught one glimpse of a rider behind us," Chuck told Jeff. "That was back on that steep grade where we could see the trail below."

Jeff nodded. "We've got a good lead. Three minutes so far, and no one else in sight. That means we've increased our starting lead."

Chuck inhaled deeply and smiled. It felt great.

"You're good to go when your mandatory fifteen minutes are up, Miss Dale," Dr. Nickerson said, giving Lancelot a slap on the side. "Take this boy over to the start now if you like. Hi, Chuck. How you doing? Having fun?" Nickerson didn't wait for an answer but put his stethoscope to Rascal's ribs just forward of the saddle's cinch strap.

"Oh, yeah," Chuck said with a grin.

"Ruby," Jeff called, and she turned to look at him.

Jeff pointed across the clearing to where a red pickup truck was pulling in. "My crew just arrived."

"You have a crew?" Her eyes widened.

Jeff laughed. "Yeah, my kid brother and a couple of friends. I didn't think they'd make it until the lunch stop, but there they are. Go over and get some water for you and Lancelot. They've got hay and electrolytes for the horses and snacks for us."

"Wow. Thanks, Jeff." Ruby studied Jeff for a long moment before she moved away.

"Trot him out, please," the vet said, and Chuck realized the doctor had already taken Rascal's pulse and counted his respirations. He gripped the lead line and ran beside Rascal for several yards away from the vet then turned him and trotted back.

By the time Dr. Nickerson had finished his examination, given Chuck the go-ahead, and teased him gently about his beautiful riding partner, Ruby was walking toward him holding three dripping bottles of water.

"Oh, that looks good." Chuck took one, uncapped it, and tipped his head back for a deep swallow. "Thanks."

"You're welcome. Bring Rascal over. Jeff's friends will sponge him down for you."

"Wow! I don't think he's even hot yet, but that will sure come in handy later on."

Ruby nodded, and her brown eyes glittered. "The secretary says we've made good time. Not record-breaking time, but pretty good." She glanced toward where the trail entered the mountainside meadow. "Hey, here comes number 4."

Chuck looked over toward the path. "Sure enough."

Jeff eased around Annabelle's head, still holding her reins as Dr. Nickerson counted her respirations. "Eight minutes. We three checked in eight minutes before number 4. Not bad." He winked at Ruby. "You and your golden boy are potential winners."

Ruby flushed. "Oh, I doubt it." She handed Jeff a bottle of water.

"Thanks. As long as you're ahead of the pack, the possibility is there."

Chuck watched Ruby closely. Of course hearing that from a champion was flattering, but Ruby just shrugged. "I'm having a blast."

Jeff laughed. "How about you, Doc? Glad you came?"

"Oh, yeah." Chuck smiled at him. "Don't feel you have to stick with us, though, Jeff. We know you'll want to move out at some point and increase your lead. Don't worry about us. Ruby and I will keep on as fast as we can, but we don't expect to cross the finish line with you."

"You never know. We could finish as the Three Amigos."

Jeff's brilliant smile made even Chuck feel it might be possible. Was Jeff humoring them? Did he do this every year—pick up some trail buddies to pace himself with? Or were Rascal and Lancelot truly among the best competitors today? The other possibility—that Jeff wanted to stick close to Ruby in a bid to win her affections—still niggled at Chuck. Jeff's earlier comment about Chuck having already won should have put that thought to rest, but Chuck couldn't help thinking some of Jeff's laughing remarks to Ruby constituted flirting.

Her wistful expression tugged at his heart. When she turned her gaze from Jeff to him, Chuck's stomach fluttered.

Dr. Nickerson dismissed Annabelle, and Jeff led the mare quickly toward his crew. They tended to the horse while Jeff grabbed a chocolate bar and offered one to Chuck and Ruby.

"Not now," Ruby said. "Maybe later."

"Are you ready to go on?" Chuck asked. "Your hold time is almost up."

"Yeah." She took another swallow of water and looked about.

"I'll take that for you." He'd spotted a trash can near the secretary's booth, set up under an awning beside a small RV. "Mount up, gal."

When he returned from discarding the bottles, Jeff and Ruby were both in the saddle.

"Hurry up, Chuck," Jeff said. "We all checked in at the same time. They're letting us go together, as long as we leave in the order we came in."

"Great!" Chuck swung up onto Rascal's back and eased in between Jeff and Ruby. The fourth rider's horse was in the veterinarian's exam area. "Okay, Ruby, lead us on to victory."

They all waved to Jeff's crew.

"Thanks! We'll see you at Mile 20," Jeff called to his brother. The secretary's assistant stood at the checkpoint's starting line with clipboard and stopwatch in hand.

"Ready. Set. Rider 1, go!"

Ruby grinned at Chuck and urged Lancelot onto the trail at a trot. Chuck moved Rascal forward and the woman with the clipboard said, "Rider 2, go."

Chuck tapped Rascal's sides, and the Appaloosa bunched his muscles and bounded forward.

ã

The trail angled upward more sharply now, slowing their pace and causing the horses to breathe faster. Ruby stroked Lancelot's withers and spoke to him frequently, encouraging him to trot when the path wasn't too steep. After a mile she pulled aside in a clearing and let the two men bring their mounts up even with hers. She'd feel better if someone else took the lead.

"One of you go first," she said, looking from Chuck to Jeff and not wanting to make the choice.

"Why don't you take the lead, Jeff?" Chuck smiled at the champ.

"You sure?" Jeff asked.

"It would be a relief," Ruby admitted. "I keep wondering if I should speed up or slow down. You have so much experience that I'd appreciate it if you set the pace for a while."

Chuck didn't seem to mind. His blue eyes held a gleam of satisfaction. "Do you need to rest?" he asked.

Ruby shook her head. "We're good to go, right, fella?" She slapped Lancelot's neck, and he tossed his head as though nodding in agreement.

"Ah, you have a trick horse." Jeff grinned and turned Annabelle forward. "Let's move, amigos!"

His quick start surprised Ruby, but she let Lancelot trot to keep up. A quarter mile later they left the trees behind and embarked on a rougher up-hill section. The next two hours required a cautious pace. When they reached the Mile 20 checkpoint, in a ravine below a waterfall, all were ready for a breather. Jeff dismounted when he rode into the hold area and took Annabelle's pulse. Ruby had fallen back a hundred yards, but when Lancelot reached the spot she, too, climbed out of the saddle.

"How you doing?" Jeff asked.

"I'm a little stiff." She did a quick pulse check on her gelding then sat on the dry grass, holding the end of Lancelot's reins and counting his respirations. "That last upgrade was tough. Doesn't the trail dip down next?"

"Right. We'll go all the way down to the valley floor and over the stream. Then there're a couple of miles of fairly flat terrain before we go up another hillside. Guess I'm ready."

Allison Bowie, the ride secretary, was on hand to do the initial gate checks in person.

"All of the riders must have left the starting gate on schedule, or you wouldn't be here now," Ruby said.

"Actually I left Tom in charge at the starting area after the first forty riders took off, and I just pulled in here a minute ago. You guys are fast." Allison smiled at Jeff and wrote the time on his vet card. "You're fine to proceed to the vet check. Your thirty-minute hold starts now."

"Great." Jeff turned to Ruby. "Tell Chuck to go over there where my brother's truck is after he checks in."

Chuck and Rascal walked the last few yards to their resting place while Allison checked Lancelot. Chuck dropped to the ground and removed his hat. "Whew." He wiped his forehead with his sleeve. "Well, we're almost a quarter done. I feel like I've already had quite a workout."

Ruby nodded soberly. "Lancelot's still eager, but I think the rest will do him good. Jeff says to join him and his crew." She pointed to where the young people who'd helped them at Mile 10 were already stripping off Annabelle's tack.

"That's really nice of him. I was counting on amenities at the noon stop but not at every checkpoint."

"I know. It seems kind of strange to me he'd help us so much."

Allison took Ruby's card. "Your horse looks good. And that's just Jeff. He's generous, and he loves the sport. He's always encouraging other riders. This year I guess you're his protégés. Be thankful."

"I don't want to hold him back."

Allison shook her head. "Don't worry about that. Jeff aims for a consistent pace all day long, not a breakneck race. If he thinks you're too slow he'll go on without you. But it's my guess if that happens he'll tell his crew to take care of you if they can do it and still be on time to meet him at the next stop."

Ruby smiled as Allison handed her card back. "He's an all-around nice guy, I guess. Thanks a lot. Chuck, I'll see you in a minute."

She led Lancelot to the veterinarian's station.

"So number 1 has dropped to number 2," the doctor said with a chuckle.

As he began his examination, Ruby looked toward where Jeff had taken Annabelle. The mare was browsing at a flake of hay hung in a net from the truck. Meanwhile three people were sponging her back and legs with cool water. Jeff was nowhere in sight.

When Lancelot's exam was completed she led him slowly toward the truck. As she approached, Jeff came from the direction of the secretary's booth.

"Hey, Ruby! We're doing pretty good. Come on over and meet my gang. Sorry we didn't have time for introductions earlier."

She followed him to the truck. His brother, another young man, and a girl who looked to be about twenty paused in their ministrations to Annabelle.

"Hey, y'all, this is Ruby," Jeff said. "Ruby, this is my brother, Kevin, and his friends, Billy and Kaye."

The young men said hi, and the girl named Kaye gave her a friendly grin. "Glad to meet you, Ruby. Terrific horse."

"Thanks."

"She and Chuck are good friends of mine," Jeff said, "so hop to and help her get Lancelot comfortable."

The three immediately surrounded Lancelot and began removing his tack. Ruby started to protest but decided that would be foolish. Jeff wanted to do this, and it would be a big help.

"His halter and lead rope are in the pack," she said.

"Terrific." Kevin located them and had Lancelot tethered to the back of his truck in seconds, with a flake of hay shaken out on the tailgate. Kaye brushed Lancelot down, and Billy followed with a bucket of water and sponge.

"You guys are great," Ruby said.

"I trained them well," Jeff told her. "Of course, when Kevin performs in his next rodeo I have to be there to patch him up."

"So you guys do for each other? That's neat."

"It's kept us close." Jeff turned and nodded toward the secretary's booth. "Facilities over there, if you need 'em. Then we've got cold drinks and snacks. I'll wait here for Chuck. Looks like he's heading over here now."

Ruby looked up into his eyes. "I really appreciate what you're doing for Chuck and me."

"I like horses, and I like people." Jeff shrugged. "That's one of the best things about these rides—making new friends."

In the next fifteen minutes Ruby made a point of chatting with Kaye and the two boys and thanking them for the extra effort they put in on Lancelot and Rascal.

"No problem," Kaye assured her. "This is a lark, compared to watching Kevin get tossed off a bull." She wasn't beautiful, but with her short auburn hair, pleasant features, and long legs Ruby could see why Kevin liked her so much. His deference to Kaye left no doubt she was Kevin's girl, and Billy was just along for the ride.

"How long have you been seeing Kevin?" Ruby asked.

"Almost a year. He's talking about making it permanent, but I haven't decided yet whether I want to be a young widow or not."

Ruby grimaced. "That bad?"

"When he's good he's very good." Kaye shrugged. "But no cowboy has a good ride every time."

"Well, maybe you'll end up spending your retirement with a crippled old bull rider."

"Yeah, that could happen. Might not be so bad. Now if Jeff could talk him into retiring from rodeo and staying home to help run the ranch I'd like that." Kaye checked her watch and called, "Hey, fellas, time to tack up. Jeff's hold expires in five minutes."

"Let's move," Jeff agreed. "Don't try to go to the next checkpoint. The road's too rough to drive up in there."

"Right," Kevin said. "We'll go refill the water jugs and wait for you at the hold after that."

"Yeah, they'll only have a timekeeper and a vet at Mile 30. You have the map, right?" Jeff asked. "The lunch stop is right where they had it last year."

"Oh, right." Kevin nodded. "Got it. We'll see you there."

"Some of my family will be there," Ruby said. "Look for my folks and two grandmas in a Jeep."

"Jeff, better mount," Billy called. He and Kaye had completed their preparations on Annabelle, and he handed Jeff the reins.

"Thanks," Jeff said. "Now make sure Ruby and Chuck take off right behind me."

The three young people scurried about with brushes, blankets, and saddles. Two minutes later Ruby mounted and waved to the trio of helpers.

"You guys are the greatest. Thanks!"

Chuck nodded and grinned at her as she turned Lancelot toward the starting area.

The ten miles to the next checkpoint tested all three horses' stamina. At one point Jeff dismounted and walked behind Annabelle as she walked up a steep, rocky grade. At the top of the slope he remounted and waved down at Ruby.

"Take your time. Let him set his own pace."

She nodded and dismounted. "Okay, boy. Up you go." She draped the palomino's reins over his neck and released him. Lancelot eyed her for a moment. "Go on." She thumped his flank, and he stepped out on the upslope.

High above them Annabelle whinnied, and Lancelot pricked up his ears. Had Jeff taught his horse to neigh on command? It certainly put a spring in Lancelot's step. Ruby rushed after him, grabbing rocks and brush for handholds. She caught up to her horse and seized a handful of his tail hair, letting him pull her along without taking too much of her weight. Holding on to his tail helped her stay upright as they climbed. She wondered how Chuck was doing but determined not to look back until they'd made it safely to the top. She couldn't see past Lancelot's hindquarters to tell whether Jeff and Annabelle still watched her ascent.

At last they reached the summit, and her horse pushed onto the flatter area, taking Ruby with him.

"Good job!" Jeff reached out his hand and pulled her farther from the edge of the steep path.

"Thanks." Ruby seized Lancelot's reins and allowed him to edge over closer to Annabelle.

"Look down there." Jeff nodded at the back trail, and Ruby followed where he pointed.

Chuck and Rascal were only a few yards below them on the trail, with Chuck leading his Appaloosa.

"Wow, they're moving right along," Ruby said. "You don't have to wait for us, Jeff."

"That's okay. But you'd better move Lancelot a little farther away so Chuck has room to maneuver here."

Chuck and his horse scrambled to the top, and Jeff reached for Rascal's bridle.

"Super. You okay?"

"Yeah." Chuck took off his hat, wiped his brow, and put it back on. "Whew. Let's hope that was the worst stretch."

Jeff's boyish smile made Ruby want to laugh. "Now comes the fun part. Down to the valley again. But on the way we stop at Mile 30. It's just a little farther now."

"A fifteen-minute breather," Ruby said.

"Right. Let's go." Chuck raised his foot to his stirrup.

"Do you need a boost?" Jeff asked Ruby.

"No, I'm good." She hopped up into the saddle and gathered the reins.

"Well, you're so chipper, maybe you want to lead again." Jeff smiled and arched his eyebrows as he scooped up Annabelle's reins.

Ruby nearly refused, but Chuck grinned and gave her a thumbs-up. She turned Lancelot toward the next checkpoint.

"One-two-three, still leading," the secretary at the cramped Mile 30 holding area said when they rode in. Ruby missed having Kevin and his friends handy with cold drinks, but she actually rested more than she had at the last stop. After their vet checks she sat quietly with Chuck and Jeff for a few minutes, holding the end of Lancelot's lead rope and letting him breathe and snatch wisps of dry grass.

"There's number 5," Chuck observed, nodding to the clearing's entry.

"He passed number 4." Jeff checked his watch. "And he's only three minutes behind us. He must have flown up that steep grade."

Their horses all passed the exam and were ready to start at the earliest opportunity. Ruby was glad. She didn't like number 5, a young man on a chestnut mare, gaining on them so suddenly.

The next few miles of trail were easier as they regained the valley floor. They trotted forward until they came to an open stretch of plains. All the horses broke into a canter, running abreast across the prairie until they picked up the path where it again entered the woods and ducked beneath a railroad bridge.

Ruby looked back but couldn't see any other riders. "How are we doing?" she called to Jeff.

"Middlin'. Are you up for another canter?"

"Rascal's okay," Chuck said.

Ruby nodded. "Let's do it."

Following the trail up a gradual slope, they wound around a gentle hillside. They reached the Mile 40 checkpoint still in the lead. Ruby was startled to see a police car in the field near where the secretary's booth and RV were set up. She spotted her parents, waving wildly to her as she led Lancelot to the veterinarian's station. Kevin Tavish and his friends were parked beside her dad, ready to help during the hour-long noon stop. Kaye was filling a hay net, and Billy carried two buckets of water toward the back of the rig.

Dr. John Hogan met them at the veterinary check with a jovial smile.

"Well, well. Still in the running."

"Hello, Dr. Hogan. Great to see you," Ruby said. The September sun shone brightly on the field, and she felt warm, though they were at least a thousand feet above sea level.

Chuck brought Rascal over to wait while his partner examined Lancelot. "We survived the first forty miles, John."

"That's a relief to me," Hogan shot back. "I'd hate to have to break in a new partner."

As soon as Lancelot was released from his exam, Ruby led him toward Kevin's pickup. She placed the reins in Kaye's hands.

"Thank you so much!"

"Relax and have something to eat," Kaye said. "We'll take good care of this guy."

"Great. My folks are right over there, so Chuck and I are going to eat lunch with them." She turned toward the Jeep. Her parents, with Grandma, Elsie Daniels, and her cousin Dylan, waved and grinned.

"Come on, Ruby," her father called.

As she walked toward them smiling, the police officer and another man approached her.

"Miss Dale?"

"Yes."

The officer nodded toward the man who accompanied him. "This is George Ware. He's the fire marshal, and he'd like to ask you a few questions."

Chapter 9

As Chuck held Rascal still for the veterinary exam, he watched Ruby lead her palomino away. This would be a high point of the day for her, he could tell. Her eyes had gleamed when she spied her parents waiting for her.

A police officer and another man intercepted her after she'd turned Lancelot over to Jeff's crew. More about the fire?

"Trot him out," Dr. Hogan said.

Chuck obeyed, keeping his eye on Ruby. When John released him with a favorable report, he hurried across the field. Now Ruby was over near her Jeep, hugging her parents. But the two men waited a few yards away, so it wasn't over yet.

"Hey, Chuck!" Billy jogged out to meet him. "Want me to take Rascal for you? Ruby said you're eating lunch with her and her family."

"Sure. Thanks a lot."

"We'll take good care of him. You can count on that."

Chuck smiled in acknowledgment and let him take the reins. When he turned toward the Dales' parking spot, Ruby was hugging a white-haired woman. That must be Grandma. He heard Ruby say, "Did you all hear about the fire at the starting booth this morning?"

"No," said her dad. "What happened?"

"I'll have to tell you later." She looked up and spotted him. "Oh, here comes Chuck. He can tell you. I need to go speak to the fire marshal." Their bewildered glances landed on Chuck. Ruby winced and said to him, "Do you mind explaining to Mom and Dad why I have to go talk to that cop and the fire marshal?"

"Sure."

"Thanks."

She hurried back to the waiting men.

Chuck turned to Martin Dale.

"What happened?" Martin demanded.

"Ruby's all right. There was a fire this morning at the starting area. She was the first to arrive, and she reported it. The fire chief told us it was arson and that the fire marshal would want to talk to her later. I think that's what this is about."

"Was anyone hurt?" Ruby's mother asked.

"No. The registration booth burned, and there was some damage to a shed the riding club had out there to hold supplies. Nothing serious."

"Well, let's get out the lunch so we'll be ready when Ruby's done," the older woman said. "By the way, I'm Ruby's grandma."

"Pleased to meet you." Chuck shook her hand with a grin.

"And this is my sister-in-law, Elsie," Grandma added. "Say, Linda, where did you put the paper plates?"

Ruby's mother turned to help her find the picnic settings.

"Who are those kids wiping Ruby's horse down?" Martin asked.

"Oh, those are some new friends." Chuck grinned and nodded toward Jeff, who was leading Annabelle across the field. "See that guy in the red shirt?"

"How could I miss him?"

Chuck laughed. "Well, that's the two-year champion, Jeff Tavish. Ruby and I have been riding with him. His brother and a couple of friends insist on taking care of our horses along with Jeff's."

"That's mighty nice," Martin said.

"Yeah."

Jeff caught Chuck's eye and waved.

"Say, we've got a ton of food," Linda said. "Maybe we should invite them to join us?" She shook out a quilt and spread it on the dead grass.

When Ruby joined them a few minutes later, Jeff had brought the cooler over from his truck and pooled his party's food with the Dales'.

"Wow! Is this a feast?" Ruby asked.

"Almost." Chuck stood until she'd chosen a corner of the quilt and sat down.

"Did you meet everyone?" she asked as he settled down beside her.

"I think we did." Chuck smiled at her parents, Elsie, Grandma, and Dylan.

"You've got a great family," Jeff said. "Can't believe your lovely grandma Margaret drives a trailer truck."

Grandma grinned at him. "Oh, you're a charmer—I can see that."

Linda looked toward Jeff's rig. "Should we wait for your friends?"

"Naw," Jeff replied. "They said they'll come over after they're finished grooming the three horses. I told them we'd save them each a chicken bone."

Martin let out a guffaw then sobered. "Right. Let's pray then." He closed his eyes and began to ask the blessing.

Chuck quickly bowed his head without looking to see Jeff's reaction. As soon as Martin said, "Amen," food containers came at him rapidly from both sides. He filled his plate with sandwiches, fried chicken, potato chips. and fruit salad. Grandma passed him a can of soda.

"So, Ruby, what did the police want?" her mother asked. "Was it about that fire?"

Ruby nodded. "I had to tell the fire marshal everything I told the fire chief this morning. And the police want me to go to the police station tonight when the ride is over to look at some pictures."

"Pictures?" Her father eyed her closely.

"Yeah, I saw a man in a pickup leaving the field this morning right before I discovered the fire. They hope I can recognize him in a photo lineup."

"That's exciting," said Grandma. "Can I go with you?"

Ruby laughed and leaned over to hug her. "It will probably be late, Gram, but thanks. You always keep me laughing, you know that?"

"Well, at the rate we're moving today," Jeff said, "Ruby will probably make it to the police station by nine o'clock."

"Thanks, Jeff." Ruby's brow puckered as she sipped her soft drink. "I told them I probably won't be able to get there until Sunday. We could be on the trail until well after midnight, depending on how Lancelot holds up."

Chuck noticed her frown remained in spite of the conversation that swirled around them about horses and Kevin's next rodeo performance. He leaned close to her ear and asked, "Do you want to drop out? I could take you to the police station now."

She chuckled. "I'd accuse you of trying to eliminate the competition, but that would take you out of the race, too. No, seriously, they said it's all right. It's just a little creepy, not knowing if the man I saw was the arsonist. I keep thinking of things I could have done differently."

"Don't. You did just fine."

"So are you guys, like, winning this thing?" Dylan asked. Chuck had learned he was in his senior year of high school and the oldest of Ruby's cousins.

Ruby turned with sparkling brown eyes. "As of right now we sure are."

"Rider number 5 checked in three minutes behind me," Jeff said. "Ruby, you need to be ready when the hour's up."

She consulted her watch. "We've still got twenty-eight minutes. Guess I have time for one of Mom's apple turnovers."

⟡

Chuck was surprised how easy the next fifteen miles seemed. Rascal stepped along as jauntily as he had at seven that morning. The trail took them deep into the hills. After a fifteen-minute hold at Mile 51 the three frontrunners sped along toward the log bridge near the junction with the old stagecoach road. Kevin, Billy, and Kaye had promised to meet them at the new Mile 63 checkpoint where the loop added this year rejoined the traditional trail.

Chuck had taken the lead, and Rascal snorted disdainfully as he approached the span over a rushing stream. He plodded steadily over it, and Ruby took Lancelot along behind him with no problems, though his hoofbeats thunked loud and hollow on the planks and the whitewater gushed over the rocks below them. Chuck looked back again in time to see Jeff and Annabelle also crossing with ease.

"This is it," Ruby called to Jeff. "We pick up the old stagecoach road here."

Jeff's eyes glittered as they turned onto the new section of the trail. Chuck felt the exhilaration, too. The path was wider and somewhat easier than the last stretch had been, and he was able to relax in the saddle and take in the vistas from every vantage point. A cool breeze off the summit reminded him winter came early in the mountains. He stopped for a minute to untie his light jacket from the back of Rascal's saddle.

"Getting chilly up here," he said to Ruby as she came abreast of him.

"Yeah, it is." She reached for her hooded sweatshirt, and Jeff pulled a denim jacket from the back of his saddle.

All too soon they reached a downhill section where places in the trail had eroded. The dicey footing required caution as they wound around the mountainside.

"This is one section Ruby and I walked yesterday," Chuck told Jeff. "Too rough to drive up, even with her Jeep."

At one point a rock slide had narrowed the trail so they had to pick their way through slowly, one behind the other.

At last they came down to the junction and the rest stop. Kevin, Billy, and Kaye were there, ready with water buckets, sweat scrapes, and cool drinks. Chuck peeled off his jacket and stowed it again, and Ruby did the same with her sweatshirt.

After turning Rascal over to the crew, Chuck chose a bottle of water. Ruby was still at the vet check, and Jeff had disappeared toward the secretary's booth for news. Chuck walked over near the rim of the trail where he and Ruby had eaten their lunch Friday and seen the riders below. All the action seemed to be up here on the mountain today. He took a long swig of water.

"No horses tied up down there?" Ruby stepped up beside him and peered down into the ravine.

"Nope. Nary a one."

She smiled faintly but continued to search the wooded area below.

"I looked over my maps last night," Chuck said. "I couldn't find any trails or old roads down in that area."

Ruby shook her head slightly. "I don't know why I keep thinking about it. Hey, it must be almost time for you to saddle up."

Two riders entered the rest stop before Chuck mounted, with number 5 being closest behind them. The young man on the chestnut mare was now six minutes behind them, and number 8, Tom and Hester Marden's daughter, Reagan, came in two minutes after him.

"How's it going back there?" Jeff called to Reagan as she held her horse for the initial check-in.

"Not bad," the young woman replied. "I think they've bunched up a little. Hey, that stagecoach road was a fantastic ride!"

They were still talking when the secretary's assistant gave Chuck the nod.

"Rider number 2, go."

He looked over at Ruby, who was next in line on Lancelot, gave her a wave, and headed out. Immediately the timekeeper called, "Rider number 1, go."

Chuck let Rascal trot out confidently, but after the first mile he pulled over to the side at a wide spot in the trail.

Ruby brought her horse up beside his. "This is where we agreed Jeff should take the lead?"

Chuck nodded. "He said it's one of the most treacherous parts of the trail. I'd as soon have the champ go first."

Ruby looked back at Jeff and Annabelle, who trotted toward them. "He's done it several times. I'd rather follow him, too."

"All set?" Jeff called as he came even with them.

"Yeah," said Chuck. "Go ahead, and we'll be right behind you."

He urged Ruby to precede him and fell in last. The trail soon narrowed between a sheer cliff towering above them on their left and a sparse stand of spruce on their right. Through the trees he could see a distant line of mountains. The horses walked, conserving energy on the slight uphill grade.

They left the trees behind, and suddenly the rim of the mountainside dropped away on their right. At least there was plenty of room to continue safely in single file. Bright orange flags along the edge of the trail warned the riders to keep their distance.

Ruby turned around in her saddle and called, "We must be right above that rock slide where the hikers went yesterday."

Chuck squinted and looked out over the valley. "Maybe. I think we're past that now."

They rounded a bend, and ahead of them Jeff had paused to give Annabelle a breather and observe the view. His bay mare stood with her front feet closer to the edge than Chuck would have liked. Ruby halted her horse a few yards back, and Rascal stopped of his own accord behind Lancelot.

"Are we holding you back?" Ruby called to Jeff.

"Nah, Annabelle needed a little rest. We're pulling some serious altitude here."

Ruby nodded. She looked over at Chuck and smiled. "I almost think I want my sweatshirt again. It's cool up here." She swiveled in the saddle and tugged at her cantle pack.

"Let me get that." Chuck prodded Rascal to slide over closer to the palomino and opened Ruby's pack with it still tied in place. He pulled out her navy-blue zippered sweatshirt. "Here you go."

"Thanks." She took it and slipped her arms into the sleeves while he fastened the buckle on her pack.

He was about to comment on the drop in temperature when a quick scuffling movement drew his attention to Jeff and Annabelle. As he looked up,

Chuck's heart leaped into his throat. A large hawk swooped just over Jeff's head, flapping its wings near the horse's ears. Annabelle leaped back and shied to the side, flinging Jeff over her left side. He hung on to the saddle but fought a losing battle with gravity. The horse's near hind foot slipped over the edge of the rocky path, and she stumbled, taking Jeff down nearly to the ground. Annabelle snorted and strained to regain her footing, but her struggle only caused her other hind hoof to loosen small rocks as she clawed to get purchase, one hoof still dangling over the rim.

"Jeff!" Ruby cried. The hawk glided off over the valley, oblivious to Jeff's plight.

Chuck shoved his reins toward Ruby and bailed out of his saddle. He ran toward Annabelle, hoping to seize her reins and steady the mare.

Jeff's face melted from consternation to fear as he slid lower along the mare's side and gave up the fight to stay in the flat saddle. He pushed off and dove down the near side, landing with a thud on the edge of the rocky trail, just inches from the precipice. His hat flew off and landed a yard away. Before he could roll out of Annabelle's way and away from the edge, the mare heaved herself forward in a desperate lunge. Free of Jeff's cumbersome weight, she leaped up, scrabbling with her hind feet.

Just as Chuck reached her head, Annabelle found a foothold with her back hoof and jumped onto solid ground, landing low on her hocks, with her haunches sticking out behind. The whites showed around the mare's eyes, and she gasped for breath, emitting a shrill squeal. In a last bid for safety she swung sideways, her hind feet swinging around and knocking Jeff toward the edge.

Chuck seized the reins and pulled her forward, hearing Ruby's scream as he hauled Annabelle toward the high cliff face on the other side of the trail. He whirled her around, stroking her neck.

"Easy, girl." He looked back toward the edge of the trail.

Jeff was gone.

Chapter 10

W hat happened?" Chuck stared at the edge of the trail where Jeff had lain a moment before.

Ruby's stomach heaved, and her head seemed to spin. "He...he went over. When Annabelle jumped up, she kicked him."

Chuck's face crumpled for a moment, then he straightened his shoulders.

Rascal snorted and crowded against Lancelot. The palomino responded by nipping at Rascal's face.

"Can you come get Annabelle?" Chuck called. "Hurry."

Ruby pulled Lancelot's head around, away from Rascal's. She looped Rascal's reins over her right hand and squeezed her palomino's sides. "Come on, boy. Move."

"Hold on. I've got something here." Chuck looped Annabelle's reins around a projection of rock. "Be good, girl."

Ruby dismounted and dropped Lancelot's reins. He would stay put, and he was in a broad spot on the trail where he would be safe. She wasn't sure Rascal would ground tie, so she led him forward. Chuck was already at the edge of the trail, lying prone and looking over the rim.

"Can you see him?" Ruby asked.

After an agonizing moment Chuck said, "Yeah. He's about forty feet down, and he's crunched up against a scrub pine." He put his hands up to his face to form a megaphone. "Hey, Jeff! Can you hear me?"

Ruby held her breath.

"Yeah!" Chuck let out a short laugh and waved. "Hey, buddy, don't try to move. We'll get you some help."

"Is he all right?" Ruby didn't see how that was possible.

Chuck shredded her temporary relief when he pushed back away from the edge and stood. "No. I think he's hurt bad, but he moved his arm. I've got to get down there."

"It's really steep."

He nodded. "It's not sheer, but it's too steep to maneuver without help. I don't want to end up hurt as badly as Jeff is. He probably fell the first five yards then slid the rest of the way. Do we have any rope?"

"I have Lancelot's lead line."

"And I've got Rascal's. Jeff has one, too, I think. I'll check his pack. If we tie them all together, I may be able to use them to lower myself down past the worst of it, to where it's not quite so bad."

Ruby picked up Jeff's hat and hurried back to Lancelot, tugging impatiently at Rascal's bridle so that he followed her. While she opened her pack to get her lead line Rascal nipped her palomino's flank, and Lancelot squealed and kicked at him.

"Would you two stop it! You're supposed to be friends." Ruby slapped Rascal's nose and put his reins in her other hand, struggling to fish the eight-foot nylon lead line from her cantle pack.

"You have your phone, right?" Chuck called.

"Yeah." She looked over at him. He'd found a cotton rope in Jeff's saddle pack. "I don't know if I can get a connection up here."

"Try." Chuck walked toward her and reached for Rascal's saddle. "I'll tie all the lines together, but I doubt they'll reach more than twenty feet once I put knots in them."

Ruby's hands shook as she handed him Lancelot's lead. Chuck tied the end of her line to his own and pulled at the knot to test it.

"Guess I'll tie a loop in Jeff's and clip the snap to it."

Ruby dug in the pack for her cell phone. When she found it she pushed the button to turn it on. While she waited for the screen to clear she hugged herself, trying to stop her shivering. "What if the snap breaks?"

He shrugged. "It's supposedly strong enough to hold a horse. I'll have to take the risk. It would take too long to get someone to hike in from the mouth of the canyon and climb up to him. We're not even sure where the nearest road is."

"There might be an easier path somewhere along here."

"Yeah. But time may be critical, Ruby." He walked to the edge of the trail again and lay down with his head sticking out over the drop. After a long moment he stood.

"He's lying right where he was when I first saw him. I need to get down there."

Ruby studied the screen on her phone and frowned. "No bars. I don't think I can reach anyone, Chuck."

He frowned and glanced up the trail. "Maybe if you go up a little farther."

"Or maybe I should take Lancelot and ride back to the checkpoint."

"Well. . .it's closer than the next one." Chuck gritted his teeth.

Ruby knew she couldn't ride off for help and leave Chuck to climb down there alone with no one spotting for him.

Lord, help us!

"Are you praying?" she asked him.

"Yeah. Big-time. Run up to the top of the rise and try your phone from there."

Ruby dashed up the path, praying silently as she ran. At the highest point she stopped and looked at her phone.

"Maybe. Please, God." She pushed 911 and listened, trying to still her ragged breathing.

"What is your emergency?"

Ruby's knees almost buckled at the sound of the familiar voice.

"Nadine! It's Ruby. I'm at the hundred-mile ride, and we've had an accident."

"What's up?"

"One of the riders fell off a cliff. We're trying to get down to him, but we need rescue fast."

"What's the 20?"

"Between mile markers 65 and 66 on the trail. Drive in at Bear Creek Road. You can get an ambulance within a mile and a half of him. The EMTs will have to walk in from there."

"You're breaking up," Nadine said, "but I think you said Bear Creek Road. Is that correct?"

"Affirmative. There are race officials at the checkpoint. Tell them we're past Mile 65. And we have a veterinarian here who's trying to get down to the victim and give first aid."

"Got it."

Ruby closed her phone and raced back to where she had left Chuck. He looked up from his effort to connect the mismatched lines solidly.

"Did you get through?"

"Yes. They'll send an ambulance to the rest stop."

"Great. Help me find a solid place to tie the end of this. It has to be close to the edge, or there won't be enough length to do me any good."

"Can we tie it to Rascal's saddle horn?"

"Not long enough."

Ruby's stomach roiled. Was Jeff dying while they debated the best way to reach him? "Chuck, I'm lighter than you are."

"So?"

"So I should be the one to climb down the rope."

His eyes narrowed. "No way."

"Yes. Think about it. You could hold the end of the rope. We'd get the maximum length out of it that way."

"Oh, no. I'd probably drop you, or we'd both end up falling down there. Look, Ruby. I have medical training. I know I'm an animal doctor, but. . ."

He looked deep into her eyes, and at last Ruby inhaled and nodded. "You're right."

His smile was only a shadow of the one he'd charmed her with earlier. "Good. We agree. Now when I get down there I want you to take these three horses farther up the trail and hitch them in a safe place. You'll have to tie them by their reins, which isn't good, but it's all we have."

"Okay, but we need signals. When you get down there, you need to let me know how bad it is and if we need a helicopter or what."

"I should be able to make you hear me," Chuck said.

Hoofbeats clattered on the rocky trail behind them, and they both turned toward the sound.

Rider number 5, the young man on the chestnut, trotted into view. He pulled his mare up short when he saw them.

"What's going on?"

"We've got a man down," Chuck replied. "We'll need help."

His eyes widened. "No kidding? Where is he?"

Ruby pointed toward the edge of the trail. "Down there."

The young man's jaw dropped.

"Can you ride back to the checkpoint for help?" Chuck asked.

He hesitated.

"Well, at least help me get down there so I can check him over and give him first aid."

"Sure." He climbed from the saddle and eyed Ruby. "I'm Cody. You're Ruby, right?"

"Yeah." The bib with the bold number 1 felt like a scarlet letter, announcing her identity to the world.

Chuck once more went prone, leaning over the edge of the dropoff. "Cody, there's a stunted tree growing a few yards down the slope over there." He pointed to the left below them. "If you can help Ruby hold the line while I climb down there, I can tie the end to that tree and use the line to get down close to where Jeff is."

Cody's eyes popped open wider than ever. "Jeff Tavish? The champ is down there?"

"That's right."

"Oh, man."

Together they braced themselves. Ruby held the knot where Chuck had hooked the two nylon lines, and Cody grabbed the flat woven strap just below her hands. Chuck tested his weight against it then eased himself gingerly over the edge of the rock.

"Easy. Let it out a little. A little more. I'm almost to the tree."

Ruby gritted her teeth. Her hands hurt, and her arms ached. If not for Cody's help, she was sure she would have flown down the mountainside.

Suddenly the weight lifted.

"I'm at the tree!" Chuck yelled. "Hold on a sec." A moment later he called, "Okay. Let go."

She let the line slide away and clasped her aching hands. Cody went to his knees and peered downward, and Ruby lay on her stomach beside him. Chuck was trying his weight against the line once more. The scrubby tree he'd tied it to looked insubstantial, but it held as he began slowly backing down the steep incline. He reached a place where the hillside spread out more, supporting small brush, and paused to rest against a jagged rock.

He was at the end of the rope. Ruby judged the distance between him and Jeff's crumpled form to be about ten yards. She and Cody watched in silence as Chuck released himself from the line and edged onward, down and over toward Jeff.

Hoofbeats sounded behind them, and Cody leaped up. Reagan Marden trotted around the bend on her pinto gelding.

"Hey! Take it easy! There's been an accident," Cody shouted.

Reagan pulled her horse to a stop near Rascal. "What's up?"

"Jeff Tavish fell over the edge," Ruby said. "Dr. Sullivan is going down to help him, and I called for an ambulance."

"Wow. Anything I can do?"

Ruby looked at the cluster of horses in the trail. "The thing that would help most would be to take our horses a little ways up the trail to where you can tie them up off to one side. The trail is so narrow here that we don't want to clog the path. Someone else could get hurt."

"Sure. Is Jeff hurt bad?"

"We don't know yet. He was moving a little."

The girl nodded. "Oh, I have some aspirin in my saddlebag if it will help."

"I'll take it," Ruby said.

Reagan fished out a small plastic bottle and handed it to her.

"If you can just secure the horses, then you may as well ride on," Ruby told her. "When you get to the next checkpoint, tell them what's happened. I expect the ambulance will arrive at the Bear Creek stop before that, though."

"I could help her," Cody said.

Ruby gritted her teeth and nodded. He didn't want to give up his advantage and let Reagan take the lead in the race. Oh well. It was a sport, after all.

"Sure. You two go ahead. I'll stay here."

Cody ran to his horse. Ruby watched as he untied Annabelle and led her off up the trail. Reagan hooked Lancelot's reins over Rascal's saddle horn and clucked, pulling Rascal along by his bridle. To Ruby's relief both horses followed her pinto without nipping or kicking.

As the cavalcade disappeared up the trail, she sighed. They were past the most dangerous point now. There was plenty of room, really. If only that hawk hadn't swooped down from the cliff above and startled Annabelle.

She went back to the edge and lay down once more, pulling herself over until she could see down to where Jeff lay. Chuck was beside him now, bending low over Jeff's form. She wanted to yell and ask him for information, but she waited silently, praying for Jeff.

After what seemed like hours, Chuck turned toward her and rose, clinging to the small tree that had broken Jeff's slide down the mountainside.

"Ruby!"

She waved. "Yeah! I hear you."

Chuck nodded.

"How bad is it?" she called.

"Pretty bad. Broken arm for sure, maybe an ankle too, and no doubt heavy internal injuries."

Ruby's heart sank. The pitiful bottle of aspirin Reagan had passed her would do no good and might make things worse if Jeff was bleeding, since aspirin was a blood thinner. "What can I do?"

"Just get the medics down here as quick as you can." He pointed to her right, along the back trail. "The slope is easier over there. They might be able to come down with a stretcher. I don't see any place a chopper could land, though."

"Okay. I'll see if I can call dispatch and tell them that."

Chuck waved and turned back.

Hoofbeats thudded again on the rocky trail, and Ruby scrambled to her feet and away from the edge.

Chapter 11

Several riders wearing racing bibs trotted toward her. She recognized the woman edging up behind them on a quick-stepping black. Dr. Heather Spelling of Laramie, the veterinarian from the last checkpoint.

"What happened?" asked the first rider who reached her.

"An accident, but help is on the way. The best thing you can do is keep moving." Ruby waved on riders 4, 6, and 9. When they'd continued up the trail the veterinarian rode up to her and dismounted.

"I'm Dr. Spelling. As soon as we got the message, I packed all the supplies I could in a backpack. Where's the patient?"

"Down there." Ruby pointed toward the rim. "Dr. Sullivan is with him. I think you know Chuck?"

"Yes, and I know Jeff Tavish, too. Is there a way for me to get down to them?"

Ruby gritted her teeth. "It's really steep the way Chuck went. We improvised a line for him to hang on to. But he thinks it would be easier if we tried back there a little ways." She pointed. "The slope is more gradual, and you can get down to their level and work your way across."

Dr. Spelling nodded. "I'm not so good with heights, but I'll do it. Can you tie my horse up somewhere? He belongs to one of the ride officials, and I don't want anything to happen to him."

"Sure. But. . ." Ruby looked toward the precipice. "Maybe we could throw your pack down to Chuck, and he could get it and have the supplies while you're working your way down there."

"Good idea. I'll take out anything breakable."

"Let me tell Chuck what you're going to do, and then I'll take your horse." Ruby crept to the edge and lay down again. "Chuck!"

He looked up at her and waved.

"Dr. Spelling is here. Can I throw down a backpack with some bandages and stuff?"

"Terrific. I can use it."

Dr. Spelling crept to her side. "Here. I took out all the glass vials and syringes."

"We can put them in my pack for you to carry," Ruby said.

"Sounds good. Do you want to toss this down there, or shall I?"

"Are you good at softball?" Ruby asked.

Dr. Spelling chuckled. "Lousy at it. You go." She handed over the red backpack. It was light and floppy. Ruby wondered if she could get it near Chuck.

"Hey!" Chuck yelled.

She looked down at him.

"Just toss it gently and let it tumble down."

"What if it doesn't get close enough to you?"

"Then I'll climb up and get it."

Ruby gulped. "Okay." She sent up a swift prayer and threw the pack out away from the edge as far as she could. It plopped to the earth and rolled several yards then came to rest against a projecting rock about eight feet above Chuck and Jeff.

"Perfect," he shouted.

Ruby grimaced. It was far from perfect, but he would act as though it were. She watched as he crawled up the hillside and stretched to retrieve the pack. Pebbles dislodged by his feet pattered down the incline. Dr. Spelling caught her breath, and Ruby waited for something worse to happen. Chuck remained still for a half minute then inched his way back down to Jeff. When he was back at the patient's side Ruby exhaled, backed away from the edge, and stood. Dr. Spelling rose and brushed off her jeans.

"Listen. I could go down," Ruby said. "Let me go tie up your horse with ours and bring back my pack. I'll carry the medications down to Chuck."

"Well. . ."

"I'm sure I can do it."

Dr. Spelling sighed. "I don't have much that will help him. Saline and some painkillers. Most everything I had along was dosed for horses, though. We don't want a medication accident, so I only put in a few drugs."

Ruby reached out to squeeze her arm. "It's okay. I'm glad you rode up here. Just having the bandages will help Chuck a lot. If you stay here and make sure the riders keep going and don't block the trail and show the ambulance personnel where to climb down, it'll be terrific."

The vet still looked skeptical.

"You think about it," Ruby said. "I'll be right back." She jogged up the trail with the coal black horse trotting beside her. Around the next bend Lancelot, Rascal, and Annabelle were tethered off to one side and browsing the meager foliage. She hitched the black near them and ran to Lancelot. "Maybe I should have brought the lead ropes," she muttered, but there was no way she could have gotten them from the scrub pine where Chuck had tied them without climbing down there. With no harness that would be far too dangerous.

She unfastened her cantle pack, checked to make sure each horse was securely tied, and ran back down the path. Dr. Spelling was talking to rider 11, who sat astride a rangy chestnut. He moved on and passed Ruby.

"Who's doing the vet check now that you're gone?" Ruby asked as she handed her pack to the vet.

"I don't know. Tom Marden said he'd have the vet come up from the third checkpoint as soon as possible. Meanwhile, the secretary's assistant at Mile 63 said she'd check the vital signs and make sure all the horses took their mandatory rest."

"I guess that's all they can do until another vet gets there," Ruby said.

Dr. Spelling pulled vials and syringes from her pockets. "Okay, that's it. Are you sure you want to do this?"

"Yeah, I'm sure."

Ruby took the pack and slung it over her shoulder. She walked back along the trail and scrutinized the terrain below her.

"Hey!"

She looked up when Dr. Spelling called to her. "Yeah?"

"Chuck's pointing farther along. Go farther down the trail."

Ruby nodded and walked several yards back, around a slight curve in the trail. The mountainside was definitely gentler here. She adjusted the pack and prepared to climb down off the path. Another horse came walking up the trail toward her.

"Hey!" called rider 12. "Number 1!"

"Yeah?" Ruby waited for him to come closer.

"I'm supposed to tell you the ambulance was on the way when I left the last checkpoint. The EMTs will be here shortly."

"Great."

"So I heard Jeff Tavish fell off a cliff. Is he alive?"

"Yes." Ruby blinked at him, wondering how much to say and at the same time wishing she had more information to give. "Uh, he's hurt, but we've got two doctors helping him." No need mentioning they were animal doctors.

The rider nodded. "Okay. Guess I'll move along."

"Best thing you can do," Ruby said.

She watched him round the curve and inhaled deeply then stepped down off the trail. Her momentum pulled her downward, and she grabbed at low-growing shrubs to slow her descent.

≈

Chuck knelt beside Jeff, bracing himself on the steep hillside as he rummaged through the backpack Ruby had flung down to him. He pulled out two rolls of gauze and a tube of antibiotic ointment.

"I don't want to move you much, but I need to roll you away from that tree just a little so I can get at your arm."

"Do it."

Chuck pressed gently on Jeff's right wrist to keep the arm from flopping when he moved him and pushed him over, uphill, onto his back. Jeff let out a quick groan then was silent.

"There we go," Chuck said.

Jeff's eyes flickered open. "How we doing?" The champ's words slurred, and he grimaced as he tried to shift his weight.

"Could be worse." Chuck glanced up the hill. No help yet. The arm really needed a splint. "I think we should wrap your ankle while we wait. It's swelling a lot."

"Is it broken?"

"I'm not sure. Could be just a bad sprain. I also think that arm will need to be splinted before you're moved."

"Hurts something wicked."

"I'll bet."

"Annabelle kicked me. Can't believe she spooked like that. Guess I jumped the wrong way when she did." Jeff looked up at the blue sky. "I'm causing a lot of trouble, aren't I? Are we going to need a Life Flight?"

"I'm not sure they could land here," Chuck said. "They could maybe lower a basket stretcher. But I think we can carry you up to the trail."

Jeff turned his head slightly, wincing as he moved. "Up there? I doubt it."

"It's not so bad over yonder." Chuck nodded toward where he'd told Ruby to send the EMTs. "Let's get your ankle wrapped." He'd already removed Jeff's boot, and he began to wind the gauze firmly around the injured ankle.

"Kevin will never let me hear the end of this," Jeff murmured.

Chuck smiled as he worked. "Well, you usually take care of him when he gets banged up in the rodeo, right?"

"Yeah."

"So let him mollycoddle you for a change."

Jeff looked up again toward where he had fallen. "Guess I could have broken my neck, easy as not."

"That's right," Chuck said. "God was watching over you for sure."

Jeff gave a little shrug and grimaced. "Uh! This arm is killing me." He brought his left arm over and grasped his right arm just below the elbow.

"That's broken, no doubt. I'd like to get your jacket off, but I don't want to hurt you, so I figured to leave it for the EMTs to cut off."

Jeff sighed. "My favorite jacket."

"Well, it looks like your arm is bleeding a little." Chuck frowned at the dark stain on Jeff's sleeve. "Compound fracture, I'm guessing, but I could make it worse if I pull that sleeve off. It's not bleeding hard, I don't think, but it seems to be oozing a little."

"How long have I been here?"

"Fifteen minutes, maybe."

"How long before the EMTs get here?"

"I don't know. Ruby got through to the call center on her cell phone, which is a blessing. I'm guessing it would take them twenty minutes to drive to the last checkpoint and another twenty to hike up here with their equipment."

Jeff bit his upper lip. "Do whatever you think is best, Chuck."

"Well, you're not going to bleed to death. I'm praying they get here soon."

"You and Ruby pray a lot, don't you?"

Chuck eyed him cautiously. "You could say that."

"I guess this wouldn't be a bad time for you to pray for me, if you don't mind."

Ruby had just started along the sloping hillside when her cell phone rang. Rather than try to balance while she talked, she sat down and opened the phone.

"Ruby, this is Nadine. How are you doing?"

"Okay. Is the ambulance on the way?" Ruby could barely believe she was receiving a signal.

"Yes. They're on Bear Creek Road now and should reach the checkpoint you told me about any minute."

"They'll still have a hike ahead of them unless they can borrow horses."

Nadine chuckled. "That would be something. How's the patient?"

"I don't know. I'm heading down there now. Dr. Sullivan is with him, and we threw down some dressings one of the other vets had along."

"Okay. I don't want to run your cell phone down, so I'll let you go, but I wanted to let you know it won't be long before help gets there."

"Thanks." Ruby put her phone away and edged along the rough ground, finding hand and toeholds before letting go of the sagebrush and shrubs that gave her meager support. "Hello," she called as she approached the two men. "I brought you some things Dr. Spelling had in her kit and a canteen and some aspirin if you think it will do Jeff any good. The ambulance should be at the checkpoint by now."

"I'd probably better not medicate him then." Chuck looked up at the trail above, and Dr. Spelling waved at them. "Can you use a drink of water, Jeff?" he asked the patient.

"Yeah, thanks."

Chuck helped lift Jeff's shoulders, and Ruby opened the canteen for him. Jeff took a long drink and moaned as Chuck eased him back to the ground.

"Your arm's bothering you a lot, isn't it?" Chuck asked.

"Yeah."

"He's shivering." Ruby eyed Jeff critically. "I should have brought a blanket down."

"I'm okay." Jeff's chattering teeth belied his statement.

"Here." Chuck pulled off his denim jacket and laid it over Jeff's torso. "I'm wondering if we should immobilize your arm now. It would make things quicker when the EMTs get here."

"How would you do that?" Ruby asked, looking around at the slight vegetation.

"I think I could find a couple of sticks." Chuck pointed in the opposite direction from where Ruby had come down. "There are a few small trees over there. Say. . ." He stared up the cliff face.

"What are you thinking?" Ruby asked. Jeff lay with his eyes closed, and she wondered if he was asleep or unconscious.

"It's going to be tough getting a stretcher down here and even harder getting it back up. I was thinking that if we could rig a stretcher now and collect enough rope we could use the horses to pull Jeff up to the trail."

Ruby frowned. "That would cut the time to get him to the hospital all right."

"Go for it," Jeff said, his eyes still closed.

Ruby smiled. "So you *are* still awake. I'm just afraid we'd hurt you worse if we bungled the job."

"I think we can do it," Chuck said.

"At least you'll have something to think about while we wait," Jeff said. He opened his eyes and squinted up at Ruby. "You ought to go on to the finish line."

"What? Leave you guys here? No way."

He started to smile but grimaced and drew in a quick breath. "No sense you both losing out on a good chance for the top ten. How many riders have passed us already?"

"Don't know, don't care," Ruby said.

Chuck stood up, balancing carefully on the slope. "If you'll be okay for a few minutes, I'm going to look for some sticks for splints and see if there are any poles long enough to make a stretcher."

Ruby watched him gingerly negotiate the slope until he worked his way down to easier going. They weren't that far beyond where they'd seen the mysterious riders tie their horses the day before.

She smiled down at Jeff. "Hey, champ, if you had to take a fall I'm glad you didn't do it back where that rock slide was. You'd have broken all two hundred bones in your body."

"Right." A brief smile flickered on Jeff's lips. "I sure didn't mean to cost you and Chuck the ride."

"Don't think about it. We're glad we were there when it happened. It might have been awhile before anyone found you."

"Yeah." He was quiet for a moment. "I guess Kevin's going to be worried when we don't show up at the next stop."

"The first riders through will tell him what happened," Ruby said.

Jeff clenched his teeth. "That number 5 will win."

"It's okay." Ruby brushed a strand of damp hair back from his forehead, noting that his brow was wet, even though he shivered. "You'll get all the attention, and you'll look great when you congratulate him graciously from your hospital bed."

He chuckled then grimaced, tightening his fist around a wad of Chuck's jacket.

"I wish we could do more for you," Ruby said.

"They'll be here soon."

"Yeah." She looked around for Chuck, but he was out of sight. A sudden panic hit her. What if Chuck fell and injured himself, too?

"You make a cute couple," Jeff said.

She blinked in surprise. "You think?"

"Yeah." Jeff laughed. "I'm a little jealous, I admit."

She smiled, feeling a flush warm her wind-cooled cheeks.

"Chuck and I were talking about God before you came."

"Were you?" Her admiration for Chuck soared to a new high. "I'm sure God put us here with you today."

"That's pretty much what Ol' Doc said." Jeff let out a deep sigh and closed his eyes. "It's something I've pretty much put off thinking about. All the really important things. God. . .death. . .marriage."

She chuckled. "One thing at a time, Jeff."

"Yeah."

She swallowed hard and shot up a quick prayer as she considered what to say next. "Sometimes God just reaches down and grabs your attention."

"Oh yeah. Like this." He lifted his uninjured arm in a gesture indicating his battered body.

"Yes. Like this." Ruby shut her eyes. *Lord, help us to get him out of here soon. And thank You for using this to turn Jeff's thoughts toward You.*

She pulled her cell phone from her pocket and stared bleakly at the screen. No service now. She looked up toward the trail and saw several people and horses clustered near the spot where Jeff fell. Dr. Spelling's lime green sweater stood out. Ruby hoped the veterinarian could discourage people from dismounting and walking near the edge of the precipice. Soon several of the contestants moved on, and she let out a pent-up breath.

A scrabbling sound on the rocks drew her attention, and she turned to see Chuck hurrying back toward them. He left the rocky area and scrambled up to their level through the low brush empty-handed.

"Couldn't find anything big enough?" Ruby called.

Jeff opened his eyes and moaned.

Chuck didn't answer until he reached them and knelt beside Jeff. "How you doing, buddy?"

"About the same."

Chuck nodded. "I found something." He glanced at Ruby, his eyes glittering, and pointed back the way he'd come, into the steep-sided valley between the mountains. "It's over there, down a ways. There are trees, and it's down in a rocky ravine."

"What?" Ruby asked.

Jeff managed a weak grin. "I'll bet it's the old stagecoach."

"Nope. You'll never guess."

Ruby scowled at him. "So tell us already."

"It's a crashed airplane."

Chapter 12

Y ou're kidding!" Ruby's brown eyes widened, and she stared at Chuck for a moment.

"Is it an old one?" Jeff asked. "I haven't heard of any aircraft accidents lately."

"It looks fairly recent," Chuck said. "I was poking along looking for a downed tree or something I could break into a usable length, and I saw it down below me. I didn't climb all the way down to it because I figured it would take me awhile to get down there and back. There's no trail or anything."

Ruby looked down the hillside. "How big is it?"

"It looks like a Piper low-wing. Maybe a four-seater. I couldn't be sure from that distance. But it's in an area that will be hard to access. I doubt anyone would see it from above even, unless they flew in close with a chopper. That plane had to be flying low and ran right into the mountain. One of the wings is off."

Ruby seized his arm. "That could be the plane the police were waiting for Wednesday night. They staked out a private airfield, but the plane never showed."

"Where was the airstrip?"

Her brow furrowed. "Not very far from here. I think it would be on the other side of this ridge, maybe eight or ten miles away."

Chuck nodded slowly, considering that. "Could be they lost their bearings and got into the mountains without intending to."

"Wouldn't someone have known?" Jeff asked. "I mean, they'd have to file a flight plan." He winced and pulled in a ragged breath.

Ruby put her hand on his good arm. "Better not try to talk much, Jeff. But we're talking drug dealers. If they crashed, who's going to tell the authorities? They must have gotten off course and disoriented in the dark."

Chuck gulped and looked back in the direction he'd come. "There could be people in the wreckage."

"Yeah." Ruby looked intently into his eyes. "Chuck, it's been three days. If that is the plane the detectives were waiting for, it's possible there could be some injured people still down there. People have been known to live for more than a week in primitive conditions after a plane crash."

"We need to call the police," Chuck said.

Ruby nodded. "My phone won't work down here, though."

"The EMTs will be here any minute, and they'll have radios," he replied.

"Good thinking. Those detectives were so disappointed. They thought the

81

tip they had was legitimate, and they were going to bust the drug ring that's been bringing in cocaine for a while now." Ruby bit her lip. "I hate to think there could be someone down there, dead or alive."

"It's only a slight chance." Chuck frowned as he looked out over the ravine. "But I think the fuselage is mostly intact."

"Go back and look," Jeff said. "You both feel strongly about it. Maybe you can help someone, Doc. You two go check it out."

Ruby patted Jeff's shoulder. "No, we're not going to leave you alone here."

"I'll be fine. Dr. Spelling is right up there." He nodded upward. Another knot of horses had gathered where Heather Spelling kept her vigil. "Man, I feel bad that so many riders have lost time because of me."

Ruby pondered a moment. "Think of it this way: Chuck wouldn't have found that plane if you hadn't had your accident. Maybe some good will come of this."

"Hey, look!" Chuck pointed toward the trail. "I think the EMTs are here." He rose and waved. Dr. Spelling and several other people waved back. Chuck put his hands to his mouth and yelled, "Have them come down the way Ruby came!"

Dr. Spelling nodded and led the others back toward the easier access route.

"It won't be long now, Jeff," Ruby said. "Do you want another drink?"

"Thanks."

While they helped him sip from the canteen again, two men headed slowly down and across the slope carrying medical bags.

"Hey, Chuck!"

Chuck turned at Heather Spelling's hail from aloft.

"Yeah?"

"We're going to lower the stretcher from up here with ropes to save them from carrying it down. Can you guide it when we do?"

"Sure."

Chuck worked his way carefully up the mountainside a few yards and waited as two men lowered the stretcher. Heather stopped oncoming riders until the task was completed. After a few minutes of maneuvering, Chuck was able to reach out and steady the stretcher against the slanted ground. He was surprised to see a man fastening on a rappelling harness. By the time the climber reached Chuck, the two EMTs had also arrived.

Ruby greeted them and moved to one side to give them room to work with Jeff on the precarious hillside perch.

"How you doing, champ?" the first EMT asked.

Jeff smiled through clenched teeth. "I've been better."

They examined him and took his vital signs. In a remarkably short time they had him strapped to the stretcher. They covered him with a blanket and gave Chuck's jacket back to him.

"Thanks," Chuck said. "Need some help?"

"Thanks, but we'll get it from here," one of the EMTs said. "I think we can lift him straight up that cliff face."

Ruby squeezed Jeff's good hand. "We'll make sure Annabelle's taken care of, and I put your hat in your saddle pack."

He gave her a weak smile. "Thanks. See you later."

Several more volunteers had prepared ropes at the top of the drop-off, and soon the stretcher lifted off the ground with a climber in harness spotting.

"Bye, Jeff," Chuck called. He and Ruby waved as the stretcher rose. Jeff lifted his hand in farewell.

Chuck sighed and turned to the EMT. "Thanks. You guys did a great job."

"Well, it's not over yet, but you did a good job, too. Thanks for stabilizing the patient and staying with him."

"No problem." Chuck looked at Ruby. "You want to take that hike now?"

"Yes, let's, if you think we have enough daylight to get down there and back."

"It'll be a tough climb out, but yeah." Chuck turned to the EMT. "Could you make a police report for us as soon as you're topside?"

"What's up?" the EMT asked.

"I was looking for some sticks to use for splints and a makeshift stretcher, and I spotted a downed airplane."

The EMT whistled. "An old one?"

"I don't know." Chuck pointed below him and across the mountainside. "It's way down there in a ravine. The thing is, Ruby works as a dispatcher. She said the local detectives were watching for a drug dealer's plane a few nights ago, and it never came in. We're wondering if this could be the one."

"Okay, I'll call it in."

Chuck gave him as precise information as he could on the location of the plane.

"If you find any survivors, you'll need to let us know right away."

"I know," Chuck said. "I doubt there are any, but we'll do the best we can. It might take us a couple of hours to get a message out."

"Could you also ask someone to check our horses?" Ruby asked. "We might not get back up to the trail until after dark."

"Yes," Chuck said. "Maybe one of the ride officials would take them back to the nearest checkpoint where you left the ambulance. I see Tom Marden up there with Dr. Spelling, and I'm sure he'd be willing to do that."

"Anything else?" the EMT asked.

"Well, if it's not too much trouble, could I give you my dad's cell phone number?" Ruby patted her pockets then unbuckled her pack. "He and my mom are going to be waiting for me at the finish line, and they'll be aw-fully worried when Chuck and I don't show up. I'm sure rumors about Jeff's accident will be flying, too."

"Yeah, I think Jeff's brother will be waiting at the next rest stop," Chuck added. "Someone should tell Kevin Tavish what happened."

"Here, I have a pen. I'll make sure Jeff's brother gets the word so he can meet us at the hospital." The EMT took Ruby's father's phone number then grinned at them. "Well, you two have had yourselves quite a day. Be careful."

"We will," Chuck assured him. "Call the police first, okay?"

"Got it." He turned to climb the rugged hillside.

Chuck and Ruby watched the volunteers guide the stretcher up over the rim and onto the safety of the trail above. From there several men immediately carried it down the trail toward the checkpoint and the waiting ambulance.

Chuck let out a sigh. "Well."

"Yeah." Ruby gave him a strained smile. "Not the way we thought the afternoon would go."

Chuck nodded, studying the terrain they would have to negotiate if they went back to the plane crash site. "Listen. I've been thinking about this, and I don't think you should do it. Why don't you go on up to the trail and go on with the ride?"

She shook her head emphatically. "We've been through that."

"It's not too late to finish respectably."

"No, I want to go with you. If people are in that plane, they'll need help as soon as possible. We've got water and a few bandages and other supplies. I have a granola bar and a flashlight. Those things may make all the difference for someone. Besides, if you got hurt down there, how would I know? It would be a long time before anyone could get to you and help you." She looked at her watch. "And we're only four hours from sunset. I say let's get started."

"Okay, I can't argue with that." Her logic and determination ratcheted up his admiration for her. If he was going to venture out on a difficult mission, Ruby was the person he wanted with him. "Let me get my rope."

The climbing volunteer had unfastened the ropes Chuck used for his descent and tossed them down the slope. Chuck worked his way up to the end of the line and pulled it in. He coiled the three attached lead lines and settled the roll over his shoulder in case they needed it at the crash scene.

"Okay, let's go."

Ruby nodded with a tight smile.

Chuck worked his way slowly down and across the steep slope toward a broad, rocky area. The ground flattened out somewhat, and they were able to maneuver steadily onward, using large rocks and low bushes as support on the steeper places. When they reached a spot where the rocks fell away again in an eight-foot drop, he scooted down then turned to offer her a hand.

"Maybe you'd better drop your pack first."

She unbuckled the strap and lowered her pack into his hands then slid down the rock face.

"You okay?" Chuck extended his hand and helped her rise and steady herself.

"Yeah, I'm fine."

Chuck squeezed her hand and released it. She stooped to dust off her jeans.

The next part was easier, and for a few minutes he imagined they were out together on a pleasure hike. Sunshine, wide-open spaces, and Ruby. He looked back at her and smiled as she scrambled over a patch of scattered boulders. Before the day was over he would ask her for a real date—a time when they were in no danger of breaking their necks. No pressure from competition. No possibility lives depended on them.

He paused on a jagged boulder and reached to assist her. When she stood beside him on the rock, he pointed.

"See it?" The slash of white that was the fuselage lay at the base of a dark rock face among scrub evergreen trees at the bottom of the ravine.

She sucked in a breath. "Wow. Yeah. That's going to take some climbing."

"Want to go back?"

She shook her head and looked into his eyes. "We can do it. I'll let you lead."

"Right. Just try your cell phone again." He shaded his eyes and looked back but could no longer see the trail above or the spot where Jeff had landed when he fell. "You could never get a horse in here."

"Nope." She pushed a few buttons and held the phone to her ear. "Not ringing." She lowered it and squinted at the screen. "No good. We'd better get going."

Twenty minutes later they stood panting above the mangled plane. Now that they were close, Chuck eyed it critically, from nose to shattered tail.

"Piper Archer, I think."

"I don't know much about planes," Ruby admitted.

Its crushed nose and propeller confirmed the theory that the little plane had slammed into the cliff face. Pieces of debris gleamed amid the dull rocks. The crumpled white fuselage, too bright among the dark neutrals of the canyon, rested with the pilot's side facing him. The windows were shattered, and the near wing of the four-seat plane had sheared off on impact. Chuck hoped the other was intact so he could climb up to the cabin door. The tail and rear portion of the fuselage were squashed and battered. "No way could anyone survive that."

She grimaced. "I'm afraid you're right, but we have to be sure."

"Yes."

"So how do you get in? I don't see a door."

Chuck squinted down at the plane again. "It's on the other side above the wing. You climb up on the wing to get in. But there's a step to help you. Looks from here like the right wing may be still in place."

She looked around then glanced at him. "We're not very close to where we saw those riders yesterday."

"It's got to be a couple of miles as the crow flies," he agreed. "From where they left their horses. . .well, I can't speculate on whether they could have hiked in this far or not. I'm guessing if they were looking for this plane they didn't find it."

"We can't be sure of that." She inhaled deeply. "Ready? That last descent looks pretty rugged."

"Yeah, let me go first."

Chuck edged down the slope, groping for handholds on the rocks.

They approached cautiously, and he reached to help her several times over rough spots. When they were only a few yards from the plane, he paused.

"Let me take a look, all right? I'll call to you if it's okay."

She nodded, saying nothing, but her dark eyes searched his face.

"Could be the plane is empty," he reminded her. "This could have happened a year ago." But he knew she was thinking it couldn't be that old. The broken limbs on the trees looked fresh. And if it was an older wreck she would have heard about it through her job at the police station. Still, it made him feel better for them both to think it was so. He had to go to the broken window on the pilot's side and look in. As he turned and scrambled down to the side of the cockpit, he steeled himself for what he might find. He glanced back to make sure Ruby waited on the rock above him.

Motion beside Ruby drew his attention and stopped him cold. A man stood up in the low brush near her. Chuck's heart lurched, and he opened his mouth to yell to her. Beside him a chilly voice said sternly, "Quiet now. Back away from the plane."

Chuck turned slowly. All he needed to convince him to obey was the glint of the lowering sun on the barrel of the pistol the stranger held.

Chapter 13

Ruby flinched as the man behind her spoke. She didn't dare turn to look at him. Her heart rate accelerated, and blood rushed to her temples. Below her, the second man forced Chuck to move away from the crumpled plane. Chuck tripped and stumbled on the uneven ground. She wanted to scream, but the touch of something hard to her spine, just below where her small pack rested between her shoulders, silenced her.

"That's it. Don't move."

She straightened, raising her shoulders a fraction of an inch, easing away from the feel of metal against her back, but the gun barrel—she was sure it must be a gun barrel—followed, pressing even harder against her sweatshirt and her vertebrae.

"Easy now." His voice was calm, reasonable, even gentle. She swallowed hard against the saliva that flooded her mouth.

Chuck had risen and stepped cautiously toward her on the trackless hillside, hopping from rock to rock, pausing after each step to gauge the best place to put his foot down next. Close behind him came a man with dark hair showing around the edges of his gray Stetson. His faded jeans looked about to give way at one worn knee, but his long-sleeved fleece shirt, topped by a quilted black vest, looked warm and serviceable. His lined face bespoke years in the outdoors. If she'd met him on the trail, Ruby reflected, she would have smiled and passed the time of day with him. Assuming, of course, he wasn't holding that gun.

When Chuck was only a dozen feet from Ruby, below her and to her left, the man behind her spoke loudly enough for all four of them to hear.

"What now?"

His partner looked up and arched his eyebrows. His tanned face wrinkled as he looked her over. At last he spoke. "Tie them up."

The man behind Ruby moved, sending the muzzle of his gun jarring against her spine. "What good will that do? They'll blab as soon as they get free or someone finds them."

The man below frowned at him. "What were you thinking then?"

"Shoot 'em both."

Ruby sucked in a breath and looked down at Chuck. In his deep blue eyes she read sorrow and regret that he'd led her into this situation. She tried to reassure him, using only her expression. God was with them. No matter how this turned out, they would be all right. In her heart she knew it was true. Still, her logical mind laid out several possibilities, and none of them was good. She gasped for the air that seemed to have thinned.

Dear Lord, she prayed, *get us out of this. Or. . .*

She couldn't finish the thought so ended merely with, *Do what is best, dear God. Only You know what that is.*

"No one would find them for years," the blond man said. "It would be easy to hide them here."

The man with Chuck let out a sharp breath. "You're a fool. There are people within sound of a gunshot. Some of those riders on the trail up yonder would hear."

Chuck glanced toward the side, not quite turning his head toward the man. "There are people closer than that. One of the competitors in the ride was injured, and EMTs came to help him."

The man with Ruby stepped forward slightly, and she could see his profile. His hat topped long, dishwater-blond hair, and a beard filled out his narrow face. "You telling it straight?" He fixed Chuck with a defiant glare.

"Yes, sir," said Chuck. "The rider fell down the rock face not too far from here. I'm sure they'd hear it if you fired a weapon."

The two gunmen locked gazes. "Come on," said the older man from his place near Chuck. "Let's tie these two up and do what we gotta do."

The blond man threw a sidelong glance at Ruby. "That'll take time."

Ruby gulped in a breath and said, "We asked them to call the police."

The dead silence lasted a good three seconds.

"And why would you do something as helpful as that?" the older man asked, glaring up at Ruby.

Suddenly she recognized him. He was the man who'd driven the gray pickup away from the fire early this morning. Did he know she was the one who had seen him then? She swallowed hard and looked to Chuck. Had she already revealed too much? Perhaps it would have been better to keep that tidbit about the police to herself.

Chuck turned toward the gunman. "I spotted the plane wreckage when we went down the cliff to help the injured rider. I couldn't tell if it was an old one or a more recent crash, so we asked the EMTs who came to radio in and tell the police. We thought there might possibly be someone in the wreck who needed help. That's why we came over here with water and medical supplies."

"Oh, Mannie doesn't need any help," the blond man behind Ruby said with a snigger.

"Shut up," his partner snapped. "Let's get this over with. The cowboy here has a rope. You can use it to tie them up." He looked around and gestured to a tree near the broken tail of the Piper. "Put 'em over there. They'll be out of the way while we get the stuff."

Chuck's eyebrows shot up. Ruby wondered, too. What kind of *stuff*?

"Come on, little lady." The blond man prodded her with an object she was sure could fire at least six rounds and swap out an empty clip for a full one in a matter of seconds. He pushed her slightly toward the drop Chuck had negotiated earlier, and she scuttled down, sliding the last few feet and landing in a heap.

Chuck reached to help her up, but the older gunman nudged him.

"Leave her be, cowboy. She's not hurt."

Ruby rose, ignoring the minor pain in the wrist she'd scraped on the way down. The blond man hopped down beside her and steadied himself.

"Come on." He herded them toward the tree his partner had indicated. "Give me your pack."

Ruby eased the straps off over her arms and handed it to him. He opened it and rummaged through the contents, tossing a few packages of sterile dressings out on the ground. He tucked her granola bar into his pocket.

"All right, sit."

Ruby sat down, shoving aside the low branches. Chuck touched her hand just for an instant then drew away, but it was enough to encourage her. They *would* survive this.

With some difficulty their captor secured them both by making them put their hands behind them and tying them to the tree trunk.

Meanwhile the older man approached the debris of the airplane, flinging branches and pieces of the plane out of his way.

The blond man stood back and eyed his restraining job critically. "Okay. Don't try anything, will ya?"

Ruby said nothing, and Chuck also ignored the question. The man moved away, turned his back, and pushed his way through the brush toward his partner.

"You okay?" Chuck asked softly.

"Yeah." Ruby squirmed until she could see him from the corner of her eye. "Where did they come from?"

"They must have been down here and heard us coming. The one guy—the older one—was behind the wing of the plane, I think. His friend was waiting over there." Chuck nodded toward a thick stand of scrub cedars. "He got behind you after you passed him."

"They must be looking for drugs in the plane."

"That's what I figure. And they haven't found them yet, or they wouldn't have showed themselves to us."

"Maybe they fell out when the plane crashed." Ruby sighed and looked up at the blue sky. Why did such a beautiful day turn out so wrong? First the fire. That was bad enough, but then Jeff's terrifying accident. Now this. "Are they going to kill us?" she whispered.

"I don't think so."

"I should have kept my mouth shut about the police."

"Maybe not. It got their attention. It'll make them work faster. And maybe it influenced them not to fire a gun."

"I suppose so." She ran over what she knew about sentencing for criminal activity. "If they get caught looting the plane they can claim they stumbled on it, like we did."

"Right," Chuck said. "But if they get caught standing over two bodies it will be mighty hard to talk their way out of that."

The older man called from the far side of the plane, "Get over here, Jack!" The bearded blond man hurried to his side.

Ruby strained her ears to hear what they said, but much of their conversation was too quiet for her to understand. After a moment the older man raised his chin and said, more loudly, "Oh, come on! You're smaller than I am."

"Uh-uh," said Jack. "What if I get stuck in there?"

Behind the wreck their voices continued, more muffled. The remains of the small plane shuddered. After a few minutes the big man said clearly, "Can't do it."

Jack stepped carefully around the smashed tail section. The other man followed, wiping his hands on his jeans. Jack looked over toward Chuck and Ruby and said something in a guarded tone. The older man looked their way, focusing on Ruby. She shivered.

"Take it easy," Chuck whispered.

"I'm scared."

"Of course you are. But God is with us."

She swallowed down the lump in her throat. "Thanks. But they're talking about me."

"I think you're right." Chuck strained at the rope and leaned toward her. She felt his elbow barely touch her upper arm. "Ruby, be strong. No matter what happens, God will take care of you."

She tried to respond, but her mouth went dry, and she trembled uncontrollably as Jack strode toward them through the brush. A sudden picture of her parents waiting for her at the finish line came vividly to mind. She saw the stark agony in their eyes once more—the same expression her dad's face surely held when they'd learned Julie was dead. And Mom. Could Mom take another tragedy? *God, help us.*

Chuck struggled against the rope, and it pulled Ruby's hands against the rough bark of the cedar. She sucked in her breath and held it, not watching the man coming toward her.

His shadow blocked the sun above her.

"We need you." He holstered his pistol and knelt beside her. "Now don't you do anything stupid, cowboy," he said to Chuck as he worked at the knots. "You hear me?" He paused and cocked his head to one side, glaring past Ruby at Chuck.

"I hear you." Chuck's voice was tight, and Ruby could feel his tension. "What are you going to do?"

"We just need the princess here to fetch something for us. The plane's pretty well squashed, and the cargo hold is ripped open in the back. My buddy and I can't quite get to what we want out of there."

"Don't you hurt her," Chuck said.

Jack laughed. "Or what, big guy? You'll beat me to a pulp? I don't think so."

The knots gave way, and the rope relaxed. Ruby pulled her hands around in front of her and massaged her wrists. The scrape the rocks had given her smarted and oozed blood. Jack immediately began to retie the rope. Chuck grunted, and she turned to watch. Jack seemed to enjoy pulling the rope tighter now that he had only one prisoner to restrain.

"You'll cut off his circulation," she said.

Jack smiled up at her. She couldn't control a tremble, and she hated that he saw it.

"Well, princess, I guess you'll just have to hurry if you don't want his poor little hands to go numb, won't you?"

Ruby looked down into Chuck's eyes. There were so many things she wanted to tell him before she left his side. But Jack's presence and his snarl as he drew his gun again kept her from saying anything.

"Get moving. Thanks to you, we need to hurry." He nudged her ribs with the gun barrel. Ruby turned toward the aircraft and worked her way around it. She stepped cautiously over a strip of jagged metal and eased sideways between the side of the fuselage and a clump of brush.

The older man waited, glowering at her as she approached. Beyond him the windows on this side of the cockpit were cracked and shattered, too. The door above the wing was open. Ruby caught a glimpse of dark fabric, and her stomach roiled. She avoided looking up toward the door. Instead she focused on the man's face. Definitely the man fleeing the fire this morning.

He nodded toward a smaller open door behind the wing and gestured to it as if ushering her to a choice seat in the theater.

"There you go. Just slide on in and bring out any bags you find."

"Bags?" Ruby eyed him doubtfully. "You mean like a grocery sack?"

"No, like a gym bag. You know. A carry-on or a duffel bag." He pushed his hat back and wiped his forehead. "Come on now. Get in there."

She squatted and looked into the small opening. The framework had buckled, and torn metal hung down into the belly of the fuselage. She glanced forward. A wall separated this bay from the passenger compartment. Though it was partially collapsed, she couldn't see into the cockpit. She was glad.

"I'm not sure I can fit in there." She looked up at him.

He jerked his arm forward and pressed the muzzle of his pistol to her temple. "Sure you can."

She caught her breath and poked her head inside the small cargo bay. It had been no bigger than the trunk of a car originally, but in the wreck the rear dividers had torn free. She could see daylight through holes in back of the compartment.

"I don't see anything."

Jack swore. "Just get in there and take a look."

"That's right." The older man gestured with his gun toward the rear of the plane. "I thought I saw something stuck back there, but I couldn't reach it. I figure when the plane hit and fell, the bags shifted. Now get in there and see if you can get 'em."

Ruby pulled in a shaky breath and eyed a sharp piece of metal protruding from the side of the craft inside the compartment.

Behind her, the older man said to his partner, "Did you tie the cowboy up good?"

"Oh yeah," said Jack.

"Wouldn't want him getting loose now."

"No, we wouldn't."

Ruby leaned forward and crawled inside. She lay on her side and slithered around the jagged metal. Behind the luggage compartment the smashed top of the tail section bowed down to within a foot of the bottom. She swallowed hard. The stench of fuel overrode the clean smell of cedar, and another smell—faint but foul—teased her nostrils. She scrunched her face up and inched forward, looking for luggage. The scrape on her wrist hurt, but she ignored it.

Ahead of her she saw something dark, wedged between broken members of the framework. She reached toward it, but it was just beyond her grasp.

"Find anything?" one of the men yelled. He sounded far away, as if he were talking through a toy tin can "telephone" like she and Julie used to make when they were kids.

"There's something, but I can't reach it."

"Try harder, princess."

She swallowed down the bitter taste in her mouth and squeezed forward. Her head wouldn't fit beneath the bent metal of the aluminum frame without her forcing it. What if she got stuck? Would Jack grab her feet and pull her out? Or would they go off and leave her here?

"I can't."

The older man's voice came, louder and more distinct. "You'd better. Because we have no reason to keep your friend alive. If you like him, get whatever bags you find and haul them out here. Fast."

She gritted her teeth and blinked back tears, praying desperately in the silence. She shoved her shoulder against the broken metal. It gave slightly, and her outstretched fingers touched the dark fabric. Nylon? More like canvas. It certainly felt like a duffel bag.

She relaxed for a moment, panting.

"Whatcha got?" Jack yelled.

"There's some kind of cloth item. It could be a bag. But I can't get it free. Do you have any tools?" Her voice sounded close and tinny.

A low murmuring behind her was all she could make out of the men's conversation. Louder came the sigh of the wind through the canyon, making the loose edges of the wreckage quiver.

The walls of fractured metal pressed in on her. *It's okay,* she told herself. *It's like an MRI machine.*

Her heart raced, and the air she gulped didn't seem to fill her lungs. She couldn't stand the closeness any longer. She had to know she could free herself. Inching backward, she scuffed her knees on the metal ribs and slid along the floor.

"Hey!" the older man shouted. "Did you get it?"

She kept going. At last her left foot found the edge of the opening to the side. She wriggled out and sat gasping on the ground.

"Where's the bag?" Jack loomed over her.

She turned her face away. "I told you, I can't get it. There's too much trash in the way. You'll need tools. Metal cutters."

"Well, darlin', we don't have any tools," the older man said. "So just make up your mind to go back in there."

"No."

Jack raised his pistol over his head and swung his arm back, as though he would strike her with it. His partner caught his wrist.

"Hold on there. If you beat her up she won't be any use to us."

Jack's scowl suddenly brightened. "The cowboy."

Ruby and the other man looked at him.

Jack shrugged. "He's big and strong."

Both men walked to the back of the plane and looked toward Chuck. Ruby stood shakily and followed.

"Think you can help us?" the older man called.

"I'm willing to try." Chuck leaned forward, pulling at the rope that bound him. His gaze locked on Ruby for a moment. She tried to smile, but tears were so close she could only grimace and sniff.

"You think we'd trust you, cowboy?" Jack yelled.

Chuck met the bearded man's glare with a level gaze. "I won't try anything. Just leave Ruby alone, and I'll help you tear that plane apart."

The two gunmen looked at each other. The older man spread his hands in indecision. "I don't trust him," he muttered.

"If we wait too long, the cops will fly in here with a chopper," Jack said.

"If they really called the cops. I think she just said that to make us nervous."

They both frowned at Ruby.

"How about it, princess?" Jack leaned toward her with his hands on his thighs, his gaze drilling into her. "Did you call the cops or not?"

Suddenly her claustrophobia was worse than it had been in the plane. She turned her face away. "Yes. Not us, but we asked the EMTs to make the call. We told them we were coming down here to see if there was anyone still alive from the crash."

Jack stretched his arms and popped his elbow joints. The wind whooshed over them, and a loose piece of metal flapped against the fuselage.

"Get the cowboy," the older man said. "We need to get that stuff and get out of here."

"What if he gets tough?"

"Then we shoot him."

Chapter 14

Chuck held his breath as the two men conferred. Would they untie him and let him help them find what they wanted in the debris? His hands were numb, and his elbows ached from his awkward position. *Lord, let them be reasonable. Please don't let them hurt Ruby. I can deal with anything else. Just please make them leave her alone.*

His stomach had churned since the moment the bearded man called Jack had come to fetch Ruby. So far they hadn't injured her, but that could change any moment. From his vantage point he couldn't see what they were doing, but it appeared they had forced her to enter the downed plane. Now Ruby was outside, and he'd heard her refuse to go in again. What horrors had she encountered in the wreckage? The haunted cast in her brown eyes moved him to promise them anything.

Jack climbed up toward Chuck again. Ruby pushed back a loose lock of her hair and followed the outlaw's progress with her eyes. Chuck refused to speculate on what would happen but focused on Ruby's pale face instead. *It's all right. God will protect us.* If only he could get that across to her.

"Hold still." Jack tussled with the knots he'd tied.

Chuck tried not to move while he worked. After a minute of failure Jack swore and pulled out a pocket knife. Chuck said nothing but made a mental note to buy Jeff a new lead rope.

"All right, move."

Chuck staggered to his feet and slapped his arms against his chest. As the burning sensation of restored blood flow hit his hands, he rubbed them vigorously.

"I said move," Jack snarled.

Chuck stumbled toward where Ruby and the other man waited by the plane.

"Come on," the older man said. "We've had good luck until this week. But if we get caught here we're looking at some serious time in the hoosegow. Let's get this done."

Ruby pressed her lips together.

Jack eyed Chuck with speculation. "Your girlfriend's scared to go in there again."

"It's too close." Her voice broke. "There is something in there—maybe the bag they want—but I couldn't get to it. It's way in the back, behind where the baggage is supposed to be. There's metal hanging down, and I couldn't get through."

Chuck eyed the fuselage and the torn wing structure. "There's a gap on the top of the tail section. Have you looked in there to see if you can spot it?"

"Can't say as we have." The older man lifted his gray Stetson and wiped his forehead with a bandana. "You're not going to cut and run, are you?"

Chuck looked down the ravine. "Where to?"

The man nodded with a grim smile. "Right. So maybe you and Jack can clear some of the trash out of that hole from above and we can drop Miss Ruby in through the rip."

Ruby shivered and hugged herself, but Chuck shook his head. "I can tell from here the hole's not big enough. But maybe we can clear the fuselage out enough so one of us can go in." Chuck watched his captors' expressions but saw no enthusiasm.

"That would take too long," Jack said. "Let's just rip off some more metal and stuff her in there."

Chuck wished he could touch Ruby, just a simple squeeze of the hand to reassure her, but Jack stood between them and clearly expected him to climb up on the plane's tail and start working.

"Where's the backpack we had?" Chuck asked. "We had a flashlight. That might be useful."

Jack flailed about in the brush and came up with the red backpack. He tossed it to Ruby. She opened the front flap and extracted a small flashlight.

"All right, let's do this," Jack said. "You coming, Hap?"

His partner shrugged. "One of us had better watch the princess, don't you think?"

"Oh, right, and that just naturally has to be you." Jack swore under his breath and followed Chuck.

Chuck tested his weight against the buckled framework on the right side of the fuselage and climbed up, straddling the tail section the way he would a horse. He slid forward to where he could peer in through the yawning hole. He looked down at Jack, who stood on the ground below him.

"Do you think the baggage is clear at the back?" Logic told him it would have shifted forward on impact; but if the plane tilted or spun when it fell, anything was possible.

Jack scratched his chin through his beard. "It shoulda been in the hold right behind the seats, but it could have shifted anywhere. The gal said she saw something in the tail, but I suppose it could even have fallen out some-place over the mountains."

Chuck shook his head. "Most of the plane is right here, and the worst breach is high. I'm betting your cargo is still inside. But getting at it may take some doing."

"Well, make it snappy."

Chuck looked around. "Get me a branch or a long piece of debris.

Something sturdy and long enough to reach down in there. Maybe I can pry things apart enough for you or Ruby to get farther back in there."

"Not me." Jack shuffled into the brush and picked up a piece of metal Chuck hazarded to be part of an aileron. He flexed it in his hands.

"Too flimsy," Chuck called. "I need to be able to push and pry with it."

Jack turned to a small pine that had been flattened by the plane. "Maybe I can break the branches off this."

While he waited, Chuck leaned down into the fuselage and moved some wires out of the way. He was also able to reach pieces of the jumbled debris inside but couldn't tell if he was making headway in the retrieval mission. At last Jack brought him a five-foot stick with stubs of limbs sticking out down its length.

"Guess it will have to do." Chuck hefted it and poked the fatter end into the hole. Bracing it against the edge of the gap for leverage, he pushed on the broken metal inside the plane. It gave and folded toward the wall. He strained to push out the caved-in aluminum walls. After several minutes he felt he'd made enough changes that a small person might be able to squeeze past the trash that had stopped Ruby earlier.

"Okay," he told Jack. "Go around to the door and see if you can get in there."

"Not me," Jack said again.

Chuck scowled at him. Ruby was the only one of them smaller than Jack. Looking across the top of the Piper, he could see the older man, Hap. Ruby must be sitting near him in the shadow of the airplane.

"Ruby," he called.

She stood and stepped away from the plane, beside Hap, and gazed up at Chuck. The sun was long beyond the mountains, and twilight was snaking into the canyon, but even in the shadows her pallor struck him.

"Do you think you can try again? I've pried some of the pieces of metal to one side."

She swallowed hard. "I. . .guess so."

"I'll be right here. Give it a go. I think I'll be able to see you once you get in a few feet, past that luggage compartment."

She nodded. "Are you praying?"

"Yes." He was surprised she'd said it aloud. Hap's eyes narrowed, but he made no comment. Ruby adjusted the visor of her baseball cap and disappeared from view. A few seconds later he heard muffled sounds from within the plane, soft thuds and a creak. The whole thing shook. Chuck put his face to the hole again. A moment later he saw her hand fumbling among the wreckage.

"Hey! I see your hand. You okay?"

"Yeah. I can't see you."

He stuck his arm through the gaping hole and waved. "How about now?"

"Oh, yeah."

"Do you see the bags they want?"

"I'm not sure. There's something about a yard ahead of me. I may be able to reach it this time."

Chuck could hear her strained breathing as she worked her way farther into the tail of the plane. Her cap appeared below him in the shadows as she worked laboriously onward.

"You can do it," he said softly. "If it's what they want they may leave us alone after you get it for them."

She stopped moving. "What if they don't?"

Her dread washed over him, and he wished he could assure her the men wouldn't hurt them, but anything could happen at this point. "Keep praying."

"Hey, quit yakking!" Jack yelled. "We need to get out of here."

Chuck turned and looked down at him. "She's doing her best. Just take it easy."

"Chuck!"

Ruby's faint call snagged his attention, and he put his face back to the tear in the metal, shading his eyes so he could see better. The beam of her small flashlight showed him her head and arms in the tight enclosure.

"I'm here, Ruby. What is it?"

"I think I have what they want. It's a travel bag."

"Will it fit through this hole?"

"I don't think so. And I don't think I could get it up there anyway. There's not enough room to maneuver in here. But I have it loose, so I think I can drag it out with me."

"Right." He wished he could transfer his strength to her.

"I'm backing out now."

"I'll tell our pals." Chuck looked around for Jack. He had sat down on the ground and was watching him from beneath half-closed eyelids. "Look alive, Jack. She's coming out."

Hap had climbed onto the remaining wing and from what Chuck could see was rifling the cabin, but he heard the announcement and pulled back from the doorway.

"She find it?"

"She's got something," Chuck said. "No guarantees."

Hap jumped down off the wing and joined Jack beside the cargo door. Chuck debated whether to keep his post or not and decided he wanted to be close to Ruby when they examined her loot. If it didn't make the two men happy, he wanted to be near enough to defend her if needed.

He slid down the side of the plane's tail and landed on the ground just as Ruby's sneakers appeared at the open cargo door.

"All right, princess!" Jack leaned forward to help her climb out. When she was on the ground he reached in and pulled out a navy blue duffel bag.

Hap grinned at his partner. "That's it."

Jack unzipped the bag and smiled. "Sure enough." He quickly examined the contents. "Good job."

"Can we go now?" Chuck asked.

Jack turned to eye him thoughtfully. "I suppose I should've said, 'Good half a job.' There's supposed to be another bag."

"Cut your losses," Chuck told him. "Be thankful you have this one."

"He may have a point," Hap said. "Those cops could be flying over any second."

"Naw, we've got to get it all." Jack zipped the bag. "We've got to buy a new plane, in case you didn't notice, and a new pilot to go with it." He turned and fixed his gaze on Ruby. "You done good, honey. Now you gotta do it one more time for Uncle Jack."

Ruby's mouth twitched. She looked down at the ground.

"Don't make her go in there again," Chuck said.

Hap drew his pistol and leveled it at him. "I'm getting sick of you, cowboy."

"No!" Ruby grabbed Hap's arm. "I'll do it. But you have to promise to let us go afterward."

Hap looked at Jack.

Jack's lips skewed in a grimace. "I'm not sure we can do that."

"Yes, you can." Ruby gulped in a breath. "We won't tell anyone. And you can leave first. We'll stay here until you have a good head start. I promise."

Jack looked at Hap, who shrugged and stuck his pistol back in his holster.

"Maybe we could just tie them up again and leave them here. Their friends would find them by morning." Hap eyed Chuck as he spoke.

Was this where he should chime in with Ruby and promise not to turn them in? Chuck knew he couldn't do that.

"They might rat on us." Jack shook his head. "I dunno. Let's see what you bring out this time, princess. If you're a good girl, I'll think about it."

Ruby took two shaky breaths, turned on her flashlight, and climbed back into the cargo bay.

Chuck climbed up onto the tail section once more and watched from above as she again crept into the belly of the plane.

"How you doing?" he asked softly as she reached the area just below him.

"I'm okay. Should we stall them or give them what they want?"

"Do you see the other bag?" The fuselage lurched, and he glanced behind him. The two gunmen had gone to the front of the plane where Hap again clambered onto the wing and leaned into the cabin.

"What was that?" Ruby's white face stared up at him.

"Hap's checking the cockpit. I don't think they can hear us right now."

"In that case, yes, there's another bag like the first one. Should I bring it out, or will that mean they don't need us anymore?"

Chuck bit his lip and drew in a breath. "Not sure. But if you don't pull it out for them they might just get angrier."

"That's what I figure."

"Ruby. . ."

She waited, looking up at him, her dark eyes huge.

"If things go bad, just remember God is in control, and. . .well, I think you're the bravest woman I ever met."

She sobbed. "Thanks. Here goes nothing." She inched ahead and lay prone, with just the back of her legs from her knees down in his view.

Chuck prayed silently and looked back. Hap was handing a small item down to Jack, who stood on the ground below the wing. Chuck put his ear to the tear in the metal again and heard Ruby panting as she struggled to retrieve the rest of the cargo. Finally she edged backward and looked up at him. She shone the beam of her flashlight on another dark travel bag.

"What do you think?"

"Let's trust God to get us out of this. Bring it out."

By the time he slid to the ground, Hap was hauling her out of the cargo bay. Jack pounced on the bag she carried.

"All right! I knew you could do it."

Hap hoisted the first bag and looped the strap over his shoulder. "Let's get out of here."

"What?" Jack stared at him. "You gonna just leave these two here? We've got to tie them up at least. You said so before."

"They did give their word," Hap said.

Chuck edged closer to Ruby, ready to step in front of her if Jack drew his gun again. He hoped Hap wouldn't recall he hadn't given his word—only Ruby had.

"Oh, excuse me," Jack said with a sneer. "Their word is golden."

"Shut up!" Hap raised his arm with fingers outspread.

"What do you—"

"Hush!" Hap glared at Jack. "Hear that? I'm telling you, we've got to move!"

Ruby raised her chin, frowning. Chuck heard it then—the distant, throbbing engine of a helicopter. Was it the state police? He didn't care. It was enough to send the two drug runners scrambling.

He watched as Jack grabbed his canteen from the grass and shouldered the second bag Ruby had found. Hap had already dodged around the tail of the Piper with the first bag.

"Adios, princess," Jack called and followed his partner.

Chuck let out a deep sigh. "Think it's the cops?"

"I don't know," Ruby said in a tight voice. "I think the nearest police chopper is in Cheyenne. Maybe it's just someone out on a sightseeing tour."

Chuck strode to the wing of the plane and climbed up. He looked into the cockpit and swallowed the bile that rose in his throat. He shut his eyes for a moment then turned and jumped down. Ruby stood silently, watching him with huge brown eyes.

"The pilot's dead." Chuck hurried to the tail and around the back of the plane. He spotted Jack and Hap rushing down the canyon, hopping over rocks. Ruby came and stood beside him. He felt her small hand touch his and closed his fingers around hers.

"They must have their horses tied up at the mouth of the canyon," she said.

"Or a truck hidden somewhere on an old trail. Ready to hike?" he asked without looking at her.

"Yeah. Think we can make it up to the rim before dark?"

"I don't know. It'll be a rugged climb, and we don't have much daylight." He turned and eyed her carefully, speculating on how much energy she had left after the ordeal. "If you're too tired I can try to get up there and call for help while you rest."

"No. Don't leave me here alone."

The helicopter seemed to be no closer, though he could still hear its thrumming motor. He nodded. "Okay, let's go." He found the red backpack and some of the scattered packages of bandages. He put them in it and held it out to her. Ruby added her flashlight. "That may come in handy later," he said. "Let's get the lead lines."

She nodded and straightened suddenly, peering down the canyon. "The chopper's louder."

Chuck caught his breath. "Maybe they really are looking for us."

"Let's get up on that rise," Ruby said, pointing to where she'd stood when Jack and Hap first appeared. "They'll be able to see us better."

They clambered up the steep slope. When they stood on the ledge she peeled off her dark sweatshirt. Her light-colored shirt would show up better, Chuck realized. He whipped off his jacket and cotton shirt, though it was getting colder, so his white T-shirt would show. He could wave his jacket if the searchers came close.

The helicopter hovered a half mile down the canyon then resumed its approach. The engine noise grew louder, almost unbearable as the echoes crashed off the cliffs around them. Ruby clamped both hands to her ears.

"They can't land here!" Chuck yelled.

She nodded, watching the chopper as it roared above them. Its wind swept over them, and Ruby waved the sweatshirt wildly. Chuck waved, too. The chopper backed off and hovered. A man leaned out the side with a speaker horn.

"Are you Dr. Sullivan?"

"Yes!" Chuck waved his jacket.

"We can't land to pick you up, but we can drop you a survival pack. Can you walk out?"

Chuck and Ruby waved harder.

The chopper moved in lower. A bright yellow parcel tumbled out and landed in a clump of juniper twenty yards away. Chuck and Ruby ran to it as quickly as they could. Inside were a water bottle, a small first aid kit, two protein bars, a pack of matches, and a radio transmitter. Ruby grabbed the radio. Chuck was surprised at how confidently she turned it on, but he supposed that was part of her training at the police station.

The chopper moved off and beat the air a hundred yards away.

"Hello," Ruby said into the radio's microphone. "Can anyone hear me?"

"We hear you," came a strong voice. "We're with the Wyoming State Police. Are you all right?"

"Yes, we're both fine."

"Are you Ruby Dale?"

"Yes, sir. Dr. Sullivan is with me. Did you see the two men leaving here a few minutes ago?"

"We did. We have ground units searching for their vehicle."

"They may have horses," Ruby said. "They're carrying two duffel bags full of drugs from the crashed plane at the head of this canyon."

"We'll do our best to intercept them," said the man in the helicopter.

"It may be a little easier if you triangulate my cell phone and use the GPS locater in it," Ruby told him. "I stuffed it into one of the two bags of contraband they recovered."

Chapter 15

Ruby and Chuck scrambled up the treacherous hillside. Dusk had fallen in the canyon, and she handed Chuck her flashlight so he could spot the best footholds as he led the way higher. A half hour later Chuck stopped and turned to help her climb up beside him.

"Look there, Ruby. See that?"

On the hillside above them other lights bobbed along, slowly progressing toward them.

"It's a rescue party, looking for us." The knowledge warmed her, but at the same time sent a tinge of guilt throughout her weary body. As rescuers, she and Chuck had become the victims to be rescued, something she'd hoped to avoid. "I told the state police we were okay."

Chuck clapped her on the shoulder. "It's okay. They wanted to come help us, so let them do their thing. Imagine your folks and the riding club members wondering what had happened to us. We had all the excitement today. Let them have a little glory."

She nodded. It was true the emergency workers and volunteers who had come out to search for them would want to feel they had accomplished something, rather than staying idly at home. "Right. And I'm starved. I'll even let them give me a chocolate bar if they have one. I think Jack ate my granola bar, and those protein bars the helicopter dropped are long gone."

Just below the spot where Jeff had fetched up against a scrub pine, stopping his fall, they met a party of three men from the local police department.

"Ahoy, Dr. Sullivan," the leader called. "Is that you, Ruby?"

Nelson Flagg's cheerful voice brought tears to her eyes. "Yeah," she yelled. "Hello, yourself, Nels!"

They sat down for a few minutes to rest, and the officers plied them with water bottles and snacks. Ruby leaned back on the hillside and sucked the chocolate coating off the candied peanuts Nels offered her while Chuck gave them a condensed version of their adventure.

"Tomorrow our detectives are going to hike in the long way from the mouth of the canyon," Flagg said. "It's too rough to try it in the dark. The state police said they saw the plane wreckage from their helicopter but can't land in there. They're preparing for an all-day expedition on foot."

"It will take them at least a couple of hours to hike in," Ruby said. "Hey, can you guys patch through to my dad's phone on the radio somehow?"

"We can be up on the trail in ten minutes," Officer Chet Baker said. "You can call him from there."

She shook her head. "I'm afraid my cell phone is either evidence by now, or else it's been ditched and I'll never see it again."

"How's that?" Flagg asked.

Ruby looked up at Chuck. All she wanted right now was her own bed and about ten hours' sleep.

Chuck smiled at her. "Ruby's about the quickest-thinking woman I know. Not only did she report the fire quickly this morning, but she also thought of a way for the police to track the drug dealers."

The men all looked at Ruby. "What did you do?"

"Not much. I just put my cell phone into the last bag of drugs they made me take out of the plane. If the state police trace it they may be able to follow those men wherever they go. On the other hand, if my dad tries to call me and the crooks discover it early on they'll probably toss it into some place that would be hard to get at, and the police will be on a wild goose chase."

They waited while Flagg radioed in a request to notify her father. A few minutes later he told Ruby, "Your folks will be waiting at the Bear Creak clearing where the endurance ride officials had the last checkpoint you visited. We can call them by phone as soon as we get back up onto the trail. Oh, and I warned them not to try to call your cell phone."

"Sound good?" Chuck asked her, smiling.

"Very good."

"Your horses were led back to the checkpoint, too," Flagg added. "Jeff Tavish's horse went back with one of the other veterinarians—Dr. Spelling. She was going to make sure his brother and friends took it home."

"Great," Ruby said. "They'll take good care of Annabelle until Jeff recovers."

A contingent of volunteer searchers joined them, and they were soon climbing up the steep hillside to the trail. Full darkness had descended, and the moon rose to the east, among the myriad stars. Every muscle in Ruby's body screamed with fatigue, but she made herself continue plodding upward, sometimes bent over and grasping at the scant bushes for support, sometimes clutching one of the volunteers' hands. When they at last reached the edge of the path and strong hands pulled her up onto the trail where she and Chuck had ridden with Jeff, she staggered and reached for the nearest arm to steady her.

A warm arm slipped around her waist, and Chuck said in her ear, "Are you okay?"

She leaned against him for an instant then pulled in a big breath. "Yes, I'm fine. Just tired."

"We can rest here if you need to."

She shook her head and pulled away. "It's tempting, but I'm afraid if I sit down again tonight I'll never get up."

"Miss Dale!" Fire Chief Ripton strode toward her, shining a powerful flashlight on the ground. "We have a couple of four-wheelers here. They aren't normally allowed on this trail, but we thought you and Dr. Sullivan might be glad to have a ride down to the Bear Creek clearing. Your parents and Dr. Hogan are waiting for you there."

Ruby let her shoulders sag and laid her hand on his sleeve. "Thank you, Chief. That sounds wonderful."

The ride to the checkpoint passed in a blur. Ruby leaned against the back of the firefighter driving the four-wheeler and dozed. When they reached the clearing she climbed stiffly off the vehicle and fell into her mother's arms.

"Baby, we were so worried," her mom murmured.

Tears filled Ruby's eyes. Her parents must have relived the hours after Julie's accident. She pulled them both into a big hug. "Mom, Dad, I'm okay. Honest."

Her father sobbed, and Ruby's tears spilled over.

They stood for a long moment together; then she eased gently away. "Is Lancelot okay?"

"He's great," her father said. "I've got him hitched to the trailer, and Dr. Hogan has Chuck's Appy. Are you sure you're all right? The policeman who spoke to us last said something about a plane crash."

"I'll tell you all about it on the way home." As she turned toward the parking area, she saw ride volunteers were dismantling the check-in and veterinary exam areas. "Are all the riders past this point?" she asked.

Her father nodded. "Doc Hogan told me the last of the contestants passed through here about a half hour ago."

Ruby looked around and saw Chuck had walked over to Dr. Hogan's truck and was deep in conversation with his partner.

"Ruby?"

She pivoted. Officers Flagg and Baker approached her and her parents.

"What's up?" she asked.

"We just got word the state police arrested two men loading horses into a trailer near the main road," Flagg said. "Your cell phone trick worked."

She smiled up at him. "I'm glad. Tell me, was their trailer hitched to a light-colored pickup? Because I forgot to mention that one of the men who kidnapped Chuck and me was the same man I saw early this morning at the site of the fire."

"Really?" Flagg asked. "I'm not sure about the truck. But it's late, and I think you've had enough excitement for one day. You can go home and rest and then come down to the station in the morning to identify the prisoners."

"Thanks. I think I'll do that." She realized Chuck had come over and was standing at her elbow as she said good night to the officers.

"Are you all set, Ruby?" he asked. "I guess your folks will want to baby you tonight."

"No doubt."

Chuck nodded with a smile. "Would you mind if I came by in the morning and took you to the police station? I know you go there all the time, but they want me to identify Jack and Hap, too. I was thinking we could ride over together in my pickup. Maybe get some coffee afterward."

"I'd like that."

He nodded. "Good night then. I'll pick you up around eight." He walked toward Dr. Hogan's truck.

"Hey," she called after him.

He turned back and arched his eyebrows.

"We did great on the first half of the ride."

He grinned. "We sure did. And there's a fifty-miler up near Sheridan next spring. You want to train for it?"

Ruby smiled. "I'll give that my consideration when I'm not about to fall asleep on my feet."

He strode back to her side and leaned close. "Consider this, too, would you? I think you're terrific. There's no one I'd rather have spent the day with, even a day as lousy as today." He stooped and kissed her cheek then backed away.

Her father ambled over. "Ready to go? I've got Lancelot loaded. You can ride with Mother, and I'll haul the trailer."

"Thanks, Dad." Ruby slipped her hand into his and walked with him toward where her mom waited beside the Jeep.

❧

"Hey, Ruby. Dr. Sullivan. Thanks for dropping by." Detective Garrett Austin sank into the chair opposite them in his office at the police station.

Chuck leaned back and watched Austin as he shuffled a few files on his desktop, selected one, and opened it. A week had passed since the Wyoming 100, but it seemed far longer.

"Just wanted to update you both, since you discovered the drug dealers' wrecked plane and were instrumental in us catching two of the gang members."

"Thanks, Garrett," Ruby said. "We've wondered what's going on with Jack and Hap."

Austin scrutinized the papers in the folder. "Well, they've admitted they were out looking for the downed plane the day before the ride."

"That's when we saw them the first time," Ruby said.

Chuck leaned forward. "Right. The day we posted the trail markers and they left their horses tied up in the woods for hours."

Austin nodded. "Yes. Hap cracked first, hoping for a lighter sentence, and when Jack knew his buddy had talked he sang, too. They knew about the cocaine in the plane, and they were desperate to find it before anyone else did. They located it, but it was too late to get down to it before dark and retrieve the drugs. They decided to come back on Saturday. You saw them when they had left the canyon and gone back to where they'd tied their mounts."

"But Saturday was the ride," Ruby said.

"That's right. Jack told us they saw a poster for the Wyoming 100 and realized on Saturday and Sunday a lot of people would be riding through the area and they would risk being seen again."

"So why didn't they wait until Monday?" Chuck asked. "Why take the risk of hiking all the way in there during the ride?"

Austin leaned back in his chair and smiled. "Because Monday was the opening day of elk hunting season. There would be hunters everywhere, even where there were no trails. Someone else might see them in the canyon or, worse yet, find the plane before they could get to it."

Ruby's eyes narrowed as she listened. "So that's why they set the fire at the starting area."

"Yes, they hoped to stop the ride. That would give them the weekend pretty much to themselves to get the job done."

"But that didn't work," Chuck said, "thanks to Ruby's showing up early. The damage was minimal, and the ride went on pretty much as planned. So they took the chance of being seen during the ride and tried to recover the drugs."

"Right. You two stumbled upon them when you climbed down to check the wreckage for survivors." Austin leveled his gaze at Ruby. "You were lucky to get out of that one alive. You know that, don't you?"

"God protected us," she said.

Chuck smiled. "She's right. I prayed constantly during the hour we spent with those guys. God was merciful and allowed us to walk out with only a few scrapes and bug bites."

"Well, someone was looking out for you all right." Austin tapped the papers on his desk to align them and put them back in the folder. "Oh, and you got your cell phone back, right?"

Ruby smiled and pulled it from her purse. "It's right here. The state police brought it back a couple of days ago."

"Good. That thing led them right to the suspects."

"I'm glad. I was afraid it would ring and the two crooks would find it before the police found them. Even though I couldn't get a signal down in the canyon, I left it on, hoping it would get within range of a tower or two so the police could track it. I knew it was a risk. If someone had called me while they were carrying it and the signal had gone through. . .well, I guess the worst they could have done was to smash it or throw it away." She shook her head. "It never occurred to me to set it on vibrate instead of ring. Maybe next time. . ."

"Let's hope there won't be a next time," Chuck said.

"It's a good thing it didn't ring while they were with you." Austin shook his head. "Guess you were pretty sure it wouldn't while you were down there near the plane. But still. Those guys have assault records. They might have gotten violent if they knew you were setting them up."

"So what about the drug suppliers up the line?" Chuck asked.

The detective inhaled briskly. "Yeah, we think we may get a break there. Harold Smith, the man called 'Hap,' gave us a couple of names. Their pilot was flying the cocaine in from Texas where they have a contact with a supplier over the border. This bust may go a long way toward stopping the flow of drugs into Wyoming, at least for a while."

Ruby smiled. "Then it was worth it."

When they left the police station, Chuck opened the door of his pickup for her. Ruby climbed up, holding her skirt expertly out of the way. She seemed as much at ease in her Sunday outfit as she had in her jeans and sweatshirt. With her hair pinned up in the back, she looked older and more pensive. He went around to the driver's side and got in.

"How are we doing for time?" Ruby asked.

"I think Sunday school is over, but we have plenty of time to meet your parents at your church before the worship service starts."

"Sounds good. Thanks. I wouldn't have minded going to your church today, but my folks are still in the smothery mood, and Grandma Margaret is there, too."

"It's all right." Chuck reached over and squeezed her hand. It was definitely all right. "They just need a little time to unwind and realize you're not going to leave them suddenly, like Julie did."

She nodded in silence, and he wondered if he'd said too much. Her eyes glistened as she looked up at him. "Thank you. I'm glad you understand. I don't think they'll be this way forever. In fact, I was talking to them last week about the possibility of getting my own place soon."

"What did they say?"

Ruby shrugged. "They're not crazy about it. I told them I wouldn't go far unless I found a place with a barn for Lancelot. Of course Dad said, 'Why bother if you're going to be over here all the time to ride the horse anyway?' But I can't just live with them forever. I love them, but I need to have my own life."

Chuck put his key in the ignition. "I'll pray about that, if you don't mind."

"Would you? Because sometimes I feel like I can't breathe when I'm around them."

After church, as they gathered their things, Chuck said, "How would you like to go out to the steakhouse for dinner? Then I could show you my place."

"Well, I—"

"Oh, Ruby," her mother said, "you've got to eat with us today. Of course Chuck's invited, too."

"Now, Linda," Martin began.

His wife set her jaw. "Grandma and Elsie are leaving tomorrow. It'll be Ruby's last chance to see them for a while."

Chuck looked helplessly at Ruby, trying to discern her true feelings. She smiled and turned to her mother.

"Okay, Mom. But Chuck and I are taking a ride afterward. He wants to show me where his ranch is."

"You have a ranch, Doc?" Martin asked.

Chuck smiled sheepishly. "It's a very small ranch, sir. Only ten acres and a very small house. But that's good. If it were any bigger I probably couldn't handle it on my own."

"Well, that's nice." Martin eyed him as if about to say more but clamped his lips together. He took his wife's arm. "Come on, Linda. Let's go get dinner ready. The kids have places to go this afternoon."

❧

Late in the afternoon Ruby called the hospital on her cell phone as Chuck drove them down the county road in his truck.

"Hi, Ruby," came Jeff's voice, more cheerful than it had been all week.

"Hey, champ! How are you doing?"

He laughed. "Better. I'm going home tomorrow."

"That so?" she asked.

"Yeah. I'm getting around really well on my crutches."

"How's the arm?"

"Still hurts like crazy, but since they put the pin in they say it'll heal completely. I won't have full use back for a while, though. I'll be going to physical therapy for at least three months."

"Chuck asked me to tell you he'd come see you tomorrow. But if you're going home. . ."

"Tell him not to do that. I'll be gone for sure. But I'll drive down and see you both in a few weeks, as soon as they clear me to drive on my own."

"That would be great, Jeff. How's Annabelle doing?"

"Kevin and Kaye are spoiling her. But it's all right. They've decided to get married, so I won't hold it against them. I'll have Kev back on the ranch full-time again."

"That's terrific. Will they be living with you?"

"I'm thinking of giving them the ranch house and building a kit log cabin down in the back field," Jeff said.

"Sounds like a plan. Keep us posted, will you?"

"Sure will. Say hi to the doc for me."

Ruby told Chuck the gist of the conversation and sat back in contentment as he drove the pickup onto a butte. She knew they were close to his home. She was curious about it, but she didn't say anything. She wanted to see it the way he wanted to present it.

He slowed and pulled the truck onto a gravel spot beside the road. He smiled over at her then climbed out and walked around to open her door for her.

Ruby hopped down, glad she'd changed her dress shoes for her loafers. They walked to a low fence at the edge of the butte and looked out over the plain.

"See that place down there? The one with the green roof?" Chuck pointed to a ranch almost directly beneath them.

Ruby swallowed hard before she spoke. The house was tiny, and the attached barn leaned toward the sunset. A few pieces of rusty farm equipment sat about the yard, and even from a distance she could see the yard wasn't well kept.

"I see it."

"Well, count over two houses. That one's mine." He nodded westward.

She caught her breath. "The one with the creek?"

"Yup. The stream flows right through my pasture."

She stood motionless, taking in the neat dooryard, the compact but inviting house, and the barn that stood a few yards away near the fence line.

"Oh, there's Rascal," she said. The Appaloosa grazed contentedly in the field.

"Yeah, he loves it out there. See the stand of trees at the far end of the pasture? He goes down there when it's hot."

"Ten acres?"

"That's right." He looked down at her, his brows arched in question.

"I like it."

Chuck smiled and slid his arm around her shoulders. "You know, if we're going to do that fifty-mile ride in the spring we need to keep the horses in shape."

"Sure. I plan to ride as much as I can. Until we get snow anyway."

He pulled her a little closer. "Since we did so well on the first half of the Wyoming 100, we ought to excel at doing a fifty-miler." He looked down toward his ranch again. "Want to drive down and see the barn?"

She suppressed a chuckle. Was he shy about giving her a tour of the house unchaperoned? His steady blue eyes were watching her, waiting for her answer. "What's in the barn?"

"Well, two box stalls, among other things."

"Two?"

He nodded. "In case you ever want to bring Lancelot over for a visit. Or something."

Her laugh burbled out. His brows shot up again, and she flung her arms around his neck.

"I'd love to see the barn."

"Would you?" he asked softly. He lowered his face toward hers and gently kissed her.

Ruby snuggled into his embrace. When he released her, she sighed. "Yes, I surely would."

Epilogue

June twelfth dawned clear and bright. Ruby leaped out of bed and pulled on her jeans. She hurried out to the barn, but her father had beaten her to it and was already measuring out feed for Lancelot.

"You get right back in the house, young lady. You are not going to muck out the barn on your wedding day."

"Oh, Dad! I'll take a shower afterward."

"No way. I'm doing your barn chores this morning, and that's final."

Lancelot poked his head out over the half door of his stall and whickered. She gave her father a quick hug. "Thank you. Just let me say good morning to Lancelot. Then I'll leave you alone."

"You'd better."

She laughed. "I promise." She walked down the barn alley and reached up to scratch the palomino's ears. "I won't be seeing you for a few days. But then we'll come get you and move you over to Chuck's ranch. You and Rascal can race around the pasture together all you want."

Lancelot rubbed his cheek against her arm, and she burrowed her fingers under his white forelock to reach another of his favorite scratching spots.

"You're really going to love the ranch. And you can drink right out of the creek."

"All right, young lady." Her father stood behind her with a lead rope. "Just because you and Chuck won that fancy ride up in Sheridan, you think you can boss the barn help around now. Skedaddle, you hear me?"

Ruby gave Lancelot a last pat and scampered for the barn door. "Okay, Dad, this time you get your way."

She stepped out into the sunshine and inhaled deeply. She would miss the home place, and she would miss Mom and Dad. But she would be only a few miles away, and she had a huge store of memories. This was the right time to step into her new life, with Chuck at her side.

A few hours later she and her mother drove to the church in Ruby's Jeep with her cousin Holly. Dylan, Aunt Ruthie, and Uncle Phil would ride over with Dad.

"Are you sure Grandma and Elsie will make it on time?" Ruby asked her mother. "I thought they'd be here an hour ago."

"Yes," her mother assured her. "When she called, Grandma said they'd had a slight delay, but they'll be at the church in plenty of time." She put on the turn signal for the church driveway.

Holly squealed. "Look, Aunt Linda! There they are."

Ruby looked down the road. Sure enough, there came the hot pink semi with gold lettering across the hood: GROOVY GRANNIES.

She leaped out of the Jeep and waited in the parking lot while Elsie expertly parked the big truck at the far side of the pavement out of the way. The jake brake gave its familiar rattle, and the passenger door popped open. Grandma climbed down from the passenger side in a stylish powder blue pant suit. Her silver white hair was perfectly coiffed. Ruby ran to embrace her.

"Grandma, you look spectacular."

"Well, so do you, dear, though I hope you're not going down the aisle in those dungarees. Now I wanted to tell you, Elsie and I took care of everything for the wagon ride. After you and Chuck have your week in St. Louis, you can go right to the Moose Valley guest ranch. We've outfitted your covered wagon for you. Here's the reservation." She slipped a folded sheet of paper into Ruby's hand.

"Oh, thank you, Grandma." Ruby gave her another hug.

Elsie, looking as pert as Margaret in a lime green outfit, came to stand beside her sister-in-law. "It was so much fun setting up the trip for you. I know you and your young man will have a wonderful week on the trail."

"Oh, you two are the best." Ruby gave Elsie a squeeze. "Chuck and I are looking forward to it."

"But hadn't you ought to be putting on your bridal gown?" Grandma asked.

"Yes, hurry, Ruby," her mother said. "You can visit after. Other people are arriving already."

Ruby scooted with Holly, her maid of honor, into the church and to the room set aside for the women to dress in.

"Just in time." Holly closed the door behind them. "I saw a black pickup pulling in right when we reached the church door. I'm pretty sure it was your sweetie and his doll of a brother."

Ruby eyed her in surprise. "You only saw Chuck's brother once."

"Yeah, but he's cute. I can dream, can't I?"

"Well, sure." Ruby reflected she now had an entire new family to enjoy, and Chuck's mom and siblings would be a big part of her life.

"Besides, I'm the one who gets to walk down the aisle with him," Holly added, pulling her dress off the padded hanger.

"True."

Holly gave her a knowing smile. "Of course it's Chuck's friend I'm really interested in."

"Which one?" Ruby asked absently while unzipping the back of her lace gown.

"Jeff. The horse trainer."

"Oh, that one." Ruby smiled. "He's a great guy."

A soft tap sounded on the door, and the other two bridesmaids entered.

"Hey, you're already dressed!" Ruby looked at her two friends and their rose-colored gowns with approval. "What do you know? I picked a color that looks fabulous on all of you."

As they hastened to help Ruby prepare to don her wedding gown, Ruby's mother and grandmother peeked in.

"Hi, Mom," Ruby said. "I'm just about to put this on. Maybe you can help with my veil."

Holly held the dress while Ruby stepped into it and lifted it. Then Ruby turned, and her cousin zipped it for her. When she turned to face the others, her mother's eyes glistened with tears.

"You look so beautiful."

Ruby hugged her. "Thank you."

"I always thought Julie would be with us on this day," her mother whispered.

"I know," Ruby said.

Grandma patted Mom's shoulder. "There now, honey. Julie *is* with us in a way. I'm sure she knows how happy we all are today."

૨&

Chuck left the study with the pastor, his brother, Jeff Tavish, and Dr. Hogan. As they entered the sanctuary, his best man and two groomsmen seemed at ease, but Chuck's stomach churned. Amazing that Ruby had agreed to be his wife. The realization delighted him; yet he felt more nervous than he had the day the drug dealers forced him and Ruby to help them recover their contraband.

He stood with his hands folded in the spot the pastor had assigned to him, trying to breathe evenly while his blood rocketed through his veins.

"You okay?" his brother asked softly.

"Yeah. Piece of cake."

"Ha!"

Chuck smiled then, but only for an instant. The organ music changed, and Ruby's friends glided down the aisle toward them. Their rose-colored dresses floated about them. All the girls looked unnatural. Their usually laughing faces regarded him soberly. Makeup perfect, hair pinned up in formal arrangements. They reached their marks at the front of the church and faced the congregation.

Again the music changed, and suddenly everyone stood. Chuck gulped and looked toward the door.

Ruby's smile beamed to him the length of the auditorium. Her brown eyes radiated joy, desire, and satisfaction. Chuck inhaled deeply. He would never regret this day.

He shifted his gaze to Martin's face. How hard would it be for him to hand over his only daughter? Instead of the pain and hesitation Chuck expected to see in his expression, he saw only contentment on his soon-to-be father-in-law's face.

Relieved, he let his gaze rove back to Ruby. Her smile became a grin, and he couldn't help but answer her silently as the music swelled. A few moments later she stood beside him where she belonged.

"Join hands," the minister instructed him.

Chuck reached out, and Ruby slipped her small hands easily into his large ones. He squeezed her fingers and turned with her to face the pastor and begin the rest of life with Ruby.

SUSAN PAGE DAVIS and her husband, Jim, have been married thirty-three years and have six children, ages sixteen to thirty-two, and six grandchildren. They live in Kentucky where they attend a Baptist church. Susan writes historical romance, mystery, and suspense novels. Visit her Web site at: www.susanpagedavis.com.

HEARTS ON THE ROAD

Diana Lesire Brandmeyer

Acknowledgments

Thanks to Pastor Vern Lintvedt for truck stop lunches, Truckers for Christ, and Roger Miesner for help with the rig descriptions. Thanks also to my pre-readers, Sara Lesire and Barbara Friederich; your help is appreciated.

Chapter 1

Sunshine caressed Randi Davis's face and poked its strong rays through her closed eyelids. Clawing her way back from the depths of sleep, she knew two things were wrong. The truck sat motionless, and it was past sunrise. "Jess, are you still sleeping?"

A grumble came from the bunk below. Jess Price, her partner, still huddled under blankets.

"Jess, wake up. We're late—again."

Covers rustled. The truck swayed gently with Jess's motion. "Late?" She groaned. "Now we're behind schedule. Why didn't you wake me up?"

"Don't yell at me. I did tell you to take over the wheel. You said okay. I assumed that meant you were. Good thing I didn't close the curtain; without the sun in my eyes, we might have slept for hours." Swinging her legs over the berth, Randi dropped to the floor and faced her driving partner of two years. "If you counted up the money we've lost from the times we've over-slept, we could afford to take a cruise."

Jess dragged a brush through her hair. "You know Dana will be madder than a two-year-old told no."

"Yeah, I know." Randi yanked the canvas privacy curtain closed. Twisting around in the tight space to avoid Jess, she snatched a clean T-shirt from a small set of drawers in the corner of the sleeper cab. She slid it over her head. "Let's call the office after we eat. We can feel guilty with full stomachs instead of empty ones. She'll want us to leave now, forget breakfast. Besides, I need my caffeine jolt."

"Jolt?" Jess slipped on a leather boot. "More like submersion."

Randi agreed as she finished tying her tennis shoe. She crawled over the driver's seat and opened the door. Grabbing the keys from the ignition and her cell phone, she jumped from the cab, wincing at the impact. The heat spiraled from the asphalt parking lot of the Wyoming Fuel and Go and curled its tentacles around her. After the coolness of the truck, she welcomed the warmth. The passenger door slammed with a bang. Randi turned, waiting for Jess.

"I'm starved." Jess ran her hand across her stomach as if to calm the beast within.

"And that's new?" Randi patted the emblem on the side of cab door. " 'Round the Clock' means we don't stop long. This has to be a fast breakfast, Jess. Not one of those famous 'I want one of everything' deals where you can't make up your mind."

"I know what I want." Jess propelled herself in the direction of the restaurant door, leaving soft taps from her cowboy boots hovering in the air.

Randi patted the back of her jeans, feeling for her wallet. "I forgot my money. Order me a large cappuccino and raspberry scones if they have them. If not, I'll take scrambled eggs."

"I love those dreams of yours. Better expect the eggs."

Randi turned back to the truck, slipping her fingers into her front pocket for the keys. Her reflection bounced back at her from the side of the polished door. Her hair resembled straw escaping from a bale. Looking for some kind of improvement, she gave it a quick finger comb.

Inside the truck, she reached under the driver's seat, her fingers grazing the smooth leather of her wallet. A stray lock of hair poked her in the eye. Grumbling at the aggravation, she wished she'd kept her salon appointment or at least brought along scissors. She removed one of many multicolored rubber bands resting on the neck of the stick shift and corralled her hair into a ponytail. Wallet in hand, she stepped onto the chrome running board and slammed the heavy truck door.

She scurried across the parking lot and pushed against the door of the truck stop. A blast of cold air from the ceiling vent sent shivers racing down her back. If they were on schedule, she'd go back for her warm shirt. She dreaded talking to Dana, the company dispatcher. Concentrating on a clever excuse, she came to an abrupt stop—against someone.

"Sorry! I didn't see you."

"That's okay." A voice warm enough to melt any iceberg wound its way through Randi.

"My fault. I wasn't paying attention." Randi stepped back to see what the brick wall she had smacked into looked like. She expected an overweight, unshaven trucker. Instead, delicious eye candy stood inches in front of her. Brown eyes met hers, and summer nights of stargazing suddenly seemed within her grasp. She knew deep inside she needed to get away from him. Fast. He made her feel too much, and he'd only said two words. Definite proof she had to give up watching classic Hepburn and Tracy movies.

"Are you hurt?" He reached out and caressed her arm.

She jerked her arm away. "Fine. I'm fine."

"Maybe I should stand back farther from the door. I'm Matthew Carter, by the way." He handed her a neon green sheet of paper.

"Thanks." Clutching the flyer, Randi fled, willing her face not to announce her inner turmoil, especially to Jess. She weaved around an aisle of mud flaps and yellow OVERSIZED LOAD signs into the attached restaurant. The top of Jess's red hair bobbed above a booth.

Randi slid into the booth, where a mug of coffee and Jess waited. She tossed the bright green page onto the center of the table with her phone then slid her hands around the mug, avoiding Jess's questioning look. She gulped the hot drink, wincing at the searing heat on her tongue. "Scones or eggs?"

"Eggs." Jess planted an elbow on the tabletop, propping her chin on her palm. "What's going on?"

Randi grabbed the bundled silverware and uncurled the paper napkin. The utensils clunked against the Formica. She smoothed the napkin and placed it on her lap. "Nothing."

"Something's up. Why is your face red?" Jess nailed her with a stare. "What have you been doing?"

"I just bumped into that guy over there, that's all." Randi straightened her fork, knife, and spoon into exact parallel lines, avoiding direct contact with Jess's all-knowing eyes.

"Must have been some bump." Jess turned halfway in her seat and peered across the room. "Where is he?"

"He's over by the door in the gray T-shirt, holding a bunch of green paper. I walked right into him." Randi shook her head in disbelief.

Jess emitted a soft wolf whistle. "If you have to run into somebody, it's nice to run into a body like that." She sighed. "Makes me miss Mike all that much more."

Randi reached across the table and patted Jess's hand. "You'll be back with him in Cheyenne soon." Jess's face lit. Randi ached at her friend's happiness. She remembered that feeling; it's what she'd wished for her own life, but now that her thirtieth birthday had slid by, she'd made a different plan for herself. Independent Randi, that's who she wanted to be, not needing anyone or anything but the open road.

The waitress arrived with a tray. "Two breakfast specials with wheat toast, right?" She slid a plate of scrambled eggs in front of Randi.

"Thanks." Randi reached for the saltshaker as the waitress set down Jess's meal.

"Randi, I thought you agreed."

Her hand stilled. She had promised to pray with Jess or at least listen while Jess prayed before meals. It wasn't that she was opposed to God—more like He didn't seem interested in her. She folded her hands. "Say it fast, Jess. I'm hungry."

Jess arched an eyebrow in what Randi knew from experience was disapproval. "You know, you're going to make a great mom someday. You have the look down."

Jess said the common table prayer and finished with, "Father God, bring a good and God-loving man into Randi's life. Amen."

"Nice, Jess. You know that's not in my life plan anymore; it's going to be me and a truck till the end." Jess could have Mike. Randi hoped it would work out. *Maybe Mike is different from Brent.* Brent had promised Randi a life together, and that's what he'd meant. While she was home, they were together, but as soon as she left to student teach, he drove into another woman's driveway.

"I want you to have what I have with Mike; you deserve that." Jess flipped over the crumpled flyer with two fire-engine red fingernails. "So let's see what he's selling." Her eyes widened. "Randi, look at this picture. It's your guy. He's a minister."

"He's not mine." Randi snatched the paper and scanned the upcoming schedule of places where Matthew Carter would hold services. "He's preaching to truckers. Wonder if anyone shows up to hear him." She checked to see if he wore that better-than-thou pastor look. He didn't; he looked rather more like a man she might have considered dating once upon a time—before Brent reinforced an old lesson first taught by her father: Love can't be trusted.

Randi pushed her plate to the side then turned over the bill to check the total. "You want to call Dana?"

"No, but I will. She doesn't seem to appreciate your wit this early in the morning." Jess took a sip of her coffee. "And she's going to be in a bad mood when she finds out we're late."

Randi squished her napkin into a ball and placed it next to her plate. "I'll pay this and meet you back at the truck." She shot a glance at the front door. The man had left, or at least he wasn't standing there anymore. For a moment she felt disappointment, which confused her. Why did she care if he was still here?

As Randi breezed through the glass doors, her cell phone vibrated in her hand. "Hello?"

"Is this the correct number for Miranda Davis Bell?"

"Yes, this is Randi."

"My name is Rachel Miller. I'm with social services. Your brother's been arrested for making meth in his home. He listed you as a guardian for his daughter, Emma. When can we expect you to pick her up?"

Chapter 2

Discouraged, Matthew gripped the bundle of flyers to his chest as he crossed the blistering parking lot. So far it hadn't been a good day for spreading the Word of God among the drivers. Most avoided him when he offered them a sheet.

"Wait up, Carter!"

Matthew turned to see one of the men who had recently begun attending his services. "Dirk. Didn't see you inside. Did you just get here?"

"Yeah, I ran into a mess. They shut down I-80 because some woman tried to make breakfast in their RV while it was moving. Caught the thing on fire."

"Did everyone get out?" Matthew shifted the stack of flyers in his arms.

"Yeah, the only fatality was breakfast." Dirk sputtered a laugh, smacking his knee with his hand. "Good one, huh? And no cursing, either."

"You did good, Dirk." Matthew slapped Dirk on the back in approval. Dirk's language had improved dramatically in the last month. He knew how hard it was for Dirk to give up his favorite adjectives, verbs, and nouns when he was surrounded daily by other drivers using those words freely.

"Yeah, but it's too bad about that couple losing their nice ride like that."

"You mean you weren't telling me one of your stories? This really happened?" He couldn't imagine the horror of watching your retirement home burn.

"I'm 'fraid so. It was one of those mega-expensive homes on wheels." Dirk nodded at the flyers Matthew held. "Any takers?"

"Not many." The image of the blond who'd smacked into him, smelling like summer, ballooned in his mind. She'd been the highlight of his morning.

"That's too bad. They don't know what they're missing." Dirk fell into step with Matthew as he walked to his pickup.

Matthew opened the door and backed away from the blast of heat that poured from the truck. "It's going to be a hot ride home." He tossed the flyers into a box overflowing on the floorboard.

"Once your air conditioner kicks in, you'll be all right." Dirk leaned against the side of the truck bed.

"It quit working about a month after the warranty expired." Matthew rolled down the window.

"Ooh doggie, that's rough. You need a new truck."

"I need another job. Hauling boats one way. . ." Matthew kicked at a lone pebble that had found its way onto the asphalt parking lot. It didn't roll far before it stopped against a wad of chewed gum someone had spat on the ground. "Anyway, I thought I'd be driving full-time by now."

"Who've you applied with? Just the big companies?" Dirk drummed his fingertips on the side of the truck bed.

"Everywhere, large and small. I even suggested I'd be a chaplain without pay."

"Free? How you going to eat and pay rent?" Dirk scratched his head above his ear, knocking his hat off center. "Nobody works for nothing."

"I meant for being a chaplain as an extra thing. They'd have to pay me for driving."

"Tell you what, give me your phone number. I'll talk to my dispatcher and see if there's any openings. Sometimes you need to know somebody to get in the door." Dirk tapped his chest with his thumb. "I'm *your* somebody."

"Thanks, Dirk. I'd appreciate that." Matthew wrote his number on a flyer and handed it to Dirk.

"All right, then. I gotta get back on the road." He straightened the bill of his black hat.

Matthew watched Dirk swagger toward his rig. A faint flutter of hope sprang inside him. Maybe this time God would answer his prayers.

❧

She should have realized A.J. was up to something. The last two times she'd asked to pick up Emma, her eight-year-old niece, for a "girlie girl" day, he'd insisted on bringing Emma to her. Fury raged inside Randi.

How could A.J. be so stupid? Drugs. Again. And this time producing them in his home, while his daughter slept in the other room. This time they wouldn't hesitate to honor him with a well-deserved extended stay in prison.

Climbing into the truck, she slammed the door. She tried to swallow her anger, but it stuck in her throat, embedded in the thickened embarrassment her brother had caused.

Jess sat behind the wheel. She adjusted the side mirror on the driver's side. "You call the next time we oversleep."

Randi chose her words with care, trying to keep her emotions about A.J. from entering the discussion. "What did Dana say?"

"The usual. Any more delays and she's going to short us on trips."

Randi snapped her seat belt. "She can't do that."

Jess pushed a button and held it for twenty seconds to warm the glow plugs. She turned the key, and the diesel started with a roar. "She knows that. She had to say something so she'll feel like she's in charge. I told her not to get her panties in a knot; the truck will be back in the yard before night."

"True—we both slept through the night, so we can drive straight through." Randi leaned her head back on the headrest. "It's going to be a long day."

"She also said to be careful because a trucker has been shot."

Randi shivered. "Where?" A crazy with a gun who didn't like truckers might be enough to make anyone think about switching careers.

"Colorado, a drive-by at the rest stop. They haven't caught the shooter yet." Jess maneuvered the truck through the parking lot. "Seems the guy stayed on the highway and shot through the passenger window of his car."

"Sounds like he's mad at somebody. Dana didn't say if it was an east or west stop, did she?" Randi worked the rubber band out of her hair. She reached into the door cubby and pulled out a brush.

"I didn't think to ask." Jess steered the slowly rolling truck onto the highway entrance ramp. "Saw you on the phone. Who called?"

"A. J.'s in jail." Randi stared out the window. "He wants me to take Emma."

Jess whipped her head around. "Are you going to?"

"She can live with my mom." In her stomach, the scrambled eggs from breakfast slammed into the toast.

"Do you think that's fair to your mom? She's not been well, Randi."

Randi bristled at Jess's words. "I suppose not, but for now it's better than being put into the foster care system."

"Randi! You're her aunt. You wouldn't do that to Emma, would you?"

Randi stared at the road ahead. "I don't know what else I could do. I'm never home. How can I take care of her?"

"You could teach, Randi. You did get your degree."

"But it's not what I want to do. Teaching was part of the plan with Brent. That didn't work."

"Maybe God is giving you another plan to follow."

◈

Standing in the doorway of her mother's kitchen, Randi held her ground. "I can't. She can't live with me, Mom. I drive a truck for a living. I can't change my life for my brother's kid." As soon as the words tripped off her tongue, she regretted them, grateful Emma was at her friend's home for the night. They would pierce her like a knife.

Her mother plunged her hands into the soapy water, scrubbed a pot for a moment, then banged it on the drain board to dry. She turned and wiped her hands with a yellow- and-blue-striped dish towel. Her lips stretched in a tight line.

Randi's shoulders tightened. She knew the look on her mom's face. She'd seen it many times. A long spell of talking about what's wrong and what's right was about to start. She didn't want to hear it. She needed to go home, get some sleep, and then think about what to do—tomorrow.

"You're her godmother, Randi."

"Exactly. I'm supposed to be praying for her—which I do—and make sure she goes to church—which I haven't since I don't have a church anymore."

"You could have one."

"Don't get going, Mom. I know what you're going to say, but what's so wrong about Emma living with you? You have an extra bedroom, and Emma will be around to keep you company, watch movies with you. . . Remember how we watched movies together? You'd make popcorn and sprinkle it with cheese, and we'd sit on the couch with Grandma's quilt spread over our laps." For a moment she longed for that feeling of belonging, knowing someone wanted to hear about her day.

"I won't forget those times, not ever, Miranda Davis Bell. But my time for raising kids has done passed. I'm old and I'm tired. I don't want to stay up late helping an eight-year-old build villages out of cardboard or practice spelling words. I don't need the worry, either. Being a parent today can't be easy, and being Emma's parent will be even harder." Mrs. Bell scooted a wooden chair from the kitchen table. "Sit down and talk to me. Maybe you'll change your mind."

"I won't, Mom. I have student loans I'm still paying, and you know driving doesn't pay very much. Quitting my job and moving into a two-bedroom isn't possible. I'll come and get her when I'm home. It's a win-win situation." Randi couldn't help but notice how thin her mom was. She must not be cooking meals for herself. If Emma were here, her mother would have to cook again. This could be good for her mom. Randi's mood brightened. Maybe her mom needed a little more time to think about keeping Emma. "I'd like to stay and chat, Mom, but I need to get home. I need to get bills paid tonight so I can mail them tomorrow."

"This isn't going to go away. Emma needs a home, either with you or the state. Maybe you could use that teaching degree instead of driving." Her mother sighed. "Guess there's no discussing it with you tonight."

"Mom, I made my choice. I like what I'm doing." Randi turned to leave. Her mom needed a night to think about having her granddaughter with her all the time. How many times had she heard her mom wishing her children were still small? Emma could fill that need.

"Just one more thing."

Randi stopped at the doorway. Her mom didn't plan to let her leave without something to think about. She never did. "What? You want me to pray about this, don't you?"

"Yes."

"That's it, then? Just pray about my decision?" It amazed Randi how her mother depended on God to direct everything in her life. Couldn't her mother make a decision on her own, just once? Still, for a moment, she longed to feel she could do the same.

Chapter 3

Randi drove her car into the only open spot, next to the huge green garbage bin. Its lid gaped, gripping a white plastic bag between its metal lips. *Home.* It didn't feel like one, but at least she wouldn't have to wait at a truck stop for her number to be called for a shower. From the backseat she collected her duffel bag, slinging it over her shoulder before slamming the door.

Overhead lights threw shadows from the trees bordering the street across the rough concrete sidewalk. The third step down to her basement apartment had lost more of its sharp concrete edge. The night-sensitive porch light flickered over her doorway like a sign from an old roadside diner. Timing its flashes, she managed to insert her key into the lock. Grasping the knob, she hesitated. Nothing really waited for her inside. *Maybe I should—should what? Bring Emma to live with me? I love Emma, but I'm not her best option.*

Inside she dropped her bag onto the floor and slid three dead bolts across the closed door. That enforced her decision. She couldn't bring Emma to live in this place. She reached over and twisted the switch at the base of the lamp next to the door. The harsh glare from the high-wattage bulb assaulted the room. The burgundy slipcover on the couch sagged, exposing a worn shoulder where a previous owner's cat had exercised its claws. With a swift tug, Randi positioned it in place.

She retrieved the few pieces of mail on her floor. Nothing but offers for credit cards. The musty smell she associated with homecoming after weeks on the road needed banishing. The first thing she would do was to light the scented candle Jess gave her last Christmas—was it seashore or forest? Something like that. Taking two steps, she stopped at the coffee table and dropped the mail next to the candle. Matchbooks collected from truck stops across the country formed a heap in a small ceramic bowl. She picked one and withdrew a match, struck it, and touched the flame to one of the three candle wicks. She blew out the match and laid it on a small heart-shaped dish. And noise. This place needed some. Scooping up the remote, she switched on the television. The news channel filled the screen, and the quiet dissipated.

Randi slipped off her sandals and tossed them into a basket by the door. She headed for the shower, pausing when the newscaster's words "rest stop" and "shot" caught her attention. Wheeling around, she tried to pick up the story, hoping they were offering more information than she and Jess had heard when they'd returned the truck. After a few seconds it was apparent they had nothing new to offer.

After her shower, she grabbed a soda from her fridge and a bag of chips from the cabinet. Settling onto the couch, she spread a blanket over her lap. The remote in her hand, she flipped through the channels. Maybe she could find a good movie tonight. Black and white flashed across the screen. She stopped. Good, a classic. They were the best, always taking her to another time, when the biggest stress in her life was a math test.

A curly-haired child in an orphanage danced across the screen proclaiming she would be okay. Her daddy would come for her; she just knew he would.

That could be Emma. She blinked back tears and hardened her heart against the bludgeoning of loneliness and guilt. *Great. Mom must be praying.* She continued scrolling through the extensive channel list for something else, even an infomercial. Her finger paused as a man sopping with sweat screamed at his audience, "Just come to God with your problems. He can solve everything."

The camera zoomed in on the man's glistening face. "Listen to your heart. Just give your troubles to Him," he whispered. "You know God can hear you. He wants you and your love. He's waiting for you. What are you waiting for?"

Randi felt his piercing glare through the screen. She squirmed, wondering if her mom had somehow managed to broadcast this man into her home, like some kind of science fiction. Mesmerized, she listened a bit longer.

She tossed the blanket to the floor. Maybe she should talk to a pastor. But who? She hadn't attended church since she started driving; it wasn't as if truckers were welcomed—or at least not their trucks. There always seemed to be a sign saying No Semi Parking Allowed.

"Call us now. What are you waiting for?" the voice from the television urged.

What did she have to lose? Leaning over the arm of the couch, she snatched the phone from the floor and punched in the 888 number. A computer voice asked if she was dialing from a touch-tone phone. If so, please press 1; if not, please stay on the line.

"Oh no you don't. I'm not playing the number punch bingo tonight. Besides, this shouldn't happen to a person in need of prayer." Randi waited for a real person to answer.

"Please wait. One of our student disciples will be with you soon."

"Sure they will." Randi soon hummed along with the canned gospel music. She glanced at the clock on the windowsill. Five minutes passed. *Must be a lot of people in need of guidance tonight,* she thought. Nestling the phone on her shoulder, she counted to ten once then started over. She made it to seven.

"This is Angelica. May I have your name?"

She paused for a moment, unsure about giving any personal information. First name should be safe. "Randi."

"Hi, Randi. What can I help you with this evening?" Angelica's silken voice massaged Randi's tense nerves.

"I've been asked to do something that would upturn my entire life. My niece needs—"

"Can you hold? I'd like to transfer you to someone more skilled than I to pray with you."

Someone more skilled in prayer? Did they have levels of prayer people? What did this woman get to pray for? Lost keys? And how did they test for praying skills? "Sure, I suppose."

"Can I have your phone number and address?"

"Why do you need those?"

"In case we get disconnected, we can call you back."

"That explains the phone number, but not the address. You aren't planning on coming over tonight to personally pray with me, are you?"

"We'd like to send you information about our ministry. We don't do house calls." Angelica's voice went from silky to thorny.

"You mean to ask me for a donation?" So much for free help; maybe this church thought money made the prayers reach God faster.

"There will be an envelope included for that purpose if you wish."

"I don't think so." Randi ended the call feeling more alone than before.

❧

The sunset cast a rosy glow over the parking lot of Boats and Moor as Matthew unplugged the trailer lights. Standing on top of the dualie tire, he stretched over the side of his truck to reach the gooseneck hitch in the middle of the truck bed and released the latch. At the snap of metal, he dropped down to the pavement. Noticing a now-clean swipe on the side of the truck, he glanced down and grimaced at the dirt smeared across his favorite 'Pokes T-shirt. He brushed it off, but a shadow of dirt remained, much like the shadow of the Wyoming Cowpokes' last game. His last clean shirt, and he was two days from home.

"Carter."

"Kennedy. I'll get your paperwork. You'll save me a trip inside." Matthew reached into the truck and grabbed a clipboard off the bench seat.

Tom Kennedy ran his hand along the prow of the speedboat. "Looks like you brought me a nice one today."

Matthew walked over next to him. "Here you go." He handed the clipboard and pen to Tom. "Sign by the Xs. She is a beautiful boat. I'm sure the new owner will love her."

Tom signed the papers and handed them back to Matthew. "I'm just about to close for the day. The wife's at her mom's, so I'm free for dinner if you want company at your table tonight."

"Yeah, I'd like that, but I'm pretty dirty," Matthew said.

"I know a great place where as long as you're decent they feed you. And I don't care if you've been rolling in mud." Tom inspected his own hands. "I'm not all that clean, either. The grease under my nails isn't going to disappear before dinner."

Inside the store, Matthew waited for Tom to close out his cash register and put his money in the safe. "Pretty trusting to do that while I'm in here, aren't you?"

"I have nothing to worry about with you. It's like having God stand behind me."

"Don't hold me up next to God. I'm no better than any other sinner."

Tom locked the door. "I know, but some people are safer than others. You can't deny that fact."

"I won't." Matthew's stomach rumbled. "Where are we eating?"

"Dandee Inn. It's just up the road on the left. Want to ride along with me?"

"Sure, if you don't mind bringing me back for my truck later. I could use the rest time. I'm planning on starting back after we eat."

Tom jumped into his pickup. He turned the key and the radio screamed to life.

Matthew startled then recognized the sounds of a popular Christian praise band. "Great sound."

"Sorry about that. I like my music loud." Tom lowered the volume.

"Me, too—drowns out the road noise that makes me drowsy."

"Don't you get tired of living out of your truck?"

"Sometimes."

"So why do you keep doing it? I'll hire you; then you can settle in, find a good wife, and have a couple of kids."

"I'm not ready to settle. Not yet. God has called me for His purpose—to teach others about Him. I'm just waiting on Him to get me into the right company where I can do that."

"But if that's what He wants, then why aren't you traveling across the country with a rolling church, like Truckers for Christ?"

"I don't know. I ask that question all the time."

"Maybe you're confused on your purpose. Maybe instead of asking, you should be listening."

"Well said, but I'm not ready to give up my dream yet."

Tom raised an eyebrow. "Your dream? I thought it was God's plan."

"It is. I'm sure it is. It will happen when the timing is right." Matthew tried to silence the questions rising in his mind. What if he had misread God's intention? What if he was following his own path instead of God's?

Chapter 4

Randi rounded the back of the truck to finish the pre-ride check. The trailer door didn't budge when she pulled on it. The signal lights were both flashing. They were ready to roll. She kicked the back tire of her cab with the toe of her boot. *Ritual completed, check.* With one foot resting on the running board, she climbed into the truck where Jess waited. "Ready?"

"I suppose. I didn't sleep well last night. I must be coming down with something." Jess yawned. "Leaving Mike for two weeks isn't fun."

"At least this way you don't have time to get bored with each other." Randi started the engine. The click of the diesel engine welcomed her back. The sound never failed to bring her joy. She was born for this. A quick look at the gauges assured her everything measured where it should.

"I hope he doesn't." Jess crossed her arms over her chest and frowned. "As long as he doesn't get tired of waiting for me to get back."

"Come on, Jess. You know he isn't going to mess around with anyone. Not Michael. He's one of the good ones. Besides, when would he have time? He has too much studying to do. Doesn't he?"

"Lots of book work this week, anyway. Taking that bar exam next month has him worried. He thinks he won't pass." Jess picked a piece of lint off her capri pants and flicked it in the trash bag attached to a hook on the dash.

"Why? He's smart enough." Leaving the truck terminal, Randi shifted into a higher gear.

"He keeps being told by other lawyers that no one passes it the first time. Mike thinks he has to be better than the rest. I don't doubt he'll pass it the first time." Jess retrieved her log book and pen from the cubby on the door and wrote down the date. "I know I don't want to be around if he doesn't. Remind me to make sure we can take a load the week the results are supposed to come back." She slid the book back into the space on the door.

"Some supporting wife you're going to make." Randi laughed. "Where's your 'stand by your man' philosophy?"

"Please. Stand by your man? You've been listening to that old country station again. I fully intend to be a good wife, but I'm not married to him yet."

"I think you will be."

"Probably. Maybe. I don't know, Randi. Maybe he's not the one. Maybe I should reconsider one of those guys we met last spring at Anne's Date-a-Minute party."

Randi frowned. She had politely smiled and asked questions for hours that night. At the end of the evening, her tally sheet remained blank. None of

131

those men held any interest for her. She'd gone only because Jess and Anne begged. Randi told them she wasn't interested. She didn't plan to settle down with a husband, ever. "Do you really think any of them are as promising as Mike? He's going to have a great career, and he's crazy about you."

"Maybe. He's said he loves me, but I want to make sure." Jess twisted around in the seat to face Randi. "You didn't call. Tell me what happened with Emma. Is she living with you now?"

"No, not now. She's at Mom's, but Mom said she can't stay. I don't know what's going to happen with her." Randi accelerated to pass a pickup dangerously overloaded with furniture topped with a mattress.

"What do you mean, you don't know?"

"It's not that I don't want to take Emma." Randi paused, searching for the right words. "If I take her, my entire life will have to change."

"And hers hasn't been changed?"

"Of course it has. But I don't even have a bedroom for her, and my lease isn't up for another five months."

"What other choice is there?"

"If Mom won't keep her?" Randi steeled herself for Jess's reaction. She knew how Jess felt about family, but Randi knew from firsthand experience that you can't depend on people who have the same last name. Better Emma learn now than later. "She goes into the foster care system until I can get another place to live and a different job. It's overwhelming."

Jess reached for her stainless steel coffee mug from the cup holder on the floor. "But isn't she worth changing your life for?" The steel mug settled with a clunk in the cup holder as Jess suddenly doubled over with a whimper.

Randi took her foot off the accelerator. Jess's face glistened with sweat. "What's wrong?"

"I don't know," Jess said. "No. I feel awful. There's a rest stop coming up. Can we stop for a minute? Maybe if I splash my face with cold water. . . I'm just going to put my head down until we get there. I feel light-headed."

Randi's heart raced. Should she call for help? She wasn't quite sure Jess knew what was best for Jess. Stopping would be the best choice. From there Randi could call for help if she needed to.

"I'll be okay." Jess's muffled voice floated up to Randi. "Might be food poisoning. We ate at a new place last night, and I had chicken."

The cab filled with silence as Randi drove. The familiar blue sign with its white picnic table flashed by the window. "The rest stop is coming up, Jess. Just another minute or two." Randi's mouth felt dry. *Food poisoning? What do you do for that?*

The exit appeared none too soon for Randi. A quick glance at the lot and she knew she'd have to park on the edge of the lot. She gripped the Jake Brake and pulled; the rat-a-tat sound of the engine compression braking system rattled her nerves. "We're here, Jess. Do you think you can walk?"

Jess sat up but anchored her head in her hands as if it might float away. "I'm better, I think, now that the truck is stopped." She popped open the door. "Maybe walk next to me?"

"Wait for me, then." Randi sprinted around the cab to help.

Jess put a foot on the running board. "I think—"

Pop. Whish. Glass shattered around her.

Jess screamed and fell on Randi, knocking her to the ground.

Jess went limp and silent.

"Jess! Are you okay?" Randi rolled Jess off her then scooted along the ground close to her.

"I hurt. My arm. It hurts." Jess began to moan.

A dark, wet stain began to form around a gaping hole in Jess's black T-shirt. Bile rose in Randi's throat; she swallowed. The sight of Jess's face, white as skim milk, impaled her with fear.

"I think you've been shot."

Chapter 5

The flashing lights of another police car pierced the gray day. Randi shook and her teeth banged together. She tried to stop both the shivering and the chattering. She tried hard. She'd tried all her life not to be weak, but this she couldn't stop.

Everything happened so fast. She didn't remember how she got to the curb where she sat. Someone draped a rough gray blanket around her shoulders. It covered her to her feet, but it didn't ease the chill that had settled deep inside. Jess had blood on her shirt; that she knew. Who called the police? And when did the ambulances arrive? She clutched the blanket tighter.

"Are you getting any warmer?"

She became aware of the man sitting close beside her. She thought she knew him, but from where? The memory kept floating out of reach. "No." He seemed familiar, but she couldn't think of his name. "Who are you?"

"Matthew. Matthew Carter. You're still cold. I'll go see if I can find another blanket." He started to stand.

She grabbed his arm. "Don't go. Tell me what happened."

"Can I put my arm around you? That might help to warm you."

She hesitated. Another fierce shiver ran through her. "Okay." Her voice quivered. "Please tell me about Jess."

"She was with you, right?" Matthew pulled her a little closer and rubbed her arm, as though trying to dispel her chills. "I don't know what happened. I pulled in a few minutes ago. I only know she's been shot and you're bleeding."

"I'm bleeding? Did I get shot, too?" Her fingers fumbled across her chest. Did she have a hole in her? Visions of blood pumping from her assailed her mind.

Matthew drew her closer, anchoring her shaky arm with his firm one. "No. I don't think you've been shot. Randi, it's going to be okay."

Someone squatted in front of her. "Randi? My name is Bill. I'm a paramedic and I'm going to help you. I need to look at your face right now."

"Is Jess dead?" Her words seemed to float over her head, and she wondered if she had even said them aloud.

"She's alive. They'll be taking her to the hospital soon. You'll follow in the other ambulance." He gently brushed her hair from her face and patted it with something cool.

"Why can't I go with Jess? I haven't been shot, have I?" She started to rise, feeling the need to get her control back. Pain shot between her eyes, and she hunched over, pulling away from Matthew. "I—I'm fine. I just need to get to Jess."

134

"You're lucky you weren't shot like your partner, Randi. But pieces of glass hit you in the face. We have to make sure all the pieces are removed, and I can't do that here."

"Then I'll go with Jess. I have to ride with her. I'm her partner." She tried to stand, but her eyes wouldn't focus. She felt light-headed, as if she had sucked a balloon full of helium. Her legs began to wobble.

Matthew reached out and steadied her. He helped her sit back down on the curb. "Maybe in a minute you'll be stronger."

"You can't ride with her, Randi. They need the room to help her." Bill cleaned her face with something that smelled like the stuff her mom used to put on her scraped knees when she'd fallen rollerblading.

The blanket slipped from her shoulder. Matthew draped it back into place. "Is there someone you want me to call? Someone you want to have at the hospital when you get there?"

"Mom is too far away to come, and I don't want to scare her. Tell me about Jess. How bad is she? Tell me the truth."

"I don't know, Randi."

"I can't feel anything. Are you sure I'm hurt?" Randi searched Bill's face for any clues about how badly she'd been cut.

"Lots of little cuts. You're lucky you didn't get any glass in your eyes."

"Miss Bell?"

Randi pivoted her head. A Wyoming state patrol officer stood in front of her. "That's me."

"I'm Officer Benfield." The leather holster around his waist crackled as he bent down in front of her. "I need to ask you what you saw."

"Nothing. Nothing at all." The need to give him details weighed heavy like granite on her shoulders. "I didn't see a car or truck or van. Nothing. Not even the sound of an engine."

Officer Benfield stood. "Maybe in a little while a detail will come to you."

"I can't tell you anything." Randi's teeth chattered.

"Let's get her inside the ambulance," Bill said. "You can send someone to talk to her at the hospital."

"I didn't even know Jess had been shot until I saw the. . ." She attempted to stand but sank back to the curb. "Blood."

"Miss Bell, someone will be in contact with you later today. I'm sorry this incident occurred."

Incident? That's what he thought this was? This was life changing, and if she weren't so tired, she would tell him so.

Matthew helped her to her feet. "I'd like to come with you."

"With me?" She stared at the pavement, her thoughts folding over each other in slow motion. Why would he want to? She shivered and felt his arm on hers. But the bigger question. . .*Why do I want him to?*

"Sorry, sir, no extra riders are allowed." Bill snapped his medical case shut. "You could follow her, though."

"Randi?" Matthew squeezed her hand. "You shouldn't be alone."

"You can come," she whispered.

❧

At the hospital, Bill and another paramedic wheeled Randi into a curtained room next to an exam table where a nurse waited. "I'm Sue, and I'll be taking care of you."

Randi propped herself up on her elbow. "Can you tell me what's happening with my partner?"

Sue grasped Randi's wrist between her fingers and took her pulse. "What's her name? I'll try to find out for you."

"Jess Price. Someone shot her."

"You first. Can you remove your shirt, or would you like me to help you?"

"I can do it." Randi looked down to unbutton the blood-soaked shirt. Jess's or hers? Her head swam in misty darkness. Taking a deep breath, she peeled the fabric away from her skin.

Sue opened a cabinet and retrieved a gown covered in a tiny geometric pattern. She held it out to Randi. "Put this on." She took Randi's shirt from her. "Do you want to keep this? I can put it in a plastic bag for you."

"No." Randi shook her head in distaste. She would never wear that shirt again.

"I wouldn't want to keep it, either. I'll try to find you something to wear home." She tossed the shirt in the trash receptacle.

"Can you see if Matthew Carter is here yet?"

"Sure." Sue spun on her heels and left the room.

A moment later, she returned with the doctor and Matthew. Randi answered a few questions while Sue took notes, and then the doctor aimed a bright light on her face. He placed a magnifying visor over his eyes. "I'll try to be gentle, but I'm afraid a few of these might sting. I have something to numb your face."

"No thanks. I can do this. Will I need stitches?"

"Possibly. I'll know soon. You tell me if this is too painful. If it is, I'll stop and get you numb." She glanced down at his ID tag as Dr. Simon proceeded to remove a small sliver of glass.

Randi jerked. "Ow." Tears stung her eyes.

Matthew squeezed her hand. "I think you should give her something."

"Should I stop?" Dr. Simon's hand paused in the air.

"How many more?"

"Enough, and I have to get in deep for some of these. I think I should give you something to ease the pain."

"But I won't be able to drive."

"I don't think you'll be driving anywhere tonight, anyway. Why not get relief for the pain?"

Randi panicked. "I don't have anything to drive, do I? Where's my truck?"

"It's taken care of." Matthew's voice softened. "I think you should let them deaden the pain."

"It does hurt more than I thought." She sniffed, hating to give in.

Dr. Simon nodded to Sue. He took the prepared needle she offered. After the injections, Randi's face stiffened with numbness.

The doctor finished removing the last piece of glass and dropped it with the rest in a stainless steel dish. "That's the last of it. Only one more thing for me to do. A few stitches on your forehead. Don't worry. It isn't going to leave a scar. I think you might have rubbed it, causing it to tear."

"I don't remember doing that."

"Well, that's not unusual." Dr. Simon knotted the thread.

Randi closed her eyes, not wanting to see the approaching needle.

"All done," he said a moment later. "Sue will give you a paper with directions for taking care of your cuts, along with a prescription for pain pills. If you have any problems, go see your regular doctor."

"Can I go back to work?"

"Take a couple of days off. You've been through a stressful event, and your body needs to recover." Dr. Simon ripped off his latex gloves with a snap and tossed them into the trash can. "Take care," he said as he left the room.

Sue patted her on the back and offered a smile. "I found a T-shirt from one of the drug companies." She handed her the folded white shirt.

"Thanks. I can send it back."

"No need." The nurse handed her a stack of papers. "Read these and sign at the bottom. Then you can go." She glanced at Matthew. "Would you step outside so she can change? Then you can be a good boyfriend and take care of her tonight."

"I will." Matthew winked at Randi.

Sue closed the curtain and waited for Randi to put on the T-shirt. "And, Randi, an officer wants to ask you a few more questions before you leave. After you talk to him, you'll find your friend on the fourth floor. She's in surgery now. You can wait in the surgical waiting room up there." As Randi signed her release papers, Sue slid open the curtain and allowed the officer inside. "She's ready to talk to you now."

"I'm Officer Perkins; this shouldn't take long."

"I don't have any new information to add." Randi handed the clipboard back to Sue.

Officer Perkins flipped open a notebook cover. "Just in case you've forgotten something, why don't you tell me what you saw."

"Nothing. I didn't see anything. I walked around the front of the truck, and when I opened the door for Jess, I heard a noise, and then Jess had blood all over her shirt."

"You didn't see a car or truck pulling away or hear tires squealing?"

"No, nothing. I wish I had seen something."

Officer Perkins retrieved a card from his pocket then closed his notebook. "If you do think of anything, no matter how small, you can call us, all right?" He slipped the card into her hand.

Randi faltered at the doorway when she saw Matthew waiting for her. She brushed past him and headed for the elevator.

"Hey, Randi, wait."

She pushed the Up button then turned and faced him, her hands scrunched in tight fists by her sides. "Boyfriend? I don't even know you."

"Technically, we've met before."

"When? I don't remember."

"You ran into me at the Fuel and Go. I handed you a flyer and told you my name. You didn't tell me yours until I asked you at the rest area. I remembered your eyes. They're—"

"I know. Family trait." That had created a host of problems on the playground. "You're the preacher? You look different."

"I haven't shaved." He rubbed his chin. "I'm on my way back from dropping off a boat."

"So you're here because it's the 'pastorly' thing to do?" The elevator doors behind her remained closed. She wondered if taking the stairs might be faster.

"At first, but now that I've been introduced to your charming wit, I'd like to stick around awhile. At least long enough to make sure you get home safely."

"I don't date pastors." The prayer hotline had wanted more from her than she wanted to give. Did Matthew as well? She moved a little farther away from him, not all that comfortable with those mocha eyes staring down at her. Why? Because he was a pastor? Or because she found him attractive?

He smiled at her. "Actually, I'd like to make sure you're okay. Besides, you do need a ride home, right?"

She swallowed hard and nodded, willing the telltale warmth in her cheeks to fade and the ding of the elevator to sound.

"Good. Then it's settled. I'll fill the role of a big brother until you can take over. Then after we check on Jess, why not let me drive you home?"

"I don't know. I guess I can trust you, but isn't that going out of your way? You'll lose paid driving time."

"I'm on my way back, and I don't have another delivery set up. Where do you live?"

"Torrington."

"I'm just on the east side of there. I can take you home, or at least help you get settled in a hotel nearby."

She looked up, the blush finally breaking through to heat her cheeks to roasting temperature. "If Jess doesn't need me." She punched the UP button several more times, willing the elevator to open up and deliver her.

Matthew leaned against the wall with a satisfied smile in place. "Good. We'll check on Jess and then head for home."

Randi caught his gaze, noting the twinkle in his eyes. "Thanks. I guess you take that Good Samaritan thing seriously."

"You bet. 'Love thy neighbor' is my motto."

A sharp ding jolted her back to reality as the elevator doors eased open. Randi ducked inside, feeling grateful the walls weren't mirrored. She hadn't prayed for herself in a long time, but something whispered that Matthew was her answer to a long-ago, almost forgotten prayer.

❧

The elevator doors slid open again, exposing polished floors. Fluorescent lighting bounced against the hard shine of the dark green tile. A blue arrow directed visitors around the corner to the surgical waiting room.

Randi stopped at the doorway. If she went inside, this would be real. She didn't have time to think it through, as Matthew, his hand at her elbow, propelled her into the room.

A pink-smocked volunteer sat behind a desk. Below her laminated name tag hung a picture of an infant with the corny phrase ASK ME ABOUT MY GRANDDAUGHTER emblazoned below it. "Who are you waiting for?"

"Jess." Behind her, someone on television yelled out a letter then screamed. Randi cringed, wondering how normal life could continue when so much had happened. Shouldn't the world have changed? "Jess Price. Do you know what's happening with her?"

"Are you a relative?" The volunteer didn't look up from the counted cross-stitch she held on her lap.

"No, but we work together. We're like sisters."

She glanced up at them. "I can't tell you what her condition is. The privacy act doesn't allow me to give out information to a nonrelative." She looked down, pulled her thread through, and prepared to take another stitch. "How do you know she's even here? They aren't supposed to give out that information downstairs."

Randi leaned on the edge of the desk, placing her hands over the counted cross-stitch chart spread on top. "We were together when someone shot her. You have to tell me."

The volunteer scooted her chair back. "No, I don't."

"Randi, you're scaring the woman." Matthew gently turned her around and led her to a row of plastic chairs. "Why don't you sit here and rest?"

Randi plopped into one. She would sit because she wanted to, not because he'd told her to.

Matthew stared at her for a moment, looking confused. Too bad. He hadn't done anything wrong, but she didn't want him to think she needed him. She watched him go back to the volunteer. Now what? Did he think he could charm information out of that woman?

"So how old is your granddaughter?"

"She's four days old." The woman grinned at him.

"She's cute. Have you been able to hold her yet?"

"No, but next week I'm flying out to Georgia. I'll be helping her parents, and I'm planning on holding that little one often."

Randi couldn't believe the change in that woman. Matthew had some kind of magic, getting her to beam like that.

"Who did you say you're here for?" the volunteer asked Matthew.

"Jess Price."

"I'm not supposed to say anything, but since you know she's here, just this once." The woman looked over her shoulder as if to make sure no one would catch her bending the rules. "She's still in surgery. They said it would be about three hours before her family could see her."

"Thank you, ma'am. My. . .my friend might be able to rest now."

Randi saw Matthew turn. She quickly closed her eyes, not willing to let him know she'd watched his every slick move. He sat next to her and touched her hand.

"Can I get you something?"

"No, thank you." Her voice was as stiff as cardboard.

"Did you hear what she said about Jess?"

"Yes." And the part about being her friend, and the way he said it, implying she was more than a friend. Didn't it? She still reeled from the boyfriend comment in the ER. He should have said something. He was a pastor, wasn't he? She closed her eyes. Maybe if she ignored him, he would go away. She'd find another way home.

The adrenaline swell from earlier had dissipated, leaving exhaustion in its wake. She leaned her head against the wall and soon fell asleep. When she woke, she looked around. Something was missing. No, someone. Matthew was gone, and she felt a sense of abandonment. Then she noticed Mike, Jess's boyfriend. He paced the waiting room floor. "Hey."

Mike turned. "I didn't want to wake you when I arrived. I thought you might need to rest. Are you okay? I met Matthew. He said you were cut and needed stitches."

"Just a few in my forehead. I'm lucky none of the glass hit my eyes." She blinked away the cloud of drowsiness surrounding her mind.

She shot out of her chair. "Jess! Tell me about Jess. They wouldn't tell me anything because I'm not related." She scowled. "I'm her partner. We drive a truck together. We see each other more than most sisters do." She wanted to rub her face. Where the numbness was wearing off, she felt prickles below the surface.

"I know. When the hospital called her parents, they told them to consider me family since we're engaged and they couldn't get here as fast as I could."

Randi blinked hard. "Engaged?"

Mike grinned. "Last weekend. We're getting the ring the next time she has a weekend off. She didn't tell you?"

"No." And she wasn't about to tell him what Jess did say.

"I think she wanted to wait until we made it official with a ring."

Randi hoped that was the reason, but right now she wanted Jess to be okay. "How is she?"

"Still in recovery, but the doctor came in earlier and said she'll be fine. They took a bullet out of her shoulder. None of the bone shattered." He checked his watch, giving it a tap as if to make the time go faster.

"She was sick before—before she was shot. Did they find out what was wrong with her?"

"They think it was caused by our celebration dinner."

"Jess did mention the chicken. I'm glad it wasn't something else. She'll have enough to deal with now. Can she leave soon?"

"Maybe in a couple of days. She'll be okay, Randi. I promise."

"Did Matthew leave?" She tried to sound like it didn't matter if he'd left her.

"He went to get me a soda. Jess didn't tell me you were dating someone."

Her relief that Matthew hadn't left was quickly replaced by anger. "That's because I'm not. Did he tell you that?" *Just wait until he comes back in here!* Just because she had a few stitches and accepted a ride home didn't mean they were a couple.

"No, I assumed you were. Why else would he be here?"

"Maybe he's just a nice guy who offered to help. That and he's a minister out to save all truck drivers from hell."

"That's different, then." Mike glanced at the clock on the wall. "I should be able to see her soon. They're supposed to call."

Randi peeked over her shoulder. A different volunteer had clocked in. "I need to call Dana and tell her what happened."

"Done."

"Did you call?"

"I did, but the police had already notified her. She said to check in when you get home."

Confused, Randi whirled around. Matthew stood holding a soda for Mike. "Mike told her you wouldn't need a ride." He handed the cup to Mike. "Did you want something, Randi?"

"No. I just want to see Jess." She rubbed the back of her neck.

A perky voice on the television behind her caught her attention. ". . .two truckers hospitalized after a drive-by shooting. Rare turtle gives birth. More in a moment."

Randi froze. "Is she talking about us?" The perky voice slowed and thickened, and overhead the lights dimmed. Randi's knees ceased to exist. She slowly slid to the floor, vaguely aware of Matthew's hands around her waist. What did he think he was doing? *He'd better not. . .* Before she could finish the thought, the room tilted, spun, then faded to black.

Matthew whispered her name. "Randi. Come back to us." He watched as her eyelids twitched. He desperately wanted them to open, revealing the most unusual eyes he'd ever seen, one blue and one green. He wanted to see them, to stare into their mesmerizing depths. He couldn't deny it; this woman had made it past his barriers. If he didn't distance himself soon, he might find he could never erase her from his mind.

"Matthew? What happened?" Her voice sounded weak and scared, a pale imitation of her normal one.

"You heard the newscast, and your body's defenses took over."

"What?"

"You fainted."

"Why didn't you say that?"

"I don't know. How do you feel now?" He cradled her head against his cheek, liking the feeling a little too much. He felt protective of her. She hadn't been out more than a minute, but she looked pale. It would be good to get out of here and take her home. Did she have someone to take care of her? He hadn't thought to ask.

The volunteer hovered nearby. "A nurse will be here in a second."

"No need, I'm fine." She sat up straighter and scooted away from Matthew.

"Maybe you are, but here she is, so let her check you out and we'll all feel better." The volunteer stepped back.

"Want to tell me what happened here?" The nurse wrapped her fingers around Randi's wrist and felt for her pulse.

"She heard the news about her partner being shot, and it must have become real to her then, because she fainted. I caught her before she fell, though. She wasn't out very long."

"Your pulse is fine. If you feel faint again, make sure you sit down and lower your head to your knees." The nurse stepped back. "You can see your friend now if you feel strong enough."

"I'm ready."

Matthew watched her waver, as if she'd just vaulted off a boat and forgotten that land stood still. He hovered next to her. He wouldn't ask if he could go with her. She'd have to accept his being there, because she didn't have a choice. He had no intention of leaving her alone.

Chapter 6

Randi closed her eyes and tried to rest against the seat of Matthew's truck, but she kept seeing Jess in that hospital bed, so pale, and no movement under that sheet. It was so unlike Jess to lie there like that. Even with over-the-counter allergy medications, she buzzed around the cab. With all her squirming, foot bouncing, and talking faster than a teenage girl with a new phone, she drove Randi crazy—so much so that Randi banned all medications from the cab. She'd rather listen to Jess's continual nose blowing.

Matthew grazed her arm with his fingertips, bringing her thoughts back to the front seat of his truck as he drove toward her home. "Are you thinking about Jess?"

She was so intent on memories, Matthew's touch surprised her. "How did you know?"

"It wasn't too hard to figure out. You haven't said much since before we left, when you made sure she was breathing."

"Guess that was kind of weird, wasn't it? Holding my hand under her nose to see if I could feel her breath?"

Matthew grinned then looked straight ahead as he maneuvered a curve in the road. "Can't say I've ever seen anyone do that."

"That's a safe answer." The pickup rattled; the diesel engine noise for once didn't soothe her. Randi stared out the window and wished she were home. He was driving her crazy, and they'd only been on the road for two hours. He was the worst kind of man. Hovering over her, asking if she needed anything. *Is the ride too rough? Do you want to stop for food? Are you too hot?* It was enough to make her wish she were back in the hospital. No one had fussed over her since she was six and had her appendix removed.

A soda can rolled from under the seat, striking against the heel of her boot. The truck reeked from fast-food bags and fries, pieces of which she found sticking out between the crack in the seat. The smell made her queasy. She pushed the can back with her toe. "Do you ever clean this thing?"

"Every other month. Ya think I need to do it more often?" Matthew gave her a sideways grin that turned to a frown when he saw her face. "Guess so. Sorry. I'd have cleaned if I'd known you were coming."

She didn't laugh at his feeble attempt at humor. She turned to face the open window, leaning forward to allow the wind to whip her hair. She'd lost the rubber band somewhere. It occurred to her that combing the tangles would not be pleasant. She gathered it into a clump with her hand and leaned even farther out the window to let the breeze cool her face. The miles rolled by, and she wondered what kind of person it took to shoot another, someone they didn't even know.

"What are you thinking about?" Matthew asked.

"Why there are evil people. Why does God allow them to live on the same planet as the good ones?" As soon as the words passed her lips, she thought about her brother. Did she think A.J. was evil? She could only think about the towheaded boy who'd played board games under the kitchen table with her. She thought about his laugh that bubbled like a spring from his chest. Emma laughed like him. Would she end up like her father?

"It's a sinful world, Randi. I don't know the answers. I do know God is giving everyone, good and bad, a chance to come to Him through His Son. Even the evil ones can change through His power." Matthew jiggled the air conditioner control as if it might miraculously fix itself.

"He's out there somewhere. Maybe even in one of the cars we just passed." Randi watched weathered fence posts sail by the window.

"The police will catch him."

"I hope so. Before he shoots someone else." She hoped the news hadn't reported their names. It would be easier to explain what happened in person to her mom, when she showed up on her doorstep later tonight. Matthew insisted she go there, rather than home, or he wouldn't give her a ride. Did he think she would wake up screaming from a nightmare or something? "Why did you want me to go to my mom's?"

"Because you're taking pain pills, and you shouldn't be alone. I'd stay with you, but men don't stay with women they aren't married to."

"Maybe in your world." Her eyes darted to his left hand. "Are you married?"

"Not even close."

"Why? You do like women, right? Or is it because you're not allowed to get married?"

"I can marry. And yes, I do like women. A lot. It's just. . ."

"It's just what?"

He glanced in the side mirror then back at her. "I don't date a lot."

She cocked her head, squinted her eyes. Was he serious? "Who's the last person you dated?"

"Karen Landowny, in my senior year of college."

"So what happened?" Randi curled her foot beneath her, happy to be discussing something less serious, something that didn't involve her.

"She dumped me."

"Oh. I see." She tried not to smile at his morose tone.

"Are you assuming it's my fault she dumped me?"

"It wasn't?" Randi couldn't resist teasing. Surely he'd moved past a gone-wrong romance in the past. *But the same could apply to me.*

He hunkered over the steering wheel with a frown. "Great. Women stick together even when they've never met," Matthew grumbled under his breath, just loud enough for her to hear.

Apparently she'd misjudged his ability to move on with his life. He'd been nice to her, so she'd forgive his arrested development and show him some sympathy. "What happened?"

"Cows."

"What?" She whipped around and stared at him. Did he actually say "cows"?

"Cows. Lots of cows."

"I don't get it. What do cows have to do with dating?"

"My parents own a dairy farm."

"And?"

"Have you ever been to one? Driven by one?" He grimaced.

Understanding dawned, and she surprised herself with a giggle like Emma's. "The smell kept you from dating?"

"My mom invited us to come back to the farm for a family celebration. Let's say Karen's reaction wasn't promising for a lifetime commitment. She told everyone my house smelled like pigs. And it doesn't smell like pigs; it smells like—"

"Cows."

His back became more erect, increasing his height. His head almost touched the roof of the truck. She stared at his profile. His jaw jutted noticeably. "Pigs smell more."

"Sure they do." Randi snickered.

Chapter 7

Matthew woke to sounds of the farm report on his radio. The first rays of sunlight had yet to streak their way into the Wyoming sky. But his room glowed from the dusk-to-dawn security light attached to the garage.

His dad would be expecting his help in the barn. Reluctantly, Matthew slid into his jeans and a T-shirt. He couldn't stay here much longer. True, he had his own place above the garage, but it was still his parents' home. He'd tried pastoring a small church after the seminary, but his heart wasn't in it. He longed to be out on the road, talking about the gospel to truckers who didn't get the chance to hear it. The longer he stayed, the easier it would be for his dream to slip away. He wasn't the kind of son who could live here and not see the need for his help on the farm. But he couldn't imagine milking cows day after day. And right now that's what his future seemed to hold. The only thing here to connect his hands to diesel fuel would be a tractor.

He pulled his Bible onto his lap. "Father, please start my life soon." Flipping it open to Psalms, he read a chapter then spent a few minutes in prayer. He asked for healing for Jess and Randi. Unwillingly, his mind evoked the picture of Randi's teasing smile and her blond hair whipping in the wind. Why did she haunt his thoughts, and now his prayers? No one else had found a way into his private life. Why her? He tried to push her image away. His work for the Lord was planned, and he didn't have time for a wife and family.

Whoa! Now I'm thinking about marriage? He shook his head to clear it and headed down the stairs. Maybe the cows would help get him centered on the plan he'd chosen.

Outside, the barn lights blazed through the windows. Once again his father had beaten him to the barn. When he walked through the huge wooden door, he found his dad, ball cap perched on his head and overalls already dusty, attaching teat cups to the cows' udders.

Matthew walked to the sink and washed his hands with disinfectant soap and water, then dried them with a paper towel. "Hey, Dad. Morning prayers took a little longer than usual today. Sorry."

"Never be sorry about talking to the Lord, Matthew. Talking to the Father is never wasted time." His father looked up and smiled. "I come down here and talk to Him while I'm getting the cows ready. Most mornings it's as if He's right here with me."

"Amazing, isn't it, Dad, how God can be with everyone at the same time?"

Matthew flipped on the radio. "Might as well catch the weather while we're here."

"Yup. But I find it's more accurate if I stand outside and look for myself."

Matthew laughed. "I have to agree with you on that one. It seems the more sophisticated systems they have for predicting the weather, the more often they're wrong."

"Your uncle Danny already washed the teats. I'll get the rest of them hooked to the machine if you would turn the fans on high. Feels like it's going to be a scorcher today."

"Do we have any cows in the maternity ward?"

"No, maybe later this week. Go ahead and turn that fan on high, too. Helps to circulate the rest of the air." His father continued his task.

"These cows are spoiled. Their ancestors didn't have it this easy," Matthew said as he strode down the concrete walkway.

"And your ancestors didn't get as much milk from those cows, either," his dad yelled to him.

After he turned on and adjusted the fans, Matthew checked the hospital ward. The cow they had quarantined the night before seemed to be feeling better. He refilled the feed trough with the special food they saved for sick cows and gave her fresh water before leaving.

The sound of the milking machines made him feel like a kid again. If he closed his eyes, he could imagine his uncles standing in the barn talking to his dad, all of them red-cheeked from the sun, tattered ball caps on their heads. And lots of laughter. Now only Uncle Danny came to help. Uncle David had had a stroke and couldn't walk well, and Uncle Ray had retired and spent his time traveling around the country with a truck and fifth-wheel trailer.

"Woolgathering again?" His dad's voice intruded.

"Dad, when are you going to retire?" Matthew spun around to face him.

"Never. You retire, you might as well be dead. I like this life, and I'm not quitting until God takes me home." He patted the rump of a cow.

"But, Dad, how are you going to keep up with this if Uncle Danny retires?" Matthew leaned against the concrete wall.

"We've talked about that, and he isn't quitting, either." His dad removed his cap and ran his fingers through his sparse gray hair. " 'Course, we've also discussed the possibility you might grow tired of preaching to truck drivers and want to come back here. If that happens, the place is yours."

"Dad." Matthew hated disappointing his dad again. "Guess you and Uncle Danny are in for the long haul, then. I won't be changing my mind."

His dad nodded. "Okay then, 'bout time to head back to the house."

"I wonder what Mom's making for breakfast."

"I requested some of her chocolate chip pancakes last night. Sure hope that's what she's doing." His father licked his lips. "Son, when you find someone to marry, you'd better make sure she can cook."

"Right. If she can't, I'll have to learn, or maybe move my family in with you." Matthew waited for his father's comeback and wasn't disappointed.

"Son, I didn't raise you to be a freeloader. You get a family. You take care of them."

"I will, Dad." Matthew slapped him on the back. "You've taught me well." He started to say more, but a nasal voice on the scratchy radio caught his ear.

". . .early this morning another truck driver was injured in a drive-by shooting. The suspect is still at large." *Randi. Has she heard about this yet? Maybe I should call and see if she's okay.*

His father removed his cap and ran his fingers through his thin gray hair. The look on his father's face said he'd heard the news also.

"I thought when you'd be driving trucks I wouldn't need to be concerned about your safety." His father's face looked pained. "Guess I was wrong about that."

"Let's go eat. They'll catch whoever is responsible. Think about all the truckers out there. The percentages of me being shot are pretty small, don't you think?" He reached out and punched his dad's arm with affection. "More likely I'll take to eating breakfast at night and wearing dirty clothes."

"Maybe. But don't mention this to your mother. She's a bit sensitive."

"Sure, Dad, I don't want her to worry that I might get hurt when I do get a job driving." Matthew swung his arm around his dad's shoulder and the two headed toward the house. Somewhere in a high tree, a mockingbird chattered, razzing him with a high-pitched whistle. Matthew clamped his lips tight and reached for the screen door, holding it for his father. *If I get a job, that is.*

Chapter 8

Since the shooting, Randi's mom had agreed to keep Emma. For a while. Randi still hoped her mom would decide it would be permanent.

Standing barefoot on her niece's bed, Randi carefully aimed a hammer at the shiny nail between her fingers then drove it into the wall. "That's the last one, Emma. Hand me your bear." Earlier she'd made loops to use as hooks and tied them to the ribbons strung like bowties around Emma's stuffed animals.

Emma handed her the polar bear. "That's Dusty."

"Hi, Dusty." Randi held the bear to her face. "I hope you like your new home." With great care she hung the bear on the nail. She sank back onto the bed, eyeing her craftsmanship with skepticism. "What do you think?"

Emma stood at the foot of the bed and tipped her head one way, then the other. "They aren't even."

"You're right, I didn't get them all at the same height. Does that bother you?"

"No. But they aren't even."

Randi looked at the wall again and understood. The bed wasn't centered under the animals, leaving enough space to put one more animal. If Emma had another one. . .but she didn't. She didn't have much of anything. A. J.'s house and its contents were seized when he was arrested. Social services had packed a suitcase and let Emma pick a few things to bring with her. The small dresser top held three books and a generic fashion doll whose hair frizzed as if she'd been vacationing in the tropics. The room looked empty. Maybe Randi could fix this one problem. "Wait right here."

She headed for the kitchen, knowing she would find her mom sitting at the table working a crossword puzzle. "Do you still have that box of stuff from when I was a kid?"

"Look in the top of the front closet. I almost tossed it out a month ago. They were collecting for the church yard sale. I didn't think you wanted it, since you'd left it here for so long. But I thought I should ask first."

"I don't—didn't want it. But I think there might be a few treasures Emma might like."

She found the box on the top shelf, pushed into the corner. It wasn't a lot of stuff, but maybe it would be enough for now. She carried it into Emma's new room.

"What's in there?" Emma asked.

"I'm not sure. Want to help me look?" Randi plopped the box on the floor and hunkered down next to it. She sat down and patted the spot next to her. "Well?"

Emma looked at her warily for a moment. "Okay."

Randi pulled the flap open. On top there was tissue paper. She pulled it out. Underneath was what she had been looking for. *Tally.* He was in perfect condition. She stroked his golden fur then handed him to Emma. "He used to be mine, but I'd like for you to have him."

"What's his name?"

"Tally. But I think he wouldn't mind if you wanted to call him something else."

Emma held the dog in front of her, turning and twisting him. "I think Tally is a good name. Who gave him to you?"

Randi's memory jumped to Christmas morning. Her father had left them that summer and she'd never heard from him again. Eventually Mom had said he'd found someone else to love. The spindly tree leaned crookedly in the corner, surrounded by silver and gold packages her mom hadn't bought— beautifully wrapped packages. Later she learned they were brought by their church. Inside one of them was the stuffed cocker spaniel she named Tally. She decided TV Dad had sent him to her secretly. It had been a long time since she'd thought of him. She and A.J. had made him up after watching *The Cosby Show.* They wanted to have a dad like Cliff Huxtable and decided to pretend they did and named him TV Dad. "I don't know, Emma. He was under our Christmas tree one year."

"Can we hang him, too?"

"Sure, we just need another safety pin. Can you get me one?"

Emma jumped up from the floor. "I'll get one from Grandma. I'll be right back."

Randi grinned when she realized Emma held Tally tightly as she left the room. She poked around in the box, wondering what else she had considered a treasure once upon a time. She heard the phone ring in the background and hoped it would be Emma's friend. She hadn't called since Emma moved.

"Aunt Randi?" Emma held the phone out to her. "It's for you. Some man."

Mike? Did something go wrong with Jess? Her heart rate increased. She leaped from the floor, forgetting the box of memories and grabbing the phone from Emma. "Mike?"

"No, Matthew."

Matthew? Her mind went blank for a split second before realization brought a rush of heat to her face. She scrunched her brows. "Hi."

"I tried your cell phone, but you didn't answer. I thought you might be at your mom's. I wondered if you would like to have dinner tonight."

"With you?"

"Well, I suppose I could arrange for you to have dinner with someone else if you want, but yeah, I guess I hoped you'd go with me." The teasing tone in his voice returned the heat to her cheeks. "I really want to see for myself that you're okay. I've been looking for you on the road."

"I haven't gone back to work yet. Not until next week." She glanced up to see Emma watching intently. "I have plans for tonight, but if you don't mind if I bring someone along—"

"Sure. Do you want to meet me, then? I thought I'd take you—we could meet at Bill's Grill. Do you know where that is?"

"Around six?"

"That works for me. I'll see you and. . ."

She let the question hang. Did she detect a jealous tone in his voice? "We'll be there." She pushed the END button a little too quickly. She blinked at Emma.

"Who was that, Aunt Randi?" Emma raked her fingers through the fur on the cocker spaniel's ear.

"The man you and I are having dinner with tonight."

"We're going on a date?" A grin stretched across Emma's face. Her eyes widened. "Do you love him?"

Randi smiled, painfully aware that her cheeks were on fire. "No, he's a friend." She chewed on her lip and tossed the phone onto the bed. At least she hoped he was just a friend. Or did he want to be more? Worse yet, why didn't she know how she felt about that? And why had she said "friend" instead of "pastor"?

❧

Matthew slammed the door and stomped down the stairs of his apartment. Who was Randi bringing? She'd said she wasn't dating. He fished the keys to his truck out of his pocket and got in, ramming them into the ignition. No, she said there wasn't anyone to call. Wasn't that the same thing? She obviously had someone in her life, and he didn't like the idea. Not one bit. Well, at least tonight he would meet the competition. *If there even is competition!* No! He just wanted to make sure she was okay, that's all. After all, that's what a pastor did, or a big brother. Right? Yeah. A pastor or big brother. But something way down deep in his heart told him he didn't want to be either of those to Randi.

Chapter 9

Randi's fingers trembled as she pushed the lock button for her pickup. The ride to the restaurant had made her long for the quiet of the road. Emma's shotgun questions had only made her more aware of Matthew as an eligible male, not a pastor. What if he was interested in her, not just her soul? Could she handle that? Did she want to drive down that road?

Emma stretched her arms wide and twirled on the sidewalk. "Do you think our date is here yet?"

"It's not a date, Emma," Randi explained one more time. "A date picks you up at your house and takes you in his car. He doesn't meet you at the restaurant, at the mall, or at the movies."

"And Pastor Carter isn't taking us. We're taking us. So it's not a date." Emma's head bobbed in agreement with Randi. "But why did we have to change clothes and curl our hair?"

"Because we're girls, and we like to look nice for us." Randi held out her hand. "Ready?"

Emma slid her hand into Randi's. "Is he cute?"

"Emma. It's not a—"

"Date. I know, but is he?"

"He is." Great. That would just add more stress to this outing. But she couldn't lie. Emma could see for herself that Matthew. . . Well, she wasn't going to finish that thought.

They pushed through the glass doors, and the smell of grilled hamburgers and onions wafted through the air. A country song ricocheted against the walls. Bill's Grill boasted ten tables. Matthew wasn't at any of them. *Definitely not a date if he isn't already waiting.* The disappointment flowed through her, but she brushed the feeling away and attributed it to Emma's pestering.

"Can we sit over there?" Emma pointed to the stainless steel bar with tomato red tractor seat stools.

"I think a table might be better. If Matthew's been driving a lot, he'll want to have someplace to rest his back." Randi knew that from experience. She never sat on stools after a long drive unless there wasn't anything else available. Someone touched her shoulder, and she spun around. "Matthew."

"You're right. I'd rather sit at a table." He wore a huge grin.

"What are you so happy about?" Something about that grin made her think he was more than just happy to see her. But what?

"I'm Emma. Are you our date?"

Randi felt the color start to rise in her face. "Emma."

"Sorry, Aunt Randi. I know he's not a date because he didn't pick us up."

"I'll be your date, Miss Emma, if you like."

Matthew beamed, positively beamed. Could he like the idea of them dating? Randi didn't know what to do with the feelings jumping around inside her.

"If he's not your date, can he be my date, Aunt Randi?"

The end of this outing couldn't come soon enough for Randi. She should have left the girl at home with her grandmother. Then Emma looked at her with hope spilling from her face. She was probably the only eight-year-old in this town to date a pastor. Her stories at school would be stupendous. "Emma."

"Please, just this once, couldn't we say it's a date?"

The kid had been through a lot. She might as well have a bright spot in her day. Randi felt her resolve melting. "Just this once."

"You may get us a table." Emma tipped her chin and stared at Matthew. "And you can sit next to me."

Matthew blinked in surprise. Emma had Randi's eyes, and Matthew must have noticed. He looked back at Randi.

Reading his expression, Randi said, "Almost the same. They're reversed."

"Fascinating family trait."

"On the playground it's anything but that."

Emma tugged on Matthew's hand and pointed. "That table by the window. Can we sit there?"

"Looks like a perfect place for my pretty date. Why don't you lead the way?"

Emma flashed him a grin. "Okay!" She raced across the room as if there were others rushing for the prime spot in the diner. In seconds she had the menu in front of her.

Matthew pulled out a chair next to Emma, across from Randi.

Randi plucked a laminated menu from the silver prongs that held it tight between the mustard and ketchup. After a moment, she made her choice. "Emma, what do you want?"

"I don't know yet." Emma slid her finger along the words on the menu. She looked at Randi wide-eyed. "What can I have?"

Matthew leaned over and whispered into Emma's ear. She giggled.

"I get to have a chocolate shake, and we're going bowling at Ten Pin Bowl-a-Rama after!" Emma bounced in her seat.

Randi fumed and focused her best imitation of her mother's "I'm not pleased" look at Matthew. She'd agreed to dinner, nothing else. Matthew should have asked her before telling Emma. She'd march right out of here after dinner if Emma wasn't positively glowing with happiness. If A.J. hadn't been an irresponsible parent, she wouldn't be in this situation. At times like this she could barely contain her anger at her brother.

&

Bowling balls rumbled down the lanes next to him as Matthew finished typing their names into the automatic scoreboard. "Emma, you're up first."

Emma stood looking at him, holding the bright pink ball she'd picked out of the rack. She watched the bowler in the next lane. When his ball left his hand, she copied his hand movement. He threw his ball. She didn't throw hers. She turned slightly and watched a bowler on the other side.

"Has she ever bowled?" he asked Randi.

She gave a slight shake of her head. "I doubt it. Her home life hasn't been the greatest."

"Should I help her?"

"Maybe. No, wait, she's trying."

Emma's ball loped down the lane and into the gutter with a plop. She walked back with her head low, wiping tears with her sleeve. "This is a stupid game. Can we go home?"

Matthew felt at a loss. He looked at Randi for help. She didn't offer any, shrugging her shoulders as if to say, "You wanted to take her bowling. It's your problem to fix." He straightened his back.

"Emma. You're doing it just right. We're playing crazy bowl."

Both of them looked at him as if he'd lost his mind. "Yeah, it's a cool way to bowl because each round you have to do something different. My grandmother is a bowler. In Illinois they play this game for fun. This frame you have to get a gutter ball. Emma, for a beginner you're really good."

He grabbed his ball, walked to the alley, and slung it down the lane. All ten pins fell over. He pasted a frown on his face before turning around.

"See, Emma? It's not easy to get a gutter ball. Randi, you're up."

As she walked by, he stopped her and whispered, "I'll be right back. I'm going to the front desk. I'm hoping they will override the automatic scoring for me and maybe have a sheet of crazy bowl ideas."

He returned waving a piece of lined yellow paper. "They have a rock 'n' roll night that sounds like fun. They have music, strobe lights, and the pins light up, but they haven't heard of crazy bowl. I explained it to the manager, though, and he helped me come up with some ideas. This is going to be so much fun. Emma, you're up, and this time you have to sit on the floor with the ball between your legs and push it with your hands. Try for the middle, because if you knock pins down, it counts."

Emma bounced from the orange plastic seat and headed for the alley with her ball.

"So are you dating anyone?"

Smooth, Carter. You might have led up to that.

She shrugged her shoulder. "Not unless you count that speed-dating thing Jess made me do. That miserable night an entire conveyer belt of men passed by, and I let them keep going."

"Are you going to watch me?" Emma stood at the ball return, tapping her foot.

"We're watching!" Matthew was thankful for her interruption. He'd asked a question and gotten an answer he didn't know what to do with.

Emma held the ball to her chest as she walked to the beginning of the lane. She sat on the floor and placed the ball between her outstretched legs, then gave it a mighty shove. The ball sailed into the pins, knocking down five. Emma jumped up, clapped her hands over her head, and spun in a circle celebrating her success. "I did it! This is fun! What's next?"

"Standing on your left leg." Randi read from the paper. "And the next one—" She laid the paper on the table next to the uneaten nachos.

"Is what, Aunt Randi?"

"I think it's time to go home. Grandma is probably waiting for us to come home and watch that movie she rented." Randi sat on the chair and started to untie her bowling shoe.

Matthew picked up the paper, wondering what caused her sudden change of interest. *"Place your hands over the next player's eyes and guide him with words."* So she didn't want him touching her? Or was it whispering into her ear she objected to?

"Afraid of me?"

"No—no. I thought maybe we'd been gone too long, taking up too much of your time."

"I'm fine. I've already paid for the game. We might as well finish." He grinned, watching emotions race across her face. "For Emma."

"Please, Aunt Randi. This is fun."

Randi retied her shoe. "Fine. Let's just get this done." She slammed her foot down on the concrete floor. "And I'll repay you later."

Matthew watched her stomp off, enjoying her feisty attitude.

Chapter 10

As the sun fell lower in the western sky, Randi consulted the truck stop guide that lay on the seat next to her. She'd driven seven hours today and needed a place to sleep soon. The last rest stop she passed was already filled, in every legal and creative parking space. No sane driver wanted to go through Cheyenne during rush hour, but it didn't look as though she'd have a choice.

She slapped the book shut. If she'd been able to get out of the last place on time—but that meant they would have had to let her unload at her scheduled time. That never happened. She'd drive hard and fast to make it on time, and they'd make her wait every time. It didn't matter who she delivered to, either. Produce, meat, or rock, they all made her wait. And that cost her in mileage, which translated into a smaller paycheck.

If she hadn't overslept. . .

Dana called her on the cell phone. As soon as she realized she'd woken Randi, she started yelling. Randi couldn't blame her, since it wasn't the first time since she'd returned to work; more like the third in a week. Driving alone was harder than she had imagined. True, she and Jess sometimes ran late, but not like this. She knew she couldn't afford to run late again, at least not for a while. Her job could be in jeopardy.

The white lines dashed by, and her mind drifted to the evening with Matthew two weeks ago. Randi wanted to think of anything besides Matthew, his hands covering her eyes, his quiet voice. Just thinking about his breath on her ear sent her heart into a panic. She couldn't allow him to get to her; she couldn't allow him into her life. She'd made her choice. "Stand alone—let no man join me" was her mantra. But she couldn't help but wonder a little what it would be like to be his wife.

She grabbed a cup from the cup holder and dumped crushed ice into her mouth. The cold helped perk her sagging energy. Had Matthew found a company to drive for yet? She couldn't seem to keep him out of her thoughts. Frustrated, she chomped on the ice and blamed Jess. If she would come back to work, there would be someone to distract her. They could talk about Jess's marriage plans.

She still hadn't told Randi about getting engaged, and Mike hadn't placed a ring on Jess's finger. Unless she didn't wear it when Randi came over? No. Jess wouldn't hide a diamond; more like her to flaunt it. Randi hadn't stayed long enough for a long conversation, but now that she thought about it, Jess didn't even mention Mike. That couldn't be good. Jess had better not mess up this relationship. If Randi had reservations before, they'd disappeared after Jess was shot. That man was by Jess's side until he took her home. Now that was the kind of husband Randi wanted, or would want if she were looking for one.

But she wasn't.

Matthew seemed to be good with children, too. At least Emma thought so. He would be a good father figure for Emma. She wouldn't stop talking about him on the way home that night. Maybe he would call them again.

Stop! This has to end. Driving alone gave a person too much time to think about future possibilities. And she didn't want to include him.

She drummed on the steering wheel with her thumb. *What else could I think about?* Not her mom. This morning when Randi called, she'd received an earful of complaints. Her mom couldn't go to the Ladies' Society because Emma needed to go to the library after school. To hear Mom, you would think she'd missed the doorway to heaven by not attending the meeting with that gaggle of gossiping women.

Still, Randi felt guilty. Her earlier promise to relieve her mom didn't seem like much if she couldn't do it. But wasn't that enough proof that she couldn't have Emma living with her? Where would Emma go for the two to three weeks Randi sometimes had to be on the road? Randi hadn't seen her own bed for days. That wouldn't be a life for a kid. Emma deserved someone involved in her life every day. The red light on the Qualcomm lit. She groaned. Jess called it the wannabe computer. The light meant dispatch had a message for her. Probably a change she didn't want to know about. It would have to wait until she found a safe place to pull over. The brake lights on the car in front of her came on, causing her to downshift. Instead of slowing, the motor raced. Randi's heart thudded. She pumped the clutch again and tried to shift lower. The engine continued racing. *The clutch.* No doubt about it, the thing was slipping and getting hotter the longer she stayed on the road. Her choice of driving farther expired as she pulled the rig to the side of the road. Dana would not be happy to hear from her.

❧

After jiggling the diesel fuel nozzle back into its slot, Matthew screwed the cap onto the tank then climbed into the cab and moved his truck forward, freeing the space for the driver waiting behind him to fuel. Leaving the door open, he swung the pickup into a parking spot at the back of the building, avoiding the front entrance where the tourists entered. He reached down to the floorboard on the passenger side and scooped up a small duffel bag holding a change of clothes. His arms felt crystallized with dried sweat. He imagined his stench had to be as bad as the farm's. He hated to spend the last few dollars he had on a shower, but if he didn't, he wouldn't get one for at least another day. It was only July, but he kept bugging God to send him a job with an air-conditioned truck. He knew it was just a matter of time—God's time, not his—but he wished he could speed up God.

He headed inside to pay, glancing down at the pavement in time to avoid stepping on a moist mound of chewing tobacco. Inside, the cool air washed over him, refreshing him like a summer romp in the hose.

At the counter he pulled his wallet from his back pocket. "How long until a shower's available?" Once again he bemoaned the fact that he was driving his own truck and not a big rig. He would have to pay for a shower because he didn't have enough fueling credits for a free one.

The clerk popped her gum. "Um, 'bout fifteen minutes."

"I'd like to buy time in one, then." He handed over his credit card to pay, wondering what the IRS thought about deductions for showers.

She ran his card through the machine and waited for him to sign. Transaction completed, she reached under the counter and handed him a small bar of wrapped soap, a towel, and a wash rag. "Number 153."

"Thanks." He wandered to the drivers' lounge to wait for his number to be called and stopped inside the doorway. It seemed to be empty except for one bearded driver smoking in the back. Then he noticed her. Randi was curled up against the wall in a booth, her blond hair glimmering like gold against the backdrop of the dark blue wall. Her arms were tightly wrapped against her chest. Both eyes were closed, and she seemed to be sleeping.

"What are you looking at, Preacher Boy? Haven't you seen a stranded trucker before?" Her eyelids barely lifted.

He slid into the booth across from her. "How's the padded-vinyl mattress?" He gestured at the back of the booth.

"Real funny. I'm stuck here. The clutch burned out and they've got it in the shop; no clutch, no air conditioning."

"How long you been here?"

"Couple of hours."

"Rough when you can't stay in your truck. Have you eaten?"

She pointed at the empty glass in front of her. "A diet cola and a chocolate bar."

He didn't think that qualified as dinner but refrained from saying it. "Where you headed?"

"Sioux Falls. I was supposed to be going to Jackson, but they Qualcommed me with the change. I've been stalling my call home. This is going to fry my mom. Emma's going to be disappointed, too, since this will put me out further from coming home."

The dark circles under her eyes alarmed him. She must be driving more hours than she was allowed. "Been gone long?"

"Couple of days. I thought I'd be home tomorrow night." She slid her legs along the length of the booth. "Are you still dragging boats behind you?"

He nodded. "Still waiting. How's Jess?"

"She's better. She's only taking the pain pills at night." She tilted her head back against the wall and closed her eyes.

Matthew wanted to tell her to go home, crawl into bed, take a bath—anything that would be good for her. He couldn't. He didn't have that right. Besides, she couldn't do any of those things tonight. Or could she?

He twisted the shower ticket in his hand. He hated to give it up, but it felt like the right thing to do. "Randi?"

"Mmm?" She didn't open her eyes.

"I just realized I can't wait for the shower to be free." He pushed the ticket across the table.

She picked it up. "You have to use it or you lose it."

"That's just it. I have to give it up. Why don't you take it?" He hoped she would. If she was getting back in a rig tonight, she needed something to waken her. He plopped the towel and soap on the table. "So?"

Tears welled in her eyes. He hadn't meant to make her cry. He wanted to make her smile. And then she did, and he felt the room brighten.

"Matthew. That is the nicest thing anyone has done for me in a long time." She reached across the table and touched his hand. "Are you sure you don't have time to use it yourself?"

He gave her hand a gentle squeeze. "I want you to have it. I've got to head back tonight." Then he let go. He felt as if he'd lost a piece of himself. Not only did he have to give up holding her hand, but he'd have to leave now, or she'd know he'd given it to her out of kindness. And he had a hunch she'd throw it back in his face if she knew. She was that type, a woman who didn't accept help from anyone. Why was it so difficult to get close to this woman?

Perplexed, Randi watched Matthew's retreating back. He'd given her his shower. Why? Did he think she needed one? Or that she couldn't get one herself? Still, since she was stuck here and had it in her hand, why not? The idea of warm water and fresh clothes sounded heavenly to her.

She reached to the floor and hauled her backpack to her lap. She checked the small bag of toiletries she carried; she had enough shampoo and shower gel. She never used the soap they handed out at the counter. If she didn't know better, she would think it was lye soap, just packaged pretty, to kill off whatever crawled around in those bathrooms.

"Shower 153 now ready. One-fifty-three now ready."

Sliding across the booth, she realized she hadn't thanked Matthew for the shower, and then realized there were a lot of things she should have thanked him for already.

Chapter 11

Randi stared across the metal desk at her boss, Dana Foster. "How can you assign a man to drive with me? The only reason I work here is because they don't make me drive with a male."

"You don't need to shout. This isn't personal, Randi. It's what needs to be done and what my boss wants done. I don't have the power to override his decision. What do you need to make this work?" She straightened the papers in front of her into a neat pile and then fanned them out.

"It won't work. I *need* to not have a man assigned to drive with me. I can drive alone until Jess gets back." Randi struggled to keep the anger out of her voice.

"Not an option, Davis. You gave that a try, and you can't do it. You oversleep and deliver late. You're lucky I suggested you for this job instead of letting you go."

"I won't make enough money if I can't drive long hauls." She twisted her hands together as she pleaded with Dana.

"You won't make as much, but the company is willing to compensate for some loss in pay."

At the word "compensate," Randi narrowed her eyes. "Why so generous?"

"They considered you would be supervising the new driver."

"A trainee? You're assigning me a novice?"

"He's a driver, but he hasn't had a lot of time in a rig. He's also a minister. He came to the company with a unique idea of combining an over-the-road ministry with the company. The owner became a Christian recently, and since then he's been checking out the Truckers for Christ program. He wants to do something for his drivers, if they want to attend some kind of service."

Randi collapsed into the wooden chair in front of Dana's desk. "Matthew Carter."

"You know him, then?"

"Yeah, he brought me home from the hospital." *And charmed my niece and gave me his shower.* "So the only way to keep my job is accepting a man into my cab?" Randi stood and paced in front of the desk, the heels of her boots clapping against the tiled floor. She stopped at the bookshelf, plucked a yellowed leaf from a philodendron plant, and carried it to the trash can. She released it from her fingers and watched it float onto a brown apple slice.

"He's not just a man. Think of him as a pastor. Or you can opt to work for another company, take unpaid leave until Jess returns, or elect to take another woman as a permanent partner. Your choice. So what's it going to be?"

"Those aren't options I can consider." She watched Dana's upper lip curve downward.

Dana tapped a pencil on the desktop. Randi heard irritation in those taps; they weren't her usual "One, two, three, move" taps. These sounded more like stiletto heels running over cobblestones.

"That's life. I have to know right now what you're going to do. You're scheduled to meet him Monday morning. All right? It won't be that bad, Randi. It's only for a few weeks until Jess comes back. Think how good this will look on your record when Johnson reads it at review time." The wheels on Dana's chair screeched as she pushed away from the desk.

Randi stared at her, willing her to change her mind. Silence bounced back, filling the space in the room. "I guess I'll do it. But I don't like it."

"So noted. But I won't write the last part on your file." Dana's laugh cracked into a hacking dry cough.

"Give up those cigarettes yet?" Randi had been trying to get her to quit since Dana had a mild heart attack a year ago.

"I'm trying. It isn't easy. I've been smoking since I was eleven, and after this discussion I could use one."

"Look, don't blame your addiction on me. There are things out there to help you quit. You"—Randi shot Dana her best evil grin—"have to make a choice. I don't want to drive with Matthew, and you don't seem to appreciate fresh air. Let's make a deal. You have six weeks, the same six I have to ride with Matthew. Six weeks of me not calling you to complain."

"And if I don't quit?"

Randi thought about it for a moment. What could bother Dana enough to make her think twice about lighting a cigarette?

"Jess and I don't drive weekends for a month."

"A four-weekend month, not a five."

"Deal. Six weeks, and your office better not smell like cigarettes." She held out her hand to seal the deal.

Back in her truck, she wished she hadn't promised to keep driving. But she had. Knowing she didn't have a choice made it harder to accept being told who was going to ride in her cab. If she had enough money, she'd become an owner-operator. She needed and wanted her own truck—not a man to share it with.

A man, any man, would not—no, could not—ever be allowed into her life again.

&

Monday morning, Randi arrived an hour early at the Round the Clock shipping yard. After checking in with Dana, she made arrangements for Dana to drop Matthew at the truck stop so she could get breakfast. Randi picked up the truck and headed down the street.

Pushing open the heavy doors of the diner, she inhaled the scent of fresh-brewed coffee.

"Yum, just what I need." She headed for the counter.

"Hey, Randi."

Randi turned and flashed a smile at the girl behind the gift shop cash register. "Hi yourself, Brenda. How's the baby?"

"Hard to leave, she's so precious."

Randi didn't like the tired lines etched across her friend's face. "Are you thinking about staying home instead of working?"

"I'd like to, just to get some rest if nothing else. Soon Angela should be sleeping all night. That will help." Brenda sighed. "Staying home just isn't possible being a single mother. I have to bring home the paycheck. No one else will."

"Marry a rich trucker." Randi smiled, waiting for Brenda to laugh.

Brenda didn't fail her. When the laughter quit, she said, "There aren't any rich truckers, but I'll get married the day after you say 'I do.' From what I've experienced, there are only two kinds of men out there: 'Love 'em and leave 'em,' or 'Once a cheat, always a cheat.'"

"Guess we'll both be on our own and in charge of our own futures."

"Fine with me." Brenda squirted window cleaner on the glass counter and wiped it with a paper towel. "Seems to me we're the only ones who really know what we need to be happy, anyway."

"Could be, Brenda." Randi's stomach growled. "I'll catch you later. My stomach is calling for Terry's early bird special."

Randi walked into the dining area and headed straight for the counter. She patted the puffy yellow vinyl seat on the stool as if in greeting. She thought of it as her stool, her little spot of sunshine. She placed her foot on the chrome footrest, hopped on, and gave herself a spin, stopping with her hands on the gray granite Formica counter.

"Why do you always do that, Randi?" A man in a white apron and cap gave her a gap-toothed smile.

"Terry, I can't help it. If I don't spin first, it's like my day hasn't started off right. And today I have to make sure it takes off in the right direction." Randi looked over her shoulder and frowned.

"What evil thing are you expecting to walk through that door?" Terry leaned his elbows on the counter and peered into her face.

"A new partner. I don't like sharing a cab with someone new. The company won't let me drive alone, and since Jess is on disability, I don't have a choice."

"What's her name?"

"It's not a she. It's a he." Not liking the gleam in Terry's eyes, Randi decided to switch the subject, fast. "Besides, turning on the bar stool is just a fun thing to do. Not like the weird things you do. Like wearing Halloween and Christmas socks and hanging streamers from your antenna to celebrate National Pig Day. So don't pretend I'm strange."

"Humph." Terry shrugged his shoulders. "At least I do exciting things. Besides, Pig Day is a big deal if your brother raises them. Tell me, when was the last time you did anything to make your blood race?"

"Every time I order your special blend hot chocolate, my blood runs hot and fast." Randi crossed her hands across her chest, tilted her head, and batted her eyes at him. "One glance at that mile-high whipped cream and I think I just might die completely satisfied."

"Need a life. You need a life." Terry shook his head. "What do you want this morning?"

"Scrambled eggs, biscuits, and to perk up my life—hot chocolate instead of coffee. Toss some colored sprinkles on the whipped cream." Randi grinned at his surprised frown. "Just needing a bit of excitement this morning, Terry."

"Need a life. You need to marry a nice man, settle down, and have a few kids," Terry mumbled as he headed to the kitchen.

Randi stood on the bar stool rungs and hung over the counter, yelling as Terry disappeared into the kitchen, "I heard that! I have a fine life, thank you very much."

At least it was fine, up till now.

❧

Matthew Carter crossed over the threshold of PJ's Truck Emporium. He stood in the gift shop, thanking God. He'd followed his dream. And now he was here, standing in an aisle surrounded by snakes in fake peanut cans, glass piggy banks, and souvenir spoons crested with cowboys riding broncos. He'd made it, and it felt good.

He dropped his backpack on the black-and-white tile floor and looked for someone who could point out the driver he would be working with.

"Can I help you?"

Matthew turned. A woman in a uniform the color of butterscotch, topped with a white apron, peeked over the top of the cash register. She was almost hidden behind clear plastic containers of combs, novelty pens, and dollar items.

"I need to page R. Davis. Can you do that?"

"Sure. What do you need Davis for?" She gave him a cool stare and smacked her gum.

"He's my new partner. We're riding together for a while."

"Sure thing, honey." Her face broke into a wide smile as she pulled a shiny microphone toward her, flicking it on with her finger then tapping it a few times. "Davis, Randi Davis. Please come to the gift shop. Someone is here to see you."

Did she say Randi? Matthew's heart beat faster. Could it be his Randi?

He swung around in time to see Randi pull a wad of money out of her jeans pocket. Her painted nails flashed as she sorted through the green then flipped some dollar bills onto the counter. Intrigued, he watched her take a sip of some awful-looking frothy concoction. She brushed her long hair behind her ears and walked toward him.

The cashier behind him giggled.

Glancing over his shoulder, Matthew looked back at her. He turned around again and caught the container of ink pens with his hand, knocking it sideways. Pens rolled across the counter and clattered onto the tile floor.

Grumbling in his embarrassment, Matthew bent down to pick them up.

"I hope you can control a rig better than your hands." Randi's soft voice, like spun honey, graced his ears.

Matthew looked up, a long way up, past long, jean-clad legs. A woman's legs. The woman who wouldn't stay out of his mind stood before him. His old inability to talk to women resurfaced as he stood. "It's you," he sputtered.

"Sure is. Are you ready to pull out?"

"I thought I'd be riding with a man. R. Davis."

She smirked. Her full lips glistened, and he caught the scent of peaches. If he kissed her, would she taste like a fresh peach? He mentally shook himself.

"This is R. Davis, woman driver." She pointed at her chest. "If you don't want to ride with me, then don't. You can call the company, and they'll tell you I'm it or nothing."

Matthew could see she was a woman. Pure woman. The blue plaid shirt she wore over a white T-shirt made her eyes sparkle. The gold locket nestled in the hollow of her neck enticed him to run his fingers under it. She brought feelings, good ones, racing through his body. Trouble, definitely trouble. God was going to have to take control of this situation, fast.

"I thought your last name was Bell." At least that was what they'd printed on her plastic armband in the emergency room.

"It is, but I use Davis."

"Why Davis?"

"Maybe I'll tell you sometime, but not now."

"I'll ride along to the next stop. Maybe by then we can get this straightened out." Matthew tossed his backpack over his shoulder and made a mental note to retrieve his Bible before pulling out of the lot. He needed God's guidance on this one. He followed Randi to the truck, trying not to watch her walk. He shook his head in bewilderment. *What could God be thinking?*

Close to the cab, Randi yelled behind her, "Don't even think about asking to drive my truck, Preacher Boy."

Matthew groaned inside. Yes, sir, trouble in more ways than one. He'd have to do some hard time on his knees trying to find a way to be grateful to God for throwing him into the hot seat. He'd almost been able to quit thinking about her every hour of the day, and now this. He looked up to see Randi staring at him. Her stance told him she was ready to battle for her right to drive.

"You have a look that says you could take on a whole football team without protective gear." Matthew smiled. "My sister looks like that when she's mad."

"My brother taught me everything I need to survive in a man's world."

"That explains why you drive a truck, I suppose," Matthew murmured.

"Excuse me?" Randi pulled her sunglasses from the V-neck of her T-shirt and slipped them on. "I didn't catch that."

"Nothing important." Matthew thought better of repeating himself. No need to get in an argument when he wasn't planning to stick around long enough to finish it. He didn't need a woman in his life, especially this one. She had already become a distraction to him. Getting to know her and Emma had been a huge mistake, because the two of them, with their unusual eyes, had him bewitched.

Matthew ran his hand over the fender of the truck. "This is a nice rig."

"It's a good company to work for. They take care of their drivers."

"What are we hauling?"

Randi's eyebrows rose at his question. Maybe she didn't consider him a part of the "we." *She may be beautiful, Carter, but she has a vicious attitude toward you.* Maybe this was how God planned to keep him safe.

"We. . ."

Matthew noticed she stressed that word.

"Are hauling concrete fountains."

Matthew stood back and admired the cobalt blue mid-rise rig for a moment. "Round the Clock Trucking. Interesting name, but it does say it all, doesn't it?"

"Sounds like an adventure, doesn't it? We'll revisit that thought in a few weeks, since we won't be taking any long hauls. Toss your stuff in back, and we'll walk through the pre-trip together."

He frowned. Long hauls were his real dream, not day trips.

Chapter 12

A minivan passed the truck. In the back, two small children frantically motioned. Randi couldn't resist the small arms trying to get her to blow the horn. "Carter, watch this."

The air horn blasted, and the kids collapsed in laughter.

"That looked like fun. Did they try long?" Matthew asked.

"No. I gave in quick." She loved driving a truck, almost being responsible only for herself. She and Jess shared that feeling, the one of being the biggest on the road and savoring the savage power that flowed through the wheel. Would Matthew Carter feel the same way?

Randi glanced at her new partner. She wouldn't know he was a preacher boy if she didn't know him. He didn't dress like any preacher she'd ever met. No white shirt with a dark tie around his neck, dress pants, and shiny loafers. This preacher boy wore nice-fitting jeans and a T-shirt that hinted at muscles made for a woman's hand to caress. For a moment she thought about touching his dark, wavy hair, and then her glance fell on the Bible on his lap.

"Are you going to read that thing all the way to Buffalo?"

Matthew turned a page before answering her. "No, I was just thinking about my first sermon."

Proved me wrong. He's a pastor hiding in civilian clothes, all right. "What's it going to be about?"

"Temptation, I think." Matthew stretched his arms over his head. "Sure you don't want me to take a turn at the wheel?"

Randi glared at him. "No. Why would I?"

"Because you might want to look at the fields of corn and the occasional cow we pass?"

"Not a snowball's chance in—never mind." Randi cringed inside. She didn't talk like the stereotypical trucker; just because it was the job she'd chosen didn't mean she had to play the part. But this man was enough to exasperate anyone. Still, she regretted almost making a slip.

"You were going to say 'hell'? I think that's an appropriate phrase. Snowballs will not survive in hell. In fact, the way I understand it, nothing we love and enjoy will survive in hell."

"Look, I wasn't asking for a sermon." Randi reached over and popped in a CD. Lyle Lovett bellowed, cutting off any conversation.

Matthew reached over and turned down the volume. "Sorry, it hurts my ears. Do you have anything softer? Classical, maybe?"

"None. Everything I have is blues or country, and loud is how I like it."

This didn't make things any easier. If Carter didn't like the same kind of music, this *would* be a long haul. The worst part was, she couldn't even complain to Dana.

"Why do you like the blues?"

"I don't know. I think because it gets down into your soul and speaks to the pain that engulfs your heart." Randi flipped on the left turn signal, shifted, and changed lanes.

He pulled out a package of gum and offered her a piece. "Want one?"

She shook her head no.

"Your brother? Is that where your pain comes from?"

"Some, but I'm no different than anyone else driving a rig. It can get lonely, even with a partner. I like sleeping in my own bed, taking Emma somewhere—"

"Bowling?"

The man was insufferable. Of course he wanted credit for entertaining Emma. She should have seen that coming. He was a pastor, and she needed to remember that.

"Why classical?" She hoped switching the topic of conversation would get his nose out of her business. If they were going to spend every day together, she was going to establish boundaries.

Matthew laughed. It was a man's laugh with a mix of little boy delight. Randi thought she could listen to that laugh forever. She scoffed at herself. Forever? Not likely.

"Why is that funny, Matthew?"

"Because I listen to classical for the same reason. It speaks to my soul, but I like it because I can supply the words. It helps me relax while I'm driving."

"But you've only been driving a big rig for how long?" She checked her speed and set the cruise control.

"I haven't even begun to drive, since you won't let me touch the wheel." Matthew's voice hinted of annoyance.

She fought the feeling of chagrin. "Look, you just finished school. I'm responsible for this load. How do I know you're ready to drive? Besides, the reason you're here isn't to drive, is it? Isn't it to get more converts on the weekends?"

Randi jumped as Matthew slammed his Bible shut.

"That's the idea, and I'm thinking I'm going to start with you."

❧

A week later, at Greenway Grocers, Randi barked orders at Matthew. "Make sure your mirrors are clean. Are they clean?"

"Of course."

"Can you see the back with both of them? Roll your window down so you can look out."

"I can do this, Randi." Matthew put the truck in reverse.

Randi held her breath as Matthew began to back up to the dock. This was the hardest thing for new drivers to accomplish. She'd seen many fail. "Careful," she muttered. "Careful."

The truck stopped. "Look, if you can't stand the pressure, why don't you get out and wait for me?"

"Don't think I wouldn't like to, Preacher Boy. But *my* job is to make sure you don't break anything."

He scowled at her and looked as though he might say something. Instead, he shrugged his shoulders then hung his head out the window.

"Come on, mate. I don't got all day," the lumper they'd hired yelled from the dock.

"I guess he's thinking he can unload more trucks today, Matthew, if you'd just back up."

She didn't really care if it took Matthew a few extra minutes. This produce company wouldn't unload for the drivers, but they wouldn't let them take things off the truck, either. You had to hire a lumper. And they knew it. There were always several hanging around the gate waiting to "help out," as they called it. *Help themselves, that is.* Their wages came from her pocket. And Matthew's. That made her mood lift. At least she wouldn't have to come up with all the money.

Crack.

Her head flung back against the seat like a piece of wet spaghetti. He'd done it. Backed the trailer smack into the dock. She'd let her guard down for two seconds, and he'd gunned it right into the cement. Dana would be furious with both of them.

"Hey! What's wrong with you? You got a license to drive that thing?" the lumper screamed through the window at Matthew. "That's gonna cost you double. I've got kids to think of."

"So think of them and start unloading," Randi hollered back as she leaned across Matthew. "You aren't hurt, so you've got nothing to complain about."

The lumper swore and jumped up on the loading dock. The rumble of the trailer door lifting filled the awkward silence in the cab.

"You don't have to defend me," Matthew said. "I'm capable of handling insults."

His quiet tone surprised her. The truth was, if someone had taken on her battle, she'd be hopping mad.

"Sure, now I know. But can you handle Dana?"

❧

Mrs. Bell handed Randi the letter as soon as she walked in the door. "It's from your brother. I saw him today, and he asked me to give it to you. You need to read it."

"And hi to you, too, Mom." She took the note, noticing it wasn't in an envelope. "Did you read this?"

"No. He only asked me to deliver that to you, not read it. It's between you and him."

She eyed her mom suspiciously. "And he didn't say what was in it?"

Her mother shook her head. "I'm so worn out between worrying about A.J. and watching Emma." She sank onto the upholstered rocker and pulled a lap quilt over her legs. "Does it feel chilly in here? Emma keeps telling me it's too hot."

"It is warm in here." Randi helped herself to a butterscotch candy from a jar on the coffee table before she sat in the chair. She read the note then read it again. "You're sure you don't know what he wants, Mom?"

"What's it say?" Her mother leaned in to listen.

Randi's foot tapped against the hardwood floor as her anger toward her brother built. "He wants me to adopt Emma. You know I can't do that. Did you tell him I would?" The note in her hand shook. "What kind of father gives his kid away?"

"One who's not going to be able to take care of her. He's doing it out of love."

"Fine time for him to think about loving her now. He should have considered that before cooking meth in his garage." She crumpled the letter and shoved it into her jeans pocket. "Too bad her mother didn't stick around."

"Don't call that girl a mother. All she did was birth that kid. Giving up her rights to Emma less than a day after she was born. . ." Her mother sighed.

"And now he wants to do the same. Well, I'm not doing it. I love Emma, but it doesn't feel right to legally say he can't be involved in her life anymore. And why me?" She jostled her leg up and down. "I know what you're thinking, Mom."

"You're the best for her, Randi. I wish you could see that. She loves you and you love her. You'd make a great mother."

"But I didn't make that choice." She hated the rush of adrenaline that made her move when agitated.

"Randi, even when you're married you don't always get to make that choice. Some women don't ever get the opportunity to have children. And here you are, not married, and you have the chance to have a wonderful daughter."

"You aren't playing fair, Mom." She had to leave before her mother entangled her deeper in her brother's web. She vaulted from the chair, ready for flight, as Emma, pink-cheeked from the sun, burst through the front door.

"Aunt Randi! You're back!"

She sucked in her breath as the joy of seeing Emma hit her heart. She looked over at her mother. Yep, just what she'd expected. Her mother's lips were moving. *Praying. Always praying.* "Hey, kid, where've you been?"

"At Samantha's. She's my new friend." Emma's smile brightened. "Are we going to meet Matthew tonight?"

"I have to go to work tomorrow and have to get up early."

"I don't like it when you're gone for days. Grandma says you're a teacher, so how come you drive a truck?" Emma's excitement was snuffed like a burning candle in the wind, and she plopped on the floor.

Because I didn't want to come home to an empty house. She wouldn't admit that, though. Her mother would say there wasn't any reason to work to avoid loneliness, not when Emma could be with her *forever*. So she said the next thing she thought of to distract Emma. "Matthew wants to take us to his farm."

Emma bounced off the floor, smacking into Randi and hugging her tight around her waist. "Cows! I get to play with cows!"

Guilt claimed another room in the chambers of her heart. She'd never counted on someone needing her. And now if she didn't want to disappoint Emma, she would have to ask Matthew if they could come.

"When? When can we go?" Emma's voice reached a note high enough to break a fine piece of crystal, if Randi's mother had owned any.

"Soon. I'll tell him you want to go when I see him."

"Can't we call him, Aunt Randi?" Emma pleaded, still dancing around the room. "Can Grandma go, too?"

"Don't worry about me. I'd rather stay here than traipse around a smelly farm." Randi's mother put the rocker in motion. "It will be good for the two of you to spend time together, though."

Randi scowled. She didn't know if her mother meant Randi and Emma, or Randi and Matthew.

Chapter 13

Th](his has to be the best food we've eaten yet." Matthew finished his last bite of garlic mashed potatoes. He wiped his mouth with his napkin and laid it on the table.

"They are good. There's a rumor the cook trained at a cooking school in France, Chez Louie or something. He had a job at a restaurant in New York but didn't like living there, so he came back home to Wyoming. But no one has ever found out if it's true or not." Randi looked at her plate, which was still half full.

"I suppose it doesn't matter where he trained as long as it's good. Guess you're ready to go?" Matthew slid out of the booth before withdrawing his wallet. He flipped it open and put a generous tip in the middle of the table. She'd come to recognize that as a signal he'd spotted a wandering sheep, as he called them.

"I think so. Yes, I'll pay yours," Randi said in answer to his unasked question.

"Thanks." Matthew handed over a ten-dollar bill. "That should be enough. I see someone I want to talk to for just a minute."

"I'll pay, but then I'm leaving." Randi snapped up the ticket from the table and crunched it in her hand. Matthew had been riding with her for only three weeks, and it seemed every time they stopped, he had someone he needed to see. It always took him longer to get to the truck than it did Randi. This time she wouldn't wait for him. It wasn't his turn to drive, anyway. If he wasn't sitting in the seat when she wanted to pull out, well, then he'd better be finding a way to meet her down the road.

She started for the checkout counter. Anticipating the heat outside, as she walked she removed the denim shirt she wore into the cold, air-conditioned restaurants.

"Randi!"

She turned at the familiar voice. "Elsie and Margaret! It's been about two months since I've seen you." Randi admired these women drivers. They each had teamed with their husbands until two years ago, when Margaret's husband died from a heart attack. After a drunk driver killed Elsie's husband not long afterward, the women had decided to team up. They chose a vivid pink for their truck and used sparkly gold paint to letter *Groovy Grannies* across the front hood. They hauled when they felt like it and stopped to visit their kids and grandkids often.

"I promised my granddaughter Kristen I would always be there the first

171

day of school," Elsie said.

"But it's not even September yet," Randi said.

"She's on that odd schedule where they rotate the kids through the system, so her first day comes early." Elsie placed her napkin on her lap. "She's such a good kid, and I've managed to keep my promise for six years."

"I bet when she hits high school she won't care if you're there the first day anymore." Margaret laughed. "They get family-independent then."

"Not my Kristen. She knows what's important. Can you sit down and visit for a moment?"

"Maybe you can help us decide on one of these fancy motor homes. Our kids want us to give up driving a rig." Elsie held up a shiny brochure.

"I'm not getting involved in that decision. You're old enough to know what's best for yourselves." Randi glanced at the picture of the RV. "It's not pink, though; that doesn't seem like one you'd like."

"Exactly what we've been saying." Elsie dropped the brochure on the tabletop.

"Ladies, it's been nice seeing you, and I'd like to slide in and talk to you, but I've got to get moving as soon as I can get my partner away from his congregation."

"We heard a rumor about you riding with a preacher." Elsie leaned forward, waiting as if she didn't want to miss anything Randi had to say.

"It's true. Jess is still on disability, and I've been assigned to have Preacher Boy tag along with me."

"You have to sit for a minute and tell us how Jess is doing. That poor girl. And I can't believe they haven't caught the person who did it yet."

Randi sank into a chair between the women. "She's struggling to get the use of her arm back. The physical therapist is making her use heavy weights, and it hurts. She told me they would make good weapons. Sounded like she might even use them like that, or threaten to." Randi smiled. "Jess is a fighter. She'll be okay."

"What about you? You aren't afraid to drive?" Elsie patted Randi's arm. "Such a frightening experience."

"No, I'm fine." Randi thought about the nightmares that woke her several times a week. Afraid her friends' maturity gave them the ability to detect a lie, she went for distraction. "Want to see a new picture of Emma?"

"Just one?" Margaret smiled. "I thought you would have more than that with you."

"If I had known I would see you today, I would have brought more." Randi flipped open her wallet and slid a photo from its plastic cover. Emma had sat behind the wheel of the rig, pretending to be a driver, when Randi snapped the shot. She placed it in Margaret's waiting hand.

"She has your smile." Margaret passed the photo to Elsie.

"Except Randi has front teeth."

"You know what I mean, Els."

"I remember my Lynn at that age. Seems like she was all teeth and ears. It doesn't seem that long ago." Elsie patted her heart. "My memories just don't let those kids grow older."

A lump formed in Randi's throat. What if her mom was right? Could it be that Emma might be the only child in her life to love? She would be if Randi didn't start letting someone like Matthew into her life. *Matthew!* Why did it have to be his name that came to mind? She had no desire to be a pastor's wife.

"I need to get back on the road, ladies." Randi waved a hand at Matthew, catching his attention, then pointed to her watch.

Matthew nodded and kept on talking to the small group of drivers gathered around him.

"Mmm, mmm, he's a good-looker, Randi. Are you thinking he might be a partner for life?" Margaret grinned at Randi. "I've always loved trucker weddings."

"Me, too," Elsie added. "Make sure you let us know when the wedding is, and we'll get there."

"No wedding! You two matchmakers will have to find another party to attend. Jess will be back soon, and Matthew will be on his way." Randi glared at Matthew. "Besides, he's way too preachy for me."

"You've got that love look in your eyes, girl," Elsie said, handing Emma's picture back.

Randi took the photo and stuck it in her back pocket. "Think again. I'll catch up with you later." As she walked to the checkout, Randi could hear the rowdy laughter of the Groovy Grannies. She felt herself flush as she imagined what they were saying about her and Matthew.

She paid the bill then decided she couldn't pass up the black licorice in the candy stand. After digging out change for her purchase and plopping it onto the counter, she gave Matthew one more pointed look and went to the truck.

She checked her watch. Five minutes. That's all she would give Preacher Boy to finish his praying. She did the mandatory pre-check, noting that the fuel level in the reefer tank maintained an acceptable level. She climbed into the sleeper cab and out of habit began to straighten things, even though she hadn't slept in back since Dana had forced her to ride long hauls with Matthew. Matthew had left his guitar on the bunk. She picked it up and started to put it in its case, then decided to practice the few chords he'd taught her. If he wasn't back by the time she finished, then she'd leave.

Her fingers burned from the strings. She'd done it, played through the chords without forgetting where her fingers were supposed to be. Satisfied with her performance, she placed the guitar on the red silk lining and closed the scratched black cover.

Still no Matthew. She opened her licorice and chewed a piece. Like a child, she stuck out her tongue to see if it had turned black. Her eyes crossed. She climbed into the driver's seat and looked into the side mirror. Not only had her tongue turned dark, but her teeth as well. Satisfied it was the real stuff, she finished it.

She checked her mirrors, hoping to see Matthew's reflection. Not there. Fine. She started the engine, put it in gear, and rolled past the front of the truck stop, slowing to a stop. No Matthew.

"That's it. A person can't be expected to wait forever." Infuriated, she let the clutch out, and the truck tires engaged. Not looking back, Randi threw the gearshift forward and rolled off the lot.

Matthew knew Randi would be furious with him for making her wait— again. He had tried to explain to her how he couldn't walk off and leave someone who'd asked him for prayer. Right now he was talking to Tim, who needed counseling because he thought his wife might be having an affair. He needed someone to talk to, so Matthew had found Brad, another Christian driver who had been through this situation himself. He volunteered to help Tim.

Outside at last, Matthew walked to where he had parked. He ran his fingers through his hair and looked around. Where did the truck go? He parked it right here, next to the rig hauling boats, didn't he? He turned in a circle, his hand over his eyebrows to shield his eyes from the sun. His sunglasses were in the truck, and the truck was. . .where? A panicked feeling hit him. She wouldn't have really left him, would she? Randi had probably pulled the truck to the other side of the truck stop to scare him. He'd be in for a lecture, no doubt.

He jogged around the outside of the brick truck stop, expecting to see Randi leaning up against the door, tapping her finger on her watch the minute he appeared.

No truck.

She had left him.

Left him without a ride.

"Hey, good-looking. Need a lift somewhere?"

Turning at the sound of the voice, Matthew found two older women smiling at him.

"I'm Elsie, and this"—she used her key chain to point at the other woman— "is Margaret."

"We're the Groovy Grannies," Margaret chimed in. "Seems like Randi done ran off and left you. We'll give you a lift if you want. We're heading in the same direction."

Offering a quick thank-you to God for getting him a ride, Matthew said, "Terrific. Which rig is yours?"

Margaret and Elsie both pointed to the pinkest truck Matthew had ever seen.

"That's, uh, a pretty bright truck."

"That's the best truck on the road. Come on, or we won't catch up to Randi anytime soon." Margaret slipped her arm through Matthew's. "I have a grandson about your age."

"You can tell him all about the grandkids when we're driving, Margaret. He'll be asking about the gallery, anyway."

Gallery? Matthew wasn't quite sure what to make of these two, but he guessed he wouldn't be bored.

Inside the truck, when Matthew climbed through the middle to sit in the sleep cab, he realized what the women meant by the gallery. He couldn't miss it. Every conceivable flat space had a picture attached to it. All of children, and not all studio shots. Most were candid, caught when the subject least expected to be photographed.

"How many grandchildren do you two have?"

"Between the two of us, fourteen," Elsie said.

"Fifteen any day now, remember?" Margaret said with pride.

"I could never forget, dear Marge. You tell me at least three times a day."

"She's aggravated with me; that's why she called me Marge. She knows I don't like that name."

"What did your momma name you? I'm sure it wasn't Preacher Boy," Elsie asked as she pulled onto the highway.

"Matthew Carter. Preacher Boy is my handle."

"And why is that?" Margaret asked. She retrieved a basket of red yarn from the floor, set it on her lap, and began knitting something with tiny needles.

"Well, that's obvious, Margaret. The boy is a pastor."

"And why is that obvious? He doesn't have a sign on his shirt, Elsie."

"Weren't you listening when Randi said he was holding church services?"

"It's about time somebody did something like that. Especially now that we have so many women drivers. Maybe it will cut down on the likes of those like Liz Martin. I wonder what happened to her." Margaret's needles clicked in time to her words.

Matthew sat back and watched the women, thinking he wished he and Randi could talk with the ease of these two.

"Liz. Oh, that girl. Keeping two jobs at once, driving a rig, and sleeping anywhere but her own sleeper," Elsie said.

"I bet she saw the ceiling of every cab from here to California." Margaret shook her head. "Such a pretty girl, too."

"Maybe we shouldn't gossip with Matthew in the back, Margaret."

Matthew was startled to be brought back into the conversation. He'd thought they might have forgotten about him. "Gossip is never a good thing. It seems to come back and hurt more people than you think."

"He's right, of course."

Elsie nodded in agreement with Margaret.

Tired from driving most of the morning, Matthew closed his eyes and leaned against the padded cab wall. In his repose he said a silent prayer for Liz.

A few minutes of silence passed. Matthew was almost asleep when the grandmas began another volley of conversation. He started to open his eyes, but then he heard Randi's name and his. Maybe he would learn something about Randi from their conversation. No, that wasn't right. Eavesdropping would get him in trouble later. Maybe if he asked the right questions, he'd get answers. After all, he wouldn't be gossiping, just trying to find a way to help Randi. At least that's what he told himself.

"Have you known Randi for a long time?" Matthew felt bad about encouraging the two women, but quickly pushed the feeling aside. After all, how could he help Randi if he had so little information about her? After weeks of driving together, he still knew very little about her personal life. She didn't seem to want to share any information about herself. She wouldn't even tell him why she used the name Davis instead of Bell, just gave him a kidlike smirk as if to say, "Wouldn't you like to know?"

"We've known Randi awhile now. Met her like you meet most truckers, at a truck stop."

That wasn't much help. "How long have you ladies been partners?" he asked.

Margaret turned sideways in her seat to face Matthew. "I started riding with my husband. Our last child had flown the coop, and I was bored at home alone all the time. All the other women had husbands to do things with. I hated tagging along to the movies or church functions, so I decided to ride with Mac and learn how to take my turn behind the wheel."

"That's why I started driving, too," said Elsie. "I was plumb fed up with the women in my town. They acted like I would steal their husbands if I was left alone with them too long. Then when I'd mention Arnie was driving to New York with a load of potatoes, I'd get this smirky expression looking back at me. As if I didn't know they were thinking, *Poor woman, her husband's off playing with those nasty women that hang around truck stops.* Then they'd pull the arm of their husband and say something cute like, 'I'm so glad you don't leave me alone the way Arnie leaves Elsie.' No, sir, I don't miss those biddies one bit. I do miss Arnie. He was a great husband. Margaret and I teamed up after they were gone." Her earnest expression reflected back to Matthew in the rearview mirror. "You ought to marry that girl and become a team."

"Marry Randi?" Matthew shook his head and laughed at the unexpected segue. "I always thought married couples should know each other well before they stood in front of a preacher, and I don't know much about Randi."

"What do you want to know? I've always favored putting two people together when they are in such obvious need of one another."

Matthew didn't think he would agree that Randi or he was in any such need. But if it would help him with Randi, who was he to stop the women? He could use the information to lead Randi back to the good and glorious Shepherd. Then again, if it turned out that Randi might have a few feelings toward him, he might not object after all. She did have the ability to steal his breath away with just a look.

"She had a fiancé once. I've never asked her about him, though." Margaret rolled the loose yarn onto the ball, tucked her needles into it, and shoved it onto the floorboard. "I just know it ended ugly."

Matthew wasn't sure how he felt about this news. It might explain why Randi didn't want anything to do with men, but what did it mean for him? Could he win her trust?

"I heard she caught him in bed with their Realtor in the house they were going to buy," Elsie said.

"Why don't you ask her about him?" Margaret said.

Stunned, Matthew couldn't answer her. No wonder Randi carried so much anger at God. *She truly is a tender bird in need of care,* he thought. But could Matthew give her the right kind of care? He didn't know. He would like to think he could with his pastoral training, but there was that attraction he felt for her. He couldn't deny the pull he felt when she smiled at him. Yet he knew better than to date with the intention of saving someone.

"No, I don't imagine that would be a good idea. The woman won't even tell me what her favorite color is. I'm thinking she'd be less likely to tell me about a past fiancé," Matthew said.

"Her favorite color? That's easy. She loves yellow. We were having a conversation one day on the radio about truck colors. Remember, Elsie?"

"That's right. She wanted to know why we picked pink for our truck."

"Bet you're wondering that, too, aren't you, Matthew?" Margaret wore a pleased expression. Matthew knew this was one of those times they'd stressed at the seminary, and he needed to express a great deal of interest.

"It is bright pink," he said with a wry smile. "Unusually bright."

"We picked it because we'd been arguing for days about the color. I wanted navy blue, and Elsie wanted green."

"We were driving east when the sun was coming up," Elsie added.

"And the sky turned the most spectacular shade of pink."

"We both said at the same time, 'That's beautiful.' Then we thought, *Why not? We're girls, so it would be appropriate,*" Elsie said.

"And since it would be our first truck together," said Magaret, "kind of like having a baby, you send out announcements. It's just that we drive ours instead of sending them through the mail."

"I get it. Why does Randi like yellow?" Matthew tried to direct the subject back to the most secretive woman he'd ever been around.

"She likes yellow because of the sun. Randi hates cold weather and gray days," Margaret said.

"That's right. Yellow is like a warm summer day, when she can take her shoes off and run in the grass. I think that's how she said it." Elsie checked her side mirror before changing lanes.

"I can see her playing in the yard, barefoot, chasing Emma." Matthew smiled. "She would be a good wife and mom." *Wife?* He must be losing a few brain cells. These two lovely matchmakers had him thinking in a direction he hadn't even considered.

"Look at him, Elsie. He's starting to think family thoughts."

"Maybe we'll be having a trucker wedding in the near future. We should start thinking about the shower," Elsie said.

"Wait a minute, ladies. Who said anything about a wedding? Don't you two go spreading rumors."

The radio interrupted the conversation. "This is Choco-Chip. I'm looking for a package I left back at Dean's Truck Stop. Did anyone happen to pick it up?" Randi's voice sounded sad to Matthew, or maybe he was just hoping she missed him.

"We've got the Preacher Boy with us, Chip. Where do you want him delivered?" Margaret answered.

"There's a friendly hamburger joint in Kelly Cove that has a big parking lot. Can we meet up there?"

"Will do."

"Out, then."

"Sounds like she's forgiven you for not being in the truck on time." Elsie smiled in the mirror at Matthew.

"Maybe. Or she doesn't want to tell Dana I'm not with her."

Chapter 14

Randi replaced the mic in its black plastic holder. She was glad Matthew had found a ride with the Groovy Grannies. Relief flooded through her as she realized he might have ridden with Notorious Liz, known for stripping a man with her eyes the instant she met him. Liz wouldn't be good company for a man like Matthew, and not just because he worked for God. She didn't want him in Liz's company. Yet wasn't she just the kind of person Matthew wanted to bring God's Word to?

The seat next to her seemed emptier than ever. She didn't miss *him*, did she? Randi didn't think that could be possible. No, she felt only calmness now that he wasn't in the truck. But she did miss the warm, rich scent of masculinity, the soft strumming of his guitar. His fragrance lingered, and she inhaled the woody scent. She hated to admit it, even to herself, but maybe she was beginning to like having this man around.

She tugged a snapshot of Emma from the visor in front of her. She missed her quirky sense of humor. Maybe she should keep her and let Mom live the life she wanted. Sighing, she put the picture back. Emma's crooked smile touched her heart. Maybe she didn't want to drive a truck forever. She'd been foolish to let one man destroy more than her dream wedding. She'd let Brent have power over the rest of her life, and he wasn't even around.

The sign for Burgers and Beyond stood high above the exit ramp as it flashed orange and red, bright even in the dusky light. Randi pulled off the interstate and maneuvered her rig into the establishment's side parking lot, built for truckers and RVs. The security lights flickered to life. One after the other reflected off a few battered farm pickup trucks.

Not quite sure how long it would be until the Groovy Grannies dropped him by the roadside, Randi decided to wait inside for Matthew. She retrieved the shirt she had thrown onto the floorboard earlier. No need to freeze while waiting for him. She picked up her log book as well. She wanted to record this rest, even if it would be small.

She'd worked double shifts the last three weeks. As soon as she and Matthew finished each day, she headed home and changed into the cream and navy Speedy Delivery uniform. With a peanut butter and jelly sandwich in hand, she'd race out the door and wouldn't return until almost midnight. It was a crazy schedule, but the money bought Emma new clothes.

Emma had come home from school upset. Girls taunted her, calling her "witch" because of the color of her eyes. Not content to bedevil her with just that, they continued with her secondhand clothes and nicknamed her "orphan witch."

Randi couldn't change Emma's eyes and her damaged feelings, but she could help her dress like the others. She understood only too well what Emma felt like, and she intended to do what she could to build Emma's self-esteem. Even if it meant driving when she shouldn't.

As soon as Jess returned to work, Randi could say good-bye to Speedy Delivery, but until then she didn't have a choice. The compensation pay Round the Clock gave her didn't cover what she'd made before on long hauls, and when Dana had pushed, Randi had reluctantly agreed to do two-day runs with Matthew. She and Jess were often paid a bonus when they delivered on time.

Inside the tiny pale green restroom, Randi set her log book on the flat top of the trash can cover. Then she draped her denim shirt over the top.

She grasped the hot water spigot. It spun without friction in her hand, and not a drop trickled from the tap. She twisted the other handle, and the cold water gushed from the faucet. Not caring, she cupped her hands under the frigid stream and splashed the stinging water on her face. Her skin reacted to the cold, flushing and turning bright red as an army of blood cells rushed to warm her. She splashed her face once more then turned off the water.

Whisking a brown paper towel that felt more like cardboard from its stainless dispenser, Randi patted the water droplets on her face and the few that had rained onto her T-shirt. Wadding up the towel, she was surprised by the sudden desire for a soft terry-cloth towel and a tub full of bubbles to soak in. Finishing the fantasy, she added to the mirror, "And the best part, to crawl into a real bed and pull the comforter up under my chin."

Not feeling any more alert, she pushed the restroom door open and headed for the counter for a large coffee with cream. Feeling a bit guilty about leaving Matthew behind, she decided to buy him one as well.

Carrying the steaming Styrofoam cups through the door became a challenge as a small team of girl soccer players came barreling inside. She smiled at the comments flying past her. It seemed they had won their game. Someday, maybe. . .no, better not to go there; she'd been morose enough today. *What is wrong with me?*

Randi looked across the parking lot as a horn bellowed. Sighing with relief, she watched as the pink truck settled to a stop next to hers.

Elsie rolled down her window. "How's the coffee here?"

"I haven't tried it yet. It's too hot. Would you like me to get you some?"

"No, we're okay for now," Elsie said.

"Is Matthew ready this time?" Randi could feel the lack of emotion in her voice. She would admit it only to herself, but she was glad Matthew was back and could drive. She needed to rest.

"He's here. We would like to keep him. He's good company."

"Elsie, you only want to keep him because he has a set of fresh ears to listen to your grandkid stories." Randi smiled, too tired to laugh. "Did you manage to get through all of them?"

Margaret yelled through the open window. "We didn't get near enough time to talk about those babies, Randi. Please. Can we keep him until the next stop?"

Randi felt her chest tighten. She needed Matthew right now. What if he chose not to ride with her tonight? "Margaret—"

Laughter spilled from the truck. Embarrassed, Randi kicked at a french fry someone had dropped on the ground.

Matthew walked around the front of the truck. "I'm here, Randi. I'd love to ride with those ladies some more, but I don't think I would get a chance to drive. They like it too much. Did you know they fight over who's driving next?"

Randi felt her mood lighten. For some reason she wanted to hug him, relieved she wouldn't have to drive. That was the reason she felt so happy, right? It didn't have anything to do with the smile he gave her. Did it? It had to be knowing he would be able to take her place behind the wheel, and nothing to do with the tremors his voice sent rippling through her.

"I bought you coffee." Randi thrust the cup into Matthew's hand. "We need to be going."

Matthew nodded. He walked to Elsie's open window. "Thanks for the lift, ladies."

"You can catch a ride with us anytime, Matthew," Elsie said. The pink truck crept forward. "We'll see you down the road."

Matthew waved as the pink truck rolled out of the parking lot. "I'm glad I had the chance to ride with them for a while. Randi, I've been thinking. Is it possible for me to ride along with different drivers sometimes? I think it would be a good way to get to know them."

"No. Not with me, anyway. After Jess comes back, you can try setting up that arrangement with the next person you drive with." Fuming to herself, Randi opened the truck door, stepped up, and settled herself behind the steering wheel. He didn't even apologize for making her stop to pick him up, or even for making her track him down. Never mind that exhaustion ruled her body. She'd drive her own truck. He could sit counting the stars for all she cared.

Randi slammed the door. If he planned to come with her, he had better be running around the truck and planting his behind in that seat right now. Ride with someone else? Why should that bother her? The scary thing was, it did. She shook off the feeling, deciding it must be from lack of sleep. She wrapped her seat belt around her. Wasting no time, she turned the ignition key.

Matthew opened the door, and the dome light flooded the cab. "Randi, I need to apologize for not being ready when you were. I'll try to be on time from now on. It's just that when someone is hurting, I find it's awful hard to walk away from them."

Whipping her head around to face Matthew, Randi said through clenched teeth, "Yeah, well, Mr. Preacher Boy, because of you, my back is hurting from the tension of wondering if I had to go back and get you. It didn't let up just because I found you with the grannies."

"Then let me drive, Randi. Please. There isn't any reason for you to be sitting there now. You could climb in the back, pull the covers over you, and sleep until we get to the motel in Casper." Matthew placed his hand on her shoulder.

The gentleness of his touch and the tenderness in his eyes did it. Tears began to well, threatening to spill over. Trying to hide her reaction to his concern, she unbuckled and jumped out of her seat. "Fine, it's yours. Don't wake me until we get there." She hustled to the back of the cab, not waiting for a reply.

Chapter 15

Pleased with finding a shortcut through Sublet County, Matthew thought about how proud Randi would be when she woke and found they were closer to their delivery point than they planned to be. The company would be pleased the trip had been made without charging a motel room. Then again, there was that rule on the contract he'd signed. Just because he thought it better to drive through the night this time, it didn't mean they would agree. He hoped when he explained that Randi had fallen asleep before they arrived in Casper and he was confident he could drive through the night, letting her sleep. . . Still, it was their rule—but maybe this once they'd be okay with it. They would have saved the price of a motel room. As he drove, Matthew watched brilliant pinks and blues fill the morning sky. He loved this time of day. He felt closest to God just as the sun peeked through with a nudge then surged into radiant light. For years he had tried to catch God painting the same sunrise, but so far, Matthew had not seen the same one twice. The colors were often the same, but never the way they were displayed in the sky. God definitely held the highest art award for creativity.

He glanced over his shoulder to see if Randi stirred yet. After she went in the back last night, he hadn't heard anything from her, not even a rustle of the bedclothes. Funny, she hadn't even bothered to pull the separating curtain between them. Soon the morning rays would hit her face unless he could reach the curtain and slide it.

Matthew stretched, catching the fabric with his fingertips. He drew the curtain and cringed as the metal grommets scratched loudly against the rod.

Satisfied that Randi remained undisturbed, he turned his attention back to the road. Or tried to. The soft sleeping face in the back invaded his thoughts as it had all night. She had kept appearing in his thoughts as he drove through the night. The sun had not managed to dispel her image from his brain. He thought about the dark circles under her eyes and tried to remember if they were there when he first met her. He didn't think so. Maybe Randi was the kind of driver who had to take a few days off to recharge. He didn't know, but he was sure he wouldn't ask her. Their relationship was tenuous now. No need to make it worse.

There were a lot of questions he wanted to ask her. But how? The two grannies had not solved any of the mystery surrounding Randi. Instead, they'd only made him more curious about this beautiful partner he drove with. If only Randi would trust him. Matthew knew she didn't, and he wondered if it was because he was a pastor. He rubbed his forehead with the back of his hand and squinted at the road before him. It was a shame, because this woman had somehow managed to creep past the barriers around his heart and begun to star in his dreams.

"Matthew, it's morning?" Her voice, soft as silk, called to him from the back. "Where are we?"

"Still headed east. I found a shortcut last night and you were sleeping so soundly, I thought I might as well keep driving instead of pulling in at a motel. Are you hungry?" He ran his hand over his stubble-covered chin. He needed a shave.

"Hungry. Did you call in and tell Dana we would be driving all night?" The curtain grommets dragged against the metal bar. Matthew caught a glimpse of a slender bare foot and red toenails as Randi plopped into the seat next to him dressed in yesterday's shorts and T-shirt.

"No. Didn't think I needed to." He tried to keep his eyes ahead, but not before noticing how beautiful she looked in the bright morning light. Her tousled hair begged him to run his hands through it. He stole a quick glance. She sat with her knees drawn to her chest, feet on the seat. She definitely looked like someone he wanted to wake up to every morning. He focused hard on the road, imagining running his hand across her face at dawn's light, placing a kiss on her cheek, and whispering in her ear how much he loved her.

Love her? He grasped the steering wheel tighter. Matthew didn't know where that feeling came from, but surely as he knew his middle name was Allen, he knew it was true. He released a heavy breath, sagging back into the well-worn seat with a silent groan. He also knew he couldn't let Randi know. It was a good thing Jess would be coming back soon. Maybe with time away from Randi, he could sort out his feelings. He wanted to make sure it was real love. Not some "I want to bring her to the Lord" love. But he wanted that, too, didn't he?

". . .trouble, you know?"

"What? I'm sorry, I drifted off somewhere, I guess. What did you say?"

"We aren't supposed to spend the night together in the truck, remember?"

"Yeah, I know, but since I was up here and you were back there. . ." He jerked his thumb in the direction of the sleeper compartment. "I figured it'd be okay. And I wasn't the least bit tired. I was wrong. I know it. Guess I thought I'd save the company some money and us some time."

"You don't have to explain it to me. You'll have to justify it to Dana. She's the one who'll decide if you keep driving or not."

"I'm not worried about Dana." Matthew watched Randi stretch her arms over her head, her bare feet to the floorboards. She reminded him of a kitten stretching in warm sunshine. He longed to reach out and caress her soft skin as he took in the silky smoothness of her bare thighs. He started reciting the verse about being unequally yoked; then he followed with the Ten

Commandments in his head, the one surefire way he had of controlling his wayward thoughts.

Only they weren't wayward, were they? Not if Randi wasn't married and he wasn't. Was this God's way of telling him he was meant to share his life with Randi? Was there more to her relationship with God than she had let him know? Sometimes hurt dimmed the light within.

"Why, Randi?" He voiced the question without thinking.

"Why what, Carter?" Randi looked puzzled.

Thinking of another question to ask, he blurted out, "I've been wondering all night why your parents gave you a boy's name. And I really want to know why you use Davis instead of Bell."

"I renamed myself. Sort of. Davis is my mom's maiden name and my middle name. I use it when I drive instead of Bell because it lacks a *feminine ring*, which I wanted to avoid on the road." Randi yawned. "In kindergarten I decided Randi was easier to say and spell. You try writing Miranda when you're five years old. Takes way too long. A.J. wouldn't even take the time to say it. He called me Mira, only I thought he was saying "mirror." The kids at school added Bell to that and I became Miracle Mirabelle."

"So as a child you exhibited independence?" Matthew sat straighter, satisfied as a tick on a dog that he'd discovered something more about her. He chuckled at the look on Randi's face. "Hey, I do know a few four-syllable words."

"I'm sure you do. I just hadn't heard you use them. Maybe you save them for your sermons?"

"Why not come Saturday night and hear for yourself?" Matthew hoped he hadn't pushed too hard. "You could keep a tally of how many I use."

"Not going to happen, Matthew." Randi retrieved a bottle of lotion from the door cubby. With a small squeeze, she poured the vanilla scent into her hand then applied it to her legs.

"But I could use you."

She stopped in midrub, her hand motionless on her leg. "Use me? For what? An example of what a Christian isn't?"

"No. I need a guitar player." Matthew flashed his most charming smile, his gaze avoiding the sleek lines of her long, graceful legs.

"I don't know the music."

"You've heard me play a few of the songs. Besides, they're easy, just a few chord changes, the ones you know."

"I don't think so." She resumed smoothing the lotion in long strokes.

"Please. It's much better when I don't have to sing alone. You could bring Emma." Matthew kept his sight trained on the road before him, not daring to look sideways.

"No doubt. You don't sing, Matthew. You howl."

"Miranda, please."

"Ouch, first-name use. You must be desperate." She snapped the lid on the lotion.

"You can learn the music while we drive."

"How many songs?"

"Maybe six?"

"So you sing instead of preaching a sermon?"

"Sometimes I just give out the message in small pieces."

"You mean, like, sneak it in there?"

"I suppose some might think of it as sneaking." He eyed her with a faint smile. "I think of it as important things needing to stand on their own merit."

Matthew waited for her response, hoping she was seriously considering learning the songs. She seemed to be deep in thought. Should he say anything? Could he say anything to encourage her to participate in a service she said she didn't believe in? If she did agree to play the guitar, could he hold out the hope that Randi wasn't as averse to God as she let on? And if that were true, could there be a chance for a relationship together? He tried to control his excited heartbeat. He said a silent prayer. *Please, God, if Randi is the wife You want for me, give me a sign, and I'll charge on full throttle. If not, please stop making her smell so good.*

Chapter 16

Randi ran her tongue over her teeth. They felt fuzzy. She hated this part of OTR driving—morning breath—waiting until a rest stop to brush your teeth and comb your hair. Pulling her fingers through her hair, she tried to at least get it to lie in the right direction. She should have braided it before going to sleep, but she'd been too tired. She would pay for that when she endured the pain of dragging a comb through the long, tangled mess.

Glancing at Matthew, she wondered what he was thinking about. He seemed stressed. Probably because she hadn't agreed to play the guitar for him. She should. It couldn't be that hard to learn the music. It seemed to her that he played the same three chords. But would he expect her to do it more than one time? That she couldn't do. But it might be interesting to hear him give a sermon. Not that she bought into that stuff anymore, not since she'd learned the only person she could count on was Randi Davis. But maybe she could think of it as live participatory theater.

She stole a wary glance at Matthew and exhaled loudly. "I'll do it, Matthew. Just this once. This time and, I repeat, this time only." Had she really said that? She needed a strong cup of coffee before she found herself agreeing to anything else.

"Okay!" Matthew beamed.

She couldn't believe it, but Preacher Boy glowed. Unreal. If agreeing to play guitar for him gave him that look, what would happen if she reached over and planted a kiss on that gorgeous face? Randi mentally slammed herself back into the seat. She had lost her mind. Gone for sure was any common sense. Jess had to come back, and fast. If she didn't, Randi would be a pulpy mess.

"Looks like flashing lights ahead."

"Portable scales ahead: Trucks use right lane." Randi read the sign along the shoulder and groaned. "I hate ugly surprises so early in the morning. Matthew, we have to get weighed and inspected before we can get our first cup of coffee."

"Looks that way. A good stretch won't hurt me any. Can you hand me my log book, please? They're going to ask for it." Matthew pointed to the floorboard at her feet. "I tossed it down there. Might as well hand me yours, too."

Randi reached into the side pocket in the door. Her breath rate increased and her hand shook as she pulled it back, empty. "Matthew." She hated how her voice sounded small, smaller than the mewling of a newborn kitten.

"I don't have mine."

"Why not?"

"I remember setting it on the trash can at the hamburger place with my shirt. I'm sure I left it there."

He glanced over at her, his eyebrows furrowed. "You have the duplicates, right? So there won't be a problem."

She squeezed her eyes tight, afraid to tell him.

"Randi?" His voice held a hint of panic.

"I don't have them. I don't like loose papers, so I don't tear them out of the book."

Matthew's fingers tightened on the wheel; his knuckles were white. "Maybe they won't ask to see it this time."

"They'll ask, and I'll be out of service for at least twelve hours." Randi examined the chipping paint on her fingernail and wished she weren't here. Jess would laugh this off, but Matthew didn't look like he found anything humorous about the situation.

"And I can't drive much longer because I've been behind the wheel for almost ten hours. That means I won't make my Saturday night service." The gruffness in his voice filled the cab.

"Matthew, I'm sorry. I've never done this before." Randi looked at him. His jaw sharpened, and his cheek was thumping. She couldn't blame him for being angry with her. If he had left his log book, she would be screaming in his face right now, not sitting there quietly biting back words.

"It's okay if you yell at me, Matthew." She leaned back against the seat and waited for an inferno of anger.

"No, Randi. Everyone makes mistakes. It will mean calling people, but I'll just have the service during the week." He slouched back into the seat.

Randi wished he would yell, smack the steering wheel with his hand, or something. She hunkered down in her seat. His quiet acceptance—the forgiveness routine—just made her feel worse.

֍

In the side view mirror, Matthew could see a line of trucks stretching far behind them. They had moved to the front, one tire length at a time. A Wyoming Department of Transportation officer stood at the back of the scales. If they were the correct weight, he would signal.

Matthew was relieved when they were waved forward. Just past the scale, another officer held up his hand for them to stop.

He stepped over to Matthew's open window. "I need to see your log books." Ready for him, Matthew gave it to him. "Here's mine."

"She a driver?" He pointed at Randi. "I'll need hers, too."

"Yes, but she left her log book at the restaurant in Kelly Cove. She's been resting for ten hours. I wouldn't lie to you. I'm a pastor."

The officer raised the sunglasses from his nose and peered at Matthew. "Then you should know what rules are all about. You may be a pastor, you might be a guy with a dot-com divinity degree, and it don't matter to me. No book, no driving. Pull your truck over to the side."

Matthew clamped back a reply. No point in making the man angry. Besides, he still had a chance to talk to the guy while he inspected the truck.

"This isn't good. He's going to find something wrong with the truck. They always do." Randi's posture was so straight Matthew thought a strong wind wouldn't budge her.

"Don't be a pessimist. I'll talk to him. Maybe he'll change his mind." He pulled the door handle.

"And maybe pigs do fly."

He ignored her and climbed out of the truck.

The WDOT officer circled the truck with a clipboard in his hand. He took the pen from behind his ear and wrote something down. Matthew leaned over, trying to read the writing.

"Back off, son."

Matthew heard the truck door close. Randi came around the back of the trailer. He waved her away. This guy was irritated about something, and the look on Randi's face didn't indicate someone who cared. She glared at him then turned back.

"Is something wrong, sir?" Matthew put his hand in his jeans pocket and rubbed the tiny cross he kept there to remind him that Jesus didn't die just for him, but even for WDOT officers.

The officer raised an eyebrow. "That's what I'm looking for. Why don't you wait over there?"

"Sure." Matthew glanced back to make sure Randi wasn't lying in wait for the guy, then headed for the office. Unease filled his mind. He had broken the rule of driving together at night, and now he was suffering the consequence of free will. If he had stopped, Randi might have remembered her log book and they wouldn't be out of service now. She would have been driving and more than likely wouldn't have taken the scenic route. Now, instead of making their delivery early, they would be a day late. Even worse, he knew he could lose his job.

Lost in thought, he didn't realize the WDOT officer stood next to him until he tapped him on the shoulder. He handed back Matthew's book.

"You have an hour left to drive, and then you're off the clock. The trailer has a light burned out. That needs to be replaced." He ripped a slip of paper from his clipboard. "I'm giving you a warning for that. See that it gets fixed. There's a town about forty-five miles from here with trucker-friendly lodging and services. See that you stay overnight and enjoy their fine food."

Matthew clenched his free fist hanging at his side, wishing for a moment he could be an ordinary trucker and let this guy know what he thought of him. He couldn't believe they were grounded. Randi had said they would be, but Matthew had thought he would be talking to a reasonable person. He wouldn't make that assumption again.

He could see Randi standing with her forehead pressed against the cab door. Her shoulders shook. She was crying, and his heart twisted at the sight. What could he do to make her feel better? He didn't think it would be wise to gather her in his arms and wipe away the tears, but that was exactly what he longed to do. He needed to run his hands through her silken hair and tell her it wasn't the end of the world.

He walked over and stood beside her for a moment before he put his hand on her shoulder. "Look, it's not so bad. I have an hour left to drive and I've been told there's a town with a trucker-friendly motel about forty-five miles from here. Think of it as one of those mini vacations. Being able to shower when you want without waiting for your number to be called. . . We'll eat at a nice restaurant, maybe even go to the movies. You like movies, don't you? I'll take you to a chick flick."

"Matthew, you're so nice to me." She turned and leaned into him, pressing her face into his chest. "Anyone else, even Jess, would have been screaming at me for being so stupid and forgetful. And I even left you, and you're still being nice to me."

He didn't think it possible, but she seemed to cry harder. He held her tighter. The warmth of Randi's body sinking into his awoke a longing in Matthew. His arms circled her small frame with ease. It felt good to hold her. Better than good. It felt right. Maybe this was in God's plan after all. Maybe Randi was the one God had set aside for him.

He caressed her back and gently placed a kiss on top of her head. "It's easy to be nice to you, Randi." He took her shoulders in his hands and pushed her away from him just enough that he could look into her eyes. With one hand, he wiped the tears streaming down her cheeks. "We have permission to leave now. Are you ready?"

"Yes."

Matthew wasn't sure from the look in Randi's eyes if she was ready to leave or ready for something else. Him maybe? He hoped so. His heart felt light with joy. This was his woman. He could feel it.

☙

Back in the passenger side of the cab, Randi slunk down in her seat. She attempted to sort out what just happened outside the truck. Had she been the one to throw herself into Matthew's arms? Her pulse raced. Maybe not throw, but yes, she did put herself right there. Pressed her face on his chest and wept. But why? And why had it brought such warmth and completeness to her? Good thing Jess would be back soon. She couldn't possibly ride with this man much longer.

Her thoughts about him were running to the dangerous side. Thoughts like these were not the kind one should be thinking about a man who preached God's Word. She had to distance him from her thoughts, banish the feel of his heartbeat from her soul. And forget the way he smelled.

"You're going to need a new log book. And you said you were hungry, so do you still want to stop at the truck stop? Or can I keep driving until we reach the town where we'll be staying?" Matthew's rich voice broke into her thoughts.

"Keep going. We'll pick up a new log at the next truck stop. I can tear a page out of yours to use until I get one. Besides, I'm not hungry anymore." *At least not for food,* she thought. *I wonder what those lips would feel like on mine.*

Shocked at her desire, Randi realized she had it bad for this preacher man. How had she let this happen? It had to be Dana's fault for pairing them together. *Maybe that's the problem. We've been spending too much time together, so naturally I would begin to find him attractive. Wonderful.* Now she was admitting even more to herself. More than she wanted to.

"I'm hungry, but I can wait. It won't take long to get there." Matthew rubbed her shoulder.

"I'd better tell Dana we're stopping for that mini vacation." Randi reached for the mic and tried to pretend she didn't enjoy the warmth left by his hand. "This won't be pleasant."

"I guess they get mad when something like this happens."

"It's not just the dispatcher; it's everyone who's listening when you call it in. Every truck stop we pull into, drivers will be snickering beneath their baseball caps."

"Only because they're glad it didn't happen to them. If you're worried about that, why don't you use your cell phone?"

"It wouldn't make any difference. The word will get out even faster if they think I'm trying to hide it." Randi took a deep breath and called the dispatcher.

Chapter 17

The back-up signal beeped as Matthew backed the truck into the only spot large enough in the rear lot of the Sleep-Inn. Behind him loomed a privacy fence.

"Don't hit it."

"Just because I hit a loading dock once doesn't mean I'll crash that fence." He didn't know if he was trying to reassure himself or Randi.

"We'll just make sure." She opened her door and hopped out.

He could see her in the mirror as she motioned him back. *Two cents and I'd ram into it, just to watch her face.* His face frowned back at him in the mirror. *Sorry, God—she frustrates me. She can lose her log book and I don't get mad, but this taunting about my driving skills is brutal. You have to help me out here.* He eased into the space and let out a sigh of relief.

Randi met him at the door. "Nice job, Preacher Boy."

He felt his eyebrow rise. She'd given him a compliment? That had to be God working. "Thanks."

Inside the small motel Matthew followed Randi to the reservation desk. He rested his elbows on the counter.

"Can I help you?" The red-haired woman behind the desk tossed a copy of *Soap Opera Review* on the counter.

"We need two rooms for the night," Randi said.

"Can't help you, then. Only got one." The woman retrieved her magazine and settled back in her chair. "You won't find anything else in town, either, not with the Bluegrass Festival going on. Everybody's booked. I only have this room because someone canceled about an hour ago."

"We'll take it," Matthew said.

He pulled his wallet out of his back pocket. Flipping it open, he grasped his credit card and slid it onto the counter.

"I need you to fill out this information before I give you the key." She pulled a form out from under the counter and slapped it down in front of him, swiping his credit card in the process.

Matthew scratched the pen across the paper to get the ink flowing.

"There's a queen-sized bed, you know," the clerk said with hesitation while waiting for Matthew's credit to be approved.

"No problem—we're truck drivers." Matthew looked up in time to see the pursed lips of the clerk.

"Well, that makes it okay then, I suppose." She handed him back his card. "We don't have automated checkout here like the big hotels, so you'll have to come back by the front desk before you leave." She took the signed slip from Matthew and passed him the room key.

As soon as the elevator doors closed, Randi broke into laughter.

"What's so funny?"

"You know what she's thinking, don't you? One bed, and it's okay because we're truck drivers?"

Matthew could see where the woman might have misunderstood. His face flushed. "Should I go back and explain that I'll be sleeping in the truck?"

"You're blushing!" Randi hooted. "Don't go. I'm sure by now she thinks I'm a lot lizard. It wouldn't be the first time someone has thought that." Randi sighed and punched 2 for the second floor.

"Who thought you were a prostitute? Why did they think that?" That anyone could think that about Randi made his blood froth with anger.

"I had to take some forced rest time, so I took a book with me to a table at a truck stop to read."

"The universal signal." Matthew shook his head in disbelief.

"I should have known better. A trucker who didn't know me came over and wanted me to check out his sleeping arrangements. I told him I was a driver, not a lot lizard."

"Then he left you alone?"

"No. He kept insisting and even tried pulling me off the chair."

Matthew fell silent. If he'd been there, he would have protected her. A woman should have the right to read a book in public. Her story reinforced his commitment to bring God's love and grace to these people.

The elevator stopped on their floor. A bell dinged as the doors slid open, exposing carpet featuring bright blue, yellow, and orange color bursts. Randi started down the hall in the direction the arrow on the wall pointed.

"So what happened?"

She looked over her shoulder with a smile. "I was about to slug him with my book, but the Groovy Grannies saw what was going on and were all over him like grease on a fire."

"I'm glad they looked after you."

"That was the first time I met them. At first they thought I was a lot lizard, too, but when they saw me struggling with him, they realized I needed help."

Matthew laughed. "So did they hit him or lecture him?"

"Lectured. Turns out they knew him. He had a wife and kids."

"That's a real problem for some drivers, isn't it?"

"For some, but not all. Most of the married drivers wouldn't even consider cheating on their wives. It's a bad-boy image stereotype that's survived from long ago."

Stopping in front of room 215, Matthew slid his card key into the slot and watched for the green light to flash. Quickly he pushed down on the handle and flung open the heavy door. He held it wide and waited for Randi to enter.

He followed her into the tight hallway, past the bathroom door. The queen-sized bed covered with a soft cream-colored spread engulfed the room. The TV sat encased in an armoire. "Be nice to catch a baseball game."

"Typical behavior of the male species." Randi pulled open the heavy dark green curtains. "What a view, if you don't mind looking at concrete and gas station signs."

Matthew turned on the television and began surfing the channels.

Randi yawned and stretched her arms over her head for a moment. "I think I want to take a quick shower to wake up and then get something to eat. That means you're out of here."

Out of here? Matthew's attention came back to Randi in a flash.

"How about you?" she asked.

"I'm for grabbing a snack then sleeping. I'll eat later." Matthew looked longingly at the bed. "Sure would be nicer than sleeping in the truck."

"And you're a man of God?" She grinned.

"It would be nice to have room to roll over. I'm tired and want to sleep in a real bed, not something that's stuck in puberty pretending to be king-sized. Why don't you let me have the room?"

"Not a chance, Preacher Boy. You'll be okay out there, I'm sure." Randi batted her eyes at him. "But since I'm the reason we're here, you can use the shower first if you want."

"Nope, you go. I'll wait in the truck."

"I'll be fast, and while you take your shower I can explore the town."

"Thanks. Why don't you find out what this festival is all about and if it's something we want to do tonight? Or at least locate the movie theater. Unless you don't want to hang around with me."

"Who else is there to hang around with, Carter?" Randi plopped her knapsack on the bed and pulled it open. She pulled out a blue T-shirt and a pair of jeans. "I hope it isn't a dress-up affair. I didn't bring my best clothes along on this trip."

"Not likely. It's a street festival." Matthew processed her last statement. "You have dress-up clothes?"

Randi threw her jeans at him. "Shut up, Carter. I do have a life besides driving a truck."

"What do you do? I haven't heard anything about a man in your life who takes you to the nice places you deserve to go."

"I make myself happy. I don't need a man to go to nice places, thank you very much. Jess and I go to the theater in New York and stay the weekend."

"The theater in New York?" Matthew found this to be another interesting facet of Randi. How many more barriers lay locked under that protective layer she wore? And how long would it take him to get the right key?

"Sure. We've been to a few Broadway shows. My favorite place to stay is the Broadway Inn. It's like a bed-and-breakfast, only not in the country. Once you leave the inn, everywhere you turn there's something fun to do—Times Square, the Manhattan Mall."

"Do you get all dressed up, too?" Matthew scratched his head. This just didn't seem like the Randi he thought he knew.

"Of course we get dressed up for shows. It wouldn't be any fun if we didn't. Slinky dresses and stiletto heels make you feel fabulous."

"Stiletto heels?" Matthew tried to stop the rapidly forming picture of Randi's graceful legs rising from those shoes.

"I'm kidding, Carter. About the heels, anyway. I can't walk in anything that high."

Matthew sighed in relief as the image of her legs popped and replaced itself with the Randi he knew, wearing tennis shoes, faded jeans, and a three-sizes-too-big denim shirt.

"I'm hitting the shower. I'll come by the truck when I'm done and give you the key before I go exploring." She took the remote from his hand.

"Guess that's a polite way of saying I need to leave." He held up his hand to silence the words forming on her lips. "I'm out of here. Enjoy the shower." He hustled out the door, desperately trying to brush away the image of a world where Randi wore high heels and a dress with slit sides. When that didn't work, he added a white apron and a pan of lasagna. He grinned, knowing he would only see that in his dreams.

Chapter 18

Refreshed from her shower, Randi felt ready to take on the town. The motel desk clerk had told her the business district was within walking distance. She intended to explore and see what it had to offer. She opened the truck door, held on to the chrome side rail, and pulled herself inside. "Matthew?"

No reply other than the sound of deep breathing. She peeked into the sleeper cab. Matthew was sprawled on the bed asleep. She hovered over him for a moment, stilling the hand that wanted to stroke his cheek. Something about his sleeping face comforted the ache within her. She couldn't understand why he should be the one to comfort her, but he did. He seemed so full of peace. She wished she could sleep that way, with the serenity Matthew had, but longing for it wouldn't change anything.

She hesitated for a moment longer then reached over and touched his shoulder. "Shower's free."

He grumbled something unintelligible.

She poked him in the side with the motel key card. "I'm leaving the key on the seat."

He mumbled something that sounded vaguely like "thanks" then rolled over with his arm stretched across his face.

Randi gave him one more look and decided not to try to wake him any more. He needed to rest. She slipped out the door and eased it shut.

She headed for the street the clerk had told her would have clothing shops and a place to get something to eat. *Interesting little town,* she thought as she turned the corner. Jess would have loved exploring it with her. At the entrance to the street stood two brick columns to block cars from entering. An iron arbor connected the two with WELCOME spelled out on the top. The street paved with cobblestones beckoned her to walk and shop.

Sweet pastry smells wafted from a bakery. She could see the sign hanging from a striped awning. Its quaint chalkboard sign boasted of freshly made apple cinnamon muffins. Adding one of those to a steaming cup of coffee or tea would be perfect before starting her search for something suitable to wear for the evening.

Muffins and cakes piled high on glass stands inside the bakery made it difficult to stick with her first choice. She hovered in front of a chocolate chip raspberry cheesecake.

"They all look so good," she said to the man behind the counter. Behind her, a bell on the door announced another customer.

196

"Don't ask me what my favorite is. I change my mind every day," said the man.

The smell of rich dark coffee permeated the air as she chose the special of the day. She ordered a muffin and took her breakfast to eat at the only outside table.

"Do you mind if we join you?"

Randi looked up to see a young woman with a baby on her hip standing behind a stroller. "Sure. I'm Randi."

"I'm Pat, and this," she said as she tapped the baby on the leg, "is Evan. Scott, the bakery's owner, should buy another table for out here. He gets enough business in the mornings. Thanks for sharing with us."

"I don't mind. I like meeting new people. You know the owner?"

"In a small town everyone knows everyone else and what they're doing, it seems. You, for instance, would be the talk of the town if the festival wasn't going on. Lucky for you, you're not the only stranger in town."

"Small towns have that reputation, don't they?" Randi said.

"In this case it's true." Pat smiled.

"How old is Evan?" Randi pulled her tray closer to allow Pat room to set her food on the small table.

Pat sat and balanced Evan on her lap. "He's fourteen months and a handful." She brushed her hand across his tawny hair. "But we love him. Are you here for the festival?"

"No, I'm a truck driver, stranded until tomorrow."

"That's rotten luck. What happened?"

"I left my log book at the Burgers and Beyond in Kelly Cove." Noticing the confused look on Pat's face, she added, "You have to write down the time you drive, and if you get caught without the book, they ground you."

"So you drive alone?"

"No, but my partner had driven almost all the hours he's allowed, so here we are in your little town."

"I suppose you noticed the signs posted everywhere for tonight's festival. You should go. It's quite a big deal around here, and it's surprisingly fun. For a small town, we do a good job. Maybe that will brighten your stay. The food is always good, and they have a band every year."

"I thought I would go, but I need to get something to wear. All I have with me are jeans," Randi said.

"Jeans are fine, unless there's someone you want to dress up for?" Pat laughed. "I'm sorry. That isn't any of my business. I'm just curious and often ask questions before I think."

"I'm with my temporary partner, Matthew." Randi paused; how much did she want to tell this woman, anyway? She missed Jess. She needed another woman to talk to about the feelings she had for Matthew. Besides, Jess would know exactly what Randi should wear.

"Nice name. Is he gorgeous?" Pat took a sip of her coffee.

"Bite! Bite!" The toddler opened his mouth wide.

Pat broke off a piece of muffin and fed it to him. "Here, sweetie."

"He is, but I'm not interested. Well, maybe a little." Randi surprised herself with her answer. "Where is a good store for something casual but cute?"

"Domm's is great. I have some free time if you want help—you know, another woman's opinion. There I go again. I'm impulsive, or so my Bob says. Of course you might not want us to go. Evan is cute, but shopping with him can be a trial some days."

The disappointment on her face made it impossible for Randi to say no. "We can try, right? If he gets fussy, you can always take him home."

"Great. I've been so lonely. My best friend moved about a month ago, and I just haven't found anyone to spend girl time with." Pat wiped a trace of milk from Evan's face with a napkin.

"I've lost my best friend, too. Not lost, exactly. Jess was hurt and can't drive with me for a while. I miss her, even though I call her. It isn't the same as being with her and doing things."

"Like shopping?"

"Exactly, and talking about movies and good books."

"You are in serious need of girl time." Pat began to gather her belongings. "I don't need any more to eat, and Evan's had enough. Let's get started."

"I'll put the trays back inside." Randi couldn't seem to move fast enough.

"Thanks. I'll get Evan back in his stroller while you do that."

When Randi returned, Pat stood waiting behind the stroller with a smile on her face. "I think I'll get something for tonight as well. Bob and I haven't been out for a while, and his mother said she would watch Evan for us."

"It's nice she's able to help you." Randi thought of her mother and how she'd reluctantly agreed to take Emma.

"She's a gem, my mother-in-law. My mom lives a few states over, and Bob's mom makes me feel like her daughter. Hey, why don't you meet Bob and me tonight for dinner?"

"Sure. I don't think Matthew will mind, and if he does, he can eat by himself."

"He won't want to if we find just the right dress." Pat grinned. "I think something to show off those long legs, and in red."

"If I do that, I'll have to buy shoes!" Randi moaned, trying to sound sad.

"Shoes! Great! And to think I almost went home to eat instead of asking to share your table."

❧

The shadows of the day fingered their way through the streets. Matthew observed how his and Randi's dusky images touched on the street. He entwined his fingers with Randi's, liking the shadow picture even more. She tried to pull her hand from his. "Leave it, will you? It's just so we don't get separated and spend the evening searching for each other."

"If that's the only reason, then I guess that will be okay." Her fingers snuggled tighter against his.

He kept her close beside him as he wove through the crowd that filled the little town's streets. He found it to be a challenge not to knock a food-laden plate or drink from someone's hand. Laughter and shouts of "Hey, didn't think I'd see you here" rang out, causing Matthew's heart to twang in longing for the town fair he would miss back home.

"Where are we supposed to meet your new friends?" He turned to Randi and leaned in close to hear her answer and inhale the pleasant scent she wore.

"Star Galaxy. It's the old movie theater. It's not too far from here."

Matthew navigated in the direction of Randi's outstretched bare arm.

Vendors called from makeshift carts, enticing all to try their special sauces. Banners in red and white stripes draped from cart edges. Raffle tickets were being sold for a fat tire bike.

Matthew inhaled the luscious smells of brats, burgers, and brisket. Wooden barrels filled with ice and sodas were in easy reach of the sellers. Kegs of beer were stacked high behind some stalls. The silver barrels dripped with perspiration, sending tiny rivers down the street. He frowned for a moment then whispered a quick prayer that no one would be hurt because of the effects of the alcohol being served this evening.

"There they are!" Randi's excited voice sent ripples through Matthew. This woman knew how to have fun, and he was the fortunate guy tonight. *Beyond fortunate,* he thought. Not everyone would have a beautiful woman by his side. Not one dressed in a yellow and white sundress, giving Matthew a hint of Randi's trim shape and plenty of slender legs to view. He would love to be able to run his hands over what appeared to be silky skin. He gave himself a mental shake and forced himself to return to the introductions at hand.

"Matthew, are you listening?" Randi tweaked his chin with her hand.

"Yes, I am. Nice to meet you, Bob and Pat. See? I heard you." Matthew breathed a sigh of relief that he hadn't blundered the names.

Bob winked at Matthew. "I can see why you might be distracted by these beautiful women."

Matthew laughed. "Thanks for the save. Of course these two blinded me with their outstanding beauty, and I lost track of the conversation."

Pat raised her eyebrows. "I don't know, Randi. Matthew may not be as special as you originally thought."

Matthew glanced at Randi. She was blushing.

"I never said he was special. Well, a special pain maybe."

Her defensive tone of voice didn't quell the happiness he felt from knowing she thought he was special.

"Anybody hungry?" Bob asked.

"I am. I saw a few things that looked enticing on our way here. Did you have a place in mind?" Matthew asked.

"Why don't you and Randi find something and meet Bob and me back here with your dinner? We'll probably have to eat standing." Pat put her hand in Bob's. "It will be nice to eat with grown-ups for a change."

"I like that idea. It should be easier to please two instead of four individual tastes." Randi tugged on Matthew's sleeve. "Let's find our dinner."

They walked down one side of the cobblestone street, overwhelmed by the choices.

"See anything you want to eat yet?" Matthew stood close to her, trying to ignore the pleasant smell of roses coming from her shoulders. She smelled like a July evening; like someone he would love to stroll across a field with and sit beside on a blanket to watch the sunset.

"It all looks good. I can't decide." Randi's face was flushed with excitement. "What if I get something and then walk just a bit farther and find exactly what I wanted? Can we explore both sides of the street, then choose?"

Matthew could feel his stomach rumble. He didn't want to wait, but he would. He would do anything this woman asked of him. If only he could turn her heart toward God. Then life would be just this side of heaven.

"Let's narrow the choices. Why don't we find the stall with the boldest barbecue sauce?"

"And corn dripping with butter." Randi spun a half turn in front of him. "Matthew, over there. Looks like they have what we're looking for."

They carried their meal to one of the small stone-walled planters that lined the sidewalk. Side by side, they sat on the flat-topped wall and waited for their new friends. Across the street in a corner parking lot, a band began to set up. Earlier, someone had pulled two farm trailers parallel to each other for the bandstand. Several sheets of plywood covered part of the asphalt lot to be used as a dance floor. A teenager set up rows of metal folding chairs with MARS FUNERAL HOME stenciled on the backs.

"What kind of music do you think they play?" Randi asked.

"Opera," Matthew said, holding his face as still as possible.

"It's a bluegrass festival."

"But there could be an opera written with bluegrass music, right?" Matthew tried to keep from smiling.

"Sure, a cast of opera singers that travels across the countryside in a bus to belt out songs from the tops of trailers. Maybe it's the band scramble Pat was telling me about. The bands don't get a chance to practice together." Randi looked down the sidewalk. "Here come Pat and Bob." She handed her plate to Matthew. "Hold my dinner, please." She climbed on top of the wall. "Over here, Pat." She waved, and the couple joined them.

Pat sat down next to Randi. "So many choices of good food. How did you decide so fast?"

"Matthew's stomach kept growling, and I took pity on him and settled for the next booth with corn."

"Seems to me you placed your order before me. Guess that makes you the hungry one," Matthew teased.

"Or made you the polite one," Bob suggested with a wide grin.

"Bob, you and I are going to be great friends. You've rescued me twice tonight already."

"Matthew thinks the band will be doing a bluegrass opera." Randi laughed. "He has to be wrong."

"Guess we'll have to stick around and see," Matthew said. "People are starting to fill the chairs, so it shouldn't take long to find out which opera singer is onstage. I think it will be a woman."

"I suppose you think all great opera singers are women?"

"No, I just think this one is."

Matthew finished his dinner and drank the last of his soda. He noticed Randi's plate still held most of her sandwich. "Aren't you going to finish that?"

"No. I'm stuffed. You want to finish it?" Randi handed her tray to Matthew. "It's good, just too much."

Matthew took the tray from her. "No, I've had enough, too. I'll toss it in the trash for you, though. Anyone else finished?" He gathered trash from Pat and Bob.

He darted in front of a stroller holding two look-alikes. Girls, he thought. He found a trash can, tossed the remains of their meal, and headed back to Randi. She was talking to the owner of the stroller. He watched as Randi bent down and caressed the cheek of the baby nearest her. That motherly touch jolted him. Matthew felt as if God had grabbed him by the shoulders and said, "What's it going to take for you to realize I picked her out for you?"

"Matthew!"

Randi's voice brought him back. He made his way to her side. "What's wrong?"

Her nose crinkled at him, much like a rabbit's. "Nothing's wrong. I wanted to tell you I asked the mother of the twins what kind of band was playing."

"Smug look on your face. Let me guess. It's not opera."

Randi laughed. "Don't be so disappointed, Matthew. It is the band scramble. So I was right. Admit it."

"Yes, ma'am, you are the current champ of Guess the Band." The first notes of a song floated through the air. "Where did the other two go?"

"Out there." Randi pointed to the dance floor. "They couldn't wait for the music to start. Something about not wasting a minute of their time without the baby."

"Do you dance, Randi?"

"Not a chance."

"Me, either." He sat close enough to her that he could feel her swaying to the music. "But we could walk around and maybe feel the rhythm through the soles of our feet?"

She smiled at him, and he felt like a king.

Matthew held out his hand to her. She hesitated then placed her hand in his. He led her toward the soda vendor. Her fingers entwined with his, and he felt like he held a missing piece of himself. He knew without a doubt he'd given his heart to her.

❧

Bob and Pat finished the dance and joined Matthew and Randi on the folding chairs; Bob handed them both sodas.

"Thanks." Matthew took a drink of the cold refreshment. "I'll get them next."

"No need. We're headed home. Evan should be sleeping. We thought we'd sit on the couch and enjoy some quiet time." Bob took his soda from Pat.

Realizing the end of the evening with her new friends had come, Randi said, "If I ever get to come back this way, Pat, let's meet for lunch or dinner, or. . ."

"Shopping," Pat finished. "I'd like that, too. Try to give me advance notice, and maybe I can get a sitter. Ah, girl time. Just can't get enough of it."

"Great. I'll call you before then, too." Randi hugged Pat.

Matthew shook hands with Bob. "If I'm still driving with Randi, I'll see you as well." He avoided looking at Randi. He didn't have to look at her to know her face would be hard and she'd be quick to deny the suggestion that he would be with her still.

The band started another song with a fast tempo.

"You want to stay?"

"Would you mind if I went back to the motel to sleep? I want to get an early start tomorrow. You can stay."

"No, I'll go back with you."

"But you're not tired yet," she protested, stroking his arm.

"That's okay. Too bad I can't drive again tonight. We could leave now."

"Well, we can't, so let's do what we can now. Before we go, though, let's find a booth selling ice cream for a bedtime snack."

The moon cast a glow on Randi's upturned face. Matthew thought a few kisses from her would be a delicious bedtime snack.

"Randi." He pulled her close to him so that Randi alone would hear the words meant only for her. "You look beautiful tonight."

"Matthew, we'd better get some food into you. You must be light-headed."

"No, I'm fine. That's not why I said you look beautiful."

"Then why would you? Why would you want to ruin a nice evening?"

He frowned down at her. "I'm confused. I tell you that I love the way you look in the moonlight, and you decide the evening is ruined?"

"Moonlight? You didn't say anything about moonlight. What's wrong with you, Carter?" She backed away from him. "I can't let you fall in love with me. Not that I wouldn't like to find out what those brown eyes would look like full of passion, or how your lips would feel against mine, but, Matthew, you're a pastor. It can't—no, it *won't* happen."

"Are you through?"

"For now."

Matthew pulled her close to him and whispered, "Don't say it can't or won't happen, Miranda Davis Bell. If God desires this attraction between us, then it will happen." Before she could protest any further, he brought his lips to hers. At first he could feel her resistance; then his heart soared as she began to kiss him back with an energy that matched his.

The kiss over, Randi pulled away, but her eyes remained locked with his.

A smattering of clapping and a few whistles of approval drew Matthew's attention from Randi. He hadn't meant to make a public display, but he smiled at their approval. Now all he had to do was convince Randi they had a chance at love.

Chapter 19

Embarrassed by the public display of affection, Randi put her hand against Matthew's chest and gently pushed him back.

"Please don't do that again."

She couldn't allow him to kiss her again. She took a step back and felt resistance from her heart, like a magnet being pulled from its mate.

"I'm going back to the room." She forced the words from her lips.

"Randi, wait. I'm coming with you."

"It's okay, really. I'm a big girl, and I can find my room."

"I'm walking you." His voice held determination.

"Whatever." Determined to remain silent while she sorted out her feelings about the excellent kissing abilities of Matthew Carter, she increased the speed of her steps. The rounded edge of the cobblestone sidewalk jarred her balance, throwing her backward into Matthew's arms.

She felt the pressure of his arms around her, helping her steady herself on her feet. The safety she felt in his arms scared and excited her.

"Thanks, I'm okay now. I'll walk slower."

"I don't mind catching you anytime you fall, Randi."

Matthew's voice soothed her jangled nerves. She gave him a tentative smile of thanks and fell into step next to him. She remained deep in thought, weighing all aspects of a relationship with a pastor.

The motel wasn't far, and they were back at the room before Randi could come to terms with her feelings. Inside, she crossed the room to the drapes. She grabbed the long plastic wand and maneuvered it until the drapes were closed.

"It's not home, but at least you won't have lights shining in your eyes all night." Matthew stood with his back resting on the closed door.

"And no road noise." She turned from the window. The room seemed small with him there. Her hands fluttered, searching for something to do, and she ran them down the front of her dress. "Do you think you'll ever get tired of being on the road, Matthew?" Randi perched on the edge of the bed and slipped out of her shoes.

"I hope not. Right now all I can imagine is driving and preaching for the rest of my life." He sat next to her on the bed. "What about you?"

"I don't know. Sometimes I think I'd like to have the dream." He didn't need to know she wouldn't mind if he starred in it.

He scratched his cheek. "The dream?"

"Yeah. Picket fence, car pool, and orthodontist appointments." *And the urge is getting stronger every day.* Randi visualized herself, Emma, and friends in her car on the way to the mall for a shopping adventure. Everyone smiling and lots of giggles.

"I'm shocked. I would never have guessed you even thought about doing something so normal." He moved to the desk and with one hand spun the chair around until it faced her. He sat across from her.

"Relax. It won't happen. I almost tried it once." She stopped. She'd done it now. He'd want to know the entire story.

"What do you mean?"

Yep, he couldn't help himself. Might as well tell him, Davis.

"I was engaged once. It didn't work out. That's all." *Please don't ask for more.*

Concern washed across his face. "What happened?"

"Not a lot to tell. We were buying a house, and I found Brent in the one we'd chosen, with the real estate agent. Not a stitch of clothes on either one of them. Didn't leave any room for doubt the wedding was canceled."

"He didn't deserve you."

"That's what I said. I decided right then to change my life. I did a one-eighty and quit applying for a teaching job and learned to drive a truck." Randi rubbed a red spot on her foot and winced. "I should have worn my tennis shoes. I think I have the beginnings of a blister."

"And ruined the effect of that dress? That would have been a crime." Matthew held out his hand. "Let me see."

Hesitantly she placed her foot into his hands. The electricity that flowed through them brought a flush to her face.

He leaned over to inspect her sole. As he looked, a lock of chestnut hair fell forward, almost into his eye.

"I don't see anything. It's just a little red. Your foot's cold, though. How about a special Carter foot rub? I'll do this one for free. The second foot will cost you lunch."

She tried to answer him. The words wouldn't come. Instead, she reached out and touched the lock of hair that hung over his eye.

Matthew lifted his face. Their eyes met. *A girl could lose herself in the depths of that creamy mocha.* He moved closer to her.

She leaned in, anticipating the warmth of his lips on hers.

At the end of the kiss, she slowly parted her eyelids. *Just one more?* she pleaded with her eyes.

Randi found her hand entwined with Matthew's as he kissed her again.

Sliding his hand from hers, Matthew pushed himself back into his chair. He looked as if he wanted to say something. Instead, he stood.

"I'm leaving. I can't be in here with you."

"Matthew, I didn't ask you to sleep with me."

"I know. But the temptation between us may become bigger than we can control."

Her mind whirled, knowing he was right. And her heart responded with joy. He respected her, maybe even honored her, and it felt good. Really good. She hopped off the bed.

"You're right. Thank you." She grabbed his hand and led him to the door, intending to send him out of her life.

He tilted her chin and gave her a quick kiss. "Good night." And then he was gone.

Randi rested her head against the door and fought the urge to throw it open and go after him. What was it about this man that had managed to unlock the door she had tightly bolted?

❧

Randi cradled the phone to her ear. Shopping with Pat made her long for Jess's company even more. She'd called, taking a chance on waking her to tell her about her evening with Matthew. Such ninth-grade behavior, but just what she needed. "So what do you think?"

"He's a keeper, Randi."

"Just not for me. He'll make someone a good husband." She twisted the edge of the comforter between her fingers.

"I think he might be the one for you." Jess fell silent.

"But it's not what I planned." What was that whine in her voice? She sounded like Emma.

"You can plan all you want, Randi, but God already did all the work for you. Just let Him lead you."

"So what happened to free will?" She heard ice clicking against a glass.

"It's there, but why take the hardest route?"

"What if I don't choose Matthew?" Randi couldn't stop the sudden image of Matthew, three little girls, and a puppy romping across a pasture. And she wasn't with them.

"What if you do?"

"Okay, so then I get a family? And the pain that goes with losing them?"

"What about the pain of never having them?"

Randi felt the tension in her neck travel down her spine. Why did all of this have to be so hard? "So if I don't do what God wants me to do, I'll be punished? Is that what you're telling me?"

"Back up—who said that? I just asked if you would be able to live with yourself if you sent Matthew away. Besides, God works everything together for those who love Him."

"But does He really love—"

"Don't say it, Randi. I know how you feel, or say you do. God loves you. He loves you enough to go around and through your stubbornness. I know you think He's too busy to bother with you, but He's not. He's there all the time, anytime you need Him. Even when you say you don't." Jess sighed. "So think about it, will you? God's plan for Matthew could include you."

Randi's ear burned from the cell phone. She didn't know how to respond, but her thoughts were confused. How could Matthew love her? She wasn't preacher wife material. Wouldn't God want that for him?

"I have other news for you." Jess's voice sparkled. "I'm cleared."

"Cleared?" Randi asked. "For takeoff?"

Jess laughed. "No. To come back. I called Dana, and next week we'll be back on the road together."

"Does Matthew know?" She knew he didn't know, or he would have said something.

"I'm sure Dana has a plan. I thought you didn't care."

"He'll be heartbroken."

"Sounds like you do care."

"I guess I do." Randi blinked back tears, surprised by the sadness she felt.

≈

Randi lay on the bed in the dark room, unable to sleep. The room felt void of fresh air. And the quiet. . .everything was so still she could hear the sound of her own breath going in and out. That and Jess's words. Even if she didn't want to think God had time for her, she could believe He would make time for Matthew.

She kicked the heavy bedspread off her legs and crawled out of bed. *Is Matthew finding it difficult to sleep tonight, too?* She slid the room-darkening curtains open, blinded for a moment by the bright lights of the gas station below. She watched a family of four climb out of a minivan.

What would it be like to travel with children across the States? She would like that, teaching them the history of the country. Showing them all the places she had been as a driver.

She gave herself a mental shake. A reality check was in order. There wouldn't be any traveling with children, especially her own. She grasped the edges of the curtains and yanked them shut. Darkness engulfed her as hot tears streamed down her cheeks. Could Jess be right? All she needed to do was follow God's nudges? Ask Him to lead her? It couldn't be that easy. Emma prayed all the time. So did her mother, and look at what their lives were like. *But they're happy, and I'm not.*

Chapter 20

Matthew whistled a popular Christian song as he crossed the empty motel lobby. He couldn't find it in himself to be angry about the way Randi's fiancé had treated her. Sure, he didn't like that she'd been hurt, but if it had saved her for him, then he was okay with that.

Randi liked him, and that felt good, mighty good. The warm night air clung to him like a mother's hug as he strode across the paved parking lot to the truck. His mind raced with the possibilities of a life with Randi, and maybe Emma. He didn't mind. He'd take all of Randi's family, including the brother in jail, if it meant a future with her.

He climbed into his bunk and tried to stretch full length, but his feet hit the wall. He rolled over and bent his knees. He closed his eyes then opened them when sleep refused to come. He couldn't lie still, not when he could still feel Randi in his arms. He crawled out of the bed. He needed a snack. That would help.

Outside the truck, he glanced at Randi's window, hoping for a light. *Maybe she can't sleep, either,* he thought. If not, he'd go back up and get her. They could get the ice cream they had forgotten about earlier. The window remained dark. He frowned. Maybe she didn't have the same confusing feelings he was experiencing.

The white twinkle lights around the old-fashioned posts gave the town a movie set feel. Soft sounds of music echoed against the empty shops through the still night air. The crowds in the streets had thinned to a mere stream. Several high school–age kids were sweeping the streets, and a few were lugging clear trash bags full of cans. The festival hadn't officially closed. Maybe he would find an open vendor. A funnel cake with a cup of decaf coffee would be nice. The first row of vendors he came to had closed their makeshift canvas doors over their serving counters.

Matthew stopped one of the can haulers. "Is anyone still open? I'm looking for something sweet to eat."

The girl pointed toward the sound of the music. "The ones closest to the band are, but not for long. Most of them are serving beer."

"Thanks. I'll check. Maybe someone has food left."

The tent where Matthew bought their dinner still remained open. He purchased his coffee and dessert then wandered back to where he and Randi had sat earlier.

He popped a piece of fried dough sprinkled with powdered sugar into his mouth while he watched the couples dancing. The ones who were left were older, about his parents' age. They looked as if they had been dance partners for life. Every move seemed coordinated to perfection. His heart ached with longing.

Matthew began a silent dialogue. *Father, I want that. I want a love so strong no one can look at us and say we made a mistake. If it's Randi You've chosen for me, please show me how to bring her to You. I've tried talking to her, but I don't think I'm getting anywhere. Oh, I know, Father, any word spoken about You is never wasted. But sometimes. . .sometimes I feel like she's bricked herself into a soundproof room. Amen.*

He brushed the powdered sugar off his jeans then added to his prayer. *Father, can You answer this one faster than the last big request I had? She's beautiful, and if she's not for me, please move me somewhere I can't see her every day.*

Chapter 21

With her backpack slung over her shoulder, Randi trotted through the lobby and out the door. She reached the truck huffing and leaned on the door with one hand. With a tight fist, she banged against the metal to warn Matthew of her impending entrance. She retrieved her key from her jeans pocket, inserted it into the lock, and turned. As the door opened, its hinges grated, matching the growl of her stomach that reminded her she should eat.

"I'm driving first," she called. The curtain was drawn tight across the sleeping area. She didn't hear a response. With both hands she yanked the canvas curtain across the rod.

He wasn't asleep. He wasn't even there. His Bible, cell phone, and guitar rested on his bunk, but not him.

She flung her backpack into the corner. *Where is he?* She didn't think she'd passed him in the lobby. It didn't matter if she did; he'd find out she had checked out. No doubt he would return in a few minutes.

And next week Jess will be back! She sighed with relief. After last night, the sooner she and Matthew parted, the better.

Despite the conversation with Jess, Randi knew Matthew couldn't be part of God's greater plan for her. Why would he be? If anyone, Emma should come before Matthew.

And yet I've denied her a home with me. She crashed onto the lower bunk. She had done just that, refused to take a little girl who loved her into her home. She wasn't any better than her brother. It didn't matter that Emma wasn't her child. She'd stood there in church and accepted the responsibility of being her godmother, praying for her, taking care of her in case her brother couldn't or wouldn't. She hadn't done any of it.

The gravity of what she'd left undone hit her in the chest. She gasped for breath. *I am so sorry, Emma.* But what could she do? Nothing had changed, other than her guilt had been left behind and replaced with sorrow. Changes had to be made. But first she had to get home, and that couldn't happen until Matthew returned. She couldn't very well leave him behind—again. Not when he'd been so understanding about her log book.

But he'd better get back soon. It's not like he had access to a shower this morning. Maybe she should go look for him. He wouldn't have gone far. He had to know she would be ready to leave early, eager to make up the time they missed yesterday. She sat up and flipped on the CD player. Sounds of Ben Glover's "26 Letters" poured through the cab. Matthew's music. She considered changing it but decided she liked the sound and left it alone.

She moved to the back and straightened the bunk. She picked up the pillow and sniffed. It smelled like him. She closed her eyes, remembering his kisses. *Enough! It's over, remember?* She shoved the pillow into the corner.

Back in the front, she switched out the CD for some blues. Where could Matthew be? Aggravated that he still hadn't returned, she grabbed a pen and pad of paper from the cubby at the front of the cab.

> M.
>
> *Came early so we could leave. You're missing so I went to the bakery down the street. Find me there.*
>
> R.

She ripped the yellow note from the pad and stuck it to the steering wheel. She hoped he wouldn't climb in on the passenger's side and miss it. She didn't have time for a comedy routine of the two of them just missing each other all morning.

She slammed the door behind her. A thick gray cloud sneaked over the sun as she walked down the street. A Danish and coffee would taste good. The small town seemed silent after last night's revelry. The booths still stood, vacant and eerily ghostlike this morning. The streets showed no signs of the crowd that had been here the night before.

As she approached the bakery, she stopped and stared. A line appeared to have grown from the front door. Randi groaned. She hadn't expected to have to wait. She looked again. It wasn't a line, but a group. What could be so exciting at a bakery this early in the morning? It seemed to be a quiet group. She could only hear one voice.

A familiar voice. *Matthew.*

Anger bubbled inside her throat as she grasped at a reason to be mad at him. How could he? How could he make her wait while he played teacher to a bunch of believers? Well, she would take care of that. After all, he wasn't hired to preach to the multitudes. He was hired to take care of his fellow truckers, and these people didn't qualify just because some of them drove pickups. She elbowed her way through the crowd until she stood next to him.

She shook his arm. "Matthew. We need to leave. Now."

"Randi. Meet some of my new friends."

"Hi." Randi stretched her lips into a counterfeit smile. "I've been waiting for you. You could have left me a note or something," she hissed at him.

"I'm sorry. I didn't realize I'd been here so long. I came down to get us breakfast and started talking to a few people, and before I knew it I was teaching a small Bible class about Paul."

"Glad you enjoyed yourself." She smiled at the group. "I'm sorry, but *Teach*

211

needs to get back on the road."

"Let us know the next time you're going to be close enough for us to drive, Matthew. We'll come to the nearest truck stop to hear you preach," said a voice in the back.

"I'll need a phone number from one of you. The rest of you get your name on a call list."

"Joe, you make the call list. You can do them on that spreadsheet you love, like you do for your soccer team." Loud snickers wafted among the men.

"Sure, I'll handle it, or rather my wife will. She's the one who puts those lists together, not me," Joe said. He handed Matthew a business card. "My number is at the bottom. Hope you get by here again soon."

"I hope so, too."

Randi couldn't believe the glow that seemed to radiate from Matthew's face. He really believed the stuff he taught.

"Matthew, we have to go." Randi stood with her arms crossed and glared at him. She moved to the side while the group of listeners dispersed with cups in their hands.

"I'm almost ready. I want to get us some breakfast before we leave if that's okay. Isn't that why you're here?"

"Not exactly. You weren't where you were supposed to be, and I grew tired of waiting. I thought I might as well eat." Randi pulled a wad of dollars from her jeans pocket and thrust the money at him.

Matthew waved it away. "No, I'll get it." He turned away from her and walked to the counter and placed their order.

"You want me to drive?" Matthew asked, interrupting her thoughts.

"No. I didn't drive at all yesterday."

Matthew held out a small white paper sack. She took it, mumbling her thanks before walking out the door. She took small sips of the hot coffee while Matthew walked next to her. Neither spoke until they were back at the Sleep-Inn.

Matthew brushed against her arm. "Are you okay?"

"Why?" She followed him between a Mustang and the minivan she'd seen pull in last night. *They must be sleeping in this morning or letting the kids work off some energy in the pool before the rest of their drive.*

"Because last night I thought. . ."

She stopped short, realizing what he was talking about.

"You thought what? One kiss and everything would be like a fairy tale?"

He turned to face her. "Not exactly. But you did kiss me back. I couldn't help but think perhaps you might like me enough not to yell first thing in the morning."

She could see the pain in his eyes. Did he think she was like that girl in college? She hadn't wanted to hurt him. "Well, if that's all you were expecting, I suppose I could keep the conversation friendly."

As they came to the front of the truck, her stomach rolled. "I didn't do the pre-check."

"No problem. I'll run through it for you."

"Sure." Randi shivered, thinking about what Matthew didn't know. She almost drove off this morning without checking over the load. If he had been sleeping, she would have left without thinking about it. She shook the feeling of doom from her shoulders. The chance of something being wrong the first and only time she had forgotten had to be small. *But something could have.* How many times had they drilled the importance of the pre-check into them in school? It was supposed to be as automatic as putting the toothbrush in your mouth every morning.

"Checks out fine. There's still enough reefer fuel to make it to the next stop." Matthew stood looking at her. "Something wrong? You've been standing there like that since we got here."

"No, it's nothing. Let's just go." She opened the door, climbed up, and plucked the note she had left for Matthew from the wheel. She crunched it and jammed it into the bag she kept for trash.

Inside, Matthew grabbed his Bible and a notebook before buckling himself into the passenger seat. "I had a great idea for a sermon back at the bakery and need to get it down so I don't forget it."

"Good for you." Through the windshield the summer sky dimmed, and navy blue and black took its place.

"I'm sorry I wasn't here when you came down, Randi. I thought I would have at least half an hour before you woke. It's still early. We haven't lost any time this morning."

"No, but who knows, we may end up behind an accident now instead of in front of one." Lightning streaked horizontally, leaving jagged white line etchings in her eyes.

"Or maybe God is protecting us from one that we might have been involved in if we had left earlier," Matthew said.

She let that pass, knowing that even though he had already taught one class this morning, he would enjoy giving her a private lesson. Maybe distraction would work. "I told Emma you would take her to your farm."

"You did?" The look he gave her was unreadable.

"If you'd rather we didn't come. . ."

"No, I want you to come. I wanted to ask you before."

"But you didn't."

"I know. My mom would have thought we were dating."

"We're not dating." This wasn't the kind of distraction she wanted. "It was one night and a few kisses. That's it." She thought fast. "Besides, I wouldn't make a good pastor's wife, and you know it."

He closed his Bible with a snap. "I haven't asked you to marry me."

That hurt in a way she didn't think possible. Before she had time to process if she would need stitches, a gust of wind battered the trailer, yanking the wheel from her hands. She quickly caught it, clutching it tight. She squeezed her biceps until she thought they would pop free of her skin. Just as she risked a glance at the side mirror, another blast rammed them. The back of the trailer lifted.

"What can I do?" Matthew asked.

"Nothing," she said through gritted teeth. "Pray?" She felt the back end fishtail. Like hot tar, the shoulder of the road sucked at her wheels. *Don't overcorrect! Take your time.* The instructions she'd learned came back to her as she wrestled with the rig, hating the sound of gravel urging her to panic.

On the other side of the interstate, the wind caught another driver. She gasped as she saw the back of his trailer lift two feet. It landed on the shoulder. The back of the trailer started to slide toward the front; then the truck jackknifed. Its cab skated across the pavement toward the median.

Then the rain came, not in soft spatters but in thick waves, bringing another slap from the wind.

"There's a message from dispatch on the Qualcomm." Matthew pointed at the red light.

"I can't play with them right now. I'm learning to windsurf." Her voice felt as tight as the tension in her shoulders. "So find out what they want."

He didn't say anything. The suspense grated her already-raw nerves. She glanced over at him. The expression on his face told her she wouldn't like what the message said.

"What's wrong?" Another gust moved the trailer onto the shoulder. The wind pummeled them as Randi tried to keep them centered between two lanes.

"Your mom is in the hospital, and they want you to come get Emma."

Chapter 22

They'd dropped their load and asked Dana for permission to turn and burn. The only time they stopped was to switch drivers, refuel, and grab sandwiches. They rolled into the Round the Clock yard and dropped the truck. Randi drove straight to the hospital, followed by Matthew in his truck.

At the hospital, Randi welcomed the pressure of Matthew's hand in hers. He'd insisted on coming with her. It would have been impossible for her to sit and do nothing while she worried.

Dr. Sommer calmly stuffed his hand into the pocket of his lab coat as if he hadn't just tossed a live grenade into her life.

"What do you mean, she's not coming home?"

"I find it's best for a patient this age to recover in an assisted care facility. A broken hip and leg requires twenty-four-hour nursing followed by therapy. Those bones are not going to heal quickly." He averted his eyes, and she wondered how many times a week, or a day, he delivered news like this.

"The nurse will help you place her." Before she could protest, his beeper sounded. With an apologetic look he said, "We'll talk later," and hustled down the hall.

"Matthew, I—"

"Miss Bell?"

Randi turned. A short, twentysomething woman pranced down the hallway. Her bright, flounced skirt bounced above her sensible black pumps. A red leather briefcase hung from her shoulder. She looked familiar.

She pressed a card into Randi's hand. "Kate Trent, social services. We've met before. I'm here about Emma."

"Where is she?" Randi felt like she was trapped in Tom's Twister. The carnival ride spun fast, plastering her to its wall; then the floor fell two feet, leaving her hanging in the air. She wanted off.

Kate wore a stern look, amplified by the black frame glasses perched on her nose. "Emma will be here in a minute. She's having a snack. Now before she gets here, I need to know what you plan to do with her."

"Do with her?" Like a parrot, Randi repeated the question.

Emma came around the corner, carrying a candy bar.

"She has to go with you, or I have to put her in foster care."

"No! I won't go!" Emma tossed her candy bar and scurried to Randi, wailing like a wounded animal.

Randi bent down, gathered her into her arms, and rocked her back and forth. "Shh, Emma. It's going to be okay." She met Matthew's eyes, silently begging him to tell her how it possibly could.

❧

Randi tucked Emma into bed and kissed her good night.

"Will you listen to my good-night prayer, like Grandma?"

"It's been a long day, kid, and I'm not very good at prayers. Matthew's still here. Do you want me to get him?"

Emma turned away from her and faced the wall. "No."

"Emma, come on, it's late."

"It's okay. You don't have to listen. God will." Emma flipped around. Her eyes gleamed with fresh tears. "But it's better if you're here."

"Let's hear it, then." Randi folded her hands like she'd been taught years ago in Sunday school.

"Dear God, please make Grandma Bell better. Please remember Daddy. He's sorry for what he did, God. He asked me to forgive him for losing our home and I did, just like You said we should. Amen." She huddled into a ball under the covers. "Good night, Aunt Randi."

"Sweet dreams, pumpkin." Randi traced Emma's cheek then turned off the lamp, pausing at the doorway as she heard Emma murmur.

"God, thank You for answering my prayer."

Randi's feet turned to stone and she froze, unsure what to do. Had He really given Emma an answer to something?

". . .making Aunt Randi my mom."

Emma's new mom? The words pricked a small fault in Randi's protective shell. The crack radiated like a web in a broken windshield but didn't break. She closed the bedroom door.

In the kitchen, Matthew waited for her with steaming hot chocolate in a rainbow mug. She quirked her eyebrow as she slid into the chair. "How did you know this is my comfort cup?"

"I didn't. Just seemed like a good size. The other ones aren't big enough to add the powder to the hot water and have room to stir."

The phone on the wall rang. Randi thrust the chair backward and dove for the phone. *The hospital?* Her heart raced as she answered it.

"Randi, I just heard about your mom. Is there anything I can do?" Jess's concerned voice came through the line.

"No, nothing right now." To Matthew she whispered, "It's not the hospital; it's Jess."

"Who's with you?"

"Matthew came back with Emma and me. So you know Mom broke a hip and a leg?"

"How long until she can come home?"

"She's not, at least not for weeks. She has to go to one of those assisted living centers. I'm taking care of Emma for now. When are you coming back to drive?"

"About that." Jess sighed. "There isn't an easy way to tell you."

Randi's stomach turned. "The day can't get any worse, Jess. Just say it."

"Mike and I are engaged."

"That's great, Jess! Good news, not bad."

"There's more. He wants to get married next month and asked me to quit driving. He wants to start a family."

"But we're partners." Randi hated the pleading tone in her voice, but if that was what it took. . .

"We were. But we never said we'd do this forever, Randi. Remember, it was supposed to be until we found our Prince Charming and decided to live happily ever after."

Randi swallowed. *Prince Charming? Happily ever after?* She didn't think that had been a serious goal when she agreed to it.

Jess continued, "I've found mine, and I think you may have found yours."

Randi noticed Matthew trying not to eavesdrop. An impossible task in this tiny kitchen. She couldn't talk about Prince Charming now, not with him in the kitchen. "Jess, I'm really tired. I'll call you tomorrow."

She hung up the phone. "Jess isn't coming back to drive. If Dana will let us keep driving together, I'll be able to take care of Emma until Mom comes home."

Matthew frowned then looked down at his cup. "I told Dana I couldn't ride with you anymore."

"What? Why? Because of a few kisses?"

He pushed back his chair and gave her an intense look she didn't understand.

"Yeah, that's it." He turned and put his cup in the sink. "It's late. I'd better be going. I'll call you."

As soon as the door closed, Randi leaned against it and let loose the tears she'd held back all day. *If You really are listening, God, I need You.*

❧

Randi dragged herself to her mother's room. She collapsed on the bed and curled into a ball. Tears flowed, and she smothered her sobs with a pillow. She told God about the guilt she carried and the fears of being responsible for Emma. She felt His hands reach out for her. And then she knew as she placed her hand in His, He'd been with her all along. He'd been there when the kids made fun of her, when her dad disappeared, and He'd even been with her the day she'd found Brent with the Realtor. She'd called Him TV Dad. The dad she'd always wanted, one who would be there anytime she needed Him. Did A.J. know that's who He was? She'd ask Emma.

Before breakfast, Emma crawled in bed with her. Randi slipped her arm around the little girl.

"Emma, last night you told God you've forgiven your dad. What did you mean?"

Emma snuggled closer to her. "Dad said he was sorry he couldn't be a real dad anymore because he has to be in jail for a long time. But he said he loves me, and he's going to ask you to adopt me because you'll be a good mom."

"And you forgave him, just like that?"

"Nope. I was mad. But at Sunday school I learned that God wants me to forgive Dad. That's why Jesus came, so everybody could forgive. I'm not sure how it works, but I felt better when I decided not to be mad anymore."

"You're a good daughter." Randi wasn't quite sure she could so easily forgive A.J. Did he know how fortunate he was that his daughter had forgiven him? Randi couldn't forgive him, not yet. But she would honor his request and adopt Emma. She'd begun praying about that, but it would take time—and God. At least that's what Jess had said. God can do it right now, but you have to choose to let Him. Free choice. It made life so much harder when you bumbled around making the wrong decisions.

Chapter 23

As they crossed through the rough field, Randi clung to Matthew's hand, and he noticed how small her fingers were next to his.

"Are we close?" Randi asked. "I don't see anything but never-ending fields."

"Not much farther." Matthew squeezed her hand.

"There really is a creek? Shouldn't there be trees around it?" She raised her hand to her forehead to shield her eyes from the sun and peered into the distance.

"There are. You just can't see them yet. Be patient. At least you aren't carrying this heavy basket." He leaned to one side to prove it weighed enough to keep him unbalanced.

"Ouch!" Randi stooped and picked at one of the tiny burrs embedded between her sock and shoe.

He watched her remove a few more. "You know you'll get more on the way back, don't you?"

She glared at him and stood. "This better be worth the trouble."

They came to the crest of the hill. Matthew set the basket on the ground. He maneuvered Randi in front of him.

"Look, Randi. See those trees? That's where the creek is, and where we can finally sit and talk."

"I can't wait." She turned and grinned. She reached her arms around his neck, tilted her head, and kissed him gently on the lips. Her eyes enticed him with their colors of blue and green. "Want to race?"

He didn't answer her but took off running, his heart racing, not from the exertion but from the excitement of love.

Randi raced after him, laughing.

"Not fair." She crashed down next to him on the creek bank. "You have longer legs."

"You ran? I had time to spread the blanket." He gestured to the rumpled mess under him.

"More like you dropped it on the ground and sat on it only seconds before I got here." She pointed at him. "Up, Preacher Man. Let me spread that so we can both sit on it."

Preacher Man? Now that was a handle he liked. He stood and grabbed a corner of the blanket and helped her smooth it. Sitting across from her, he unwrapped the sandwiches and handed her one. He raised his turkey sandwich to his lips.

Randi's eyes widened. "Aren't you going to pray first?"

"Almost forgot," he said, embarrassed. "Not good for a pastor, is it?"

"I'll say it, since you've forgotten how."

Matthew watched in stunned silence as Randi placed her lunch on her lap, closed her eyes, and folded her hands.

After the prayer, she reached out and touched his hand. "There's something else I need to tell you."

"Like you hate picnics?" He started to take a bite.

"This is serious, Matthew. You promise you won't say 'I told you so' or laugh?"

Matthew felt his breathing slow, and he put the sandwich down. Serious couldn't be good. "Okay."

She cocked her head at him and lifted an eyebrow.

"I promise." He put a hand over his heart for emphasis.

"I get it. I mean, I get that God loves me and He does listen to everything. I've even been asking Him for help."

"I would never laugh at you for asking for God's help." Matthew's lips lifted into a smile. "Why would you think I would?"

"Maybe not laugh, but get that satisfied grin on your face."

"Can't help it." The smile on his face grew into a huge grin. "So has He helped you?"

"Let's see—Dana is letting me out of my contract, and your mom is watching Emma." Excitement almost made her jump up and down like a child, but she decided she'd probably break an ankle if she did that. "And I got the teaching job. Too bad it took me so long to find Him. I wasted a lot of time." Randi took a bite of her sandwich.

"So what brought all this change, Randi?" Matthew brushed an ant from the blanket.

"The night you said you wouldn't ride with me anymore." She looked away for a moment then whispered, "Then you left."

More than anything he wanted to hug away the hurt etched on her face. He wanted to, but he didn't. A small voice told him she needed to say it all.

She took a breath. "I felt abandoned. First my dad, then my brother became undependable, and then my fiancé, even God, I thought. I gave up. But then you came along, and I thought you were different." Tears rolled down her face, and she sniffed.

This was one of those times he wished he could whip a handkerchief from a pocket like the men in those old movies his mom watched. Instead, he reached into the basket for a napkin and held it out to her.

She took it and blew her nose. "Sorry. I didn't think I would cry."

"That's okay, but you have to tell me the rest of the story."

"I don't know if I can explain it. I was crying, and I remember asking God if He was listening. It's weird, but in my mind I saw Him standing in a boat and offering me His hand. Then I knew. All this time, He was TV Dad."

"Huh?"

"Crazy, I know. TV Dad started out being someone A.J. and I pretended was our real dad. We knew it was the church dropping off gifts at Christmas, but we wanted to feel loved by a dad. Now I realize TV Dad for me was really my true Father, and He's always been there for me."

"Are you telling me that you believe in God, that He loves you enough to have sent His Son to die in your place?" Excitement charged through Matthew's heart.

"Yes. I always did believe in God, but I felt like He didn't care about me. I was wrong. He cared about me every second of my life. I was just too stubborn to see that."

"I'm glad. Glad that you found your way back to Him." *Thank You, God, for an answered prayer.*

"Mom and Jess were praying for me, and lately Emma, too."

"And me, Randi." Matthew slid his arms around her shoulders, pulling her close. He felt nothing but love for this woman as he kissed her.

"Marry me, Randi, please. I want more than a kiss here and there. I want to go to sleep next to you at night, be the father of your children, go on vacations together, and worship with you."

Her eyes seemed to dance with joy; then her face grew serious. "Can you give up driving?"

Matthew felt as if ice water had been dumped down his back. This was the woman he'd felt sure God wanted him to love. She couldn't be asking him to give up what he'd been called for, could she? He pulled away from her. "I can't."

"Sure you can."

A cow mooed in the pasture somewhere behind him. Devastated, Matthew felt the trap of his youth squeeze him. His dad's offer to work the farm with him roamed through his mind, but he couldn't be a farmer, not even for Randi.

"Only when you pry my stone-cold fingers from the steering wheel."

"Then I can't marry you. I've seen too many marriages ruined in this business."

"But, Randi, this is what I've been called to do." Matthew knew God had answered part of his prayer, too. But was he ready to give up his dream of traveling across the country?

"I know, but I've been called to be Emma's mother." Randi began flinging the sandwiches back into the basket. "I think it's best if you take me home."

She tried to hide them from him, but he saw her blink back the tears before she hid her face. Still, he couldn't do what she wanted; he just couldn't.

Chapter 24

A few weeks later, Randi held open the door of her new home and embraced her best friend. "Jess, I'm glad you came."

Jess removed her sunglasses and entered the house. "It *is* small. I thought you were exaggerating when you said it wasn't much bigger than the sleep cab."

Randi eyed the room. "It doesn't look too bad, does it?" The corner shelf unit held books, Barbie dolls, and cows, which had become Emma's new hobby after she'd found a ceramic one at the thrift shop. The new couch hugged one wall, and the television sat in the other corner on top of an old trunk. "It's nice to have a garage and a backyard. But the bonus—"

"No trash bin outside your door." Jess finished the sentence for her. "It looks nice, Randi. I love the pictures on the wall." Jess walked over for a closer look. "These are new. From Matthew's farm?"

"Cows gave it away?" Randi laughed. "Emma loves the cows and Matthew's mom."

Jess sank into the couch with a puzzled look. "Doesn't she love Matthew, too?"

"He's not around much, but when he is, yes, she does," Randi said with dissatisfaction in her voice. "How did the interview with the florist go?"

"Still can't decide on my bouquet. Roses or daisies?"

Randi wondered if she would ever experience a walk down the aisle, much less a ring with a diamond that size on her finger. "You'll figure it out. I made tea. Would you like some?"

"Sure." Jess popped off the couch. "I'll come with you. I want to see the kitchen. Can you really touch both walls at the same time?"

"Almost," Randi said as she led Jess into the galley-sized room.

Randi laughed at the expression on Jess's face when she turned around.

"You weren't kidding."

"We don't need a lot of space." Randi poured a glass of iced tea and handed it to Jess. Picking up her glass, she said, "It will take less than five seconds to see the rest of the place."

After the tour, Jess settled on the couch once again and asked, "Any change in Matthew?"

Randi set her glass on the coffee table. "No. He's still insisting he can drive and be a good husband and parent. I don't know, Jess. I'm having trouble sticking to my decision."

"You don't love him enough to give in on letting him drive?" Jess sank back farther into the couch and slid off her shoes.

"I have to think of Emma and any other children we might have. I look into the future and see me, frazzled from taking care of the kids for days. Matthew will come home, and I'll fly out the door to experience some kind of life. He won't want to get a babysitter because he'll have been away from them all week."

"So now you can see into the future? Why don't you let God take care of what will happen? If you love Matthew, you have to trust things will turn out the right way."

"I'm not ready to do that. There has to be a way for this to work. I don't want to be a single mom while he's gone so much. I'm doing that now, and it's harder than I thought."

Jess leaned forward. "Are you sorry you adopted Emma?"

"No. Not at all. I'm grateful every morning when I wake up and realize she's in the room next to me. I just want—no, need—a husband who's here to love them, play with them, and assemble toys."

"Assemble toys?" Jess looked at her with a frown.

"Just wait. Barbie's mansion is a nightmare to put together."

"How many houses can Barbie have?"

"It's not that, not really. I want a normal family life. I want to have dinner on the table and have a husband to feed. I want to wake up every morning next to Matthew. I want to be disgusted by clothes on the closet floor." Randi squeezed her eyes tight for a minute to stop tears that threatened to spill. "I want a marriage."

❧

An envelope with a return address from Blessed Savior Church sat on top of Matthew's mail. He ripped it open and pulled out the letter.

> *Dear Mr. Carter,*
>
> *Blessed Savior Church has been made aware of you through one of our members. We are interested in talking to you about starting a ministry at our local truck stop on a permanent basis. If you would be interested in discussing this further with us, please call.*

He shook his head in disbelief. "Who could have given them my name?"

Matthew paced the kitchen. "Tied down, that's what I'd be. Stuck in one town forever. But I could still work with the truckers. . . . No, I can't. I just can't give up the road." He shoved the letter into his pocket. Unable to think, he left the house.

Hot and sweating from the exertion of trying to walk away his thoughts, he stopped at the end of the pasture. He wiped the moisture from his face with his shirttail then tramped along the creek bank until he came to his spot. He'd come here to make major decisions since he was old enough to escape his mother. Decisions about what car to buy, whether he would go to prom, where to go to school, and even whether to drive a truck or take over the farm for his dad.

That's the problem. He didn't want to live in one small town forever. Too many towns remained out there for him to explore—for him to preach the gospel in. He wanted the life of the apostles.

Matthew climbed into his tree and crawled out onto the branch that hung over the creek. The water whispered as it raced by. His thoughts kept pace with the rush. He pulled the crumpled letter from his shirt pocket and spread it on the branch before him.

An answer to a prayer, right, Father? But it wasn't the answer he wanted. He'd spent nights asking God how he could marry Randi. He didn't contemplate even for a moment that the answer might mean that to make it work he had to give up his dream.

Too much to ask. He'd worked too hard to become a driver, to have the chance to see the world. He balled the paper into his fist, pulled his hand back, and aimed at the creek. At the point of letting go, he changed his mind and stuck it into his pocket. If only he didn't love her so much, he could walk away. But he *did* love her. Was he man enough to give up his dream for her?

He spent an hour in prayer asking for guidance. Stiff from lying on the branch, he lowered himself, hanging from the branch before he dropped. He landed on his backside. *Funny, that never happened before. Kick in the pants from God?* He stood and brushed the dirt from the back of his jeans. *There is still time to work this out,* he thought. He needed to spend more time in prayer on this one. Meanwhile, he'd see Randi and Emma when he could. They would have to understand.

Chapter 27

Saturday afternoon Randi slowed the car as she drove through the rest stop. The sunshine danced through the window, its warmth belying the fact that it would soon be October and snow would soon fall. She looked for Matthew's truck. Spotting it, she zipped into a parking spot just past it. She checked in the mirror to see how she looked. Her hair, now cut short, would be a surprise to him. But it looked so much better and she wanted a more professional style that was easier to maintain now that she was teaching.

Someone tapped on her window. She looked up to see Matthew posed there with a big grin on his face.

She opened her door and jumped out. "Hi," she said, feeling shy about her new appearance.

"I saw you pull off the interstate." Matthew reached up and skimmed his fingers along the bottom of her hair. "You cut it," he said.

"I had to, to survive. Getting both Emma's hair and mine done takes more time than I ever imagined."

Matthew pulled her into his arms. "You look great. I like short," he whispered into her ear. He continued to hold her. "I've missed you so much."

"I've missed you, too, Preacher Man." She reached up and kissed him gently on the lips. She had missed him these past few weeks. Phone calls could warm you on the inside, but nothing could replace a hug from the person you loved.

"I didn't expect you to be alone. I thought Emma was coming."

"She has a new friend, Jenny, who asked her to spend the day with her. She thought that would be more fun than coming with me." She heard Matthew's stomach growl. "Hungry? I brought a picnic lunch."

"You cooked?"

She almost laughed at the disbelief on his face. "No. But I put the meat between slices of wheat bread." She grinned at him. "I even brought some of those big pickles you like so much." She reached into the car and grabbed a brown sack.

"What, no basket? Not very romantic, are you?" Matthew teased.

"Hey, you should be grateful I was able to assemble a lunch with my morning routine." She gave him a playful shove and walked toward the covered picnic tables, glancing over her shoulder to make sure he followed. Only a few colored leaves clung to their branches.

Handing Matthew a sandwich, Randi decided she liked the feeling of taking care of him. "I wish I could make lunch for you every day."

Matthew didn't eat it, though. Sitting on the bench, he just held it and stared at her for a moment. Then he drew a deep breath.

"Randi, please marry me. Being apart from you doesn't feel right." Matthew reached out and grasped her hand tightly.

Her heart beat faster. She plopped down beside him and squeezed his hand. "I want that, too, but unless you give up driving, I can't marry you." She wouldn't let tears fall from her eyes. She wouldn't. She blinked faster.

"Why? Tell me why this can't work for us. Other men manage a marriage and keep driving."

"Temptation, Matthew. I'm talking about temptation. It's happened to me before, and Brent wasn't a trucker. You're even more at risk. I won't go through it again." She looked him in the eye and squeezed his hand. "It's just too easy to fall into someone else's arms if your husband or wife isn't around enough. People will reach for comfort when they need it."

"But if we both cling to God and look to Him for all comfort—"

"I know, Matthew, but we aren't perfect. We can fall into sin."

"So you're not willing to take a chance that I can be faithful to you while I'm on the road?" Matthew set his sandwich down on the paper plate Randi had brought. "I don't know how to prove to you that I love you enough never to endanger our marriage."

"How can you be so sure? There are plenty of female truckers who need counseling. A few tears, a hug, and before you know it, there might be chemistry between the two of you."

"So what do you want from me, Randi?"

"Find a job here so we'll be together every night."

"I don't think I can do that. I told you I didn't want to be stuck in one town the rest of my life. If I do that, I might as well go back and work on the farm." Matthew's face was downcast as he avoided looking at her.

"Then I guess there isn't anything else to discuss. I love you, Matthew, but Emma needs me."

"Come with me. Work by my side," Matthew pleaded.

"And Emma? I want to be there for her—every day." Randi withdrew her hand from his. "It's not like I don't miss driving, too, Matthew. But my life changed, and I'm glad."

"Don't give up driving, then; bring her. Other families do it. You can homeschool her."

"No. That's not a life for her. She's been uprooted enough. She needs a home, a school with friends, maybe a dog. I've spent a lot of time thinking about this. I can't do what you're asking."

"Where does that leave us, then? Do we throw away our feelings and just move on?"

Heartsick, she could hardly force the words from her constricted throat. "Sounds that way, doesn't it?"

"But I love you."

"Not enough to let go of your dream." Randi stood. She brushed the tears from her cheeks, wishing she was important enough to him that he would be willing to give up anything for her. "I love you, Matthew. I always will. But I guess this wasn't meant to be after all."

Before he could say anything else, she turned and ran toward her car in the truck parking lot.

Matthew's heart ached as he watched Randi's car pull out of her spot. No longer hungry, he gathered his sandwich, plate, and napkin and shoved them into the paper bag. He sat for a moment, thinking about what had happened and how it had happened so fast.

He smashed the bag of lunch and tossed it into the trash bin. He didn't even try to save it for later. He had lost a treasure.

A gift God sent me.

He knew he could have the gift back, *if* he gave up something dear to his heart. *Gain one, lose one.* How could he? He didn't want to choose. God had called him to reach out to others, hadn't He? Wasn't he supposed to give up all and follow God, just like the disciples?

His conscience nagged at him. If that was true, shouldn't he be happy about his choice? Instead, his world looked dark and joyless. He'd lost not only Randi, but Emma, too.

He walked back to the picnic table, held his head in his hands, and prayed. *Why, Father? Why can't I have it all?* He cried in silence to God for answers.

With a heavy heart and no easy solutions, he walked down the hill to his truck.

As he got closer to the parking lot, he noticed a group of people huddled together. Curious to see what was going on, he picked up his pace.

"Matthew."

He turned toward the voice and saw Brad, his partner.

"Get over here," Brad called softly. "That nutcase is here, and he's pointing a gun at Randi."

Randi? But she had left. Matthew had seen her drive off. Air left his lungs and didn't want to return. He tried to push through the group, but hands held him back. Brad stood next to him.

"We radioed the police. They'll be here in a minute."

"Let me go." Matthew pried at the hands that held him until they released him. He elbowed through the small crowd to the front.

Randi huddled next to Reb, another female driver. Randi must have seen her as she was leaving and stopped to talk. Behind them was a man holding a pistol trained on the two women. His mouth went dry as he struggled for words to call out.

What can I do, God? A plan came to him. Adrenaline propelled him back through the onlookers. He inhaled in a failed attempt to put his body in control. He found Brad. "I'm going behind the truck next to Randi and Reb and see if I can get the guy with the gun to talk to me. Maybe they'll be able to inch back to the side of Reb's truck. Think you're up to going on the other side of her truck and motioning to them if they look at you, see if you can get them to move?"

"You bet," Brad answered.

Please, God, keep us safe. Give me the words to disarm this man. Matthew raced around the back end of the trucks. He slowed his pace, but his heart continued its rapid rhythm. He walked down the side of Reb's truck. As he arrived at the front, he could hear the man's voice. He was close to Randi. Too close.

"Just tell me where I can find some trucker that goes by the name of Bingo, and I won't hurt you."

"Why do you need him?" Matthew called out. He crept closer. "Maybe I can help you."

"Don't come any closer, or I'll shoot the women. Trash—that's all they are, anyway."

Matthew stopped walking. He wouldn't look at Randi. If he did, he knew he would lose all control of his emotions. "What's your name?"

"Doesn't matter. I just want the man who killed my wife with his truck."

Matthew took a step closer. "Can you tell me what he looks like?" He heard Randi whisper his name. He felt his gaze drifting her way. He willed himself not to look. *If anyone gets hurt today, dear God, let it be me.*

"Big guy. Wears a hat."

If he wasn't so scared, Matthew might have laughed. That described over half the truck drivers in Wyoming. "Why do you think he's here?"

"I'm checking every place trucks stop. I'm going to find him and settle this."

"If he killed your wife, why isn't he in jail?"

"The jury let him go. Said it was an accident." The man started waving his gun around. "I'll kill all of you. It doesn't matter to me who dies." The man spit a hunk of chewing tobacco onto the pavement.

"What's your name?" Matthew said.

After a moment of silence, the man said, "Al."

"Al, do you think your wife would have wanted you to take revenge like this?"

"Doesn't matter what she thinks anymore. But yeah, she would have wanted me to avenge her death."

"By shooting Randi and Reb, Al?" Matthew hated to draw attention to them, but maybe if Al saw them as women, he wouldn't shoot them.

"They're truckers. They're part of it. They might even have been in the truck with him."

The man was more out of control than Matthew thought. Surely he would have known from the trial if anyone else had been involved in the accident. Matthew grasped for anything to say that might make a difference.

"Somebody better talk soon, or I'm killing the skinny one."

Randi. Not an ounce of fat on her. *Dear Jesus, help us, please.*

"Al, her name is Randi. If you shoot her, you're going to leave a beautiful little girl without a mother. That's not what you want to do, is it? Bring grief to her precious daughter?" Matthew could see that Brad hadn't done what he had suggested. Instead, he was creeping up behind Al.

Matthew needed to distract Al so the gunman wouldn't hear Brad, but he wanted to be near enough to Randi to protect her. He took a deep breath and stepped closer to Randi.

"What are you doing? Don't go over there," Al shouted. The gun wavered in the air.

"Why not? If you're going to shoot her, I want to kiss her good-bye before she goes to heaven. Yeah, heaven—that's where she'll go. You won't kill her, Al, just her body, because she's a Christian. And I'm kissing her because I love her just like you loved your wife. I bet you'd like to have had a chance to kiss your wife good-bye, wouldn't you, Al?" Matthew tried to think of the next thing to say. He had to talk loudly to cover Brad's moves and keep Al's attention pointed at him. "Well, Al? Aren't you going to answer that question?"

"Yeah, I would have kissed her good-bye. But I didn't get the chance, and you won't, either, if you don't tell me where Bingo is." Al raised his gun hand just as Brad smacked into him, knocking him to the ground. The gun fell out of Al's hand and spun away.

Brad jumped onto Al. Several truckers rushed to help restrain the gunman as Matthew grabbed the gun.

He breathed a sigh of relief as he heard sirens in the air. Brad stood, and others took over holding Al on the ground until the police arrived.

Matthew raced to Randi and wrapped her in his arms, realizing how close he had come to losing her. What if Al had shot her? What if she had died? Could he have lived with the knowledge that his selfishness had kept him from the woman he loved? He didn't think so. But now was not the time to tell her. He knew her too well. She would think he was reacting to the emotion of the day and not to his true feelings.

"Are you all right?" He smoothed a strand of hair from her face, much like a father would do to his little girl.

"Matthew, I've never been so scared before. Even when Jess was shot. That just happened. I never saw a gun. I've never had a gun pointed at me before." Her eyes widened with every staccato sentence.

He could feel her shaking in his arms, and he held her tighter. "Everything is okay now. You don't have to be afraid. Randi, I love you so much. I almost lost you."

She pushed away from him. "I love you, too, Matthew, but nothing has changed. You'll be back driving that truck as soon as the police get finished talking to us. Right?"

Matthew knew he wouldn't be driving it long, but he didn't want to tell her now. When he told her, he wanted it to be a good memory, not one tainted with shouting, guns, and police sirens.

She walked away from him. His heart broke with every step she took. He would have to tell her soon.

૨ঌ

The next morning Matthew pulled his pickup into Randi's driveway. The newly painted lavender door of the little house brought a smile to his face. It was another piece of evidence that she wanted to settle into a domestic life. For a moment he thought about how he had almost lost her. Not to a man with a gun, but because of his own selfishness. *Thank You, God, for showing me how much I want her in my life.*

He reached over and unbuckled the surprise he had brought for the girls.

Randi answered the door. The sadness on her face broke his heart.

"Matthew? Why are you here?" She made an attempt to neaten her hair, pushing it behind her ears. "And why is there a puppy with you?"

"I brought him for Emma. You do like puppies, don't you?" He tried to untangle himself from the leash wrapped around his legs.

"I don't have time to take care of him," Randi said, disapproval in her voice.

"I'll be taking care of him for a little while. He's just here to visit today." Matthew resisted the urge to pull her into an embrace. "Can I come in?"

Randi stepped back from the door. "Of course, but if that"—she pointed to the puppy—"makes a mess, you're cleaning it up."

"His name is Jack. He's a golden Lab, and yes, I'll clean up after him." Matthew shortened the leash in his hand to keep Jack close by and out of trouble.

"Emma's at a friend's house."

"I came to see you." He grinned at her. "I wanted to tell you something."

"What?"

"I accept."

"Accept what?" He loved the look of confusion on her face.

"Your demand."

"Demand?"

"The one you flung at me when I asked you to marry me."

"You do?"

"Yes. So can we get married now?" He reached for her hand, grasping it as he went down on one knee. "Miranda, please let me be your husband and a father to your children."

Matthew watched the emotions play across Randi's face. He could barely breathe. What was taking her so long to answer? Didn't she know he couldn't live without her? He needed her in his life every day. Then he noticed the tears welling in her eyes. "Miranda, Randi—"

Jack yelped and knocked him to the floor and began licking his face.

Randi began laughing. In a moment she said, "I think Jack wants to marry you."

"I don't want to marry Jack," Matthew sputtered and held out his hand. "Please, your answer."

"Yes."

They stared at each other for a moment. A perfect moment, Matthew thought. He could hear his heart beat in the stillness of the moment.

"But what will you do instead of driving?" she asked at last.

Matthew clasped her hand and pulled her to the floor next to him. He held her close, and she melted against him. "We'll have to move. I've been offered a ministry position at the Flannel Shirt Chapel in Thermopolis."

"Flannel Shirt Chapel?" Randi snorted. "That's the name? I guess it would make some truckers less reluctant to try it out. I haven't heard of it before."

"They're just starting it."

"You won't be driving?"

"Not at all, except to get to work."

"But your dream. . ."

"You are my new dream," Matthew said just before he kissed her. And when he did, he realized this was the dream God planned for him long ago.

Epilogue

Matthew sat at the picnic table at his parents' farm. Emma sat across from him. "Emma, I'd like to discuss something with you."

"Am I in trouble?"

Matthew reached across the table and grasped her hand. "No, Emma, you're not. I have something important I want to ask you, though." He and Randi had discussed this moment earlier, but now he felt tongue-tied.

"Do I have to do something, like chores, to get an allowance when you're married?"

Emma swung her foot under the table and it connected with Matthew's leg. "I'm sorry!"

"That's okay; just try to sit still for a minute." Matthew took a deep breath. "Emma, at the wedding, I—your aunt and I—would like you to be a part of the ceremony."

"I know already. Aunt Randi told me I get to carry flowers and walk in front of her."

"Yes, but there is something else. I'd like to promise you that I'll be a good father to you, and so you'll remember that promise, I'd like to give you a ring that day, too."

"Can I change my last name to Carter like Aunt Randi?" Emma's brow wrinkled as she said, "Emma Carter. I like that name better than Emma Bell."

Matthew grinned. He hadn't expected her desire to have the same name, but it made sense. He liked the idea. "I think that would be a fine idea, Emma, but I think we should ask your dad how he feels about that."

"Maybe he'll say yes because you're going to be my newest dad and he's my old dad. Can I get a wedding dress?"

Matthew looked into those eyes and knew she would be wrapping him around his finger by the end of the day. "A wedding dress?"

"Yes. I should have one. So when are we going shopping?"

❧

The trailer that housed the Flannel Shirt Chapel smelled of roses. Jess had worked magic to make the dark brown room special. Lilac bows graced the sides of the folding chairs, and vases of flowers adorned the small altar.

Emma twirled, and the tulle of her white dress billowed in a circle around her. "I'm getting married today!" Randi and Emma were busting with excitement when they came home from their shopping trip. Matthew even bought Emma a short veil to go with the dress. Randi smiled and then said, "I'm getting married, Emma; you're getting a dad. I think it's just about time for you to walk down the aisle, so let's get your veil on those shiny curls."

Music floated from the doorway, and Randi whispered to Emma, "It's your turn."

Emma took tiny steps, looking every bit the bride she wanted to be. Then Randi took a step inside. Her mother and Matthew's parents were in the front row. They stood, turning to watch her entrance. Randi knew Jess and Mike were there, and Brad, the driver who helped save her, but she didn't see them. The only person she saw was the man waiting for her at the end of her walk. Matthew Carter, soon to be her very own Preacher Man. Her day had come; her dream was a reality.

After the ceremony, Emma led the way out. She burst through the door shouting, "We're married!"

Randi and Matthew walked through the doorway. Matthew turned Randi toward him and leaned in for a kiss. A line of trucks led by the Groovy Grannies in their bright pink rig began blowing their horns, issuing a wedding salute, trucker style, as they circled the truck stop.

DIANA LESIRE BRANDMEYER, a multi-published author, lives in Southern Illinois with her husband, Ed, and their cats, Wendell and Oliver. They have three grown sons and two terrific daughters-in-law. Diana is a graduate of Webster University in St. Louis. She spends her spare time quilting, scrap-booking, bike riding, and reading, but not at the same time.

A WAGONLOAD OF TROUBLE

VICKIE McDONOUGH

Dedication

This book is dedicated to Mike and Kathleen Rasco. They've been our closest friends for as long as I can remember and are a very kind and generous couple. My husband, Robert, and I have laughed with them, gone to myriad dinners and movies together, and Kathleen and I enjoy beating Robert and Mike at Canasta and board games. Good friends are a blessing from God, and I thank Him for bringing Mike and Kathleen into our lives.

Chapter 1

I'm sorry, ma'am, but there are not sufficient funds in your account to cash this check."

Bethany Schaffer stared at the young female teller, confusion clouding her mind. Why would her father send her a check for traveling expenses back home if there was no money in the ranch account? And how could that be? The dark-eyed bank clerk handed back her check and a receipt with the balance of the account imprinted on it then glanced down at the counter and fiddled with a pen.

Bethany stared at the paper. *$56.38? There's no way this can be right.*

She glanced up at the teller. "Are you certain you entered the correct account number? For Moose Valley Ranch? I'm Bethany Schaffer, and my father owns the ranch."

The woman nodded. "I'm sure, but I can check again if you'd like."

"Yes. Please do."

The teller tapped on her keyboard, her lips pursed. A few seconds later, she turned the monitor so Bethany could read it.

As if she'd jumped into a frigid lake in late December, a cold numbness seeped through her. She double-checked the name at the top of the screen and the account number. How could the ranch's balance be so low? Dad hadn't mentioned any financial troubles, and there had been at least forty thousand dollars last time she checked the account. Her dad had never been great with numbers, but to allow that bank account to get so low—it didn't make sense. Could something be wrong with him? Bethany thanked the teller then turned away, still trying to make sense of the account balance. The ranch had been through many hard times in the eighty years her family had owned it, but to be scraping the bottom of the barrel. . .

She stuck the useless check and her ID back into her purse. She hadn't even planned to cash it, but a nail in her tire had caused an added expense on the way home. She walked over to the ATM, pulled out her debit card, and made a withdrawal from her personal account so that she'd have enough cash to fill her gas tank and make it to the ranch. Then she returned to her Jeep.

Her father sure had some explaining to do. How could he have used up so much money? Had there been some big emergency that he hadn't told her about? As long as she'd been old enough to help with the bookkeeping, Moose Valley's balance had never even been close to zero.

Concern battled irritation. Bethany popped the Jeep into gear, squealing the tires as she pulled out of the parking lot. She'd wanted to leave Moose

Valley Ranch and its boring life in the Upper Wind River valley of western Wyoming, and she had. She slapped the steering wheel and pulled into the gas station. Her heart suddenly constricted. Had Dad called her home to tell her he was bankrupt? Could they lose the ranch?

The ranch had been the only home she'd known until she had gone away to college. As much as she had wanted to leave, she hated the thought of not having a home to return to. She studied the small town as she pumped the gas. In the four years that she'd been attending college in Denver, little had changed. Many of the old, familiar businesses were still there behind the Old West storefront facades, but new ones had also sprung up in the scenic tourist town. With the badlands to the east and mountain peaks surrounding the town on the west, south, and north, there were endless things for visitors to see and do. Bethany rubbed the back of her neck and stuck the nozzle back into the gas pump. Her family's guest ranch was just one that competed against many others for the tourist dollars that saw them through the long winters. Why, she couldn't begin to count the number of trail rides she'd led or accident-prone greenhorns she'd doctored.

But she'd hoped all that was in her past.

She paid the clerk inside the store and headed back to her Jeep. In just three weeks she would start working as an accountant for a big manufacturing plant in Denver. She'd have health insurance and benefits. She had less than a month to get things straightened out at the ranch so that she was free to begin her new life.

She started up the engine. Yep, just three weeks. Then she could kiss the Wyoming wilderness good-bye and return to the big city and all its amenities. Her thoughts traveled back to the bank account as she pulled onto the highway. Her stomach swirled as her mind was assaulted with concerns. What could have happened at the ranch to deplete their whole bank account? Why hadn't her dad called her sooner? What if she couldn't fix the problems in such a short time?

❧

Evan Parker leaned toward his computer monitor and maneuvered the tiny video game character—a character who looked amazingly like himself—through a maze of challenging hazards and over a hill to a tree abounding in colorful fruits labeled with the names of the fruits of the Spirit. The little man leaped up and plucked an apple labeled LOVE off a branch and dropped it into the basket that sat under the tree. The counter at the top of the screen added another 100 points to his score. The character snagged another fruit marked PATIENCE.

"C'mon, keep going. Don't crash on me now." He jiggled the game controller, and the man grabbed a rotten apple and yanked it off the tree. A spiraling sound echoed from the speakers, and the monitor screen went blank. Evan flopped back in his office chair, the weight of his body sending it rolling backward. *Not again.*

"See, I told you the game was still crashing at that spot," said Ben Walker, a member of the game design team, through the speaker phone. "Several of the programmers here at headquarters looked at it, but they can't find the problem."

"I've redone the code on that section three times, but I must have missed something. I'll have another look at it after dinner." Evan rolled his head around to work the kinks out of his neck, leaned back in his chair, and looked at the ceiling of his home office. He needed to get past this problem and work on the next section of the Christian video game he was helping design. He had to succeed. His dream was riding on this.

"Hey, sweat not," Ben said, "we're a little ahead of schedule."

"Thanks. Listen, I'm having dinner at my sister's house tonight, so I've got to go." Evan started the shutdown on his computer and turned off his monitor.

"Mmm. . .home-cooked food. Lucky you. I'm having my usual three-course microwave supper tonight. Talk to you tomorrow."

The line went dead, and Evan clicked off his phone. He ought to be working tonight, but Erin had wooed him with not just one of his favorites—chicken and dumplings—but also with butterscotch pie.

What could his sister want to talk about that required her to make two of his favorite foods? He searched his mind, trying to remember if she'd mentioned something to him before about watching the kids or doing a job he'd forgotten about, but he drew a blank.

He took a quick shower then gelled his short hair, raking his fingers through it until it looked passable. He rubbed his hand over his five o'clock shadow. "Better to skip shaving than be late to dinner, dude."

He grabbed a shirt off the back of a kitchen chair and sniffed to make sure it was still clean. Five minutes later he was on his way. As he drove past the quiet University of Wyoming campus, he felt his tense neck and shoulder muscles begin to relax. "No classes to teach this summer. No, sir."

No more lesson plans to prepare or projects or papers to grade. He turned the vehicle onto Erin's street, grinning. And if things went as planned, he'd never have to go back to teaching. Not that teaching was bad, but he wanted more freedom with his schedule—and landing the gaming contract was just what he needed.

He stopped at a red light. In the two weeks since the spring semester had ended, he'd gotten quite a bit of programming done on the video game. Not as much as he'd hoped, but at least he wasn't behind schedule.

Five minutes later he pulled into Erin's driveway. But his ten-year-old nephew didn't come flying out the door upon Evan's arrival like he usually did. He climbed out of his new hybrid SUV and beeped the lock and alarm on the remote then ran his hand along the blue paint, marveling at the fact that he'd finally purchased his dream machine. As he walked up the driveway, he noted again that Erin's house needed to be painted. Somehow he'd have to squeeze in time for that while the weather was warm.

He stepped into the modest home that smelled like fresh-cooked chicken. His stomach growled, and he was glad that he'd taken the time to come. He crossed through the entryway and noted the empty kitchen. The pot on the stove beckoned him, and he couldn't resist swiping his finger along the top and sticking it into his mouth. "Mmm. Awesome!"

"It's not the same, Mom. He'll ruin everything." Taylor's loud voice reverberated down the short hallway.

What had Jamie done to upset the finicky fourteen-year-old girl now? Evan wanted his own kids one day but wouldn't mind if they could just skip the whole teen scene. Being a single mother, Erin had her hands full and didn't need Taylor acting up. He could hear Erin's soft, patient voice replying to Taylor but couldn't make out the words.

"But, Mo–om. He's such a geek."

Ouch! Geek didn't begin to describe sports-minded Jamie, so Taylor must have been upset about someone else. He didn't know whom Taylor referred to, but he felt sorry for the guy. He returned to the kitchen and set the table. What was so bad about being a geek anyway?

Footsteps echoed behind him, and he glanced over his shoulder. His sister's lips were pressed into a thin line, but her blue eyes lit when she saw him. "Hey! I didn't hear you come in."

"I get to sneak bites that way." He grinned.

Erin looked at the pot on the stove, where its lid sat crooked. "You did steal a bite, you rascal."

Evan held up his hands. "Guilty as charged."

His sister pulled down three bowls. "Jamie isn't eating. He's got chicken pox." The last word came out on a sigh.

"That stinks." Evan scratched his arm and then crinkled his brow. Two days ago he and Jamie had been roughhousing, and he'd seemed fine then. Evan sure didn't need to get sick this summer with all he had to do. "Have I had them?"

"Yeah, we both have. Although, if I remember correctly, you only had a very mild case. Taylor had them in kindergarten, so she's safe. Don't you remember how she cried when she missed so much school that fall? Oh, how times change." Erin shook her head. She pulled the lid off the chicken and dumplings, and the kitchen filled with the fragrant scent, making Evan's mouth water as she dished up the three bowls. Erin added a scoop of green peas to each bowl and set them on the table. "Taylor, dinner's ready."

Evan fixed two glasses of water and one of milk for Taylor and set them beside the bowls; then he took his spot at the head of the table. He didn't like sitting in the place that had belonged to Erin's ex-husband, but the small table only had four places, and that was Evan's regular spot.

Taylor stomped into the kitchen, gave him the evil eye, and slumped onto her chair. She crossed her arms and stared at her cup. "I hate milk."

Evan lifted one eyebrow. "Since when?"

Taylor rolled her eyes. "Since like forever."

He resisted responding. It would only make things worse. For as long as he could remember, Taylor had loved milk. Everything about her was changing. The sweet, happy girl he'd played board games with had morphed into a snobbish teenager with a bad attitude.

He grabbed her cup and swapped it with his.

"Hey!" Taylor scowled.

"Hey what? You said you hated milk, so I graciously traded with you."

The teen looked as if she wanted to argue, but he had her, and she knew it. Erin sat down and made eye contact with him, letting him know not to encourage Taylor. He crossed his arms over his chest. "I'm only trying to keep her happy."

Looking tired, Erin bowed her head. "Just pray. Please."

With dumplings awaiting, he made short work of the prayer and picked up his spoon. "Mmm-mmm. Delicious as always."

"It's a bribe," Taylor spouted then filled her mouth.

Evan didn't want to examine what she meant and quickly devoured his meal. With his stomach warm and nearly full, he leaned one arm over the back of his chair. "Too bad Jamie got sick with summer just starting. Guess that means he won't be going on that wagon train trip with you."

Erin set her spoon down and stared at him.

Uh-oh. He knew that look. "I can't watch him. You know I have to finish that video game by mid-August, plus, what do I know about caring for a sick kid?"

Taylor snorted, and Erin's mouth twisted in a wry grimace. He looked from mother to daughter. What had he missed?

"You're not getting off that easy." Taylor grabbed the glass of milk and gave him back his water.

"I thought you hated that."

Taylor shrugged. "It goes good with this meal."

Erin stood and collected the bowls, took them to the sink, and filled them with water. She pulled the pie from the fridge and set it on the counter. All manner of thoughts raced through his mind. Could he watch Jamie and still do his work? Erin lifted a fat golden triangle topped with white meringue, and his mouth watered.

His sister didn't have an Internet hookup. After dealing with her husband's pornography problem, she refused to have online service, even though Taylor constantly complained that it made doing her schoolwork more difficult. Maybe if Jamie wasn't hurling all the time, he could stay at Evan's house. He scratched his neck. Did kids hurl when they had the chicken pox?

His sister set a heaping slice of butterscotch pie in front of him, and he picked up his fork. His mother's recipe was the best he'd ever eaten. He closed his eyes and let the sweet caramel flavor tease his senses. Maybe if he agreed to watch his nephew, she'd send the rest of the pie home with him. He didn't mind eating pie for breakfast, lunch, and dinner.

Erin cleared her throat and glanced at Taylor. Evan realized that neither had taken a bite of her dessert.

"Just tell him, Mom, and get it over with." Taylor sighed and rolled her eyes again. "This really stinks."

Erin heaved a sigh. "I need to ask a big favor of you."

Here it comes. "Well. . .shoot."

"Since Jamie is sick, we can't go with Taylor on the wagon train trip we've planned for all year. Jamie is heartbroken. I want to know if you'll go with Taylor." She turned her fork facedown and then faceup, over and over, but didn't look at him.

Evan let the words process in his mind for a minute. She wasn't asking him to watch Jamie—and he'd nearly had that all worked out in his head. She wanted him to leave Laramie and drive out west toward the Tetons—out in the sticks.

Nobody said a word. They all knew it took him time to process a decision like this. Taylor wolfed down her pie, but Erin didn't touch hers. Evan felt his eyes widen. She was asking him to go on a two-week wagon ride in the wilds of Wyoming. Him, a bona fide geek, who hated bugs, snakes—nature—and had hardly traveled anywhere. "You can't be serious."

"See?" Taylor curled her lip at him. "I told you he wouldn't do it. He's such a nerd."

"Taylor. That's no way to talk about your uncle, especially after all he's done for us."

"Well, it's the truth." She flung down her fork and stood. "Just cancel the whole trip. I didn't want to go anyway."

Numb to her insult because it was the truth, Evan watched his niece stomp out of the room.

"She doesn't mean that." Erin sighed and pushed her uneaten pie toward the center of the table. "You know how her American history class at school worked the whole year to raise money for this trip, and she can't go without an adult escort. I wouldn't ask you to go, but Taylor has had her heart set on this for so long. It's the only thing I've seen her excited about since Clint left.

I can't go because I need to be here to care for Jamie."

"I could keep Jamie." How did he go from *No way am I watching Jamie* to acquiescing? It was the lesser evil, that's how.

"You wouldn't know what to do to make him comfortable. He'd be complaining and bugging you all the time to play video games and keeping you from your work."

Evan leaned forward, elbows on the table. "And how will I work if I go into the high country? They probably don't even have Internet at this place—what's it called?"

"Moose Valley Ranch, and I'm sure they do since they have a Web site with an e-mail link. I know it's a lot to ask, but it's only two weeks. It would do you good to get outside and get some sun."

"So it's about me now?" Evan stood and took his plate and cup to the sink. "Besides, I get sun every morning when I go jogging."

"Sorry, I didn't mean to lay a guilt trip on you, but this trip wasn't cheap. You know the jillions of fund-raisers Taylor did. You contributed to all of them, and I've saved for a year because Taylor wanted to go so badly."

"Can't you get a refund?"

"Maybe. I don't know." Erin threw up her hands and sighed. "I don't want Taylor to be disappointed. She's had so few things to smile about lately. Besides"—Erin looked to the left and right then leaned forward, her expression pleading—"I need a break from her," she whispered then looked at the ground. "I know that sounds horrible, but it's true."

Evan felt as cornered as his video character when it had stumbled into Daniel's lions' den after making a wrong move. Without Daniel's level of faith, his character hadn't survived. Evan wanted to help his sister and niece, but could he give up two weeks and still finish his project on time? Maybe he could work on the game in his free time, and if the guest ranch had Internet access, he could still turn in his progress reports and contact the others on his team if he had a question. "When is this trip?"

His sister's lips pursed, and she seemed to be studying something fascinating on the wall. "Uh. . .ten days from now."

Evan's eyes widened, then he schooled his expression. *When* didn't really matter. Anytime this summer was a bad time. Erin didn't know he wanted to quit teaching and work permanently from home for the computer company so that he'd have more time to help her out with the kids. There was no way of escape without disappointing someone. It might as well be himself. "All right, I'll do it."

Erin's tense expression morphed into a smile that made him glad he'd agreed. He'd have to remember that grin when he was knee-deep in wild-flowers and bugs, and stuck with a cranky teenager with a Teton-size attitude.

Chapter 2

A familiar warmth tugged at Bethany's heart as she drove up the mile-long dirt road leading to the main lodge of Moose Valley Ranch. Home. So familiar, but so vastly different from the city where she now lived. An array of wildflowers painted the meadow on her left yellow and white, while conifers, aspens, and lodgepole pines rose up on her right, creating a natural windbreak. She hadn't been back to Moose Valley since last year's Christmas holiday. She should have come home on spring break, but instead she'd gotten a job and worked. The excuse had felt legitimate at the time. Rolling her head, she tried to work loose her tight shoulder muscles.

"Why should I feel guilty? Wasn't that the whole reason for going to college?" *So I could get an education and support myself—and leave Moose Valley behind?*

If nothing else, she should have returned sooner just to see her dad. But it wasn't as if he were all alone. Anywhere from six to twelve employees helped with cleaning the guest cabins, cooking, caring for the horses, and managing the wagon tours and trail rides. Bethany heaved a sigh and honked her horn at the small herd of Black Angus moseying across the dirt road. Leaning out her window, she yelled, "C'mon. Move it."

Taking out her frustrations on dumb cattle and rationalizing that her dad had plenty of help didn't drive away her guilt. The bottom line was that she had neglected him. If only he'd step into the twenty-first century, then she could have e-mailed him. A lot of good it did to have a Web site for the ranch and e-mail contact if he wouldn't learn to use it. Maybe he'd be more willing once she hooked up the new state-of-the-art computer she'd brought home with her.

As the last calf bawled and trotted after its mother, Bethany pounded her fist on the steering wheel and stepped on the gas. She topped the final hill, and Moose Valley spread out before her, mountains jutting up high on her left and in front of her, and the forest on her right. The sight certainly was magnificent and rivaled anything Colorado had to offer. So why wasn't she content to stay here?

Shaking off her nostalgic melancholy, she sped down the dirt road and parked in front of the main lodge. The near-empty parking lot, which should have been packed with the vehicles of summer visitors, captured her attention. Where were all the cars? Summer was their busy season—the time they earned enough money to run on the rest of the year. Trying not to worry, she slipped out of the Jeep, lips pursed, and jogged up the steps to the main entrance.

A WAGONLOAD OF TROUBLE

Inside, nothing had changed. The woodlands decor of the three-story building was the same, but no one stood at the registration desk to welcome her. Maggie Holmes had occupied that job last summer and was supposed to be back this year. "Hellooo. . .Maggie? Dad?"

No reply. "Weird." Bethany slipped behind the counter and into the back office. Her father sat at his desk, one hand forked into his hair, studying a ledger book. She didn't want to startle him, so she edged beside him, shuffling her shoes.

He lowered his hand and looked up at her, his dark eyes staring blankly for a moment. Then he blinked and suddenly focused on her. A smile tugged at his lips. "Beth, you're home. At last."

He stood, and she fell into his arms, just as she'd done so many times before. Why had she stayed away so long?

After a warm moment, she stepped back, crossed her arms, and leaned against the desk. "So. . .where's Maggie, and why is the bank account so low?"

A smile tilted one corner of her dad's mouth. "Always one to get right to the point, huh?"

Bethany shrugged. "And while we're at it, why aren't there many cars in the lot? I thought we were booked solid for the summer."

Rob Schaffer ran a hand through his thick silver hair, which contrasted nicely with his Wyoming sun-baked skin. Tiny lines crinkled in the corners of his dark brown eyes, and she realized for the first time that he was starting to age. When had that happened?

He sighed and dropped back into his chair.

She lowered her hip to the side of his desk. "You told me last time I talked to you that we had a full slate of customers lined up—even had to turn some folks away."

He fiddled with a pen but didn't look up at her. "We were booked solid, but the past couple of weeks a lot of people have called and canceled their reservations. Almost like an epidemic. I don't know if it has to do with the economy or something else."

He ran his hand through his hair. "I had to refund so many deposits that I had to let some of the workers go." He glanced up, then his gaze darted away. "Maggie, too."

Bethany felt her eyes widen. They had never laid off employees before. "How many?"

He huffed a sigh so heavy that it fluttered the papers on the desk. "Eight."

She tried to wrap her mind around how they could function with so few remaining workers. She stood and paced to the wall that held pictures of past guests then turned and walked the few feet to the other wall. "What about the customers who came the past few weeks? What happened to their payment money?"

"Bills. Payroll. You know the routine. I'm sorry you had to come home and find things in such a mess. Your mother never would have let things get like this." He rubbed his hand across his jaw. "I know you're planning to start work at that new job soon, but I didn't know what else to do except to call you home. I can't run this place by myself anymore and tend to the cattle, too."

Concern washed over Bethany in waves, mixing with the confusing thoughts assaulting her. Was he sick? Was the ranch too much work now that he was getting older? "Dad, you're not sick, are you?"

His head jerked up, eyes wide. "No, of course not."

She eyed him, but he looked sincere. "Are we in any danger of losing the ranch?"

He shook his head. "The ranch has been paid off for years, but things may be lean for a while."

Bethany flipped through the pages of the receipts ledger. Income was definitely down. "I don't understand. We had plenty of money in the bank when I left here at Christmas. What happened to it all?"

Her father looked away. A muscle in his jaw tightened.

"Dad?"

"I suppose you'll find out anyway." He glanced up and stood. "I probably should have just made payments, but I wanted to get those loans off my books and off my shoulders." He looked out the office door as if gathering his courage then faced her again. "It went to pay off your college loans."

Her head swirled with thoughts as she tried to grasp what he'd said. He'd paid off her student loans? She'd never asked him to cover them. She'd planned to pay them off herself. Sure, it would take awhile, but she'd get it done. But now there were no loans, only a ranch—a family legacy—on the brink of financial disaster. The floor seemed to shift under her. Bethany reached out to a nearby bookcase to steady herself.

The deplorable state of the ranch's finances was all her fault?

Evan eased up on the gas and guided the SUV around a pothole the size of his bathtub. He'd saved for years to buy his new vehicle, and he wasn't going to ruin it driving on a gravel road at a ridiculous speed just to please his niece.

"We'll never get there at this rate." Taylor stared out her window, arms crossed, and slouched back in the seat. "I don't know why we couldn't have caravanned with my class."

"We should be there any time now, and then you can see your friends. The sign where we turned off said it was just another mile."

They crested a hill, and an eye-catching valley spread out before them. He wanted to take a moment to savor the panoramic view, but he had a restless teenager prodding him on. He steered the SUV toward the largest building, an Alpine lodge with a parking lot out front. A sign identified the place as the dining hall and registration building. He parked, climbed out, and looked around as he stretched the kinks out of his stiff back. A large barn sat off to his left with tall mountain peaks jutting up behind it. As much as he'd dreaded coming on this trip, he had to admit the place looked like it was straight out of an Old West movie, all except for the alpine architecture.

"Nice, huh?" Taylor stopped beside him and leaned against the SUV.

"Yep. Not as rustic as I'd expected." Evan glanced at her, hoping the snaps on the back of her jeans didn't scratch his paint.

"Should we unload?"

He shook his head. "Let's check in first. We may not be staying in this building."

Taylor used her foot to push away from the vehicle, and Evan winced. He followed her up the steps and into the lodge. Fragrant scents of something cooking greeted them.

"Too cool! Look at that moose head." She pointed over the registration desk. "You think they shot that here? I wonder if we'll see a live moose."

Evan shrugged. A pretty blond walked through a door behind the counter and smiled.

"Welcome to Moose Valley Ranch. I'm Bethany Schaffer."

Evan held out his hand. Warm brown eyes captured his and sent his pulse skyrocketing. The woman's honey blond hair draped around her shoulders in pleasant waves. She scowled, and Taylor nudged him in the side. He realized he still held the woman's hand and released it.

"And you would be?" Miss Schaffer's brow lifted, making those chocolate eyes look larger.

Taylor cleared her throat. "I'm Taylor Anderson, and this is my uncle, Evan Parker. I'm part of the Oak Hill Junior High class."

Evan shifted his feet. He should have introduced himself instead of letting Taylor do it, but his tongue didn't want to work for some strange reason. Must be the fresh mountain air.

Miss Schaffer pulled out a thick ledger book and ran her finger down a list of names. "I have a reservation for an Erin, Jamie, and Taylor Anderson, but not a Mr. Parker." She looked up without raising her head.

Evan forced his voice into action. "Erin's my sister, but she had to stay home with my nephew—Jamie—who has chicken pox."

"Hmm. . .well, that may create a problem."

Evan's gaze wandered to the huge moose head on the wall behind the counter; then the woman's words registered. "What kind of problem?"

Miss Schaffer straightened and tapped her pencil on the counter. "Miss Anderson requested a single room with a king-size bed and a rollaway. I assume you would prefer a room of your own rather than sharing one with your niece. Am I wrong?"

He digested her words and suddenly realized what she meant. Heat warmed his face as he thought of sharing a single room with his cantankerous niece. He wouldn't get a lick of work done, not to mention it didn't seem proper. "Uh. . .do you have a two-bedroom suite by chance? With wireless Internet?"

The young woman's pink lips puckered as she checked a file box filled with colored index cards. "I have a two-bedroom cabin available with a kitchenette. It doesn't have Internet service but has a color TV. The cost is more than what you were charged for a room in our Muskrat Lodge." She waved a hand over her shoulder. "That's the wide, two-story building behind this lodge. Of course, your niece will be farther from her friends, since they're all staying at Muskrat."

Evan considered what she said. It was logical that a cabin would cost more, but since Jamie wasn't here, they should still get a refund. He couldn't expect full reimbursement at this late date, but surely they should grant a partial one. Maybe he could get the cabin and still get back some money for Erin. But then the cabin didn't have Internet service.

"Since my brother couldn't come, shouldn't we get back the money we paid for him? It was an awful lot." Taylor lifted her chin and boldly spouted the very words that had crossed Evan's mind, although she used less tact than he would have. She tapped her neon blue nails on the counter.

Miss Schaffer's brown eyes widened, and a look of panic dashed across her face before she schooled her expression. She gazed at him. "Surely you can't expect a refund at this late date, Mr. Parker. We reserved a place for your nephew, and while I'm sorry that he got sick and couldn't come, it isn't our fault."

Evan straightened. He hated confrontation, but it was Erin's money that was on the line. "I think some kind of reimbursement is in order. You won't have to feed a growing adolescent."

"And can Jamie ever pack away food! Consider yourself lucky." Taylor nibbled at the nail on her index finger then looked down at it.

Myriad expressions passed over Miss Schaffer's pretty face.

"We can wait if you need to check with your supervisor," Evan said.

The woman narrowed her eyes. "I don't have a supervisor, Mr. Parker. My father and I own this facility."

Evan swallowed, feeling thoroughly put in his place. Why hadn't he considered she might live here?

Her expression softened. "How about I let you have the cabin and not charge you extra, and we'll call it even?"

Evan shook his head. "I've got to have a room with an Internet connection. Don't you have any at all? My sister said you have a Web site and e-mail address, so you have to have a Web connection somewhere."

She pursed her lips. "Part of the reason people come to Moose Valley is to get away from things like the Internet. You'll only be in your room two nights before the wagon train starts. Surely you can do without the Internet for that short amount of time."

For a resort owner, the gal sure wasn't very hospitable. Evan straightened. The fragrant aromas wafting from the direction of the dining hall tugged at his attention and made his stomach grumble. His mouth watered, but he forced his mind back to the business at hand. "I'm on a short deadline at work. I hadn't planned to make this trip, but I did it to help out my sister."

"Humph." Taylor glared at him then walked over to a rocker facing a large picture window with an inspiring view and plunked herself down.

"*And* to help my niece." Too little too late to pacify the finicky teen, but he had to make the effort. He didn't want her to think that he didn't want to be here, even though she already did.

Miss Schaffer rummaged through the file box again. The buildings at the ranch looked fairly up-to-date, but the place was so backward they hadn't even computerized their registration information. So much for twenty-first-century living. The woman pressed her lips together until they turned into a thin line. She was pretty, in an earthy way, with her sun-kissed tan and golden hair.

She looked up and caught him watching her, and her brow crinkled. "I do have a luxury suite available that has two bedrooms and Internet. It's on the second floor of this building. I suppose I could let you have it—if we called things even."

He wouldn't get any money back for Erin if he agreed. He looked around the lodge as he considered the offer. The inside was filled with thick pine furnishings with woodland animal decorations. Off to his right was a small gift shop and snack bar with a sign on the window that read MOOSE VALLEY MERCANTILE. The door was open and the light was on, but nobody was inside. Maybe he could get a caffeine fix in there.

Miss Schaffer cleared her throat. "Will that do, Mr. Parker?"

Taylor stopped rocking and glanced over her shoulder. "You have to give him a minute to think things through. You know that Bible verse that says to be slow to speak? Well, that was written for my uncle."

Evan scowled. She made him sound like an idiot. He couldn't help that he had to look at things from different angles before making a decision. His brain functioned more like a ten-year-old PC than one of the new quad-core processors now available on computers. Since the woman didn't seem willing to grant Erin a refund no matter what, and he did need Internet service and two bedrooms, he might as well accept the offer. It sounded like the best he was likely to get. He nodded. "All right. It's a deal."

Miss Schaffer stared at the hand he'd extended in her direction for the second time and finally reached out and shook it. Evan felt as if a power spike surged through his body at her touch, and he stared at the woman. Her curious gaze captured his, then she frowned and tugged her hand away.

"Yes. . .well. . .I'll need to make sure that suite is ready since we didn't have anyone booked in there. Let me get the key, and I'll check it while you two have a look around. Would you like to purchase a snack to eat while you wait?"

Evan looked over his shoulder at Taylor, who stood and faced him. She nodded.

"Sounds good."

They followed the young woman into the tiny store, and Evan couldn't help noticing her shapely figure and easy gait. He forced his attention on the glass refrigerator, which held a variety of pop and bottles of juice. He and Taylor each selected a can, and she snagged a candy bar while he chose a granola bar. Evan noticed several packages of computer cables hanging on the wall and selected one. Obviously, he wasn't the first to show up expecting wireless Internet. Miss Schaffer rang up their purchase, and he paid her.

"You're welcome to look in the barn, but don't handle the horses unless one of the staff is around."

He thought about his odd reaction to Miss Schaffer's touch. Though twenty-eight, he'd had few dates. Not that he didn't want to date; he'd just never met a woman who stirred his interest long enough to maintain a long-term relationship. Evan watched her turn and walk back into the other room. Her black capris and pink knit top looked out of place for a dude ranch, and she sounded well educated. Where could she have gone to college way out here? She mumbled something to an older gentleman in the office behind the counter.

The man leaned back in his chair and waved at Evan. "I'm Rob Schaffer. Welcome to Moose Valley."

Evan nodded and popped the lid of his Coke can. It hissed and sent up a sweet scent. He took a swig, and his gaze followed the young woman as she climbed the stairs to the right of the mercantile. In spite of their rocky start, Evan hoped that he might get to know Bethany Schaffer better. Not that there was any reason to. But she intrigued him. And that was enough to make him want to learn more about her.

*

"Thought you said you weren't ever going on another one of these tours." Big Jim Reynolds gave Bethany a cocky grin and stacked the last crate of supplies into the back of the ranch's Jeep.

Heat warmed her cheeks. "I know what I said. I'd hoped I'd seen my last trip, but it wasn't to be." If she didn't have to lead this tour, she'd be assembling the new computer and inputting their records onto the new accounting program she'd purchased, but that would have to wait until she returned.

Bethany slung her gear onto the back passenger seat and glanced at the crates of supplies. She'd checked through all the boxes last night and made sure they had everything on the list. She closed the side door, grateful to have the vehicle leading the way. There had been a time or two on past treks that the truck had been needed in case of an emergency. She hoped they wouldn't have to deal with anything that severe on this trip.

"Hey, kiddo."

She spun around at the sound of her father's voice. "Where are you going?"

He patted his chest pocket and smiled. "The bank. That schoolteacher gave us a nice, fat check."

"Whew! Let's not cut it so close next time."

"Hopefully there won't be a next time."

She watched him amble to his pickup, and then she turned to study the group of guests gathered round, waiting to leave for the first day of the two-week tour. A boy who looked to be around thirteen sneaked up behind two girls and waved a lizard in their faces. The girls squealed and chased him around a parked car.

Bethany scanned the crowd of teenagers, mostly decked out in new cowboy or mountain boots, jeans, and long-sleeved shirts. Several sported fleece-lined vests or had jackets tied around their waists. It may be summer, but at an elevation of over seven thousand feet, the days could be cool and the nights just plain cold. Satisfied that everyone had complied with the rules to bring some type of outerwear, she headed for her wagon.

"You get him, Lacy," a tall boy yelled at the girls who were still trying to catch the boy with the lizard. Suddenly he stopped and turned around with the lizard pointed outward in one hand. The girls skidded to a stop on the rocky ground, screamed, and ran the other direction. A group of boys howled with laughter.

Bethany shook her head. They wouldn't be so loud and feisty tomorrow morning after the excitement wore off, their iPods had run out of power, and they grew bored with the view of the forest and mountains. It was always the same, trip after boring trip. She rubbed the back of her stiff neck. The only workers staying behind besides her dad were the dining room cook, one maid to clean the rooms of the few ranch guests not going on the wagon tour, and the ranch foreman. Never in her memory had they ever been stretched so thin.

And it was all her fault.

No, it wasn't completely her fault. Dad could have made payments on those loans or left them for her just as she'd planned. The check from the school group would help, but they weren't out of the woods yet.

Bethany crossed the graveled parking lot and examined the wagon she'd be driving. She checked the harnesses, knowing Big Jim didn't need her supervising, but it was a habit she'd formed at fifteen when she'd first helped lead tours.

"Gather around, everybody." Behind her, a woman shouted at all the school kids and their parents. "I have your wagon assignments." She rattled off a list of names, and a noisy group of adults and teens headed for the first wagon.

Bethany wasn't sure why she was relieved when Evan Parker's niece headed for the second wagon instead of the final one that Bethany would be driving, but not having to ride with the computer geek and his bad-attitude niece was fine with her. She double-checked the ties that held up the sides of the wagon's canvas top to allow their guests to enjoy the breathtaking views. The wagon creaked as it filled with passengers. The rubber tires, which provided a smoother ride, looked fully aired up. Everything was a go.

She climbed up to her bench seat and noticed a small tear in the canvas canopy. That would have to be repaired. If it got much larger, the whole wagon cover might have to be replaced. Bethany picked up the leather reins and watched the city slickers climb into wagon number two. Taylor Anderson was the last in line and chatted with another girl about the same size as her. Taylor looked over her shoulder as if searching for someone. A boy, probably. Wasn't that all most junior high girls were interested in?

Bethany had enjoyed meeting the boys who came to the ranch, but she'd never dated until she'd gone away to school. College. She exhaled a heavy sigh. If only her dad hadn't felt it necessary to pay off her college loans. She had never expected him to do so. Must go back to his heritage of caring for his own and not wanting to owe anybody anything. A man had to stand on his own two feet, he often said.

She breathed in a chest full of fresh air—so much cleaner than Denver's—and pulled her hair back, wrapped a thin elastic band around it, and stuck her hat back on. It might take her longer than she had planned to get things running smoothly again at the ranch. Would her new boss be willing to let her start a few weeks later than originally scheduled?

Big Jim stood outside the first wagon, next to the teacher who appeared to be counting heads. Her totals would have to agree with his before they took one step out of the parking lot. One of Bethany's draft horses shook his head and pawed the ground, eager to be off. The chatter level in the back of the wagon was high enough to send any country girl out into the wilderness in search of quiet. She'd learned long ago to put it out of her mind—but back then she'd been dreaming of her future away from the ranch.

"Someone's missing from this group," the teacher said. She held up her index finger and counted the people in the second wagon again and then looked at her chart. "There are only twelve in this wagon, but there should be thirteen."

A WAGONLOAD OF TROUBLE

Jim ambled over and counted, confirming that someone was missing.

Taylor Anderson leaned back in her seat and crossed her arms. Now that Bethany thought of it, she hadn't seen the girl's uncle once this morning. The memory of how her heart jumped as she looked into his startling blue eyes still made her pulse kick up a notch even now. Maybe he was tall and appealing with his lightly tanned skin and messed-up hair, but he sure was an oddball. A door slammed, and a man came jogging out the front door of the main lodge. He cradled a backpack in his arms like a baby and had a sleeping bag dangling from one hand and a duffel bag hanging over one shoulder.

Bethany shook her head as Evan Parker hurried toward the group, wearing a wrinkled oxford cloth shirt, khakis, and a worn pair of tennis shoes. On every trip she picked out the greenest of the greenhorns, and on this trip, it was definitely Evan Parker. Oh, he was cute enough with his short brown hair sprouting in different directions as if he'd just run his hand through it and those sky blue eyes, but he was city through and through.

The teacher saw him coming and glared in his direction, but she sashayed to Bethany's wagon and started counting. Big Jim cast a glance over his wide shoulder then looked up at Bethany, brows lifted. He shook his head and seemed to be stifling a smile.

A movement near the barn snagged Bethany's attention. A familiar reddish brown Rhode Island Red rooster strutted out of the barn, as if to say he was being left behind. "You forgot Ed."

Jim shook his head. "I didn't forget him. I just didn't want to have to listen to him squawking any longer than I had to. Soon as we're done counting, I'll catch him."

Ed added a dose of realism to the trip with his early morning cock-a-doodles. Some of their patrons loved the effect while others despised the crotchety old bird. Bethany pulled her attention back to Mr. Parker. He slowed his pace as he crossed into the parking lot, a look of relief on his face.

Ed suddenly made a beeline for the man, squawking and flapping his wings. Taylor's uncle didn't see the bird, which was coming up fast behind him.

Bethany stood, hoping to stop the man from getting pecked.

"Look out!" someone yelled from the first wagon.

Mr. Parker glanced over his shoulder at the same time Ed attacked his heel. He high-stepped toward the wagon, slapping the sleeping bag at the aggressive rooster and holding his backpack tight against his chest. Bethany bit her top lip to keep from laughing, but that didn't stop the teens in the wagons. Kids leaned out from the two wagons ahead, and Bethany felt her own tip to the left as people rushed to see. Cheers erupted, for both the bird and the man.

"Oh dear. Help me up." The teacher hurried into the back of Bethany's wagon with the assistance of one of the guests.

Mr. Parker glanced wide-eyed from wagon to wagon, and Bethany pointed at the one ahead of her. He pranced toward the wagon and leaped up the steps, collapsing in the seat across from Taylor.

Big Jim shook his head and grabbed the flapping rooster from behind as the laughter slowly died out. Taylor Anderson leaned back on the padded seat that ran along the right side of the wagon, looking as if she'd like to disappear. Evan Parker peered out the back of the wagon, and something like relief passed over his face when he saw Jim snag the rooster. He smiled at his niece and said something that made her roll her eyes and look away. He dropped his duffel bag to the floor and opened his backpack.

Bethany felt her eyes go wide as he pulled out a laptop. Never in all of her years at the ranch had anyone taken a computer on one of their tours. He leaned back on the seat, lifted his left ankle, and rested it on his knee. Then he set the computer on his lap, lifted the top, and waited until the screen lit up. After a few moments, his fingers zipped along at a fast pace, and the man seemed oblivious to his surroundings. What was so important on that computer that it couldn't wait for a few weeks?

She'd known the first time she saw Evan Parker that he'd most likely be the greenest of the city slickers. But not even she could have imagined this.

Chapter 3

Evan pursed his lips and hit the SAVE button. His last battery pack was almost out of power, and it was better to save the work he'd just completed and shut down the system than risk running totally out of juice and losing it. The computer fan ceased blowing. He closed the lid on his laptop and looked around. When the wagons had first left the ranch yard, the noise level had been so high he'd found it difficult to work, but once in his groove, he was able to tune out everyone. Typing while riding in a jostling wagon on a rutted road had been a whole other issue.

He stretched his arms, working the kinks out of his shoulders, and smiled at Taylor. She glared at him, crossed her arms, and looked out the back of the wagon. *Uh-oh, looks like I've done something wrong. Again.* He turned sideways and stared out the back of the wagon at the amazing view. A thick forest of dark green gave way to a trio of peaks that lifted their faces high into the sky. They were so tall that they still had snow on them. Were they the Tetons? He should know.

Following his wagon, Bethany Schaffer drove the last wagon. The pretty woman leaned forward with her elbows on her knees and the reins dangling in her hands. A dark brown Western hat shaded her face, and she appeared deep in thought. He figured it didn't take much effort to drive one of the Conestoga replicas. The horses were probably used to following the wagon in front of them.

"Whoa!" a man's voice called out from somewhere up ahead. Evan's wagon slowed.

"Sure is pretty out here, isn't it, Mr. Parker?"

Evan glanced across the wagon at Mrs. James. The thirtysomething brunette had been making eyes at him ever since she arrived at Moose Valley and had learned that he was single. He didn't want to encourage her but neither did he want to be rude. He shoved his laptop into the padded backpack, picked up his duffel bag, and glanced at her. "Uh. . .yeah. Real pretty."

She blushed. His gut twisted. She must have misconstrued his comment.

"What do we do now?" Mrs. James's daughter asked.

Taylor leaned forward. "I heard there was a lake we could swim in. I'm ready to get out of this wagon and do something fun."

Make that two. Evan climbed out and looked around. More than a dozen tents were mounted on wooden platforms in the grassy field. A brilliant blue lake was nestled at one end of the narrow valley and surrounded by mountains. He'd never been anywhere so. . .wild. He hugged his laptop nestled in his backpack. Surely there had to be a power source up here somewhere.

Taylor stood behind the black Jeep and waited her turn to claim her duffel bag. She smiled at Misty Chamberlain, her best friend, and Evan's heart warmed to see her happy. If not for her, he'd hightail it back to civilization.

Next month he'd be twenty-nine. On the same day, Taylor would be fifteen. She'd always been special because she'd been born on his birthday, but in the past year she'd morphed into someone he barely recognized. He hiked his duffel bag onto his shoulder. He was praying hard that this rebellious stage she was going through would be a short one.

Sighing, he watched Bethany Schaffer hop down from the wagon. She patted her team of horses and fiddled with one of the leather harnesses. What about her attracted him? After Sheri Carson dumped him for Mike-the-muscleman his sophomore year in college, he'd rarely dated. Keeping his nose in a computer was safer than risking his heart and letting it crash like a hard drive infected with a nasty virus.

"C'mon, Uncle Evan. Aren't you going swimming?" His niece's dark brows lifted in challenge.

"Uh. . .shouldn't we find out where our tent is first?"

Taylor hoisted her backpack onto her shoulder and tucked her sleeping bag under one arm. She pointed toward the middle of the tents. "It's that one over there. Number five. We're sharing it with Alison Perry and her dad."

He followed his niece up a trail into a tent erected on top of a three-foot-high wooden platform. How was he supposed to share this single room with two teenage girls?

"Chill, Uncle Evan. Look." Taylor pointed toward the tent top. "There's a room divider we can unroll. I'll sleep on this side with Alison, and you and her dad can have that side."

Evan set his bag on one of the cots, feeling only marginally better. A thin cloth didn't seem like enough of a barrier between him and two noisy teens. How was he supposed to get any work done?

Outside, he heard a rooster crow and looked down at his tennis shoes to see if the crazy bird had left peck marks. He sure hoped they left that crazy attack-critter in its cage. He shook his head and let out a heavy breath. Was he ever out of his element!

The tent held four cots, and its sides were rolled up to let in the warm breeze. A gas lantern that sat on a small table separating the two beds on each side was the only source of light. Stairs leading out the back of the tent platform pulled him that direction. Behind and off to the left was a bath-house and restroom facilities. The big man who captured the rooster walked behind the building, and a moment later, Evan heard the roar of a generator kick to life. Maybe they'd have warm water for showers—and a plug-in for his battery pack.

Mountains rose up in splendor behind the bathhouse. God sure had made this place beautiful. His gaze lifted to the sky, and he thought of how he'd skipped church the past two Sundays to work on his project. Guilt wormed its way through him, not for the first time. "Sorry, Lord. I promise to do better."

"What did you say?" Taylor peeked around the curtain and held it against her chin.

"Tay–lor!" Alison squealed, even though he hadn't so much as a glimpse of her.

"Nothing," he said.

"You'd better get ready if you're going swimming."

He shrugged. "I didn't bring a swimsuit. Didn't know I'd need one."

"Too bad." The curtain dropped back into place, and Taylor disappeared again. He heard her whisper something to her friend but couldn't make it out. Both girls giggled.

A short, thin man clomped up the front steps. He nodded and dropped his pack onto the empty cot. He held out his hand. "Charley Perry."

"Evan Parker."

The man's brows dipped. "Are you Taylor's father?"

Taylor snorted on the other side of the curtain—at least he thought it was her. Evan shook his head. "I'm her uncle."

"Nice to meet you. I was sitting in the front of your wagon, but you never looked up from your laptop."

"Sorry." Evan shrugged. "I'm on a tight deadline."

"Good luck with that up here. Don't know where you're going to find power for the next two weeks." He turned away and pulled some clothes and a flashy swimsuit from his duffel bag.

Evan wasn't ready to give up working on his project just yet, but things weren't looking too good. They weren't even a full day away from the ranch, and already they had no electricity.

He heard another generator fire up and walked to the front of the tent. Suddenly a thought sparked in his mind. Where there was a generator, there had to be power. All he needed now was a power strip.

⁂

Bethany finished her walk around the perimeter of the camp, satisfied that everything looked in order. The scent of pine mixed with the fragrance of hamburgers cooking over an open flame on the grill her dad had made years ago.

Squeals and shouts of people at play echoed across the green valley. She stopped to watch the teens and their parents splashing in the cool water of the lake. If only she could recapture the joy of her youth, a time when worries and concerns didn't weigh her down.

"Here I go, ready or not." A husky boy took a running start and jumped off the end of the dock onto the colorful water blob. A skinny boy with lily-white skin flew high into the air, arms swirling, and landed in the lake with a splash. Bethany smiled, remembering the fun she'd had after they'd first installed the giant inflatable pillow.

Evan Parker's niece was next in line to jump on the blob. Taylor said something to the girl behind her and then ran hard, jumping into the air with a shrill squeal and onto the blob. The heavyset boy didn't go up into the air nearly as much as the skinny boy had, but his smile showed he still enjoyed the ride.

Behind the lake, the sun was already heading downward, its light soon to be blocked out by the tall mountains. She turned to leave and saw Mr. Parker tiptoeing his way, barefoot, over the rocky ground. His pants were rolled up, and Bethany sucked in her top lip to keep from grinning at his pale legs. She lifted her gaze to his as if drawn by an unknown source, and her heart skipped a beat at the vividness of his eyes. They were as blue as the sky, and at this elevation, the sky was even bluer than in the low country.

He spied her, waved, and jostled toward her, backpack in hand. "Hey, I was looking for you. Is there someplace I could charge the batteries for my laptop? I used up the juice on all three of the ones I brought with me."

Bethany resisted the urge to sigh and shake her head. The deadline the man said he was working toward must be really important for him to feel the need to use his vacation time. "I would imagine there's an outlet in the cookhouse that might be free."

"Great!"

She glanced down at his pale feet. "You really shouldn't be going barefoot. You might cut yourself on a rock."

He grinned, sending tingles dancing in her stomach. "I thought I might go walk around in the water."

"Don't say I didn't warn you." Without indicating for him to follow, she moseyed over to the canteen and cookhouse and entered through the back door. The sweet odor of cooling baked beans circulated around the smell of a freshly baked cake. Jenny Campbell, the trail cook, looked up from the bowl of coleslaw she was stirring and smiled.

"How's everything going, Jenny?" Bethany asked. Evan Parker padded in behind her.

"Good. The cake just needs to cool some, and then I can frost it. Everything else is ready if you want to ring the bell."

"Jim has a mess of burgers ready." Bethany glanced around the small kitchen and spied a power strip on the counter where the mixer and the light were still plugged in. She looked over her shoulder. "Looks like you're in luck."

Evan Parker must have spied the power strip, too, because his face lit up like a kid seeing his first Christmas tree. Bethany sucked in a breath at the difference it made. He was a handsome man when he wasn't scowling and his head wasn't buried in his laptop. His tan proved he spent time outdoors, even if his legs hadn't seen the light of day for a long while. Wide shoulders tapered down to a narrow waist. She forced herself to quit staring.

Jenny lifted both brows and gave her a knowing smile. Heat charged to Bethany's cheeks. She searched for something to do and grabbed the stack of Styrofoam plates and napkins and hurried toward the door.

"Um. . .you don't mind if I used your power strip for a while, do you, ma'am?" Evan's voice sounded behind her.

"No, I'm nearly done. All I'll need is a plug-in for the mixer."

"Great. Thanks. I'll just plug in my charger and get out of your way." He rustled through his pack, pulled out a charger with a battery attached, and plugged it into the strip. "I'll come back later and swap out the battery for another one."

Hugging the plates and napkins to her chest, Bethany waited at the door to make sure he didn't get in Jenny's way. Mealtimes observed a strict schedule.

He walked toward Bethany and grinned. "Thanks for allowing me to use your power."

She stepped outside, and he caught the screen door and closed it without letting it bang. She walked toward the picnic tables that sat between the tents and the lake, circling the campfire where Jim cooked the burgers.

"Can I carry that for you?" Evan glanced sideways at her.

She shook her head, pleased that he'd offered. "It's not heavy. If you're going in the water, you'd probably better do it now. We'll be eating soon, and the temperature will cool down fast once the sun sets."

"Yeah, I suppose I should check on Taylor." He looked toward the lake then back at her. "I can't imagine being able to enjoy such a view every day. Have you lived here long?"

"All my life. My great-grandparents bought the place and ran cattle. Not long after my dad took over the ranch, people started learning about the awesome beauty up here, and my parents decided to branch out. They started inviting city folks to visit."

"That must have been hard on you. To have to share your family and home with so many strangers." He stared at her, as if looking into her soul.

Bethany swallowed and broke the connection. As she'd grown older, she'd tried to be friendly and yet distance herself from their guests. As a teen, she'd longed for a close friend, but every time she got to know a girl and made a connection, her new friend would leave and go home. Maybe they'd write for a while, but usually by the time school started, the girls would quit contacting her. Losing a friend hurt more than not having one at all.

Most visitors talked about the view, the animals, or the ranch, but no man had ever considered how living in such an isolated place had affected her. His gaze was clear and curious.

"Sorry—didn't mean to venture into taboo territory." He shoved his hands into his pockets and stared at the lake.

"It's all right. I'm just not used to people asking me personal questions. Sharing the summers with others is all I can ever remember. I loved going on the trail rides as a kid and riding my horse."

"Do I sense a *but* coming?"

She shrugged one shoulder, not sure why she was confessing to this stranger. "I guess I got tired of it as I grew older."

"Yeah, I've seen that with Taylor. She used to be happy playing board games or going to the park, but she seems to change every time I see her. She's not a little girl anymore, and I don't know this stranger who's inhabited her body."

Bethany peered sideways. Light brown stubble enhanced his jawline, making him look more manly. For some odd reason, she wanted to offer him encouragement. "It won't always be like that. Give her a few years, and she'll get her feet back on solid ground. I know I did."

He turned toward her and smiled. "Thanks. I needed to hear that."

"Maybe this time together will help your relationship with her."

Jim clanged the old-fashioned triangle, signaling that the burgers were ready. "Guess I'd better go help."

"Yeah, and I think I'd better get some shoes on before I cut my feet to shreds."

She smiled. "See you at dinner, tenderfoot."

His return grin warmed her as she hurried back to the kitchen for the pot of baked beans. Jenny was coming out the door with her arms filled with a huge bowl of coleslaw and bags of buns.

"Did you have a nice chat?" The cook waggled her brows.

Bethany rolled her eyes. "I was just being friendly to a guest."

"Uh-huh." Jenny pushed past her, chuckling.

Bethany grabbed the pot of beans and stood in the quiet of the small kitchen for a moment. Why was she attracted to Evan Parker? He was nothing like the few outgoing guys she'd dated in college. Outside, she set the beans on the serving table and went to pass out plates to help keep things moving quickly. Dripping teens lined up with their parents and took a plate and bun as fast as she could pass them out. They slathered on mayonnaise, ketchup, or mustard and then helped themselves to an array of garnishes.

"Mmm, sure smells good." One of the fathers smiled at Bethany and took a plate.

Three adolescents plopped down at the table nearest her and bit into their burgers. She liked to watch people's expressions as they tasted the homegrown beef for the first time. Her father prided himself on his quality cattle. But instead of eye-closing delight, all three faces scrunched up. The two boys leaned sideways and spat out their bites, while the girl swallowed hers then chased it with half a can of pop.

Bethany's heart lurched. What in the world could have caused such a reaction?

Glancing around at the others who'd gotten their burgers, she watched for their reactions. Every one was the same. Disgust. Revulsion.

She strode over to the table with the three teens, and they all stared wide-eyed at her. "What's wrong with the meat?"

The girl grabbed her can of root beer and took another drink. Bethany shifted her gaze to the biggest of the boys. He guzzled his drink and fanned his mouth. "It's too hot. Blazing hot."

"Yeah," the other boy said. "I guess we just aren't used to eating things as spicy as you guys out here do."

"They're not supposed to be hot at all. Not spicy hot, anyway. Let me see what I can find out."

She marched over to Big Jim, noticing more and more people were shoving aside their hamburgers. She didn't need this trouble.

"Stop serving the meat."

Both Jim and the next kids in line stared at her as if she'd gone crazy. She grabbed a plate and took a patty right off the grill. She sniffed it, savoring the beefy fragrance, then pinched off a small piece and put it in her mouth. Blazing fire ignited her senses and set her tongue burning. She leaned sideways and discreetly spit the half-chewed bite into her hand and dropped it on the ground. Her eyes watered, and she raced toward the drink table and grabbed a bottle of water. Her nose ran, and she sniffed as the fire in her mouth lessened.

Jim stomped his way toward her, the metal spatula still in his hand. "What's wrong?"

She held up her index finger and took another swig. "The meat is burning hot."

He shook his head. "Yeah, well, that's what happens when you take one right off the fire and cram it into your mouth."

"No, I mean it's loaded with hot sauce or cayenne pepper or something."

Jim's fuzzy gray brows dipped. "How is that possible?"

Bethany shook her head. "I don't know, but we have to do something fast. Look around you."

Not a soul was eating a burger, but they were scarfing down the baked beans and slaw.

"What do you want to do?" Jim crossed his arms over his massive chest.

"Can you run back to the ranch ASAP and have Polly fix up a bunch of sandwiches? The last thing we need is all these people leaving early and demanding a refund."

He nodded and marched back to the grill. "Folks," his deep voice boomed around the camp. "Let me have your attention. I apologize for the meat being so hot. Someone goofed somewhere. If you can hold out for a while longer, we'll have some sandwiches for you guys. There'll be a couple of cowboys singing 'round the fire in an hour. We hope you will join us."

Groans and grumbles sounded all around. Jim removed the remaining half-cooked patties from the grill and dumped them back on the baking sheet with the rest of the raw burgers. He carried the pan to the kitchen then made a beeline for the Jeep. Bethany appreciated his making the announcement, although she should have done it. One round-faced boy piled his empty plate with sliced dill pickles and sat back down, while most of the people finished their side dishes. Some were leaving the tables and heading for their tents. It was best they shed their wet clothes before the temperature dropped, anyway.

Jenny hurried her way toward Bethany, her long brown braids bouncing on her chest and her eyes snapping. "I didn't do it. Just so you know. I never put hot sauce in the ground beef—at least not unless I'm making chili. Too many of the city folks can't tolerate it. I can't imagine what happened."

Bethany stared at the peaceful lake. The surface, no longer broken by rowdy kids, rippled gently from the light wind. "I don't understand how a mistake like this could have happened. Did Polly help with the meat this time?"

Jenny nodded. "Yes. Polly ground the meat in the ranch kitchen and shaped them into patties then stuck them in the freezer. I suppose she might have left the meat unattended at some point, since she sometimes had to help at the front desk when your dad was gone. I didn't even season it until we got here. Just added salt, pepper, and a little garlic. I'll go check the containers to make sure that I didn't get the wrong condiments in them somehow."

Bethany shook her head. It made no sense, but she had to get to the bottom of this. They needed this trip to be perfect so these folks would return someday and recommend Moose Valley Ranch to their friends. With the ranch's finances being stretched tight, they couldn't afford another mistake like this one.

Chapter 4

"You girls quiet down over there."

Charley Perry's deep voice seemed out of place with his short stature, but Evan long ago learned not to judge a book by its cover. Giggles sounded from the far side of the curtain.

"You 'bout ready for lights-out?" Charley slipped on his flannel green plaid pajama shirt and tucked it into the bottoms. "Being out in the wilderness sure can wear a body out."

"I hear you." Evan grabbed his cell. "Just let me make one quick phone call, and then I'll be ready."

"Good luck with that. I tried earlier but couldn't get a signal up here." Charley yawned and scratched his belly then plopped down onto his cot.

Dressed in a long-sleeved gray pullover and comfortable navy sweatpants, Evan stood on the top step and flipped open his phone. The message SEARCHING FOR SERVICE shone on the screen. After a moment he lifted the phone higher in the air. "C'mon. C'mon."

The NO SERVICE message flashed. "Great."

"What's so important that you've gotta call tonight?" Charley asked from inside the tent.

Evan flipped the phone shut and then opened it again. Still no luck. "I'm working on a project and need to make regular reports. Too bad they don't have Internet service here, or I could just e-mail them. I think I'll try getting away from the tent."

He slipped on his socks and shoes. Using his phone for a flashlight, he followed the path to the picnic tables. When the light on the display screen dimmed, he snapped the phone shut and climbed onto one of the picnic tables. He tried again, and this time when the ROAMING sign came on, he punched in the project manager's number. The phone was quiet for a moment, then he got a busy signal. He looked at the screen and realized the call had disconnected.

Sighing, he closed the phone and shoved it into his pocket. The picnic table creaked under his weight. A short distance away, soft lights flickered behind the canvas walls of the tents, reminding him of the ceramic Christmas village his sister set up every holiday season. Pine trees rose up black against the sky, illuminated by the moon just rising. He lifted his face to the sky and sucked in a breath at the myriad stars shining like diamonds against black velvet. "You sure made some majestic places, Lord."

He felt torn between wanting to spend this time with Taylor and being faithful to the company that contracted him as a video game developer. Trying to do both wasn't working too well. After dinner he'd worked another hour and a half outside the cook shed while he still had daylight. The singing cowboys around the campfire and the dirty looks Taylor cast his way had finally pulled him from his work.

Evan heaved a sigh. He didn't like disappointing family. Maybe he should forget his work and try harder to join in the activities. He'd just have to put in extra hours when he got home to make up for it. With his eyes on the sky, he spent the next few minutes in prayer. Somehow he needed to find some answers.

Evan yawned and started to jump off the picnic table, but a noise halted his steps. Big Jim had warned them all about venturing away from the group during the day or straying from camp at night. Bears inhabited the area, as well as mountain lions, but Evan never thought they'd stray into the camp with so many people around. His heart pounded. Could he outrun a bear to his tent? But then what good would a bit of canvas do in deterring a determined beast—and he couldn't very well lead it straight to his niece. Swallowing hard, he strained to hear the creature again.

Soft whispers and giggles sounded to his right, and he spun around. The table creaked again beneath his weight.

"What was that?" a shaky female voice called out.

"I don't know. Maybe this wasn't a good idea."

Evan recognized the male voice as belonging to one of the boys who rode in his wagon. So, he'd interrupted a little romantic tryst. He couldn't help grinning as his heart slowed back to a normal pace. After so long outside, Evan's eyes had become accustomed to the dark, but he barely made out the shape of a boy and girl standing a dozen feet away. He considered growling and sending the kids screaming back to their tents, but that would be too mean.

"Shh. I heard something again," the girl whispered.

Evan bounced on the table, making it squeak. The girl let out a yelp and took off running with the boy close on her heels. He chuckled and stepped down to the bench seat and onto the ground. Nope, no bear this time, but as he neared his tent, he couldn't help thinking again how that flimsy canvas wouldn't keep out a determined bear if it wanted in.

⁊⁊

The morning sun erupted over the eastern ridge in brilliant glory, bringing with it the promise of clear skies and warmer temperatures. Bethany stretched and made her way to the cookhouse. Today would be a good one. She could feel it.

Ed had been crowing off and on for a good hour, and Bethany couldn't help remembering how the old bird had attacked Evan Parker's shoes. She smiled at the mental picture of the prancing man trying to get away. She shook her head. "Shame on me for taking pleasure in someone else's distress."

She'd been raised a Christian and had attended church until age twelve, when her mother died, but after that her father had rarely taken her. He missed his wife and buried his sorrows in work. She thought of the small community church she sometimes attended in Denver. The people were friendly enough, but she hadn't been able to find what she needed to fill the emptiness inside her. She stared at the trio of peaks glistening in the morning light. Why was it she felt closer to God when she was outside and away from town and church?

The door to the cookhouse squeaked as she pulled it open. Jenny, always an early riser, was hard at work browning a mess of bacon and sausage. The scent of the meat and biscuits baking filled the room and made Bethany's stomach grumble. She snitched a slice of cooked bacon. "How are things going? What can I do to help?"

"Fine, and you can fill that other baking sheet with biscuits. The ones in the oven are about done."

Bethany did as ordered. She might be the boss's daughter, but out here each person had a job she or he was responsible for, and she didn't mind helping the others. They'd help her if she needed it.

"Are the city slickers stirring yet?" Jenny tucked her spatula under several rows of bacon and laid them in a serving pan layered on the bottom with paper towels.

"Some. They've hardly done anything and are already tuckered out."

"Must be the fresh mountain air getting to them." The women shared a chuckle.

Bethany removed the golden biscuits from the oven and placed them on the counter then slid the uncooked batch in. She stacked the hot biscuits in a large, rectangular pan and set it on the warming tray.

"Just wait until next week. I'll have to serve breakfast a whole hour later because they'll be so pooped out." Jenny chuckled, and Bethany shook her head. It was an ongoing joke, though the cook always stuck rigidly to the meal schedule.

Jenny shoveled the remaining sausage links into the stainless steel serving dish then dumped the bacon at the other end of the rectangular pan and set it in the warming tray. "I just need to pour the gravy into the serving pan and scramble another batch of eggs. You want to ring the bell?"

"Sure. Everything looks great. Can't wait to eat." Bethany went outside the cookhouse and unlatched the upper half of the wooden wall on one side of the building. With the wall down, their guests could walk right up to the buffet and serve themselves. She tugged a stack of plates closer to the edge so they'd be within easy reach and then checked the silverware and napkins.

"I guess you're eager to see that good-looking greenhorn again." Jenny glanced up from her cooking eggs and sent Bethany a teasing glance.

Evan Parker invaded her mind, and her heart flip-flopped. She glanced over to where his batteries were still charging then peeked back at the cook. "Which greenhorn are you referring to? There are several nice-looking men on this trip."

Jenny grinned, her eyes sparkling. "Did I say it was a man?"

Bethany opened her mouth to respond then closed it. "Uh. . .no, I just assumed that's what you meant."

"Well. . .for the record, he is cute, even if he is a bit technically minded."

Bethany resisted commenting because it would only stir up Jenny to teasing her more. How had the cook noticed her interest in the computer geek? Other than when he first came to the cookhouse to ask about charging his batteries, she and Evan Parker hadn't been together where Jenny might have seen them. She scratched her head and walked outside where she picked up the metal striker and ran it around the inside of the triangle. The strong, clear ring brought the few folks sitting around the remains of last night's campfire to their feet. Others scurried out of their tents and down the steps. Bethany couldn't help searching for Evan Parker. Would he be at breakfast? Or had he stayed up late last night working on his project?

She hooked the striker to the bottom of the triangle and went back inside the cookhouse. The man wasn't her type at all. She preferred tall cowboys with dark eyes and dark hair, like her father had been when he was younger. Okay, Evan Parker was tall, she'd give him that—and had shoulders wide enough to lean on and blue eyes to die for. Gritting her teeth, she shoved thoughts of the computer geek aside. They had nothing in common, so why did he keep straying into her thoughts?

She poured a pot of coffee into the large carafe and started another pot brewing. With everything in order, she filled a plate and sat down at the small table to eat with Jenny while the guests filled their plates. They were close enough if anyone needed help.

The salty bacon teased her tongue and crunched in her teeth. A swig of coffee filled her stomach with its soothing warmth. Murmurs of conversation battled the clank of the big serving spoons and tongs as the guests helped themselves to the array of food.

"Are things ready for lunch?" Bethany held her mug with both hands and peered over the top at Jenny.

The cook nodded. "I've got fixings for sandwiches and am making a pot of chicken noodle soup to go with it. I'll clean up here and cook the soup then meet you at the lunch site by noon."

Bethany nodded, grateful that her father had the wisdom to keep Jenny on staff. The woman had cooked for them for the last five summers. With her kids grown and her husband deceased, the job gave her something to do, as well as a much-needed income.

They ate in companionable silence for a few minutes, then Big Jim banged through the back door, filling the whole entryway. A muscle in his jaw ticked, and he stared at her with narrowed eyes.

Bethany's heart sank down to her belly. "What's wrong?"

He glanced at the line of guests at the buffet and motioned his head toward the door. "Got something to show you."

Thankfully, she'd just finished her breakfast. She had a feeling the news he had to share would have affected her appetite. Big Jim was normally lively and jovial, but not this morning. He didn't even take time to grab a cup of coffee.

Outside and away from the guests, she turned to him. "Tell me straight. What is it?"

"Better that I show you." He strode toward the wagons, and she searched the area for signs of trouble. Occasionally, some critter wandered into a tent when a guest had left food exposed, but that rarely happened with so many people around.

Jim strode around the back of the last wagon and pointed to the wheel. Bethany pursed her lips. A flat tire. Well, it wasn't the end of the world or the first time a tire had gone down. "What's the big deal? Just air it back up."

Jim gave her an exasperated shake of his head like a father might give a troublesome child. He gently grasped her upper arm and propelled her forward. He stopped beside the next wagon, and her eyes drifted downward. This wagon had not one but two flat tires.

Her gaze flew up to his. "This can't be an accident. One tire, maybe, but not three."

"Oh, it's not just three. The back tires on the Jeep are flat, too."

"Why would someone do this?" Evan Parker leaped into her mind again. Surely he wouldn't do something like this just so he could stay near a power source. No, he didn't seem the kind of man to play pranks, but what did she really know about him? "Maybe some of the teens couldn't sleep last night and got bored."

Jim shrugged one big shoulder. "Maybe, but I can't help feeling there's more to this than meets the eye."

"I'll air up the Jeep tires and then start on the wagons," Bethany said. "You go on and get some breakfast."

"You sure? I don't mind doing it."

She smiled and nodded. "Go on. This won't take too long, and let's try to keep it quiet and not let the guests know there's been trouble."

"Good idea. If it is some of the teens, maybe we can catch them if they don't know that we're on to them." He turned and strode toward the cookhouse.

Bethany opened the back of the Jeep and found the long hose that hooked to the small air compressor they always brought along. A hiss of air escaped as she attached the other end to the Jeep's right rear tire. She turned on the rumbling compressor and started the air pumping.

She looked back toward camp to see if anyone was watching her. If one of them had done this, surely they'd want to see the reaction of whoever discovered their deed. But nobody seemed to be paying the least bit of attention to her.

Thank goodness they hadn't damaged the tires. If they'd been slashed, the whole trip would have come to a quick halt until replacement tires could be provided.

First, the too-spicy food, and now this. Was someone deliberately trying to mess up this trip? Or was it just some strange, unfortunate coincidence?

Chapter 5

Bethany rubbed lotion on her hands and worked the soothing cream into her cracked fingertips. Washing dishes for fifty people did a number on her hands. She stood at the door of her tent and scanned the crowded campsite. Teens and their chaperones sat listening to Steve spin a yarn about the olden days while two other cowboys played a banjo and a harmonica.

The sun had already set on the second day of their tour, but the sky was still a dark blue and hadn't yielded to the blackness of night that would soon surround them. Bethany longed for some quiet and grabbed her rifle. With all the noise in the camp, it wasn't likely a wild animal would venture close, but she would be prepared if it did.

She zipped her tent shut and then her jacket and strode past the rows of tents. Lantern lights flickered behind a few of the canvas sides, but most people were still down at the camp, making s'mores and enjoying Steve's tale about a lost gold shipment. The ground crunched beneath her boots, and she angled over toward the horses. Under lantern light, Big Jim was brushing down a bay mare, one of the dozen head they kept on hand for horseback riding.

"How's it going?"

Jim turned her direction, but his face was blotted out by the growing darkness. The light shone behind him, outlining his silhouette. "All right. The horses weathered today's trail rides okay, even though a few of the kids ran them more than they should have."

"Kids like to gallop, that's for sure." A gray gelding nickered at Bethany and stuck his long head over the fence, looking for a handout. She patted his forehead then smoothed down his forelock, remembering with a smile how one girl had called them bangs. "Sorry, boy, I don't have any treats for you."

"There's something I've been meaning to tell you ever since breakfast." Jim patted the mare he'd been brushing and turned her loose in the corral. He rolled up the lead rope and stared at Bethany. With his left side facing the lantern, she saw a muscle tick in his jaw. He studied the ground then looked up. "It wasn't any of these kids that let the air out of the tires."

Bethany sucked in a breath. "Then who was it?"

Jim shrugged. "I don't know for sure, but I found a set of hoof prints close to the wagons."

She huffed out a half laugh and relaxed her shoulders. "The horses have been all over this area. What's so unusual about that?"

"I found where the horse had been tied up. There were quite a few prints there, all belonging to the same animal and someone wearing boots. The horse was wearin' egg bar shoes, and you know we don't use those on our horses."

"Isn't that a shoe that is shaped like an oval and has a bar across the back?"

Jim nodded and leaned his arms over the top rail of the corral. "I'll make some calls and see which ranchers around here use egg bars. Whoever let out the air rode a long ways to play a prank."

Bethany lifted her boot to the bottom rail and set her rifle against the gate post. "But who? And why?"

"I don't know. But I think we should be extra watchful on this trip."

"Yeah. I agree." She thought of their neighbors and the people in town, but not one person stood out who might want to cause them trouble. People in the high country generally stuck together and helped each other. "Well, I'm going for a walk before it's totally dark. I'll keep my ears open."

"It's already dark. Want some company?"

She smiled. "Thanks, but I need some time alone. These teenagers make too much noise."

A loud laugh from the edge of camp sounded, followed by a girl's squeal.

"I hear ya." He took the lantern and headed back toward the campfire.

Bethany pushed away from the corral and picked up her rifle. The tire incident couldn't have been by chance. They were miles away from anyone else, so someone would have had to deliberately seek them out. Someone who knew their schedule. A shiver raced down her back.

She walked along the path the horses used during the trail rides. She knew this area by heart and didn't need a light to guide her. The music and chatter of the guests faded, and the sounds of nature soothed her with their serenade.

She topped a hill and walked down the other side, effectively blocking out the glow of the campfire. A strange light flickered ahead in the navy twilight. Bethany slid to a halt. What in the world? It fluttered around like a giant firefly; then it faded and disappeared. Her heart stampeded, and she lifted the rifle. The light reappeared, closer than before. She took a step backward.

Scuffling footsteps drew nearer. The light dimmed again, disappeared, and then shone bright once more. Her breath grew ragged, and she clutched the weapon tighter.

The blue glow looked unnatural in the wilderness setting. Suddenly, she heard whistling. A tune that pulled her back to church. One of the worship songs she'd learned as a kid.

The footsteps stopped about fifty feet in front of her. The light dipped down and moved around about a foot off the ground. Bethany's limbs grew weak with relief as she realized what she'd been seeing. A cell phone.

"Are you lost?" she called out, glad the darkness covered the red on her cheeks.

The light jerked, and whoever it was must have straightened. The phone stayed black, and the person didn't answer for a few moments. "Uh. . .a man never likes to admit such a thing to a lady."

Her heart constricted. She recognized that voice. "Mr. Parker?"

"Busted."

"What are you doing out here?"

A cool breeze whipped her hair into her face. She brushed it back and looped it over her ear. Laughter drifted her way, and she strained to hear where it was coming from. Definitely not camp.

"I was climbing trees."

"What?"

"Trees. You know. Climbing." He flipped open the phone, illuminating his face in the stark darkness.

"You're serious."

He nodded.

"Why?"

He shrugged and looked to his right. "I. . .uh. . .was trying to get up high enough to get phone service."

Bethany shook her head. "That's crazy. You could have gotten hurt. And you're not supposed to leave camp alone, especially at night. Did anyone even know where you were?"

"No, not really." The light faded, and he left it off. "I'm not exactly used to reporting in to my fourteen-year-old niece."

Having an argument in the dark was weird, but she wasn't about to ask him to turn on the light. So much for time alone. "We have rules for a reason, Mr. Parker."

"Call me Evan."

"Woo-hoo! That's what I'm talking about." A loud voice carried across the quiet landscape, and a fire flamed to life in the distance.

What now?

She reached out and grabbed Evan's arm, tugging him up the hill. "Come with me."

"Who's out there?" he asked.

"I don't know, but I'm going to find out." As they topped the hill, the soft glow of the campfire illuminated the horizon. She released her hold on him. "There's camp. You can make it fine from here."

"You're not going out there alone."

"I'm not alone. I have my rifle."

He snorted a laugh. "I'm going with you."

"No."

"Yes."

She walked toward his voice. "You're a guest. I do this for a living. Go back to camp."

He didn't say anything, but his warm breath fanned her face. Given another day and time, she might have enjoyed a walk at night with the handsome man. She shook her head and stomped down the hill. What had gotten into her?

Dreaming of walking in the dark with a man who climbed trees in hopes of making his cell phone work. Oh brother. She missed the comforts of the city, too, but this guy was really out there. Her pace slowed as she neared the small campfire. Illuminated by the fire, a lanky boy from the junior high group passed a bottle to another teen.

"Whoo-wee, that stuff sure has a kick."

"Hey, give it back. I only got a little swig."

Bethany ground her teeth together. She ought to go get Jim, but then she ought to be able to handle two kids on her own. She hoisted her rifle and marched into camp. Maybe she could scare some sense into them. "Just what do you think you're doing?"

On the far side of the campfire, the tallest youth spun around looking startled, and then a cocky smirk lifted one side of his mouth. The shorter boy stuck a bottle behind his back.

"We're just havin' some fun. Come and join us, why don't you?" The tall boy ran his hand through his hair. "My name's Donny. Aren't you Miss Schaffer?"

Bethany ignored his unskilled attempt to flirt and lowered her rifle. The boys may have broken several rules by taking off alone, starting a fire, and drinking liquor, but she certainly wasn't going to shoot one of them. The campfire popped and flickered, stretching its fingers of light into the night, illuminating the teenagers and casting spooky shadows in her direction.

"It's dangerous to be out here alone, especially after dark, and this is a family camp. Liquor isn't allowed."

Donny hooked his thumbs in his front pockets and swaggered toward her like a cowpoke. If she hadn't been angered by the tomfoolery, she might have laughed. Did the youth actually think she'd be impressed?

"Put out that fire, and let's get back to camp. You two are in a world of trouble."

The shorter boy kicked a little dirt onto the fire but not enough to snuff out the flame. Donny smiled, reminding her of the serpent that tempted Eve in the Garden of Eden. "Why don't you just sit down and have a drink with us? Nobody would have to know."

"Don't be ridiculous. Kill the fire, and let's go." Bethany's heartbeat galloped. This kid didn't look as if he'd go easy. She heard a twig snap to her right and glanced into the inky blackness.

Donny yanked the rifle from her hand, jerking her gaze back to him. "C'mere, Fred."

The boy by the fire hesitated. Donny glared over his shoulder, putting

Fred's feet into action. Bethany swallowed the lump in her throat and took a step backward.

"Oh no you don't." Donny grabbed her wrist.

A shiver charged down her spine. She could get away easily if she ran into the darkness, but she wouldn't leave her rifle with this delinquent and possibly put others in harm's way. Fred, almost as wide as he was tall, with pimples all over his face, stopped beside his friend. Donny held out the rifle, and Fred looked at it as if it were poison.

"Hold this for a minute."

When Fred didn't respond, Donny shoved the rifle at the boy. If she could distract Donny, maybe she could snatch the Winchester from Fred and run for help. Big Jim would come looking anyway if she didn't return soon—unless he was too busy working to notice. Or maybe she could fire the rifle into the air. That would bring Jim fast.

She tried to wrench her arm free, but Donny was stronger than he looked. A good five inches taller than she, he was lean and solid where Fred was wide and dumpy. He tightened his grip and forced her closer then grabbed her other arm.

Her pulse skyrocketed. "Let me go, boy. So far you've just broken the rules, but now you're bordering on assault."

"Aw, don't you want to have some fun?" He pulled her against his chest, and the stench of the liquor on his breath forced her to turn her head.

She shoved against his torso. "Let me go."

"Yeah, Donny. Turn her loose."

"Shut up, Fred." He lowered his face to hers. "You're a hottie with all that golden hair sparkling in the firelight."

She spun her face away, and his moist lips slid across her cheek. One hand raced around her back, anchoring her body against his, and he used his other hand to force her face back toward his.

She wasn't about to give him what he wanted. She lifted her foot behind her and slammed it into his shin. He cursed and hopped on one foot but didn't release her. He called her a foul name and grabbed her hair. "You'll pay for that."

She heard the scrabble of hurrying footsteps and saw a man step into the light of the campfire. Hope emboldened her. Donny was still hissing from pain and didn't notice the man.

"Turn me loose, kid, or you're going to be sorry."

"Ooh, you're scaring me." He chuckled and angled his face downward again. "Like you said, it's dangerous to be out here all alone."

"She's not alone."

Donny froze. Slowly he lifted his head and released her. Bethany scrambled away and looked for Fred. He sat by the fire with his head in his hands.

Suddenly, Donny spun around, his fist colliding with Evan Parker's jaw. Evan stumbled backward but regained his balance and held up the rifle he'd somehow taken from Fred. Donny halted and glared at the man. The boy's hands lifted slowly into the air.

"You okay?" Evan glanced at her.

"Yeah." She tried to calm her trembling hands. "But let me have the rifle. How about you?"

His smile warmed her insides and calmed the jagged edges of her nerves. "I'm fine."

She reclaimed her Winchester. That had been a close call. She didn't want to think how far Donny might have gone. Evan grabbed Donny by the arm. The fight must have gone out of the boy, because he just stood there looking at the ground.

She glanced at the campfire. "Let's take them to base camp, then I'll come back and deal with this fire. It looks contained for the moment."

"Come on, we're heading back." Evan looked at Fred.

The boy lumbered to his feet, looking repentant. He shuffled toward them. "Nobody was s'posed to get hurt. We just wanted to have some fun."

Bethany thought of the archery lessons, swimming, and horseback riding that had been offered that day. She knew they couldn't please everyone who came to the ranch, but they tried hard, and it bothered her that this boy had been dissatisfied.

They escorted the boys back to camp and found two relieved fathers.

"I was just heading out to search for them—and you." Jim gave her a scolding glare.

"I'd have been back sooner, but I ran into trouble." She told them what happened, getting stern looks from Donny's father. "I'm sorry, but you'll have to leave the tour. The boys knew the rules and willingly broke them our second day out. If Mr. Parker hadn't happened along when he did, these boys could be facing charges for something worse than assaulting him and me. Jim can drive you back to the ranch in the morning, and my father will have our attorney contact you."

Four sets of worried eyes stared back. "Surely we could work out something without getting the authorities involved," Donny's father said.

Bethany shrugged. "You need to realize the seriousness of what your son did. I'll let my father decide what to do, but you'll be leaving come morning."

As everyone drifted away, Evan gently rested his hand on her shoulder. She flinched but didn't move. "Are you sure you're all right?"

She looked up, surprised to see one side of his jaw swelling. "We need to get some ice on that."

He wriggled his jaw then grimaced. "Guess he got me better than I realized."

In the cookhouse, she flipped on the light. The flickering bulb that normally didn't throw out enough light looked bright after the darkness of the night. The generator hummed just outside, but the cookhouse seemed unusually quiet without Jenny bustling about. Bethany opened the freezer and grabbed two ice cubes then put them in a plastic sandwich bag and sealed it shut. She placed the ice inside a dishrag and handed it to Evan.

"You'll probably be a little sore in the morning. Does it hurt much?"

He shrugged one shoulder and held the pack against his cheek. "My jaw's a little sore and my head aches, but it's nothing I can't live with." In spite of everything that had happened, a smile lingered in his azure eyes.

Bethany pulled out a chair. "Have a seat. I'll get you some aspirin. Would you like some coffee? I could make some."

He glanced at the refrigerator. "I could really use a pop. I prefer my caffeine cold."

"Pop it is." She snagged two cans, got a couple of aspirin from the medicine box, and sat down across the table from him. She popped the lid of one can and slid it and the pills toward him.

"Thanks." He threw the pills into his mouth and swigged down half the can of pop. "Mmm, that tastes good. I have to admit, I've been having caffeine withdrawal."

She smirked. "I don't see how. I've noticed that you're usually first in line when the snack bar opens."

His shy smile sent pleasing tingles racing through her.

"Don't let those two bad apples spoil your trip, okay?"

Bethany blinked and opened her mouth, but nothing came out. He took a hit for her and had the bruises to prove it, yet he was concerned for *her*? She stared into his eyes, unable to look away. "How can you be so upbeat after what just happened?"

He cautiously opened his mouth, worked his jaw sideways, and pressed the ice pack against it again. "Just a God thing, I guess. God's grace is sufficient for any situation."

"If you hadn't wanted to use your phone so badly, you wouldn't have been out there to help me."

"Bingo! God put me there because He was watching out for you and knew you'd need help. He sees our needs even before we're aware of them."

He stared into her eyes, as if begging her to believe him. Her mouth suddenly dry, she broke her gaze and downed a third of her pop, then set the can down. "I'd better call my dad and let him know what happened."

She walked over to the satellite phone that was plugged into the charger right beside Evan's computer battery. Behind her, his chair scooted across the floor.

"You have a sat phone?"

She couldn't help smiling at the reverence in his voice.

"Yeah, it's necessary in case of an emergency." She lifted it from the charger and turned to face him. "Would you like to use it when I'm done?"

A wide grin tugged at his lips, and he nodded. His stunning smile made her legs go weak. If she didn't watch herself, she was going to be in for a world of hurt when Evan Parker returned home.

Chapter 6

Bethany sat down on a log bench that overlooked a scenic view of the mountains. She sipped her coffee and watched the drifting clouds. One looked like a dolphin and another like a long-faced man with a hooked nose and open mouth. Her mother had played the game with her when she was young. Bethany sighed.

How many weeks had passed since she'd thought of her mama? She no longer endured the stabbing pain she'd once felt but could now cherish the memories. Most girls seemed closer to their dads, but she had always had a special bond with her mother.

Maybe it had something to do with the fact that her mom homeschooled her. Or maybe because they went to church together. She'd never considered that before.

Evan Parker's words once again lingered in her mind. *"God put me there because He was watching out for you and knew you'd need help. He sees our needs even before we're aware of them."*

Could that really be true?

But how? If God saw their needs, then why were they in such a financial bind? Why did He take her mother away when Bethany loved and needed her so much?

Bethany wanted to believe—to grasp the peace she'd had as a child, but it was so hard. Still, there was something awesomely appealing about the almighty God seeing and anticipating her desires. Is that why Evan was on this tour? Because she needed him?

She snorted a laugh and shook her head. The last thing she needed was a geeky city boy who couldn't leave his toys behind long enough to take a vacation with his niece.

An eagle screeched and drifted high above her, pulling her gaze upward. She watched as it lowered, wings spread wide, and glided to a stop. From this distance she couldn't tell if it had a nest on the craggy mountain ridge, but eagles had always fascinated her.

Girlish squeals sounded behind her, and she stood. Time to get to work. With Jim gone to take the two boys and their dads back to the lodge, she had extra chores. They'd have to spend another day at this camp since they couldn't leave until Jim returned. Trail rides were scheduled next, and horses needed to be saddled.

She returned her cup to the kitchen and made sure Jenny had the breakfast cleanup under control, then headed toward the corral. Evan's words returned to taunt her mind. If God was watching out for her, that meant He still cared about her. Her stomach twisted. He'd never left. She was the one who'd gotten angry after her mother's death. She was the one who'd walked away from Him. But how could she find her way back after so long?

She shook her head and smiled at some teens singing and doing a silly dance around the campfire. Most of the kids who visited Moose Valley were great kids just out for an adventure. From time to time, they'd get the troublemakers like the pair who'd been drinking.

Glancing at her watch, she noted the time. Almost nine o'clock. She'd take the riders on a different trail that would make the rides longer and kill more time today. Since they weren't supposed to be in this camp again today, she hadn't planned activities, but she could always wing it.

Footsteps sounded behind her, and she turned. Evan jogged toward her, the sun gleaming off his brown hair. Her heart flip-flopped and her limbs suddenly felt weak. His megawatt smile revealed straight, white teeth, and his injured jaw looked puffy and purple in the daylight. He was looking less and less like a nerd to her and more and more like a man she'd like to get to know. But what for? He'd be leaving soon.

Her smile slipped, and he slid to a halt. His grin dimmed in response to hers. "Hey, I uh. . .just wanted to say thanks again for letting me use the sat phone. I let my boss know that I'm out in the boonies and can't get reception on my cell. He said not to worry about checking in until I get back to civilization."

For some odd reason, her heart sank. She didn't like how he referred to her home. His attitude just proved that there was no reason to lower her guard.

"No problem. Are you going riding today?"

He walked beside her and stared ahead at the corral. She glanced at him, and he looked as if his jaw was set. Must not hurt him too badly if he could clench it.

"You're not afraid of horses, are you?"

His gaze darted sideways, and she grinned.

"You are!"

"No, not exactly scared of them. But they *are* the biggest animals I've ever encountered."

Bethany shook her head. "Most of these trail horses are just big babies. They want snacks and to be cared for like any other pet. Not that they are pets."

"I don't even have a dog."

"Do you have a roommate?" Bethany opened the door to the tack shed that held all the riding equipment.

"No, I live by myself."

She looped three bridles over one arm and handed another three to him.

"You've been drafted to be my assistant since Jim's still gone."

His vivid eyes widened, but he reached out and took the bridles. "I have no idea what to do with this—other than to use it to steer the horse."

"Well, city boy, looks like you're going to learn."

She opened the corral gate and whistled. Evan came in behind her and closed the gate. Bethany suddenly stopped. Her heart jolted, and she counted the horses. "What in the world?"

"What's wrong?"

"Half of the horses are gone." She paced the wide corral, checking the railing for breaks, with Evan close on her heels.

He glanced back toward the cookhouse. "Could some of the teens have taken them?"

"I hadn't thought of that." She marched toward the tack shed and looked inside. Enough light shone through the door to illuminate the small room. "All of the saddles and bridles are still here, so it's not likely any kids are out riding."

She closed the door, thankful that at least none of their equipment had been stolen, but then saddles and bridles were cheap compared to horses.

"So, what do you think happened?" Evan asked. "How could they have gotten out if the gate was shut?"

"That's what I'm trying to figure out. The rails look fine." She stopped and faced him. He was a guest and shouldn't even know about their problems, but she needed an ally. "They couldn't have gotten out unless someone released them on purpose."

He shoved his hands into his pockets. His saddle-brown hair jutted up in cute spikes, reminding her of a porcupine. "Why would anyone release some of the horses and not all of them?"

She pressed her lips together and considered how much to tell him. Normally, she never got this friendly with a guest, but he'd come to her rescue, and for some reason, she wanted to tell him. "I think someone has been sabotaging this trip. First, the food was tampered with, then someone let air out of several tires on the wagons and Jeep the first night we were here. Now the missing horses. Too many problems to be a coincidence."

"Hmm." He placed his index finger over his lips and tapped them. Then he ran his hand over his swollen, purple jaw and winced. His hand dropped to his side. "You may be right, but why would someone want to cause you problems? Do you have any enemies?"

"No. None that I know of. I can't imagine who could be doing this." Bethany lifted a bridle off her arm and trapped a black gelding against the rails. She slipped the bit into his mouth and slid the headpiece over his ears, then hooked the throat latch. "I'll take this horse and see if I can find the others. I don't want the other guests to get wind that there are problems." She looked down at the ground. "I shouldn't even have told you."

He stood there for a moment with his face pointed at the sky. Had she offended him? Was he praying?

He rubbed the back of his neck and looked deep in thought. Bethany remembered what his niece had said about him needing time to process his thoughts. She led the gelding over near the gate and tied the reins to the railing. If she were lucky, she could find the horses and bring them back quickly. She'd have to get Steve to start another archery session to distract the guests—or maybe a fishing contest, and by the time they were finished, she should have all the horses back and saddled.

A sudden thought buzzed in her mind. "You know, the horses must have been released in the past few hours, or else Jim would have noticed them missing when he fed them earlier."

"We could question the campers and see if anyone would confess."

Bethany shook her head. "Teens aren't the best at admitting their faults. I doubt that would work unless someone saw the horses being released."

"You want me to ask around?"

"No. Let me go see if I can find them first." Patting the gelding, she stared at the camp. She had hoped her problems would disappear with the two troublemaking boys Jim took back first thing this morning. These guests would never want to return if they knew all that had happened.

Evan went back to watching the sky. Suddenly he snapped his fingers and strode toward her, still carrying the bridles. "I have an idea."

She ran her hand over the gelding's rump and met Evan in the middle of the corral. "What idea?"

"What if we make the campers think that the horses gone missing was planned? We could pretend rustlers stole them and let the campers hike out in groups to find them. Maybe even offer some kind of reward to the winners."

She shook her head at the crazy suggestion, but even as she did, she saw the beauty of his plan. It could work. The three wagon drivers, Steve, Benny, and herself, could each head up a group and make sure none of the greenhorns got hurt. It could actually be fun. A smile worked its way to her lips, and she refrained from reaching out and hugging the man who'd just solved her dilemma. He was a pleasant surprise, and she enjoyed his quiet company. Now they were partners in crime—sort of. "I like it. Let's do it."

❧

"I bet the horses are over this hill." Taylor raced Alison, Misty, and Sarah James to the top of the hill.

"Yeah, we'll be the winners for sure." Sarah heaved a breath, and her short, stubby legs pumped as she tried to keep up with the taller, leaner girls.

Evan walked with several other chaperones and parents, following at a much more relaxed pace. He didn't want to admit it, but the altitude must be getting to him. Though he jogged regularly, this morning's walk had left him winded and feeling more tired than it should have. He scratched his arm and massaged his achy forehead.

Knee-high grass swished as they plowed through it. Wildflowers in yellow, white, and purple dotted the area, and with the mountains ahead, it was a scene worthy of a painter's canvas. He lifted his digital camera and snapped a picture. If only he could capture such a scene in his video games, but that was the job of the graphic artist, not the computer engineer.

Mrs. James jogged up beside him, breathing hard, and Evan resisted rolling his eyes. It seemed like every time he stepped outside, she managed to worm her way up next to him. "This is quite an adventure, isn't it, Mr. Parker? Just imagine. . .rustlers. Why it's enough to make a woman faint."

He glanced sideways at the slightly overweight brunette, hoping that she wasn't serious. He'd be more than winded if he had to help carry her back to camp. She wasn't a bad-looking woman, but he wasn't interested. A honeyblond with brown eyes so dark he could barely make out the pupils lingered in his mind. He'd hoped that he and Taylor could have been in the group Bethany Schaffer led, but at the last minute, Taylor decided she wanted to go with Alison's group, and he couldn't very well go in a different one than his niece.

The balmy sunshine warmed him, and the high altitude made catching his breath more difficult after the vigorous walk. A nagging pain stabbed his head. He swiped at a trickle of sweat, rolled up his shirtsleeves, and scratched at a red spot on his arm. Must be a bug bite. The difference in the nighttime and daytime temperatures amazed him. Short-sleeve weather by day, but he needed a jacket after the sun set, taking the day's heat with it.

"What kind of work do you do, Mr. Parker?" Mrs. James fanned her face with her hand and blinked her gray eyes at him like a schoolgirl. Her cheeks were bright red, but he didn't know if it was from exertion or a blush.

"I'm a computer engineer. I've been an instructor at the University of Wyoming, but now—"

High-pitched shrieks pulled his attention to the top of the hill. Ahead of them, four girls squealed and bounced up and down.

"There they are!"

"I see three of them."

Taylor looked over her shoulder and seemed to scan the group. Her eyes locked with his, and she actually smiled at him. Evan's heart tightened. He smiled and waved back.

Benny, the young man on horseback who was leading the group, rode up the hill and reined to a stop. The girls looked up at the handsome young man, as if seeking his approval.

"Those girls sure do have an eye for that hot ranch hand," Mrs. James said.

Evan scowled. "Yeah, I noticed." Benny may not be near Evan's age, but he was far too mature for a fourteen-year-old. Still, he had to give the man credit. He'd never once encouraged the girls' attention whenever Evan had seen him out among them.

Benny spoke something into his satellite phone and turned his horse toward the adults. "Looks like we're the first ones to locate any of the horses."

Cheers rang out among the group, and the adults quickened their pace and soon joined the girls at the top of the hill.

"The boys in Miss Schaffer's group will be so jealous that a bunch of girls beat them." A red-haired girl whose name Evan didn't know rubbed her hands together and grinned.

Benny dismounted and looked at Evan. "Could you hold my horse for me? Those horses down there know me, so I'd best approach them on foot alone. You guys stay here so you won't scare them away."

Evan looked at the reins and then the horse. He reached out and took the reins in spite of his nervousness at being so close to an animal with such big teeth. Taylor smiled and walked over. She petted the horse, but an ornery sparkle gleamed in her eye. "You're not afraid of him, are you?"

"No." *Okay, so maybe that was a half-truth. A man's got his pride, after all.* He steeled himself and touched the horse's nose, amazed at its softness. The black horse sniffed his hand, blowing its warm breath across his palm.

"Isn't it cool how God made such big animals, and yet they can be so gentle?" Taylor combed her fingers through the horse's black mane. "I love riding. Can we go again?"

"Yeah, if you want."

Taylor clapped her hands.

The horse jerked his head, and Evan nearly dropped the reins. He shot a warning glance to Taylor, and she giggled. Evan shook his head and patted the horse's neck. He had tolerated the trail ride but had never felt completely comfortable. Still, if it made Taylor happy, he could endure another hour on the back of a horse.

Benny strode down the hill, carrying three lead ropes. He reached into his vest pocket and pulled out some feed, and the nearest horse lifted its head and walked toward him. Benny allowed the horse to eat, then snapped on the lead rope and led the gray horse up the hill toward them. The other horses followed at a good distance.

"Is it true what everybody is saying?" Taylor flicked a strand of her dark hair away from her mouth and gazed up at Evan with clear blue eyes. The wind picked up, blowing her shoulder-length hair in all directions. She grabbed it and held it in place behind her head with one hand.

Evan frowned. "What are they saying?"

"That you saved Miss Schaffer from. . .well, you know."

He should have realized word would have gotten around about him coming to Miss Schaffer's rescue. Evan shrugged. "I was just in the right place at the right time."

Taylor blinked and looked up, something like awe on her face. "God put you there, didn't He?"

"That's what I believe."

The widest grin he'd seen in months brightened Taylor's face. "You're a hero."

She wrapped her arms around him and laid her head against his chest. "Thank you for bringing me here, Uncle Evan. I know you have important work to do, but I really appreciate it."

Before he could respond, she darted toward Benny. Warmth flooded through him as he realized that his sacrifice of time had been worth it.

The horse beside him whinnied as loudly as if someone had blown a trumpet in Evan's ear. He lunged backward three feet and nearly dropped the reins. Chuckles mounted around him.

Evan had never been so out of his comfort zone before, but seeing Taylor so happy and relaxed made all the hassles of this trip well worth it. He just had to keep reminding himself of that.

Chapter 7

Bethany set the heated syrup on the serving counter and uncovered the massive pile of pancakes that Jenny had cooked. Teens in hoodies and jackets huddled together at the front of the serving line, chatting and gently shoving one another. Bethany lifted the lid off the sausage and eggs then waved to the leader. The savory scent of grilled sausage filled the air, as well as the odor of fresh coffee. "Come and get it."

She stretched her back to rid it of the kinks and took another sip of her coffee. The screen door screeched as Big Jim strode in and made a beeline for the coffeepot. He swigged down a whole steaming cup and poured another, then turned to face her. He leaned back against the counter, making sure to stay out of Jenny's way.

"Got fresh hotcakes. Want some?" Jenny swiveled her spatula in the air.

Jim smiled. "Sounds good." He pulled out a chair and sat at the table, then heaved a big sigh and looked up.

Bethany's heart jolted. What now? "I looked everything over early this morning, right after Ed woke me with his crowing. Everything seemed fine. I know that look. What's wrong?"

Jim took another sip of coffee and stared at her over his cup. "That computer geek you like is sick."

She sucked in a breath. Evan? He'd been fine the day before. "What's wrong with him? And I never said I liked him."

Jim lifted his fuzzy brows and gave her a knowing stare.

"Okay, I like him. He's a nice guy, even if he's a bit weird. How bad is he?" She glanced at the power strip, and her heart stumbled. Evan hadn't recharged his laptop batteries.

"Fever. Headache."

She rested her forehead on her palms and gripped her hair. What could he have? She peeked over her shoulder at the line of guests filling their plates. Was it contagious? "Is anyone else sick?"

Jim shrugged. "Not that I know of. His roommate, Mr. Perry, I think, came and got me. Wanted to know if we had any medicine."

Bethany stood. "There's some acetaminophen in the medicine chest. I can take it to him."

Jim smirked and lifted one brow.

She straightened and stared him in the eye. "I'm the boss's daughter, so it's only right that I check on him."

"Uh-huh." Jim sipped his coffee.

Jenny smacked down a plate of food in front of him. "You leave her alone, you big ox."

Jim chuckled and cut his pancakes with his fork. He got up and helped himself to the syrup then sat down again. "You know someone will have to take him back, so that means we can't move the wagons again."

Bethany shook her head and looked at Jenny. "We're okay on food, right?"

The cook nodded. "I think so. I'll check the inventory after breakfast and call you if I need anything; then you can bring it when you come back."

"All right, I'll go check out our patient. Jim, can you come up with something different for the guests to do today? They all seemed to enjoy hunting for the horses yesterday."

"Yeah, I'll set up the volleyball nets and get out the ball equipment. Maybe see if I can get an adults versus kids game going. That always stirs up interest, but if that doesn't work, we'll have a fishing tournament."

Bethany got the pills from the medicine kit and grabbed a can of pop. Outside of Evan Parker's tent, she halted. She'd cleaned the tents plenty of times but had never gone in when one of the guests was present. Through the netting of the door, she could see a shadowy bundle on the back cot. Nobody else was around. She cleared her throat. "Mr. Parker, it's Bethany Schaffer. May I come in? I have some medicine for you."

He groaned, threw back the blanket, sat up, and dropped the cover over his lap. "Yeah."

His voice sounded croaky. She slipped inside and pulled a chair close to his bed. His head hung down, resting in his hands, and he looked cute in his University of Wyoming sweatshirt with his hair all messed up. He scratched his chest and looked up.

Bethany's heart melted. At first she'd thought maybe he was just sunburned from spending the day outside without a hat, but his eyes held pain. She reached out and touched his forehead. "You've got a fever."

"That stinks."

Her lips tilted up. "I brought you something that might help." She opened the bottle of acetaminophen and handed two of them to him. His hand felt hot as her fingers touched his palm. She popped the lid of a can of 7UP and gave it to him. He stuck the pills in his mouth and took a drink, then passed the can back to her.

"Thanks."

"Do you think you could eat anything?"

He swayed then scooted under the covers and lay down. "No."

"Besides a fever, are you sick to your stomach? Do you hurt anywhere else?"

He stuck an arm under his pillow. "My head and back ache."

Maybe he had a virus, but it could be something more serious. She remembered the boy who had been here the year she turned sixteen. He'd had a low-grade fever and a stomachache. Nothing major, but after a few days, his mother insisted they go to town to see a doctor. The boy had appendicitis, and the doctor told his mother that he could have died if his appendix had ruptured. Since then they'd taken no chances. If someone got sick, he or she returned to the ranch.

Bethany stared at the man. Even with a day's growth of his dark beard and his eyes shut, something about him tugged at her. But it was his sky blue eyes that took her breath away—them and his kindness. Evan scratched his chest.

"Why do you keep scratching?"

"I itch." His mouth cocked up in a weak grin.

"Let me see your chest."

His lids lifted halfway, and his brows arched.

"Mr. Parker. . ."

"Evan."

Bethany sighed but secretly smiled. "Evan, there are things out here that you don't encounter in the city, and some people are highly allergic to them."

He shoved the blanket away and lifted his sweatshirt. Bethany resisted gasping out loud. Angry red spots dotted his flat stomach and mixed with the brown hair on his chest. What in the world? *I've got to get him back home.*

She indicated for him to pull down his shirt. "You rest, and I'm going to make arrangements to take you back to the ranch. You need to have a doctor check you over."

"I can't go. This trip means too much to Taylor." He shook his head. "I'll be better tomorrow."

She rested her hand on his arm. "Maybe, but we can't take a chance that what you have could be contagious. You need to be isolated."

"I'll stay here, in this tent."

She shook her head. "You would still have to use the bathroom facilities, and besides, you seem too weak to even walk that far."

"I'll manage," he growled.

Bethany stood, distancing herself from him. "I'm sorry, but for your own well-being, we can't let you stay."

He ran his hand through his hair. "Taylor will be so disappointed."

"Let me see what I can do." It was normally against ranch policy for a child to be there without a parent or guardian, but maybe Taylor could stay with another family. Bethany strode across the campground, half angry with herself. Why was she willing to bend the rules for Evan Parker's niece when she wouldn't do it for someone else?

Taylor hurried toward her, carrying a plate of food. Her brows lifted when she saw Bethany leaving the tent. "I thought I'd see if Uncle Evan could eat something."

"Good luck with that." Bethany smiled. "I don't think he feels up to eating, especially something like sausage."

Taylor glanced down. "Oh, I didn't think of that. Maybe he could eat a little of the eggs."

"Yeah, that might help him. I left a can of pop in the tent and gave him something for his headache and fever." She looked down, steeling herself for the girl's response. "I'm sorry, but we're going to have to take him back to the ranch. We need to get him checked by a doctor. I have no clue what's wrong with him."

Taylor pressed her lips together and stared off toward the mountains. "Yeah, I was afraid of that."

Bethany laid her hand on the girl's arm. "I'm going to see if another parent would be willing to take responsibility for you so you can stay with the tour."

Taylor's eyes sparked for a moment then dulled. "Thanks, but I should stay with my uncle in case he needs me."

"You sure?"

She nodded. "I'll see if I can get him to eat and then start packing our stuff. I guess I just wasn't meant to go on this trip."

"All right, if you're positive. I'm going to call my dad and see if he can get the doctor from town to come and check your uncle."

They parted, and Bethany strode back to the cookhouse. She couldn't help being worried about Evan. Nobody had ever had a rash like that, as far as she could remember. It seemed isolated to his chest, which was odd, since she'd never seen him go anywhere without a shirt. That probably ruled out an allergic reaction.

She thought about her first few meetings with him. Why had she considered him such a geek, just because he lugged his computer around? She smiled. Because he was.

A large crowd of guests sat at the picnic tables, laughing, talking, and devouring their breakfast. *Good, keep things as normal as possible.* Maybe if she hurried, they could get Evan and Taylor away without too many people asking questions. She hoped the Perrys would not get sick since they shared a tent.

Back inside the kitchen, Jenny and Jim stared at her with curiosity. Bethany grabbed the phone. "I'm taking Mr. Parker and his niece back to the ranch."

Jim lifted a brow. "*You're* taking them?"

"Yes. Why don't you see about getting the net up?"

Jim's thick lips twisted into a humorous smirk. "Yes, ma'am. You're the boss."

Bethany stuck out her tongue at him and grinned.

An hour later, she drove the Jeep toward the ranch, taking it slowly so as not to jar Evan too much. He sat beside her, hunched against the door, eyes closed. Every so often her gaze would meet Taylor's concerned one in the rearview mirror.

Bethany had to admit that she admired the girl for sacrificing her trip to stay with her uncle. She hadn't expected the teen to respond in such a mature way. In fact, Bethany realized that she had wrongly judged them both.

Why was that?

She swerved to miss a pothole. She didn't think of herself as an overly judgmental person. For the most part, she liked people.

Barrett Banner invaded her thoughts, and she clenched her jaw. Why would her ex-boyfriend come to mind now?

She glanced over to check on Evan, and it hit her. The men somewhat resembled each other. Barrett was about the same height, around six feet, but he was stockier than Evan. Barrett had been the only man she'd considered marrying—until he dumped her for a redheaded biology major with a cheerleader's body. Her grip tightened on the steering wheel as she remembered Barrett's blue eyes.

Bethany scowled. Had she somehow subconsciously considered the two men the same?

But they weren't, not by a long shot.

Barrett had been a taker, moving in and forcing a relationship she hadn't wanted at first, and then when she decided that she did, he dropped her cold.

She drove into the ranch yard and pulled around to the side entrance so Evan wouldn't have to walk so far. She hadn't known him long, but she couldn't imagine him treating a woman as Barrett had. Too bad she'd never get a chance to find out. Once she got him settled and heard what the doctor had to say, she'd return to the tour and would probably never see Evan Parker again.

The doctor straightened and eyed Evan over the top of his black-rimmed glasses. "Well, Mr. Parker, it seems you have the chicken pox."

Confusion swarmed Evan's already foggy mind. Chicken pox? Hadn't Erin said he'd already had them? "But I thought that was a kids' disease."

"Usually it is, but adults do occasionally get it, and it can be quite severe. Until all your spots crust over, you're highly contagious." He ran a long, thin finger over his mustache and looked around. Evan followed his gaze. The large bedroom sported a king-sized bed, two nightstands with lamps, a recliner on the far side of one nightstand, and a large wardrobe with a television hidden behind double doors. Bear and moose statues accentuated the wallpaper around the top of the walls, which displayed log cabins and woodland creatures.

"You're fortunate to have such a nice suite here. I suggest you stay in your room for the next week or so and take things easy. Enjoy the room service and relax." His expression softened. "I'm sure that's not the vacation you had planned when you came here."

Evan shrugged, but he suddenly realized he'd just been handed hours upon hours in which he could work on his program—just as soon as his raging headache dimmed. *Please, Lord, make it so.*

Of course, that wasn't fair to Taylor. Maybe he could talk her into going back to the tour with Miss Schaffer.

Dr. Franklin scribbled something in his black leather notebook. "When did you first notice the rash, Mr. Parker?"

"Last night when I took a shower." Evan cleared his throat. It hurt, and he longed for something cold to drink.

"Hmm. Since the rash just appeared, I'm going to prescribe an antiviral drug for you to take. It may lessen the severity of your symptoms." Dr. Franklin packed away his instruments and lifted his black bag. He tugged on his gray goatee. "You can expect to have a few uncomfortable days. Calamine lotion may help with the itching, but see to it you don't scratch. It only makes things worse and can cause scarring."

Great. Half of his body itched as if he'd rolled in a poison ivy patch and scratching wasn't allowed. He relaxed against the soft pillow and stuck his hands behind his head. At least he was in a comfortable bed and partway back to civilization.

"Miss Schaffer has my phone number. If you get worse in any way, have her call me. Chicken pox is rare in adults, and it can cause serious complications. Make sure you drink plenty of liquids, and you can take ibuprofen for your headache." He tipped his Western hat and left the room, carrying his worn black bag with him. The man reminded Evan of Doc Adams from *Gunsmoke*, a TV show he'd watched as a kid.

The second the doctor closed the door to their suite, Taylor bolted out of her room and into his.

"Hold it right there, young lady." He dropped his hand back to the bed.

She lifted one hand like a princess and swirled it around. "Oh, I had the chicken pox back when I was in kindergarten, so I'm immune. Let me see your spots."

"No." Evan leaned back against his pillow. Just lifting his head to look at his niece made it throb. "I'm really sorry about this, sweetie."

Taylor sighed and sat on the foot of his bed. "It's not your fault. Like, if it's anybody's, I blame Jamie. He's the one who gave you the chicken pox."

"And who gave them to Jamie?"

She shrugged and sighed. "Got 'em at school, I imagine."

Evan smiled. "So we can blame some nameless fifth grader."

"Yeah, I guess." Taylor's lips turned upward. "So, are you hungry? I could get you something from downstairs."

"Thirsty, and I could use some ibuprofen."

Taylor hopped up as if happy to find something to do. "I'll be right back. You want a Coke?"

"Apple juice or ginger ale if they have it. I might take some soup later." Evan rolled onto his side and stuck a pillow against his stomach. He nudged his chin toward his pants on the desk chair. "Get some money out of my wallet. Get yourself a snack if you want one, and take enough money for what we need now and some for you to have if you want something later."

Someone knocked, and Taylor opened the hallway door. Evan thought he heard Miss Schaffer mumble something but couldn't make out the words. Taylor ambled back into the bedroom. "Bethany wants to see you if it's okay."

He nodded and made sure the hunter green blanket covered most of his body. He saw her shadow moments before she stood at the door with a shy smile on her lips. Her honey-colored hair, which had been blown haphazardly by their Jeep ride earlier, had been tamed once again.

Those dark chocolate eyes stared at him with concern, then her lips danced as if she were holding back a grin. "Chicken pox?"

Evan shrugged. "What can I say? Guilty as charged."

Bethany pressed her lips together, but her eyes still glimmered. She fiddled with the doorjamb with her fingers. "I'm sorry. It's just that when I saw that rash, I thought maybe you were having some horrible allergic reaction to something you came in contact with. Can I get you anything?"

Evan's gaze took in her red cotton shirt tucked into her jeans, revealing her narrow waist and womanly figure. Dust-covered boots completed her outfit, making her look every bit the Western woman she was. "Taylor has money to get me something to drink and for some pills for my head. Maybe you could open the store?"

Bethany nodded and waved her hand in the air. "Of course I can, but get whatever you want. It's on the house. I'm driving to town to get your prescription filled and need to know your birth date and home address. I have your sister's address on record, since she made the reservation, but not yours." Her cheeks reddened. "The pharmacy always asks for that info."

His head felt as if it was caught in a vise, and he longed to scratch his whole body. "Have Taylor show you my driver's license. It's got all that info. Could you maybe pick up some calamine lotion?"

Bethany's golden brows lifted.

"The doc said it would help with the itching."

She smiled, sending his stomach into spasms. Or maybe it was because he hadn't eaten all day. "Sorry to be all this trouble. We'll get out of your hair just as soon as I feel like driving."

"Just get better and don't worry about that."

"Yeah, this is one of those times where we have to trust that God knows what He's doing."

Her smile dimmed, and she waved. "Be back soon."

She left his room but not his mind.

He couldn't help admiring how in-charge she was around the camp and didn't let bugs or critters bother her, but she seemed to get flustered when things didn't go as planned or when he mentioned God. What could have happened to cause such a reaction?

"Lord, help her come to know You. Let Bethany see that You can ease her load if she'll only let You."

Chapter 8

Bethany smacked the wheel of her Jeep as she spun onto the highway, squealing her tires and scattering pebbles behind her. She ought to be heading back to camp to see if anyone else had fallen sick, but she needed to pick up Evan's prescription and get him on the road to recovery so he could go home. Still, deep down, if she were honest with herself, she'd admit that she was glad to be able to do something to help him. He'd looked so helpless lying in bed with his hair all messed up and blue eyes filled with discomfort.

He was right about trusting God when things went wrong. She knew that in her heart, but getting her mind to align with that truth was something else. Her father was a tough, quiet man who worked hard. He didn't show affection easily. Bethany rarely saw her parents kiss except for a little good-bye peck, like a bird snatching a crumb. Her dad had always been busy, and after her mother died, it seemed as if he'd worked even harder to drown his sorrow. She'd had to figure things out herself and find answers to her problems rather than relying on her father to help her. When had she quit relying on God, too?

Chicken pox. She shook her head and grinned. She'd never heard of an adult catching that. Suddenly, her smile faded. Had she ever had them?

She couldn't remember, but maybe her dad would know.

The doctor had said Evan already had the chicken pox in his system before he came to Moose Valley—that a person could be contagious before they even knew they had it. What if she had already contracted the disease? She moaned. "Wonderful! Just wonderful."

How many others would come down sick before the end of the tour? She'd better get several bottles of that calamine lotion and keep the doctor's phone number handy.

He had also said that the chicken pox took ten days to two weeks to incubate. That meant it wasn't likely anyone else would come down with it before the end of the tour. Still, she'd need to notify each family that they had been exposed to the disease. But what if a bunch of them wanted to leave and asked for a refund?

Concern chased her like a crazed bull. She guided the Jeep along the road, passing wide valleys of wildflowers, going up and down steep hills and around sharp switchbacks. The drive to town was as pretty as anyone would see on the tour, but today her mind was elsewhere.

If she had to, she could use her savings to give partial refunds to a few of the guests, but she hoped it wouldn't come to that. If only Evan Parker hadn't come to Moose Valley. She wouldn't have this worry, and the man wouldn't be bugging her mind like a bad case of the chiggers.

And why was he always on her mind?

Yeah, he was cute and tall. But there was something about him that drew her like a butterfly to a flower. He exuded peacefulness.

She pulled into the pharmacy lot and parked. That was it. While she wrestled with the turmoil of the ranch's finances and the problems on the wagon tour, Evan was calm and peaceful. Never rattled.

Just like her mother had been.

She opened her door and stepped out of the Jeep. Well, maybe that worked for him, but she had an ongoing mystery to solve. It was a good thing she was going back to the tour this afternoon and that Evan Parker would have gone home by the time she returned. Too much peacefulness could drive a woman crazy. She knew that for a fact.

An hour and a half later, Bethany tramped into the lodge and set the sack of medicine on the counter. When you lived so far up in the mountains, there was no such thing as a quick trip to town.

Her dad mumbled something into the office phone and hung up. His chair squeaked as he rolled backward, and then he stood. His warm smile settled her worries as he exited the office and leaned on the counter. "As of this moment, we are filled up for the next tour."

"That's great news." She stretched and rolled her head, working the kinks out of her shoulders. "Have you had any more cancellations?"

He nodded. "Two, but I had a waiting list, and those folks were thrilled to fill the openings."

"Good." She smiled. "I got Mr. Parker's medicine. Hey, have I ever had chicken pox?"

Her dad rubbed his chin and stared at the ceiling. After a moment he nodded. "I think so. I know you had something that caused spots all over you."

"Let's hope it wasn't the measles."

"Why?"

"Because Mr. Parker has the chicken pox."

Her dad fought a grin. "Seriously?"

She nodded and rattled the paper bag. "I'll just run this up to Evan's room, then I'm going to take a shower and head back out to the tour."

Her father shuffled his feet and studied the floor. "Well, about that. . . I think you should stay here in case Mr. Parker needs you."

"What?" Bethany straightened. "Why me?"

He leaned his full weight against the counter and tapped a pencil on a notepad with the Moose Valley logo on it. "I don't know nothin' about caring for sick folks. Besides, Scott is back and needs something to do."

She frowned. "I thought you laid off Scott."

He shook his head and looked confused. "What gave you that idea? His grandma died, so he went home for a week to attend the funeral and spend time with his family."

"Oh, guess I misunderstood. I'm glad he's still around." She thought of the good-natured cowboy who played guitar and led the singing around the evening campfire. When she was younger, she'd wanted to grow up and marry the handsome man, but as she got older, she realized the difference in their years was too great. He was closer to her dad's age than hers.

A playful grin tugged at her dad's lips and danced in his eyes. "Besides, I thought you might like some time to get that fancy computer of yours set up. Not that I'll ever use it once you're gone from here."

Her heart somersaulted, and her mind immediately started assembling the computer. "Really? I'd love to get started on that project."

He slapped the counter so hard that she jumped. "Good! I'll tell Scott to get packed. Are there any supplies we need to take with us?"

"Us?"

"With all the problems this week, I thought it might be good to have an extra set of eyes up there."

She nodded. "Might not be a bad idea. As far as supplies, I don't know of any, but you might call Jenny or Jim. Someone is going to have to survey all the guests and find out if everyone has had the chicken pox. Or at least inform them that they've been exposed."

"What if they haven't? We sure can't offer them all a refund."

Bethany crossed her arms. "I don't know. If they've just now been exposed, then maybe they won't be contagious or break out until they return home. The doc said it takes a week and a half to two weeks to incubate."

Her dad stood and scratched his head with both hands, leaving his short gray hair pointing in a jillion different directions. Kind of like someone else's. "Okay then, I'll go hunt down Scott."

"After you do that, could you get those computer boxes from our living room and cart them down to the office while I get a shower?"

Ever the Western gentleman, he tipped an imaginary hat. "Yes, ma'am. I can do that."

She jogged up the steps, her excitement growing. Finally. She'd be able to bring her family's record-keeping system into the twenty-first century. She slowed her steps outside Evan's suite; the television hummed through the walls. Maybe she could recruit Taylor to help her. The girl must be bored.

She thought of her foreman's daughter. *That's it. I can introduce her to Cheryl.*

She reached up to knock on the door then lowered her hand. If Bethany stayed here, she would probably see more of Evan. She would have to face her feelings instead of running back on tour as she'd planned.

But then what was the point of it? He'd leave in a week and go back to his home in Laramie, and she'd go to Denver. She'd learned years ago that long-distance relationships never worked out. Oh sure, there were sworn promises to e-mail or call, but the longer two people were apart, the rarer those contacts became. Better just to nip things in the bud.

She knocked on the door, and after a moment Taylor answered, eyeing the sack in Bethany's hands. "Hi."

Bethany held it out to her. "I've got your uncle's prescription and calamine lotion. I also picked up a bottle of ibuprofen for him so he can take them as he needs. Is there anything else I can do for you guys?"

Taylor shook her head. Without the sassy teen attitude pouring forth, the girl was pretty with her dark brown hair and blue eyes almost as vibrant as her uncle's.

"Let me set this down and get the money. Uncle Evan said to be sure I paid you for the medicine."

Bethany waited while the girl fished around in her pockets and held out the money. "Thanks."

Taylor leaned against the doorjamb as if in no hurry to get back to her show. Bethany ought to leave, but she wanted to ask about Evan. "How's he doing?"

"Sleeping, moaning, and trying not to scratch." Taylor grinned. "Men can be such babies when they're sick. Mom always said if Dad got a paper cut on his finger, he'd have to go to bed for two days."

Bethany shared a chuckle with the teen. Her dad had always been hale and hearty, and she knew nothing about men being sick. "I'm going to put together a new computer downstairs. If you get bored and want something to do, feel free to come and help."

Taylor's eyes sparked with interest. "Thanks. I might just do that after I give Uncle Evan his medicine."

Walking down the hall, she thought how fortunate Evan was to have his niece to care for him. The few times she'd been sick, Polly, the ranch cook, had tended to her, but it wasn't the same as having family care for you. Bethany sighed. She wished she could have checked on Evan herself, but it hardly seemed proper now that they were back at the lodge. She ran down the stairs, thankful to have a project that would occupy her mind and rid it of Evan Parker.

❧

Evan very gently rubbed—not scratched—an itch through his T-shirt. As soon as he quit rubbing, the sore started itching again. Now that the spots had scabbed over, they itched even more. He grabbed the bottle of calamine, put a glob on his finger, and lifted his shirt to paint the offending area. He looked as if he'd been the loser in a paintball battle against a bunch of girls using pink paint.

Taylor had gone downstairs to chat with a new friend she'd made. Lucky her. There were so many other things he'd rather be doing besides lying in bed that even chatting sounded fun. Being laid up was kind of like going on a fast. Food he'd rarely eaten, like hot dogs and fish, sounded good. Now, just about anything would be fun. Even the wagon train ride didn't seem so bad. Had Bethany returned there? He hadn't seen her since the day he came back to the lodge.

But hadn't Taylor mentioned something about helping her put together a new computer? The days swam into one, and he couldn't remember much about the past few, but now that his head was clearing, he needed to try to get some work done.

He glanced at the bird clock on the wall. The incessant chirping every hour on the hour had driven him crazy until he'd finally crawled out of bed and removed the batteries. Sure, it looked great with the room's decor, but it was annoying.

His stomach growled, reminding him that dinnertime was just an hour away. A woman named Polly had delivered meals to him the past few days, but Taylor had met Polly's daughter, Cheryl, and decided to eat downstairs with her.

He glanced at his pink-splotched belly. With his sores healing, he was no longer contagious, and fortunately, none had formed on his face. Maybe he could clean up and eat downstairs this evening and then get some work done on his project tonight. He stood and made his way to the bathroom. If he hurried, he just might surprise Taylor and Miss Schaffer.

An hour later Evan sat back in his chair in the dining hall. "You have no idea how good it feels to leave that room."

"I know I sure got tired of it until I met Cheryl. She's a lot of fun." Taylor took a sip of her pop and followed it with the final bite of apple pie. "Mmm, that was really good. I'm going to the barn and see if Cheryl's there. She said I could help her brush down the horses this evening. Then we're going swimming."

Evan leaned forward. "I know it's summer, but isn't it a bit too cool for swimming after the sun sets?"

Taylor grinned and stood. "The pool is heated."

"Be careful around those horses. They're—big." He shivered at the thought of his niece anywhere close to those big teeth and hooves, but she'd occupied most of her time down at the barn while he recuperated. Now he understood better what Erin went through watching her oldest child grow up and away from her.

Taylor put her tray on the conveyor belt, and it rolled into the kitchen.

She dashed out a side door. Evan knew she'd been surprised to see him downstairs and even a bit relieved. Silverware clinked at the few tables with guests, and the soft buzz of conversation floated around the room. A wide two-story window offered a magnificent view of the mountains. If he had to be stuck somewhere recovering, this place was much better than most.

"Well, look who decided to rejoin the living." Bethany stood beside him holding a tray of food.

His heart did a little flip-flop. "Yeah, I'm AAK."

"What?"

"AAK—alive and kicking."

"Oh, I get it. Geek speak. Mind if I join you?"

He waved his hand toward a chair. "Not at all."

She set down her tray, took a seat, and stared at him. "You're not contagious anymore, are you?"

"The doc said I could be in public once all the sores had scabbed over, and they have."

She wrinkled her nose and grabbed the salt shaker. "Such lovely dinner talk."

He sat with one arm over the back of his chair and watched her eat. Her hair was pulled back in one of those stretchy bands, but rebellious wisps hung enticingly around her tanned cheeks. She glanced down to cut her steak, and her long lashes fanned across her cheeks. Evan sighed. Too bad he wouldn't be here much longer.

She peered up at him, an ornery smile making her eyes glisten. "You look like you had a wreck with a Pepto-Bismol truck."

"It's not that pink, is it?" He held out his hand. Several healing sores were covered with pink lotion, and he knew the ones on his neck also showed. "If I was smart, I'd invest in calamine lotion stock."

She giggled and forked another bite into her mouth. After chewing and taking a drink of her tea, she glanced up. "Can I ask you something?"

"Sure."

"I've been trying to figure out ways to better market Moose Valley and come up with more activities to draw people here. We've had some cancellations lately, but I have no clue why. I thought maybe if we had more to offer. . ."

"Well, let me think for a minute." He focused on activities since he knew little about marketing. After a few minutes, he leaned forward. "At the county fair, they had a hot air balloon that people paid to ride in."

She scowled and wiped her mouth with her napkin. "Sounds like a lawsuit waiting to happen."

"Not really. It was tethered. People just rode up, had about a fifteen-minute look around, and came back down."

"What about on windy days?"

"You leave it tied down on the ground."

"Hmm. . .it might work. What did they charge?"

"Fifteen dollars for fifteen minutes—per person." Evan took a sip of his pop and crushed the empty can. "You could even get a balloon made with the ranch's logo on it."

Her eyes sparkled. "I *love* that idea. Wonder how much something like that would cost."

He shrugged. "No clue."

Evan pushed his tray to the center of the table and leaned his arms where it had been. "Do you ever open the place up for guests in the winter?"

She shook her head. "No. It's too hard for tourists to get here when the snow is deep."

"Well, maybe you should rethink that. You could offer sleigh rides and maybe some winter sports."

She smiled at a couple who walked past their table. "I'll have to think on that for a while. I'm not sure we want people here in the winter, not that I plan to be here."

"Where would you be?"

She fiddled with her cup of tea then finally looked up. "I have a job in Denver that I'm supposed to start in another week."

Evan felt his brows tug upward. "You're leaving the ranch?"

She was silent so long that he didn't think she'd answer. "It's been a dream of mine for a long time."

"Wow." He looked around the large dining hall and out at the mountains, their snowy tops glistening in the sun. "I can't imagine living in a place like this and just walking away from it. It's like being five thousand feet closer to God."

She pursed her lips and heaved a breath through her nose. Then she stood. "Yeah, well, just imagine how lonely this place is when there's nobody around for months on end. And try making new friends, only to watch them leave every few weeks."

She snatched up her tray and stormed away.

"Wow. Did I ever hit a sore spot." He'd never thought about it before, but even with so many people around, Bethany Schaffer was lonely. How could she not be when everyone she met stayed only a few days to a few weeks and then was gone from her life like snow under the summer sun?

Chapter 9

Bethany pursed her lips. Setting up the new computer was proving to be more complicated than she'd expected. Once she and Taylor had unloaded everything from the boxes, there had been a plethora of wires to connect, not to mention making room on the counter for the monitor and keyboard. She tapped a pencil against the granite counter and waited for the professional accounting software to install. The printer that her college roommate had given her had saved some money, but it didn't match the rest of the equipment. Oh well, who would even notice?

"Hey, you got a computer."

Bethany peered up into Evan's eager blue eyes, and her limbs felt as boneless as spaghetti. The pencil flipped out of her fingers and rolled across the counter. She owed him an apology for storming out after dinner last night. He was just being friendly, but he'd hit too close to home.

"So, are you working the registration desk *and* the gift shop?" He glanced at the store. "I need a caffeine fix."

"There's free coffee in there." She nudged her chin toward the open doors of the dining hall.

Evan scrunched up his lips in a cute way and waved a hand in the air. "I've never had a cup of coffee. Can't stand the taste."

"If you've never had any, how do you know you don't like it?" Bethany eased off the stool she'd been sitting on.

He grinned wide, revealing even, white teeth. Her stomach felt as if a flock of butterflies were trying to escape. "Okay, so I tried it in college. Once." He grimaced and shuddered. "I just prefer my caffeine cold."

She chuckled at his performance, grabbed the key to the gift shop, then opened the door. She needed a break anyway. "A cold drink sounds good."

Inside the store, Evan opened the small refrigerator's door and grabbed a can. He looked back over his shoulder. "What's your pleasure, ma'am? I'm buying."

"You don't have to do that."

He lifted up a hand, silencing her. "What kind do you want? Or should I just pick?"

She sighed. "Root beer, please."

He snagged a brown can and meandered along the row of candy bars.

"Are you one of those junk food addicts?"

His head was lowered as he studied the selection. His hair looked more orderly than normal. "Guilty as charged." He chose two bars and plunked them on the counter with the pop cans. He reached into his pocket and pulled out a five-dollar bill.

Bethany rang up his purchase and handed him his change.

"Care to join me on the porch for a few minutes?" he asked.

She had plenty of work to do, but until the computer was finished doing its thing, she was at a standstill. "Just let me check the progress of the software I'm installing, and I'll take a short break."

With the program at just 47 percent loaded, she figured she might have five minutes to spend with Evan. She dashed into the office, grabbed a brush from the top drawer, and ran it through her hair. She wasn't primping for him, she fibbed to herself.

Outside, Evan had pulled two of the wooden rockers close together. Her root beer lay on the seat of the empty chair. She snatched it up and sat down, popping the top of the can. It hissed and sizzled, sending a sweet scent into the air. The snowcapped mountains rose up before them. She'd grown so accustomed to seeing them that she pretty much took the view for granted. She needed to take time to appreciate the beauty around her—and the heritage that would one day belong to her.

"Choose one." Evan held out the two candy bars.

"Oh, no thanks. This drink is plenty."

He tossed one at her then tore the paper off the other and started eating. Bethany grabbed at the bar as it slid down her leg. "You don't take no for an answer, do you?"

He shrugged, giving her a charming look. Maybe he wasn't as unaware of his appeal as she'd first thought. She tore back the paper and bit into the sweet confection.

"Are you planning on putting your registration system on your computer now that you have one?"

She took a drink of her pop and peered at him. "We've had a computer for a while, but it's an older one. We keep it in our private quarters. But yes, I do hope to get the registration on the new computer soon, although I plan to install the bookkeeping program first."

"That should make things much easier for you and will save time."

"That's what I'm hoping." She bit off a small piece of her chocolate bar.

"You know, that printer you have isn't going to work with your new operating system."

Bethany nearly choked on a peanut and leaned forward, coughing. Evan patted her back and looked concerned. She washed the bite down with a drink of root beer, thinking about the money she'd saved by not buying a printer. "Why not?"

"Those new operating systems don't have drivers for printers as old as yours."

"That's just great."

"The dealer should have explained it when you bought your computer. Basically, the manufacturers wanted people to have to buy more printers, so they didn't write a printer driver that would allow older printers to work on the new system."

"The clerk asked if I needed one, but I told him I already had one." She leaned back, allowing the view to comfort her.

He fiddled with his can then looked at her. "I saw your Web site. It's a nice, basic one. I, uh. . .wouldn't mind designing a fancier one for you—as a way of saying thanks for allowing me to stay here and for caring for me while I was sick."

Bethany waved her hand in the air. "Thanks, but that's not necessary."

He lifted up his rocker and jiggled it around to face her. "No, seriously. I'm a computer engineer. Designing a Web site would be simple. I like doing it, and maybe a fancier one would help draw more business to your place."

Their Web site was plain but functional. She'd designed it using a basic template that the Web host offered. If they redid it, they could add pictures and all kinds of features. Hope building, she reconsidered. "Could you maybe add one of those animations? Like a moving wagon train or a galloping horse?"

His wide grin warmed her insides, and she was glad that the chicken pox hadn't marred his fine features. "You bet. Or we could videotape a real wagon and show the mountains behind it. Maybe even with the sun setting."

Excitement growing, she jumped up. "Let me get some paper and make notes."

Evan stood and followed her inside the lodge and behind the registration desk. "I could take some pictures with my digital camera to show the awesome countryside and the main lodge. Might even take a photo of that old tree trunk with the mother and baby bear carving, with the stairs to the lodge in the background."

Bethany checked the monitor. "My accounting software's done loading, but let's work on the Web site idea. I'd love to have a site that lists our prices and shows everything we have to offer."

She pulled a pad of paper from a drawer and grabbed a pencil. She wrote down several items then tapped her pencil against the paper as she considered what else to add. Since Evan was more than willing to build a new Web site, she wanted the best one possible.

૱

Evan couldn't help smiling. Once she'd decided to proceed with the new Web site, Bethany jumped in with both feet. Standing beside him, her chin rested in one hand with her elbow on the counter, her other shoulder pressed against his. She'd leaned in at one point and never moved away.

He liked her nearness and the feel of her arm touching his. Wisps of blond hair flittered around her tanned cheeks. She was organized, reliable, cute, and lively—when she wasn't worrying about everything. And she'd been very kind and nurturing when he'd first become sick. He knew then that he wanted to get to know her better. To have a relationship with her.

But as an unbeliever, she was off-limits. He sidestepped and put some distance between them, not that four inches was all that much. At least she was no longer touching him.

He zeroed in on the notepad and refocused on the job at hand. If he could get the basics of what she wanted, he could hide himself back in his room and get to work. This job should only take a few hours.

He cleared his throat. "I can add a counter if you like. That way you will know how many hits you're getting and where the visitors live."

She turned those doelike eyes on him. "You can do that? Tell where people live?"

He nodded and forced himself to look away. His heart pounded, and he watched myriad dust motes floating along on a beam of sunlight. Picking up his pop can, he moistened his dry mouth.

"That's about all I can come up with," Bethany said. "What do you think?"

Evan forced his gaze back to the notepad. "Looks good. What would you like for your dominant colors?"

Her gaze roved the lodge. "I guess we should stick with woodland colors: brown and dark green mainly."

"Great." He tore off the top sheet with all her notes. "I'll get started on this right away and have a prototype for you to view by dinnertime."

"That's wonderful. I never dreamed when I got up this morning that we might have a whole new Web site by evening. I don't know how to thank you." She stared into his eyes.

Warning bells went off as he longed to embrace her. He cleared his throat. "I, um. . .can't work on my project until I hear back from my boss and he approves of the section I just completed, so I might as well get started on this now."

She smiled shyly up at him. "All right. I'm anxious to see it."

His gaze lowered to her lips, and he felt as if a mainframe computer rested on top of his chest. *"Submit yourselves, then, to God. Resist the devil, and he will flee from you."*

Okay, so Bethany wasn't the devil, but she was a temptation. She licked her lips, and his heart stumbled. He may be a geek, but he was still a man—a man who'd spent little time with a member of the opposite sex, especially one who intrigued him so much.

Using every ounce of strength left in his body after nearly a week's illness, Evan stepped back. "If I get done before dinner, I'll come down and show you what I've worked up."

She nodded, looking confused. Maybe she'd felt a similar attraction to him. Thinking that did not help. Not one bit.

He strode toward the elevator, grateful when the thick metal doors closed and blocked his view of Bethany Schaffer. If not for Taylor wanting to stay the full two weeks, he would pack up and be gone as soon as he finished the Web site. But he owed his niece that much.

He'd just have to find a way to steer clear of the tempting Miss Schaffer until then.

Chapter 10

The phone jingled, and Bethany picked up the receiver. "Moose Valley Ranch."

"This is Marilyn Bochner. My family has a reservation for your July nineteenth tour. I need to cancel that."

Bethany's mouth went dry; she clutched the receiver. "May I ask why?"

"It doesn't really matter. We aren't going to be able to come. I understand there's no penalty for canceling. Is that correct?"

Disappointment and the loss of income made Bethany's stomach swirl. "Yes, ma'am. That's right."

"Good. Now, please cancel my reservation."

"Just a minute, please. I need to find your information card." She put the woman on hold and closed her eyes. That was the second cancellation this afternoon. What was going on?

Digging around in the old file box, she located Mrs. Bochner's index card, which had her contact info and reservation date on it. The reservation was for a family of five. Ouch. With tours costing over fifteen hundred dollars per person, Moose Valley was taking a big hit. They definitely needed a cancellation policy. She made a big X across the card and stuck it in back with the terminated reservations, and then she erased the Bochner name from the July 19 tour list.

She picked up the phone and forced a smile into her voice. "All right, ma'am. I've taken care of everything. I hope in the future you might consider trying us again."

The phone clicked without so much as a thank-you from the woman. Bethany exhaled so hard that she fluttered a sticky note that clung to the counter. Why were so many people canceling on short notice? Sure, it happened now and then because emergencies occurred, but not this frequently.

The spicy-sweet scent of barbecue wafted from the dining room, reminding her that dinnertime had arrived. The elevator opened, and Evan shuffled out carrying his laptop. He almost looked as if he were afraid to approach her, as if she wouldn't like his creation.

"How's the Web site coming?"

"Ready for you to approve—or not." He laid the computer on the counter. "Where's your Internet hookup?"

She pointed under the counter, and he plugged in his cord. They'd had the lodge wired for Internet several years back, but she'd never been able to talk her dad into getting a computer for the reservation system and bookkeeping.

She'd finally just decided to buy one and make him learn to live with it, and she was glad now that she had. If nothing else, it gave her something in common with Evan.

He logged on and waited for the Internet to come up. His eyes narrowed, and he peered sideways at her. "You know, you really ought to consider getting a wireless setup."

"I'm counting my blessings as it is, just having a computer. Things move slower up in the mountains than in the lowlands. When I was little, we didn't even have electricity."

Evan shook his head and typed in her Web address. "I'd be out of work without that."

Bethany gasped as a beautiful home page filled the screen. An image of the Alpine lodge with the mountains in the background created a masthead with the ranch name in letters that looked as if they'd been created out of pine boards. "It's awesome! Where did you get that picture?"

Evan studied her face as if to gauge her response. "I took it." He leaned close to the screen and pointed at something. "It's real small, but you can see the bear statue right there."

She leaned closer, and sure enough, there it was.

"I have a bigger picture of it on a different page. So, what do you think?"

Glancing up at his boyishly expectant expression, she wanted to lean in and hug him, but she didn't. "I love it so far. Show me more."

"Once we videotape the wagons moving with the mountains in the background, I'll add that here." He pointed to a blank area. "If you want, you or your dad could even narrate the video and tell people about your ranch."

"Dad might enjoy doing that. Besides, he's the real-deal rancher and would draw people's interest."

"We can add more links. I wasn't sure what all you might need. I've made pages for the wagon tours, horseback riding, directions, and your rates, which I need to get from you."

"One thing I do want to add is a cancellation policy. For some reason, we've been getting a lot of them lately."

"Really?" Evan straightened. "You mean more than normal?"

She nodded and clicked on the wagon tours link. "Yeah."

"Do you have the cancellation policy written down? If so, give me a copy, and that will be easy to add."

She turned to face him. "Well, that's the problem. We've never had one. Dad wanted to keep things simple for our guests, and he thought the friendly thing to do was not to have one. We discussed it last night and decided we were losing too much money, so we just came up with one."

"That's probably a smart idea, and you ought to have a nonrefundable deposit. That would make people less likely to cancel." He leaned against the counter. "Just give me the info, and I'll make a cancellation section below the rates."

She pulled the paper from her pocket and studied it. She hated being such a stickler about things, but they couldn't afford to get stuck with empty wagons when they normally had a waiting list.

Evan tapped his index finger against his front tooth and looked deep in thought. She laid the paper on the counter beside him and clicked on another link. Evan sure knew his stuff. This Web site was way more than she ever could have hoped for. He was kind to put so much effort into it.

A movement outside the window snagged her attention. Taylor and Cheryl bumped shoulders and giggled as they climbed the front steps to the lodge. Cheryl held the door for Evan's niece, and the girls ambled toward them. Where Taylor was a willowy brunette, Cheryl was blond, short, and a bit on the chunky side.

Pulled from his thoughts, Evan looked up and smiled at the girls. "Long time, no see."

"So, the patient has emerged from his recovery room again. It's good to see you back among the living." Taylor set her elbows on the counter and rested her chin in her hands. "So, what are you doing back there?"

"Your sweet uncle made a new Web site for us."

Cheryl glanced sideways at Taylor. Both girls had ornery expressions on their faces. "Sweet, huh?"

Bethany realized her error. "Well. . .it was sweet of him to design the site, especially after he's been so sick."

Taylor straightened. "I for one am glad he found something to do. He was about to drive me crazy. Why is it men are such babies when it comes to being sick?"

"I wasn't a baby." Evan looked insulted.

Bethany smiled and patted his shoulder. "It's okay. You had a good reason to be fussy."

"How about buying us something to drink, Uncle Evan?" Taylor lifted her brows expectantly.

"Sure, if the store is open."

Bethany grabbed the key and wiggled it in the air. "Always, for a paying customer."

She walked behind the counter and through the hallway toward the store. The others followed, and Evan mumbled something.

She opened the door and held it back for them to enter. The girls skipped in and bounced over to the pop fridge. Evan ambled in after them, his head down.

"What did you say?" Bethany asked.

His gaze darted up and collided with hers. He stifled a laugh and broke eye contact. "Nothing. Just that I wasn't fussy."

Bethany chuckled under her breath and slid behind the cash register.

❧

Outside, Evan sat on the porch with Taylor and Cheryl. The two girls giggled and chattered like magpies. After a few moments, they turned to face him.

"You ought to see how well Taylor can ride a horse now, Mr. Parker."

"Yeah, I'm turning into a regular cowgirl. I'm actually glad you got sick so we had to come back."

"Me, too." Cheryl smiled, then her eyes widened. "I mean, I'm not glad you got sick, but I am glad that Taylor is here."

Evan chuckled.

Taylor tilted her head back and took a drink of bottled water. In the porch lighting, he could see that her skin was darkening, and her cheeks held a healthy, rosy glow. She seemed happier than she had been in months.

"Cheryl's even teaching me how to rope. Do you want to come and see me?"

"I'd like that, but the sun has already set. How about we wait until tomorrow?"

Cheryl popped up from her rocker and glanced at her watch. "Uh-oh, I'm in trouble. Mom'll be wanting me home since it's getting late. See you tomorrow, Taylor. Thanks for the pop, Mr. Parker."

Taylor watched Cheryl trot to the side of the lodge. The girl waved as she headed toward the cabin she shared with her parents. Taylor turned back and looked at him. "This place sure is peaceful. No traffic sounds, no sirens."

"No teenagers playing their car stereos as loud as they can."

Taylor snickered. "Everybody has an MP3 player now."

"Excuse me for being an old geezer," Evan teased, even though he had his own MP3 player in his room.

Taylor laughed out loud. "You're not that old, Uncle Evan." Her blue eyes twinkled and dark brows waggled up and down. "At least Miss Schaffer doesn't think so."

Evan tightened his grip on the chair. Had Bethany noticed his interest? He'd tried to keep from letting his attraction to her show. He was a city boy and she was a country gal. There was no future for them as a couple. "What do you mean?"

Taylor elbowed him in the arm and grinned. "She likes you. Can't you tell?"

Evan laid his head back against the rocker. He had noticed that the impatience and irritation present in Bethany's gaze when he first met her had dimmed, and her defensive shields had lowered. He *had* noticed her interest in him, but he'd thought her softening was merely gratitude because he'd helped her several times. But maybe there was more to her actions than he'd realized.

He ran his hand through his hair and pushed thoughts of Bethany

Schaffer aside. He pulled his gaze away from the darkening mountains and back to Taylor. "It's great to see you smiling again."

She leaned back and crossed her arms. "I like it here. I can't imagine how wonderful it would be to live here."

"You'd get bored. No malls. No movie theaters. No ice cream shops."

"I can get ice cream from Cheryl's mom or in the store."

"Ah, but it's not the same thing."

"If I lived here, I wonder if Mom would let me get a horse of my own."

Evan didn't want to throw cold water on the fires of her dreams, but nothing would come of such thinking. "I'm just glad you're having a good time, sweetie."

"I am. Cheryl's dad is taking us fishing tomorrow." Taylor nibbled her lip. "I can go, can't I?"

That she was asking him and not telling him meant they'd crossed an invisible barrier somewhere along the way. "As long as you're careful and he doesn't mind you tagging along."

The cool evening breeze whipped across his face, bringing with it the fragrant scent of pine. A lodgepole pine on the other side of the parking lot waved its limbs as if in praise to God. How was it that he felt closer to the Lord out here, away from the city?

"Do you think Dad would have stayed with us if we'd lived somewhere like this?"

Evan clenched his jaw as anger surged through him at the way Clint Anderson had hurt his family. He leaned forward and placed his hand on Taylor's arm. "No, sweetie, I don't. Your dad loved your mother and you kids, but he was never one to settle down."

She swiped at the tears on her cheeks. "I used to think it was my fault. That he left because I was bad or something."

Evan stood. He pulled his niece up and into his arms and kissed the top of her head. "Nothing you did caused him to leave. Trust me. He just wasn't a man who could handle responsibility well."

Taylor's tears dampened his shirt, and she clung to him. "Why couldn't he be more like you?"

Joy flooded Evan's heart. She'd just given him the ultimate—albeit indirect—compliment. He squeezed her tight. "God knows how you feel, Taylor. You can always talk to Him and cry on His shoulder if I'm not there."

She ducked her head and stepped back. She wiped her face and then looked up. "Thanks. I don't know why I suddenly had that meltdown. Maybe because I'm jealous that Cheryl's dad is so nice and friendly."

"Well, I'm not a dad, but you can use my shoulder anytime you need it."

"Thanks."

She smiled, and he wrapped his arm around her shoulder. "I don't know about you, but I'm hungry. Let's go see if there's any pie left over from dinner."

Chapter 11

The elevator doors opened, and Evan turned left toward the registration desk instead of the dining hall. His stomach rumbled in complaint as he sniffed the scents wafting up from the lunch buffet. Burgers would be his guess. After being sick and then getting back on normal food, he'd been amazed at the flavor of the beef served at Moose Valley. He'd never tasted fresh beef raised locally before, and he seriously considered asking about buying some to take home with him.

Bethany leaned down, looking at something on the monitor, and her hair hung around her face, blocking his view of her pretty features. He liked it down much better than pulled back with one of those elastic bands wrapped around it. Her loose purple top hinted at her womanly shape and hung down over her jean-clad legs.

"Hey." He leaned his arms on the counter.

She slowly looked up, and dark chocolate eyes met his. Something in them sparked, spinning his insides in circles, and she smiled. "You won't believe this. We've already had twenty-two hits just since the new Web site went online last night, and I've received two reservations for next month. One visitor was from New York, and another was from Vancouver. Isn't that amazing?"

The expression on her face was amazing. Evan returned her smile, glad that he'd been able to help. He liked making her happy. "Yeah, it is. You might even have to add some more wagons if this keeps up."

She swatted her hand in the air. "Yeah, sure."

"I'm serious. I've got something I want to talk to you about. Can you take a lunch break?"

She glanced into the vacant office behind her. The chair was shoved back, and the new computer boxes still littered the floor. She closed the door, hiding the mess. "I usually watch the desk when Dad's not here, but I guess I could if we eat out here or sit in the dining hall so I can see the desk. You never know when someone will want something."

She walked beside him into the dining room and toward the buffet line. He wished he had the right to hold her hand, but he didn't, and she'd probably go ballistic if he tried in front of her guests. Several tables held families who were staying at the lodge or awaiting the next wagon tour. Taylor sat with Cheryl and her father near the two-story window that showcased the mountains. Both teens seemed to be talking at once and waving their forks at each other. Girls sure were strange at times. If he ever had kids, he'd only have boys. They were much easier to handle and understand.

Evan handed Bethany a tray, then they each gathered their silverware and moved down the line. He took a thick beef patty and topped his bun with mayonnaise, lettuce, and pickles. Bethany slathered hers with mustard and ketchup, then put two slices of cheese on it and added every condiment offered *except* pickles. He shook his head. They were polar opposites in more than one way.

Bethany waved at the cook, who was in the kitchen slicing a pie. It wasn't butterscotch from the looks of it, but he knew it would be tasty, as everything else he'd eaten at Moose Valley had been—except for the meat that had been tampered with. Why would someone want to cause trouble at Moose Valley? It would take a lot of effort to come to such an isolated place and to hang around without being noticed, just waiting for an opportunity to stir up trouble.

They sat down at a table where they had full view of the registration desk. Around them the soft buzz of conversation and the clink of silverware filled the room. Evan said a quick prayer of thanks and closed his eyes as he bit into the thick beef patty. "Mmm. . .this is the best meat I've ever eaten."

A soft smile tilted Bethany's lips. "Yeah, that's one of the things I miss when I'm not here."

"I know you guys raise cattle, since we've seen a lot around here, but who do you sell the meat to?"

"Dad has some contracts with stores and restaurants in nearby towns, but most of what we raise stays here."

He took a swig of his pop. "Have you ever thought about making your beef available to your guests?"

Her brow crinkled then lifted. "Just what do you think you're eating?"

"That's not what I mean." He popped a chip into his mouth. "What if you sold packaged beef to your guests?"

She shook her head. "I don't see how that would work. Most of them fly to Jackson and then rent a car to drive here."

"So? You could ship it to them."

Bethany gave him a patronizing stare. It was the same look Erin gave him whenever he tried to talk computers with her. As if he were dumb to even bring up the subject.

"It can be done. There are companies that specialize in shipping meat to customers."

She stirred her baked beans. "Sounds like a lot of work."

He shook his head. "Not really. You just have to have some of the beef packaged in specific weights. Maybe like five-pound or two-pound packages."

"Well, that works for ground beef but not cuts like steaks."

He shrugged. "I didn't work out all the details, but it seems to me you could stand to make some decent money from such a venture."

She glanced toward the desk then leaned back in her chair and crossed her arms.

"The customers could pay for the shipping cost and the packing. All you'd have to do is box up the meat, invest in some dry ice or frozen packets, and deliver the boxes to a shipper. Sounds pretty simple."

"Uh-huh, and someone has to keep track of those orders and record the information."

"Yeah, there's that." He took another bite of his burger, realizing that there was more involved than he'd first thought.

She leaned forward, arms on the table, eyes focused on his. "You know, you may be on to something. I'll talk to Dad about it tonight."

"I have another idea, too. You want to hear that one?"

Bethany grinned. "I thought you said you didn't know anything about marketing."

"I don't really." He fiddled with his fork, trying to look nonchalant when he felt anything but that. Why was helping her so important to him?

"So. . .what other ideas do you have?"

"I noticed that you don't have any souvenir items with your logo on them."

"Dad never liked the idea of forcing folks to buy stuff like that when they pay so much money to come here."

"Many parents go looking for souvenirs to get for their kids. It's not forcing if they want them. Kids would love little stuffed animals like they see on the wagon tours—moose, deer, beaver, and maybe even a bear."

She sat up straight. "You saw a bear?"

He grinned. "No, but I sure thought about them and how that tent canvas wouldn't keep one out if it wanted in."

"Just so you don't worry, we've rarely had problems with them—not during the summer anyway. The smell of so many people usually keeps them away."

"Usually?"

She lifted one shoulder. "We did have a bear—at least that's what we think it was—break into one of the cookhouses in May. I guess the bear must have smelled food, although we hadn't equipped the cookhouse yet for this summer's tours. It sure made a mess."

Evan tapped on the table, his thoughts running rampant. "What if it wasn't a bear and was the same person who's been causing trouble?"

She opened her mouth then slammed it shut. "I never even considered that, but in light of the problems we've had lately, I probably should."

He laid his hand on her arm. "I'm praying that you'll figure it all out."

"Thanks." She pulled away and leaned against her chair. "Back to your great ideas. Got any more?"

"You might consider having some T-shirts, sweatshirts, or jackets for sale with your logo on them. You could even keep a small stock of those at the cookhouses, so if someone should find out they left their jacket in the car"— he grinned—"they could buy something to keep warm."

"Are you talking about yourself?"

"Maybe."

Bethany shook her head. "You're something else, you know it?"

He wasn't sure if that was a good thing or not, but she *was* smiling. The phone at the registration desk beeped, and Bethany jumped up and ran toward it. He carried their trays to the conveyor belt and set them down. They disappeared under a dark green flap. Spinning around, he noticed Taylor was gone and strode out of the dining room. Now that he was well again, he ought to do a better job of watching her, but Bethany had assured him that Cheryl was very mature for her age and would see to it that Taylor didn't get into trouble. He needed to get back to work. They'd be leaving in a few days, and he was still behind on his project after being sick. His steps slowed as he reached the front desk.

"I can't believe that. Who was it?" Bethany said into the phone. "Did they leave a name?"

Bethany listened, brows furrowed like a plowed field. "Thank you for calling and letting me know. If you remember the name, please call me back. Okay?"

She listened a moment longer and then hung up. "You won't believe this."

"What?" He moved around behind the counter and stood beside her. He couldn't resist holding her shoulders. "Tell me."

"That was one of our best repeat clients, who's booked for our mid-July tour. He just received a phone call from another guest ranch offering to beat our price if they'd change their reservation. Ooh!" She slapped the counter then rubbed her hand. "That makes me so mad. Stealing customers is unethical."

"Well, now you know why you've had so many cancellations."

She gazed up at him with hurt in her dark brown eyes. "People out here watch out for one another. Who would do such a thing?"

Evan shook his head. "I'm sorry, but that's one thing I can't help you with since I don't know anyone around here. You'll have to discuss that with your dad."

Her eyes blurred with unshed tears. "Looks like I won't be starting my new job anytime soon."

Evan stuck his hands into his pockets, wishing he could pull her into his arms and comfort her. "Sounds like you're needed here."

"Yeah, it does." She sighed and swiped at a stream of tears running down her cheeks. "I just wish we knew who was causing all this trouble."

Evan snapped his fingers. "What if I registered under a different name and left my cell phone number? Now that I'm back here, it's working again."

"That might work. But how in the world could they be getting our reservation info?"

"Who has access to your cards?"

"Nobody. Just Dad and me."

"That's not totally true. The cards were here on the counter while you and I were eating. Anybody could have looked in the box while we were getting our food."

Her shoulders drooped. "You're right. Dad and I can't watch the desk constantly. We used to have a girl who worked here, but Dad. . ." She bit her lower lip as if she'd said too much.

He didn't want to push her to share more information than she was comfortable with. "So, basically anybody could have snooped in the box at a time when you and your dad were gone."

She nodded. "Yep. At least once all that information is on the computer, nobody will have access to it."

"Did you assign yourself a password?"

"No. I didn't think it was necessary with just Dad and me using it."

He laid his hand over hers. "It's necessary. That way you can leave and nobody else will be able to access it. I can help you set up a password if you don't know how."

"All right, let's do that and get you set up for another tour. What name do you want to use?" She opened her wooden file box and pulled out a blank card.

He tapped his finger against his lips and stared at the ceiling. "Daniel Lionheart. Group of four."

She lifted one eyebrow and looked at him as if he'd gone crazy. "Lionheart?"

He grinned. "Yeah, Daniel and the lions' den is one of my favorite Bible stories. Can't you just imagine how scary it must have been to be thrown into a pit with a pride of hungry lions?"

She shivered. "I don't even want to think about it."

"I've always admired Daniel. He refused to bow to anyone except God, and it could have cost him his life. I want to be that bold in my walk with the Lord."

"I remember that story from when I was younger. I think I had a picture book that my mom read to me."

"Yeah, me, too."

She seemed to snap out of her melancholy moment. "Okay, Mr. Lionheart, what's your cell phone number?"

He rattled it off, wondering why she'd looked so sad for a moment. "I'll let you know ASAP if they call me."

"Okay, thanks. I think I'll call one of our regular clients and see if she and her friend would mind if I booked them, too. We might be more likely to hear something if there are two fake reservations."

"Good idea. Have you known those clients very long?"

She nodded. "You'd probably like them. Elsie and her friend Margaret—they're known as the Groovy Grannies—drive a hot pink semi and haul products."

"Seriously?"

Bethany smiled, warming his belly as much as the hot apple cobbler he'd just had for dessert. "Yeah, Elsie used to come here with her husband, but after he died, she brought her friend Margaret, who is also a widow. We love them both. Dad's been encouraging them to retire, but I can't imagine Elsie being happy staying in one place for any length of time." She sucked in a deep breath. "Listen, thanks for everything. It helps to have someone to talk things out with, and I'll tell Dad about your *marketing* ideas."

He chuckled at her emphasis on marketing. "I'm glad I could help. I'd better head upstairs and get some work done." He walked away, wanting nothing more than to stay and spend more time with her. Too bad he was leaving so soon.

❧

Bethany watched Evan stride away. He wasn't as broad in the shoulders as the ranch hands who had done hard physical labor much of their lives, but he was tall and well built for a city boy. The elevator doors closed, but not before she saw him smile and wave. A warm sensation spiraled down her chest to her stomach.

Evan was thoughtful and logical, which was why he was probably very good at his job. He certainly was dedicated to his work—but not so much that he couldn't take breaks or come talk to her. He wasn't the nerd she'd first thought he was. She couldn't help grinning. "Well, he is a bit of a nerd."

"Who is?"

Bethany glanced up. "Maggie!"

"Hi. I was driving past the ranch and thought I'd stop in and see how things are going."

"Well, they've definitely been better. I'm so sorry Dad had to let you go."

Maggie shrugged. "Everyone's been hit by the bad economy. I'm working in town at Gertie's Café."

Bethany smiled. "I'm sure glad you found some other work. Are you interested in coming back here when things turn around?"

"When? Don't you mean 'if'?" Maggie leaned on the counter and propped her chin in her hands.

Bethany shook her head. "No, I mean 'when.' I have to believe things will get better."

"I suppose. Is your dad here? I wanted to say hi to him, too."

"He's gone on a tour, but you can hang around and talk to me if you want."

"Okay, I will. So, how do you like living in Denver?" Maggie tucked a strand of her black hair behind her ears. Her green eyes glistened with curiosity.

"I like it, I guess. I miss Dad and even have to say I miss the ranch at times."

Maggie laughed wryly. "I don't think I'd miss living in the sticks if I ever got away from here."

Bethany knew exactly how she felt, but her own desire to leave seemed to be fading. Maybe because her dad needed her or because of the ranch's problems. "Well, you'll be a senior next year, right? Got any plans for college?"

Maggie curled her lips. "As if my parents could afford it."

The girl's clothes looked new and of a high quality, not something a blue-collar worker like her father could afford. She was getting money from somewhere. "Well, maybe things will work out."

"Oh, hey. I've got a new boyfriend—Ryan Ogden. His family moved to Wyoming last year and started Ogden's Outfitters. It's a new guest ranch east of here on the old Scroggins land."

"Yeah, I heard someone talking about them, but I haven't met the owners yet." Bethany leaned forward. "Listen, I got a phone call just as I was finishing lunch and didn't have time for a pit stop. Would you mind hanging around a few minutes while I run to the restroom?"

"Sure. No problem."

Bethany logged on to the ranch's Web site. "Here, have a look at this while you're waiting. Let me know what you think."

Maggie slipped behind the counter. "Oh, wow! This is awesome. I love the animated wagon train."

Still listening eagerly to Maggie's excited responses, Bethany walked down the hall and into the restroom. She was glad that Maggie wasn't upset with them for laying her off. The girl had always been happy, and Bethany would have hated losing her friendship. Maybe they'd be able to rehire her when Bethany returned to Denver.

Back at the desk, she said good-bye to Maggie. She hated not being able to employ the cheerful teenager who loved people and had made a perfect desk clerk.

Bethany tapped on the keyboard, trying to set up a password. Finally, she sighed, giving up. That was another thing she needed Evan's help with. How would she have gotten her computer up and running without his assistance?

She thought about what he had said about Daniel refusing to bow down to anyone but God. She missed the closeness she felt to God as a child and young teen. If she hadn't walked away from Him, would the ranch be having the problems it was?

No, she couldn't believe that God worked that way. It was unfortunate that her father drained the bank account to pay off her college loans. Why had he done something so foolish when they could have made monthly payments?

Somehow, she'd pay back every penny. But not anytime soon. She didn't even draw a paycheck while working the ranch. Of course, there had always been plenty of money in the account to pay for the things she needed. She picked up the receiver and set it back down. She didn't want to do this, but she had no choice. Dad needed her. The ranch needed her. She punched in the phone number. Time to call her new boss and see if she could postpone her starting date.

Chapter 12

I sure hope I'm not making a big mistake here." Bethany climbed out of the Jeep and looked at Evan as he closed the passenger door.

"Trust me, you're not. Your guests will be thrilled that you've switched over to a wireless network. They'll be able to sit on their balconies or the lodge porch and check their e-mail or conduct business." He grinned, making her heart turn somersaults. "Welcome to the computer age."

"Well, I'm not there yet. We still have to find the right equipment, and that can be hard to do in these small Wyoming towns."

Evan met her in front of the Jeep and gazed around. "This town is a lot smaller than Laramie."

"Ya think?" Bethany blew a sarcastic laugh between her lips. "Try comparing it to Denver, where I've been living the past four years."

"It does kind of look like something out of a cowboy movie."

"Well, it's a tourist town. What else would you expect?" She tried to view the town from his eyes. No town in Wyoming even came close to what Denver had to offer, but that's what the locals loved about it. You could get close to nature here like you never could in a big city, and there was no quiet like that of the mountain valleys. She shook her head. She was getting nostalgic in her old age.

"Point the way, tour guide."

"Yes, sir, city slicker." Bethany smiled and pointed. "It's that store across the street."

They walked to the corner and waited for the light to change. The streets were crowded with vacationers strolling along, carrying packages, and dodging in and out of stores.

A car started to turn left in front of a pickup. Tires screeched, and the truck driver laid on his horn. Bethany jumped and stepped closer to Evan. She liked the amenities a town had to offer, but she hated traffic and congestion. In truth, she *was* a country girl at heart.

The light turned green. Evan grabbed her hand as if it was a common occurrence and tugged her forward in the crosswalk. She liked the feel of her hand in his bigger one. It felt solid and strong. She doubted he even realized what he'd done, and she shouldn't enjoy feeling as if she belonged to him, but for this one moment, she would.

He opened the door, allowing her to enter first. His hand rested lightly on her lower back as he looked around the store. He pointed in the air. "Over there."

Evan guided her toward the back of the store where the wireless routers were located. As he studied the few available, she watched him. He looked like a wide-eyed child riding his first horse, minus the fear element.

"Okay." He picked up a box. "I recommend this one. Do you want the Muskrat Lodge to also be wireless?"

She hadn't considered that yet, but the cost of the router wasn't as much as she'd expected, and they'd be offering wireless Internet access to more of their guests. "How many routers would you need if we did the main lodge and Muskrat?"

"Two, probably. What about the cabins?"

She thought for a moment then shook her head. "I think we should leave those as they are for people who are coming to get away from the rat race."

"Okay, then two should be enough." He grabbed a package of cables. "We can hook the router for the main lodge to your new computer, but we'll need to find a closet or utility room for the one at Muskrat Lodge."

They selected a new printer and then checked out. She could almost imagine them as a married couple in town to do their shopping for the week. She probably shouldn't have spent the money for the routers, but Evan was right—they needed to offer top-of-the-line service to be competitive with other outfitters. Besides, who knew how much she would have had to pay if she'd hired someone to do the work? Evan seemed to enjoy helping her with her computer woes. Was she taking advantage of him?

Suddenly he stopped in the middle of the sidewalk, his nose tilted in the air. Tourists gawked and made a wide clearing around him. He looked one way then another. His sky blue eyes sparked. "Pizza. I smell pizza."

Bethany couldn't help giggling. He was like a big kid. He tucked the sack of computer supplies under his right arm and looped his left arm through hers.

"C'mon. I'm buying lunch. Two weeks is too long for a man to live without pizza."

"You don't have to buy lunch. We can eat at the ranch," she protested but couldn't help the pleasant feeling swelling inside her. This was almost like a date. An impromptu date.

They took a seat in a booth, and Evan looked at her. "What's your pleasure, ma'am?"

"Hamburger."

"Just hamburger? Where's your sense of adventure?"

"Oh, I have all the adventure I can handle, thank you. But maybe I will get something different today." She tapped her finger on her lips. "Hamburger with black olives."

Evan grinned. "I like a woman who's not afraid to step out and take a chance."

A skinny young man with big ears and teeth stopped at their table. "You guys ready to order?"

"Give us a large thick crust. Half supreme and half hamburger with black olives. I'll take a Coke, and the lady wants. . ." He lifted his brows.

"Iced tea." The waiter nodded and walked away as Bethany plucked two packages of sugar from a little dish near the salt shaker. "So, I guess you'll be happy to get back home."

"Yeah, all this fresh air is clogging my sinuses."

She shook her head.

"Seriously, though. There are things I will miss about this place. I can't believe I've lived my whole life in Wyoming and never visited the mountains before. My parents never traveled much, and I've been busy working." He tapped his fingertips on the table as if he were typing on his keyboard.

Bethany couldn't help wondering if she was one of the things he'd miss. How had she gone from crowning him the greenest among the greenhorns to hating to see him leave? His gaze lifted from the table and collided with hers. For a moment she couldn't breathe at the intensity of his stare.

"I'll miss *you*, Bethany."

He glanced away, as if fearing her rejection. She ought to nip things in the bud, but the truth was, she'd miss him, too. He'd sneaked in under her radar and stolen a piece of her heart. But like all the others she'd befriended or cared about, he'd be leaving—soon. Still, she couldn't lie to him. "I'll miss you, too."

His hopeful gaze swerved back to hers. His lips tilted upward, and he slid his hand across the table. Hers move forward to meet his, as if it had a mind of its own. He clutched it tight. "So. . .what are we going to do about this?"

She shrugged and pulled her hand back. "Nothing. You'll go back to your world, as I will."

Scowling, he repeatedly flicked the edge of his napkin with his index finger, and she thought he'd drop the subject. The waiter delivered their drinks, and Evan captured her gaze again. He sighed. "I won't lie to you. I don't have much experience with women. I dated a few times, but most girls prefer jocks to geeks. I don't want things to end like this. At least we can e-mail each other and stay friends."

"Yeah, sure. We can do that." She knew how e-mailing worked. The first week or two there would be a ton of messages, but as the weeks drew on, there'd be fewer and fewer. Maybe it was better to play along, knowing how things would eventually end. That way he'd be hurt less than if she just dropped him now. She had to protect her heart. No one else could do that job.

❧

Their pizza arrived, and they ate quickly, talking little.

He'd pushed too hard, and now she was pulling back. But he didn't have much time left.

Maybe this was God's way of telling him that she wasn't the woman for him. A Christian shouldn't be yoked with an unbeliever—he knew that—but for a short time he'd allowed himself to run on emotions instead of logical thinking.

Bethany flicked her hair out of her face, and he longed to touch it, to see if it was as soft as it looked.

Stop it, Parker. How could he lose his heart so fast, and to a country girl who didn't want to live in the country? He straightened. If she didn't want the country, would she consider living in Laramie? It wasn't Denver, but maybe it could be a nice compromise. Nah, he'd better just be happy that she agreed to be friends.

Bethany shoved back her plate and finished her drink. Evan jumped up. "Ready to go?"

She flinched, as if surprised by his sudden movement. Nodding, she grabbed her purse.

He walked toward the checkout register, ready to get back to the ranch and away from her. He'd been a fool to bare his heart when he knew things could never work out. What was he thinking?

He'd seen what happened in Erin's life when a Christian married an unbeliever. Sure, things had been bearable for a while, but in the end, Clint had walked away from his family, leaving behind a debris trail as wide as an EF-5 tornado and a hurting wife and children. Evan had been the one to step in and clean up that mess, and he wasn't about to make the same mistake.

He'd been stupid to think things could work out between him and Bethany, to even consider a relationship with a woman who wasn't sold out to God. He just had to face reality and make his heart stop aching.

Chapter 13

Bethany tapped her finger on the phone receiver. *Should I call him or not?* She needed Evan's help with another computer problem but hated calling him after he'd all but given her the cold shoulder then stayed in his room after they'd returned from town yesterday. He hadn't even come down for dinner or this morning's breakfast.

She couldn't exactly blame him.

The elevator doors opened, and Bethany's heart jolted. She was half disappointed and half relieved when Taylor got off instead of Evan. The teen waved and stopped at the counter. Almost two weeks in the sun had tanned her skin to a golden brown, highlighting her blue eyes. She was a pretty girl who would grow into a beautiful woman as long as she kept her attitude in check.

"Hey, Miss Schaffer."

Bethany smiled. "Looking for Cheryl again?"

Taylor nodded and glanced out the front window as if searching for her friend. A black SUV pulled into one of the parking spaces, leaving a cloud of dust trailing behind it.

"Um. . .I probably shouldn't say anything. . ." Taylor glanced up, an intensity in her eyes. She nibbled on her lower lip, revealing front teeth with the tiniest of gaps. "My uncle may be a geek, but he's a really nice guy. I don't know what we would have done after my dad left without Uncle Evan's help." She looked back at Bethany. "He doesn't have a lot of experience with women. I hope you'll give him a break. He really likes you."

Bethany felt as if her mom had just given her a well-deserved lecture. "I like him, too, but I don't want to lead him on. You guys are leaving, and so am I. Soon. There's no future for us together."

Taylor raised her gaze, probably up to the moose head on the wall behind Bethany. "Never say never. God can do amazing things. Just give Uncle Evan a chance, will you?"

An older couple walked up the front stairs, and the man held the door open for his female companion, probably his wife. In that split second, Bethany wondered what it would be like to grow old with Evan.

Taylor peeked over her shoulder then flashed a tight-lipped smile. "I probably shouldn't have said anything, but I hate to see my uncle looking sad. He does so much for others that he deserves some happiness of his own."

Bethany watched the teen walk toward the dining hall. *How had the girl changed from Miss Attitude to Wise Sage so quickly?*

She shook her head, putting Evan and Taylor out of her mind as she registered the new guests. Five minutes later she escorted them to their room on the same floor as Evan's. "I hope you have an enjoyable stay here at Moose Valley Ranch. Please let me know if you have questions or if there's anything I can assist you with."

"Thank you, miss." The man closed the door to the room.

As Bethany walked past Evan's door, her steps slowed. She ought to keep walking. She could figure out the problem herself, but it might take hours. Sighing, she lifted her hand and knocked.

The door handle jiggled, and then Evan stood before her, a slight scowl wrinkling his forehead. His hair was messed up, as if he'd been running his hands through it. His eyes looked tired and red, as if he hadn't slept the night before.

Was she responsible for his rumpled state? Hadn't she only been protecting her own heart? It pained her to think she might have hurt him. She ducked her head.

He reached out, lifting her chin with his index finger. "Hey."

Every fiber of her body seemed happy to be in his presence again. She cleared her throat. "I was, uh. . ."

Evan's brows lifted.

"I was wondering if I could buy you a pop."

His eyes sparked; then wariness descended, stealing away her hope that he would agree. "Why?"

Pulling away from his stern gaze, she noticed a frayed edge of carpet at the door's threshold. *Better let Dad know about that before it gets worse.*

She took a strengthening breath. The discomfort between them was her fault because she had tried to distance herself from him. Could they actually be friends and leave it at that?

Bethany shrugged. She could really use a good friend. She summoned a smile to her face. "I thought maybe you'd need a caffeine fix about now. . .and I could use some help on the computer."

He faked a brief laugh. "Ah, so the truth comes out." He rubbed the back of his neck. "I guess I could use a break. Just let me save my current work."

She watched him walk over to the coffee table where his laptop sat. He made a couple of swift hand movements and stood. Beside the couch on the end table was a tray of dirty dishes. "Mind if I grab that tray and take it downstairs?"

"I'll get it." He snatched up the tray and held it so high she couldn't reach it, even standing on tiptoes.

"You're the guest. I should be carrying that."

He pulled his door shut. "Maybe, but I was the one who ate the food."

A WAGONLOAD OF TROUBLE

Bethany sighed and trotted down the stairs with Evan beside her. Their being together felt right somehow. Like wearing matching shoes or hitching the correct team of horses to a wagon. She was in dangerous territory, allowing her thoughts to travel along such lines.

At the counter, Evan lowered the tray and she grabbed for it. He raised it over her head again, sidestepped around her, and grinned. "How about you unlock the store, and I'll return this to the kitchen?"

"Fine." She conceded her loss with a smile of her own. She liked this playful side of Evan Parker. In the store she grabbed two cans of pop and a bag of chips. She wrote a note that she'd taken them so she could deduct the items from their inventory later, then locked the door. Evan joined her at the counter.

"So. . .what seems to be the problem this time?"

She told him and stood beside him, watching the master at work. She was no dummy concerning computers, but he seemed to know them inside and out. It amazed her how he could fix something in five or ten minutes that took her hours, if she could fix it at all. Leaning toward the monitor to get a better look, her arm touched his. He'd rolled up his sleeve, and this arm was free of spots. The warmth of his skin soaked into hers and made her hands tingle. He seemed oblivious but shifted his feet and leaned a bit closer, all the while jiggling the mouse and working the keyboard. His milk chocolate hair hung across his forehead, and his lips moved as if helping him.

The doors opened, and her father strode in. Bethany hopped back a half step, putting distance between her and Evan. He glanced sideways and grinned. The rascal had been aware of her nearness all along if she wasn't mistaken.

"What are you doing back, Dad? There haven't been any more problems, have there?"

He shook his head. "Nope. Jenny's running low on sugar and some other stuff, so I made the run back here. Got another problem with that crazy computer?" Her dad barely glanced at them as he walked around the counter and into the office. "Don't know how you expect *me* to run that thing when you can't even get it working. I'm going to have to build a house for Evan so he can stick around and help keep that computer working."

She wasn't sure if her dad was just mumbling to himself or complaining loud enough for them to hear on purpose. Teaching him to run the computer was a big concern. He was a skilled man, but with horses, cattle, and ranch equipment, not electronics. Maybe she ought to figure out a way to rehire Maggie. Having the teen work the counter as she had last summer would free Bethany to do other jobs.

Something that sounded like a foghorn blasted outside. Evan jerked his head up and stared out the front window at the same time Bethany did. What in the world? A huge pink RV stopped along the back edge of the parking lot.

"Talk about Pepto-Bismol. I can honestly say I've never seen anything quite like that." Evan stared openly at the huge vehicle.

Bethany rounded the counter and squinted at the lettering on the side of the motor home. In fancy gold script, she read, THE GROOVY GRANNIES. "Oh my goodness! Dad! Elsie and Margaret are here—and they're not in their semitruck."

"Two grandmas drive that thing?" Evan's surprised expression made her giggle.

Her dad came out of the office and strode toward the door. "What do you mean they're not in their semi?"

"Well. . .look!"

He muttered under his breath. "I tried to talk them into selling that pink semi last time they was here, but I never expected them to buy something as hideous as that."

She hugged him. "Be nice, Dad. They're entitled to live their lives the way they want."

Bethany dashed out the door and jogged down the steps. Elsie had traveled the country hauling freight the past few years with her friend Margaret even though both of the women's families had tried hard to get them to retire. It looked as if they finally had.

"Howdy!" Elsie climbed out of the RV and waved, her silver hair sparkling in the sunlight. Wearing leather boots, a pink tank top, and shorts, she stepped to the ground. She enveloped Bethany in a bear hug. "My, just look at you. You're so lovely."

"And look at you. You're retired." She pushed back to see Elsie's wrinkled face. "You are retired, right?"

Elsie nodded as Margaret, wearing a lavender sweat suit and black sunglasses with shiny sequins along the top, rounded the front of the RV. "That's right. We are officially retired."

"Then what's this contraption?" Bethany's father waved his big hand in the air.

Elsie shoved her fists to her slim waist. "What did you expect, Rob? That we were just going to retire in some old folks' home?"

Bethany grinned. "I don't think he ever expected you to retire at all. So, what brings you out here?"

"We came for our wagon tour."

Bethany glanced at her dad. "But that was just a test registration to see if anyone would call and offer you a better deal at some other ranch. That hasn't happened, has it?"

It was Margaret's turn to get her feathers ruffled. "Well, if they did, we'd have given them what for. Imagine stealing your customers. Why that's unethical."

Bethany looped her arm through Elsie's and tugged her toward the lodge. "Still, I never meant that you actually had to go on the tour."

"We want to. We have all the time in the world now."

Her dad offered his arm to Margaret, and the two followed them inside. "Let's all go get something cool to drink. My treat."

"You're so generous, Rob," Elsie joked and patted Bethany's arm. "I thought you were starting a new job in Denver, dear."

Bethany darted a glance at her father and noticed his lips tighten. "We can talk about all that later. I want to hear what you've been doing."

They marched inside, but as Bethany turned toward the dining hall, Elsie tugged her in the other direction, toward the counter.

"My, my. I'd say that young man is quite an improvement over that young tart you had working here before."

Evan's vivid blue eyes widened as he looked up from the monitor.

"Whew! And look at those eyes. Just like Paul Newman's." Elsie turned to Bethany and whispered, "I do hope you're planning on keeping him."

Her cheeks felt as if they'd been torched. "He doesn't work here, Elsie. Evan's a guest who's helping me get the new computer system up and running."

Elsie turned loose of her arm and walked up to the counter. "Come along, young man. We're taking refreshment in the dining hall."

Evan's questioning gaze rushed to Bethany's. She didn't mind him joining them and nodded toward the dining hall. He looked down and made a few quick taps on the keyboard then offered one arm to Elsie and carried his pop can in the other. "I already have a drink, but I'd enjoy the company."

Margaret took Evan's other arm. "You can't have him all to yourself, Els."

Bethany suppressed a grin. Evan looked bewildered but smiled down at the two older women and led them into the dining hall as if he were escorting royalty.

Over tea and pie, they caught up on all that had been going on at the ranch. Elsie pushed back her empty plate. "I don't like that all these strange things have been happening."

"Maybe the prankster has gotten tired. You haven't had any problems here while I was gone, have you?" Bethany's father looked across the table at her, and she shook her head.

"Nope, nothing but some cancellations."

"Good, maybe that's over with." Elsie smiled at Evan as he took a swallow of pop. "Are you married, young man?"

Bethany stifled a gasp as Evan worked hard not to spew his drink. He pounded his chest and coughed. "Uh. . .no, ma'am."

Elsie winked at Bethany, and Margaret smiled as if she'd won the lottery. Bethany shoved back her chair and stood. "Don't you think we should get back to work, Evan?"

He nodded and stood. "Nice to meet you both."

If Bethany hadn't been as anxious to leave as he was, she might have laughed at his hasty escape.

❧

Evan leaned against the corral and watched Taylor lead a golden horse out of the barn. She'd called it a palo-something. She waved, warming his heart. If nothing else, this trip had brought them closer together. He prayed that when they returned home she wouldn't cop an attitude like before.

The setting sun sent lances of light into the pink and orange clouds, creating a view that took his breath away. Only the almighty God could have created such a magnificent sight. He forced his gaze away so that he could concentrate on Taylor.

"Watch me, Uncle Evan." She nudged her horse in the side, and it jolted into a trot. Taylor bounced up and down.

He clenched the railing, afraid that at any moment she'd fall to the ground and he'd have to call Erin to explain how Taylor had broken her arm. He climbed up on the bottom rail and was ready to yell at her to stop when the horse broke into a smooth lope that settled Taylor into the saddle.

Someone slapped him on the shoulder, and he jumped. "Easy, city boy; she's doing fine."

He lowered himself to the ground and glanced at Bethany before turning back to watch Taylor. "Tell that to my heart."

She chuckled.

Near the barn door, Cheryl bounced up and down. "Yee-haw! Ride 'em, cowgirl."

Taylor's megawatt grin could have lit up the whole city of Laramie.

Bethany climbed onto the fence and placed a hand on her brow to shield her eyes from the sun as Taylor rode around the corral. "She's gotten quite good at riding in a short time. You might want to think about finding a place for her to ride when you go home."

He tightened his grip on the wooden rail. He didn't want to think of leaving in two days. Of never seeing Bethany again—but she'd made her position clear. She would be his friend, but she wasn't willing to risk her heart on a computer geek from the city. His pride took a nosedive, but it wasn't the first time.

"Has Taylor talked to you about tonight?"

His niece made several circles around the corral then rode the horse back toward the barn. Cheryl walked out and took the reins while Taylor slid off.

Evan turned to face Bethany. The sky was darkening, but he could still see her well in the twilight. "What about tonight?"

She pursed her lips then looked up. "I guess it's no secret that Taylor and Cheryl have become good friends. Polly asked me earlier if you might consider letting Taylor spend the night with Cheryl."

Evan's gut tightened. Should he let his niece stay with people they barely knew? Sure, they seemed like decent folk, but what would Erin do?

Bethany must have sensed his concern, because she laid her hand on his arm, warming it through his sleeve. "I've known Shep and Polly Wilkes most of my life, and I can vouch for them. They're good folk. Taylor will be fine with them."

Cheryl handed the horse off to her dad, and the two girls raced toward him, their eyes lit up as they climbed over the corral fence.

"Did you ask him?" Cheryl directed her question to Bethany.

She nodded.

"You'll have to ask your mother." He didn't mind passing the buck to stay out of trouble.

Taylor grinned. "I already did, and she said I could if you thought it was okay."

He was cornered. He'd met Shep Wilkes once and liked the man, but the bottom line was that he trusted Bethany's judgment. Evan nodded, and the girls squealed and high-fived each other.

"Let's go pack your stuff," Cheryl said, bouncing up and down.

Both girls took off running, but Taylor slid to a halt and jogged back. She wrapped her arms around Evan's waist. "Thanks!"

Before he could return her hug, she was gone.

"You did the right thing. They'll have a blast." Bethany smiled. "Cheryl gets lonely living here. Trust me, I know."

Something about the melancholy in her voice touched a spot deep within him, and he longed for her to know God more closely—to know Him as the Friend who was always there. Who would never desert her. Maybe she could never be his, but if he could introduce her to his Savior, he wouldn't worry about her so much once he was gone. He stared out at the darkening sky. "Would a country gal be interested in taking a walk with a city boy?"

She cocked her head. A smile danced on her lips. "Why not? Dad's gone back to the campsite, so there's nobody waiting for me."

He stuck out his arm, and she looped hers through it. "Which way?"

She tugged him toward the barn. "There's a hill we can climb and see the sunset better."

They walked in silence, and when the climbing became more difficult, she let go of his arm but he captured her hand. Friends could hold hands, right? Her skin was soft and warm, and she didn't pull away. As they topped the steep hill, the sky brightened a bit. The sun had already disappeared behind the mountains, but the distant horizon glowed like a pinkish-orange neon rope light. "It's beautiful."

"Yeah. I haven't been out here in a long while." She stood quietly for a few minutes then cleared her throat. "I, uh, have something to ask you."

"Yeah?" He turned to face her.

"Dad and I were wondering if you might be willing to stay on a few more days to help make sure the computer is up and running. We can't pay you anything, but you could keep the suite and we'd feed you. He also wanted me to tell you that we'd like you to come back with your sister and her kids and take another wagon tour. You've been such a big help that we wanted to do something for you." The words seemed to rush out of her, as if she were afraid to voice them.

Evan shook his head and grinned. "No thanks on the tour, at least for me."

He considered her offer to stay longer. He was making excellent progress on his project now that he was feeling better, and with Internet service, he'd been able to do several video conferences with his team. As far as he knew, Taylor didn't have anything that she had to do once they returned home, but he should probably call Erin to make sure.

"It's okay if you can't. Dad wanted me to ask you."

His excitement at spending more time with Bethany spiraled down like a marble on a twisting slide. "Your dad—or you?"

"Both of us." She shrugged in the waning light. To her right, the lodge and buildings glowed as lights popped on. "Okay, it was my idea, but Dad is in full agreement."

Evan smiled then. "I'd like that, but I do need to check with Erin."

She nodded and turned back toward the mountains. Feeling brave, Evan wrapped his arm loosely around Bethany's shoulders. She glanced up at him then focused back on the sunset.

"God sure made some beautiful sights," he said. "I can't believe I've lived my whole life in Wyoming and never been here before."

"It's like any other place. When you live here and have seen it so often, you take it for granted. I know I do at times."

"Yeah, just like people take God for granted."

She stiffened but after a moment relaxed. "I was close to Him as a child, but after Mom died and Dad wouldn't take me to church, I drifted away."

"It's never too late to make things right with God." He tightened his grip on her shoulders.

She sighed loudly. "I don't know how to."

"All you have to do is pray. Acknowledge your need for God and believe that Jesus died for your sins. God is always waiting for you to come to Him."

She shrugged. "You make it sound so easy."

Evan turned to face her again and rested his wrists on her shoulders. "It is easy. All you have to do is express your need for God and ask Him to come into your heart."

"Seriously?"

"Yep." With the sky nearly black, Evan could barely see Bethany's face. "All you have to do is ask."

She sniffled. "I've been angry with God for so long. I still don't understand why He had to take my mother away when I needed her so much."

Evan stroked her hair, wanting to comfort her. "People get sick. They have accidents. But God can give us the strength we need to make it through those rough times."

"I want to make things right with God." She ducked her head and leaned it against his chest. "Will you help me, Evan?"

His heart took off like a racehorse from a starting gate. "I'd love to."

He said the words, and she repeated them after him, asking God to forgive her sins and to come into her heart anew.

Bethany looped her arms around his waist, and Evan couldn't resist hugging her back. "Now you never have to be alone. God will be your Friend."

"Yeah. That's pretty cool."

He could feel her tears dampening his shirt. She may not be his, but she would always be the Lord's.

After a few minutes, Bethany loosened her grip and stepped back. Reluctantly, he let her go. She lifted up on her tiptoes and placed a brief kiss on his lips. Evan felt his eyes widen in the dark and longed to keep her from leaving, to hold her tight and let her know the depth of his feelings. But now wasn't the time.

"Thank you. I will always appreciate how you brought me back to the Lord."

They walked down the hill. Evan knew he should be thrilled that she'd reconciled with God—and he was. But he wanted more. He wanted her in his life.

Maybe staying longer wasn't such a good idea, after all.

Chapter 14

You're sooo lucky. I wish I was staying longer." Misty Chamberlain hugged Taylor before climbing into the school van.

Evan watched his niece saying good-bye to all her friends, glad that he had decided to stay on a few more days. He opened his laptop, ready to do some work on the lodge porch while enjoying the warm sunshine.

Sarah James walked out of the lodge with another girl, carrying a Coke and a sack of chips. "I can't wait to get home and eat junk food again and watch TV."

A boy carrying a duffel bag jogged down the steps past her. "You would, you couch potato."

Sarah scowled and stuck out her tongue at him, then walked down the stairs. Chuckles sounded all around as two boys tossed gear into the van.

It was no wonder Taylor struggled with attitude problems when she was around these kids all the time at school. Evan wished he could afford to send his niece and nephew to a Christian school. He typed in his password.

Taylor waved good-bye to her friends and teacher, then walked toward the corral where Cheryl sat on the top railing waiting for her. His niece had been ecstatic when Evan asked if she wanted to stay a few more days. He wasn't quite so thrilled, but after praying, he felt it was what God wanted him to do. Maybe things could still work out between him and Bethany—or maybe the Lord wanted him around to help strengthen her new walk with God before he left.

He sighed and tapped on his keyboard. The van driver honked as the tires crackled on the gravel and pulled away, leaving behind a trail of dust. Fortunately, the dirt cloud floated away from him instead of toward him.

Staring out at the mountains glistening in the morning sun, he heaved a sigh. He just wasn't in the mood to work today. Maybe he could go riding with Taylor and Cheryl, not that the teens would want a greenhorn uncle tagging along. If he had a swimsuit, he could enjoy the pool. With the school group gone and a new group of guests already on the second day of a new wagon tour, there were few people about the ranch.

He stood and stretched. What he needed was a jog. He'd been idle too long after being sick, and his muscles were tight and stiff. A cloud of dust still lingered over the valley the van had just driven through. If he jogged down the road, would the cows bother him?

Shaking his head, he closed his laptop. Bethany would certainly tease him if she thought he was apprehensive of cows. Not cows exactly, but more the unknown. His mood soured, and he realized this was just another way they were incompatible.

He picked up his laptop and headed toward the front door.

Bethany nearly knocked him down on her way out. Her eyes were wild with worry, and she stared past the barn, not even noticing he was there.

"What's wrong?" He grabbed her arm until she looked at him.

Her gaze took a moment to register his presence. "Dad's been hurt."

"How?"

She turned away, keeping her vigil again. "Steve's bringing him in. He just called and said Dad was unconscious."

Evan's heart lurched.

"Jim hitched up the teams this morning, but afterward, someone cut the traces and several other parts of the harness on Dad's wagon. When Dad ordered his team to go, the horses walked forward, but the wagon didn't move. Dad was jerked off the wagon seat. . . ."

She clutched his arm, tears in her eyes. "Oh, Evan. I can't lose him. He's all I've got."

Evan set his computer back on the table and held her shoulders. "He's not all you have. You've got God now—and you've got me."

Leaning against his chest, she sobbed. Evan was stunned to see this woman who was normally so in control of her feelings falling apart. He held her until she pulled away and looked again toward the wagon trail.

"Listen, sweetheart. I'm going to run my laptop up to my room. Why don't you get your keys and purse? That way we can take your dad to the hospital as soon as he arrives." Evan picked up his computer. "There is a hospital in town, right?"

Bethany nodded then spun around. "No, but there's a clinic."

"All right. I'll run upstairs. Could you call Shep and see if he'd keep an eye on the girls? I don't know his number."

"Yeah." She raced past him and through the front door, seeming happy to have something to do.

Evan glanced toward the trail. No sign of the Jeep yet. He ran up the stairs, taking two at a time. "Please, Father. Let Rob be okay. Bethany needs him. Don't take him from her."

❧

"I'm not going to no doctor." Bethany's dad slid forward from the back of the Jeep where he'd been lying down and sat on the tailgate. He listed to the left, and she reached out to steady him. He swatted her hand away, and with one of Jenny's towels from the cookhouse, he swiped at the blood dripping down his temple. He stood, wobbled, and sat back down. Steve stood beside the Jeep scowling.

Her heart ached. Her father's jaw was swollen, and blood seeped from a goose egg on his forehead. He held his left arm close to his chest and weaved sideways as he tried to stand again.

"I'm not taking no for an answer. Get in my Jeep, Dad."

She gently reached under his right arm and helped him to straighten as he mumbled something about her being bossy. Steve stayed close to Rob's side and stood ready to assist if needed, but with her dad's confounded pride, she should count her blessings that he was allowing her to help him at all.

Evan ran out the front doors with something in his hands, and Bethany's nerves settled a measure just having him near.

"Polly cornered me and sent an ice bag. How is he?"

"He's fine," her father growled.

The fact that he let her put him in her Jeep instead of going into the lodge proved that he wasn't as well as he claimed. Her heart stumbled at that thought. He leaned his head back, and she buckled his seat belt and closed the door. Evan handed her the ice pack, and she passed it to her dad through the window. "Keep this on your forehead."

He mumbled something else but did as he was told.

She motioned Steve to the front of the vehicle. "How long was he unconscious?"

The ranch hand shook his head. "Hard to say, because I was driving and his wagon was in the back. He was out from the time he fell until after we got him in the Jeep and I was well on my way back. Twenty minutes maybe."

Bethany winced. "That's a long time."

Evan took her hand and squeezed it. "We'd better get going before your dad changes his mind."

She nodded. "Anything else I need to know?"

Steve shrugged. "The wagon was hitched up properly. I know because I did it myself." He lifted off his hat and scratched the back of his head. "I just don't see how anyone could have gotten in and cut the harnesses without any of us noticing."

Bethany sighed. "You guys be careful. It's obvious that someone is sabotaging our trips and stealing our customers. I just wish we could find out who it is before a guest gets hurt and we find ourselves facing a lawsuit."

Evan took her shoulders and propelled her toward the driver's seat. "Don't worry about that right now. Just get in and drive."

Steve lifted his brows, and she knew he wondered why this guest she'd poked fun at was ordering her around. She obeyed and climbed into the Jeep, more to avoid Steve and his questions than anything else. Evan crawled in the backseat and closed the door.

She started the engine, backed out, then stepped on the gas. The Jeep shot forward, and her dad moaned. Feeling guilty for causing him pain, she slowed down. *Please, God, he has to be okay. I'll even come back and stay at the ranch if that's what it takes. Just let Dad be all right. I need him, God.*

An hour and a half later, Bethany paced the waiting room of the small clinic. She gulped down the last of her coffee, crumpled the paper cup, and tossed it at the trash can. She missed. "What's taking so long?"

Evan stood and stretched, then put the cup in the trash. "They're probably just being thorough."

She heard a shuffling noise and watched the doorway. Dr. Franklin ambled in, drying his hands on some paper towels. He caught her eye and smiled. "He's going to be fine."

She strode across the room toward him. "How bad is it?"

The doctor nodded at Evan as he joined her, his shoulder touching hers. "He has those cuts on his head and a concussion. He also broke his wrist in the fall."

"Oh," she gasped, and Evan wrapped his arm around her shoulders. She leaned her weight into his side. "Dad is so independent. How will he ever tend to himself with a broken wrist?"

"Well, you've answered your own question, young lady. Rob comes from tough stock. He's independent and will manage, although I suspect he may need your help with some things for a while."

"I know. I'm just overly worried."

"I gave him something for the pain, and it will make him sleep for a while. Why don't you two go grab something to eat, and maybe you could show this young man some of our town."

"There's not that much to see."

The doctor lifted his brows. "People sure pay a load of money to come here."

She ducked her head and studied the cracked tile at her feet. "Yeah, I know."

Evan squeezed her shoulders. "I could use some lunch. I think we'll take your advice, Doc, since Rob will be sleeping."

Bethany wanted to argue, but the fight seemed to have oozed out of her.

The doctor looked at Evan. "You're sure looking better than the last time I saw you. How are you doing? Everything healing all right?"

Evan nodded. "Yes, that medicine you prescribed sure did the trick. I was better in a few days."

"Good. You're fortunate. Chicken pox in adults can be severe and cause shingles." He offered a tired smile. "Well, I'd better get back to my patient."

Bethany allowed Evan to guide her out of the empty waiting room, past the check-in desk where a nurse was busy working on charts, and outside. The sun made her squint after being inside for so long. The hum of cars greeted her as they passed on the street. She heard someone honk and yell. Scents from a nearby café made her stomach gurgle, and she glanced at her watch, surprised that they had missed lunch. She hadn't even noticed. Evan's arm slid off her shoulders.

"So, what will it be?"

She shrugged. "I don't care. Anything is fine."

"Are you okay?"

When she looked up, he ran his finger down her cheek. She was surprised that it had a rough feel to it and wasn't as soft as she'd expected. Could a guy get calluses from typing so much? She smiled.

"What?"

"Nothing. That café across the street has pretty good food—unless you'd rather have pizza again."

"Whatever. You choose." He tucked a strand of windblown hair behind her ear and rested his hand on her cheek.

Her heart swelled with affection for him. He was a good, caring man. Why couldn't their lives be more similar?

His eyes darkened, and she wondered if he would kiss her. Instead, he pulled her into his arms and held her tight. She buried her face against his clean shirt and smelled his spicy aftershave. He was warm and solid. His hand crushed her head against him, and he kissed her hair. Bethany clung to him, wishing she could stay forever in the shelter of his arms without worry or concern.

Evan's phone chirped. He loosened his grip with one arm and reached into his pocket. "H'lo."

She could hear the hum of someone talking but couldn't tell what they were saying. Evan stiffened.

"I might be," he said. He gripped her shoulder and pushed her back. "Tell me more."

He motioned for her to get a pen and paper.

"Yeah, that is a much better deal. What did you say the name of your place was? Ogden Outfitters?" Bethany felt as if she were falling face-first off a cliff. He must be talking to the competing guest ranch. Why did that name sound familiar?

"Can I think about it and call you back?"

The voice on the phone buzzed.

"I understand. I realize you can't give everyone such a great deal. Let me talk to my friends and see if they'll agree to make the change to your ranch. I'll call back in a few hours. What's your phone number?"

He waved at the paper and quoted a number. She wrote it down along with the ranch name.

Evan hung up and grinned. "We got 'em."

"How in the world did they get your number?"

He shrugged. "Obviously, someone went through your file box again."

Bethany pursed her lips and forced her feet to move. "C'mon. Let's get lunch. I want to be there when Dad wakes up."

Evan took her hand, and as if they'd decided together, they both walked toward the café that had a two-foot hamburger painted on the window in vivid colors. Something was nagging at her memory. Where had she heard that name before?

Suddenly she halted and pulled Evan around to face her. The wind whipped at his nut brown hair, making it even more unruly than normal. She clutched his forearm. "Now I remember. Maggie, the desk clerk Dad laid off last month, stopped by this week to say hi. She said she was dating a guy whose father owned Ogden Outfitters, a neighboring guest ranch that's only been in business a short while. That's why the name sounded so familiar."

Evan scowled. "How well do you know this Maggie?"

Bethany waved her hand in the air. "Oh, she's a sweet girl from town who worked for us last summer. She wouldn't do anything to hurt us."

Evan's brows lifted. "Your dad laid her off, and she's dating the son of your newest competitor. Talk about motive."

She opened her mouth, but her gut clenched with disbelief. Surely Maggie couldn't be involved. Bethany gasped and lifted her hand to her mouth, a feeling of betrayal slicing through her. "I left Maggie alone at the counter the day she visited so I could—uh. . .never mind." She looked up at Evan, shock fogging her brain. "I left her at the counter, Evan."

Chapter 15

I think we ought to call the sheriff rather than handle this ourselves." Evan held on to the door frame as Bethany drove her Jeep like a maniac. The wind whipped his shirt like a flag, and grit coated his teeth.

"We handle things ourselves out here."

"I don't believe that for a minute. These people could be dangerous. Look at all the pranks they've pulled. Obviously, they don't care if they hurt people." The engine roared as she gunned it up a steep hill. A sign indicated a right turn onto Ogden land.

She careened around the corner, barely slowing down. Evan flung out his foot as if to hit the brake and used his left hand to brace himself against the dash.

Bethany peeked at him and smiled. "You're such a city boy. Don't you enjoy a drive in the country?"

"Not when I feel like I'm riding in an ambulance minus the tires. All that's missing is the siren." He shook his head. "Remind me not to ride with you when you're upset."

Ten minutes later, she pulled into a crowded parking lot. White buildings and cottages with green roofs dotted the hillside. A huge barn sat off to the side and down a hill with a creek running not far from it. A trio of rafts floated down the creek with several people in each one. The view of the mountains was spectacular but farther away than the view from Moose Valley.

"Looks like business is good here," he said.

Bethany sniffed a laugh. "Yeah, it ought to be, the way they've been stealing customers."

Two long-legged cowboys walked out of the building in front of Evan and Bethany. She fired out of the Jeep like a cannonball, and he leaped out, hurrying to catch up. The crazy woman was going to get them shot.

The taller of the two men glanced at them and said something to the other cowboy, who nodded and walked toward the barn. The tall man started toward them, a wide smile on his face. Evan couldn't help feeling a bit sorry for the guy, not knowing he was about to encounter a rabid she-bear. But then again, if he was guilty of the crimes committed at Moose Valley, he deserved Bethany's ire.

The man's smile dimmed as Bethany stalked toward him. Evan jogged up beside her and grabbed her arm. "Calm down, okay?"

She lanced him with a scathing glare and jerked away. With his hat on, the man stood more than a foot taller than Bethany, but somehow Evan felt the unsuspecting man had the disadvantage.

"I'm John Ogden, owner of this place. Can I help you with something?"

"Yeah, you can stop stealing our customers and pay for my dad's doctor bills." Bethany stomped right up to the man and halted, her chest heaving with rage.

Mr. Ogden darted a confused glance at Evan then refocused on Bethany as if he was afraid to take his eyes off her too long for fear of what she might do. *Wise man.*

"Excuse me?"

Evan stepped in front of Bethany and nearly looked the man eyeball to eyeball. She snorted and tried to squeeze past him. He elbowed her back. "We're from Moose Valley Ranch. Someone has been sabotaging the Schaffers' operation and causing all kinds of problems, as well as calling their booked guests and offering them a better deal to change wagon tours."

"I can talk for myself, Evan Parker."

Mr. Ogden scowled. "I resent the implications you're making. We run a clean operation here and have enough business that we don't have to steal from our neighbors."

"That's a lie."

The man narrowed his eyes at Bethany. "Now see here, ma'am. You can't come onto another man's property and call him a thieving scoundrel with no evidence."

Evan pulled her back and got in her face. "Let me handle this. You're too upset."

She pursed her lips like a woman sucking on a lemon and crossed her arms. "Fine."

Evan spun back around. "We have evidence." He pulled out his cell phone and showed the man his phone with the caller ID showing Ogden Outfitters.

The man lifted his brows and shook his head and crossed his arms, too. "So, you received a phone call from us. What does that prove?"

"The man who called offered me a special deal if I'd cancel my reservation with Moose Valley and sign up for a wagon tour here. He gave me a number to call him back." Evan pulled the paper from his pocket and handed it to Mr. Ogden.

The man's irritation immediately turned to shock, if his changing facial expressions were any indication. Evan knew he recognized the number.

Mr. Ogden sighed and stared toward the mountains. He ducked his head then finally looked back at them. "That's my son's cell phone."

Bethany stepped forward. "Is his name Ryan?"

"How did you know that?"

"He's dating a girl named Maggie, right?" Bethany's stance seemed to relax now that they were getting some favorable responses.

"Yes, that's correct." John Ogden nodded.

"Well, Maggie used to work for us." Evan noticed she left off the part about Maggie being laid off.

"So. That doesn't prove anything." Mr. Ogden crumpled the paper in his fist.

"We think Maggie stole the names from our reservation file. Your son must have been the one to make the phone calls."

The man shook his head. "But why? We have plenty of business."

"Maybe you have plenty of business because of the people who came here instead of our ranch. Do you have any idea how much money in lost fees we're talking about? Tens of thousands of dollars, not to mention that whoever tampered with our equipment and supplies put people's lives in danger. My own dad is in the clinic right now with a concussion and broken wrist because of it. And if someone stole *our* guests, who's to say they didn't steal some from other ranches?"

Mr. Ogden blanched. "I can't believe Ryan is involved, but there's only one way to find out." He spun around and marched toward the barn. Instead of going inside, he bypassed the structure and strode out to a grove of pine trees where someone was waxing a shiny red convertible.

"Ryan Ogden, I presume." Evan hurried to keep up and held on to Bethany's arm to prevent her from running ahead.

"Let go of me," she hissed. "I want to be there when that man confronts his son."

"We're there." Evan hoped he never got on Bethany's bad side. It was a fierce thing to behold.

"This is your phone number, right, Ryan?" Mr. Ogden said as he handed the piece of paper to a handsome young man who looked about seventeen.

"Yeah, so what?" Ryan glanced at Evan and Bethany as they approached, then back at his father. He shifted from foot to foot, looking as if he was ready to bolt.

Evan moved closer, determined not to let the youth get away. He recognized the boy's voice from the phone. Bethany needed all this to be over so she could get on with her life.

"These folks say someone called and tried to get them to change their reservation from Moose Valley Ranch to ours. You wouldn't know anything about that, would you?"

Ryan's face paled, and he backed up against the car. "No, Dad. For real."

"Then why do they have your cell number? And how is Maggie involved?"

Ryan straightened, and a look of panic engulfed his face. "Maggie told? Why that. . ."

"So you were part of this?"

The tall teen shrugged. "I heard you talking on the phone. You said we might have to leave here if business didn't pick up. I was only trying to help."

John Ogden hung his head. "Did you also pull pranks on the wagon tours at the Moose Valley Ranch?"

"What pranks?"

Mr. Ogden looked at Evan, as if he hoped his son wasn't involved in that part of the situation.

"Tampering with the food, turning horses loose, letting air out of tires, and cutting harnesses on the wagons."

Mr. Ogden's eyes widened more with each item Evan rattled off.

"I didn't do those things, Dad. Really."

"Whoever did rides a horse with an egg bar shoe," Bethany said. "We found tracks."

Mr. Ogden ran his hand through his hair. "My son's horse is the only one here that wears them. We recently bought the animal, and it already had those shoes."

"So," Ryan said, "lots of other horses around these parts wear them."

Bethany shook her head. "I've lived here my whole life and don't know another rancher who uses bar shoes. Face it, kid, you're busted."

"You don't have any proof that I did anything." He crossed his arms.

Evan pulled out his phone and showed Ryan his number. "I recognize your voice from when you called me earlier today."

"C'mon, Evan." Bethany grabbed his arm and tugged. Confused by her sudden desire to leave when they were making headway, he dug in his feet.

"You were right about coming here without the sheriff," she said. "Let's go to town and talk to him."

"No!" John and Ryan Ogden yelled at the same time.

The father removed his hat and scratched the top of his balding head. "What if we agree to pay for everything that was damaged and for your father's medical bills?"

Bethany crossed her arms. "That doesn't help us with the loss of income."

Mr. Ogden sighed. "I'd like to keep the law out of this, if possible. Ryan can sell his car and give you the money to make up for what you lost, if that's agreeable to you."

"Da—ad! You can't be serious. I paid for this car myself."

John Ogden lifted his chin. "You paid for it working for me at a ridiculous salary. You will sell it to make restitution to these people, and if that doesn't cover what they've lost, we'll sell your horse. Now get in the house before I do something I'll regret."

Evan watched the young man skulk toward the house. Calling the sheriff may have been the legal thing to do, but putting the young man in jail with truly hardened criminals wouldn't help him any.

"If you'll be so kind as to make a list of all the damages, medical bills, and lost income, I'll have my accountant cut you a check, and I'll deliver it myself." Mr. Ogden paused and took a deep breath. "I hope you will seriously consider not prosecuting my son. His mother died in a car accident when Ryan was learning to drive. He blames himself for her death. Coming here was a way for us to start over."

Bethany studied the ground, and Evan wondered if she'd cut the poor man some slack now that she knew he wasn't involved. Would she give Ryan some measure of grace since she herself knew what it was like to lose a mother?

She looked up. "I apologize for blaming you for our troubles, Mr. Ogden. My father was just hurt today, and I'm worried about him, but that's no excuse for the way I spoke to you."

"Don't worry about it. You had just cause. I'm sorry that we had to meet under these circumstances."

"Me, too. I'll have to discuss this with my father and see whether he wants to press charges against Ryan or Maggie."

Mr. Ogden nodded, shook Bethany's then Evan's hand, and they parted.

Evan guided Bethany back toward the Jeep.

"What a relief to have that over." She rolled her head and glanced up at Evan. "Thank you for being here with me and helping me keep a lid on my anger."

Evan hugged her. "Anytime."

He opened her door then walked around the front of the Jeep. Bethany's mouth moved, and he thought she mumbled something about him staying forever. He shook his head. Probably just wishful thinking on his part.

Chapter 16

Bethany fluffed the pillow and placed it under her dad's injured arm. "Anything else I can get for you before I go?"

"No. I'll just sit here in my recliner and rest for a while. Maybe watch some television later."

She patted his shoulder. "Okay. I left the bottle of pain pills there by your glass of water in case you need them."

"Thanks. I'm glad to have that mystery cleared up and for things to get back to normal. I'll call our lawyer tomorrow and see what he recommends."

Bethany nodded, wishing they could forget the whole ordeal but knowing they couldn't.

Her dad lifted his arm and winced. "This confounded cast is going to make things mighty hard for me."

She leaned down and kissed his leathery cheek. "You deserve a good rest, Dad. You work too hard as it is."

"I work hard because there's so much to do." He ran his good hand through his hair. He didn't show emotion often, and the look on his face now made Bethany realize how much her father had aged since she'd first gone off to college.

"You just rest and get better. I'll take care of your chores, and what I can't do, I'm sure Shep will be happy to help with."

"But you're going back to Denver soon. How will I manage without you?"

She scooted around the recliner and sat on the edge of the sofa, hating that her normally tough father sounded like a lost little boy. "I called my boss yesterday and told him that I couldn't take the job because I'm needed here."

Hope glistened in her dad's eyes. "You're staying? For how long?"

"Indefinitely. My boss needed someone for the position and said he was sorry but he couldn't hold it open any longer. He's hiring somebody else."

A muscle ticked in his jaw, and he looked away. "I'm sorry. I know how much you wanted to leave here and live in Denver."

Turning to face the big picture window, she stared at the mountains. The ones she could see looked gray because of the cloudy sky that threatened rain. The curtains fluttered at the open window, and a chilly breeze cooled the room. "I guess I just needed to grow up, Dad. This place is my heritage, and I need to be here to help you run things. Don't take me wrong." She grinned. "I don't care if I never go on another wagon tour, but I want to be here. Guess you might say I've grown up."

His warm smile stole away any apprehension that she was making a mistake. Maybe she could get him to start going to church with her one day.

He leaned back and closed his eyes. "I can't tell you what a relief that is."

She placed her hand over his. "There's nothing more important in this world than God and family. It just took me awhile to realize that."

He grunted, but there was a hint of a smile on his lips. She stood, unfolded a light blanket, and laid it over him. "Get some rest, okay?"

He mumbled a thank-you.

Her hand was on the doorknob when he cleared his throat. "Have you got that computer all set up?"

"Yeah, it's up and running. Since you can't do much of your ranch work until you heal, you'll have more time to learn how to run it." She couldn't help grinning at his disinterested grunt.

"Let your young man know how much I appreciate his help, and if his family wants to come and take another tour, let them do it. No charge."

"He's not my young man, and I already made him that offer, but I don't think you have to worry about Evan taking us up on it."

"Why couldn't you fall in love with a cowpoke? And don't bother denying it; I was in love once. . . ."

As his last words slurred, her breath froze in her lungs. Was it obvious to her dad that she'd lost her heart to Evan when it wasn't even clear to her?

She watched him, waiting for him to say more, but his lips fluttered with a heavy breath as sleep descended. She closed the door and stood in the hallway looking out the window. The views from their private quarters on the third floor were majestic, and she never tired of seeing them, but today her thoughts were on a certain man.

Did she actually love Evan? *Do I, Lord?*

Something inside her quickened, and she knew the truth in that instant. A silly grin tugged her lips. She did love him!

She walked down the hall toward the stairs, amazed by the happiness she felt at that revelation. And if Evan loved her, they could work out their differences.

She had no clue how, but with God's help they could.

Feeling lighter than she had in years, Bethany wished she could slide down the banister like she had as a child. Instead, she trotted down two flights of stairs to the main floor of the lodge. She had to find Evan and talk with him—see if he felt anything for her.

No, she knew he did. It had been written on his handsome face and in his touch. He'd respected her choices enough that he hadn't forced his interest. And that made her love him more.

How was it that her love could be so strong now when an hour ago she wasn't even aware of it? She shook her head, marveling at the mystery of it all.

Evan was leaving in the morning. She couldn't let him go without him knowing how she felt.

She checked the porch and noticed his laptop sitting there by itself. How odd. As protective as he was of his computer, she'd never seen him go off and leave it.

She scanned the area, and her gaze zeroed in on Evan's back where he stood in the parking lot. Her heart flip-flopped. He opened the door of a blue car and helped a woman out. She fell into his arms, and he held on, hugging her head to his chest.

Warning bells screamed in Bethany's head. *No! Not now.*

The hug went on entirely too long for the woman to be unimportant to him. Bethany's hopes and dreams plummeted like a stone kicked off a cliff. Evan kissed the woman's cheek.

Bethany grabbed the door frame. The back door opened, and a boy who looked ten or eleven climbed out. Evan released the woman and high-fived the boy, then wrapped him in a hug. Bethany held a hand to her heart.

Her first thought was to flee, but she had more faith in Evan than that. Curiosity propelled her out the front door and down the steps. Evan glanced in her direction and smiled. He released the boy and walked toward her. "Come and meet my sister and nephew."

She resisted closing her eyes in relief as he took her hand and pulled her toward his sister. The woman had the same blue eyes, but her hair was darker than Evan's.

"Erin, this is Bethany Schaffer. She and her dad own the ranch here. I've been helping her with some computer problems she's been having."

Erin nodded, but her gaze dropped to Evan's and Bethany's linked hands. One eyebrow lifted. Evan must have noticed, because he cleared his throat and turned loose of her.

"Nice to meet you, Miss Schaffer. It is Miss, isn't it?"

There was more to that question than was asked. Bethany smiled. "Yes, and it's a pleasure to meet you, too."

Evan clapped his hand on the boy's shoulder. "And this is my favorite nephew, Jamie."

"I'm your only nephew." The boy gave Evan a playful shove, and they pretended to be boxing with each other.

Erin shook her head. "I can't take those two anywhere."

Jamie jabbed at Evan, who dodged him then charged. The boy took off running with Evan close on his heels, and Bethany smiled at their silliness. Erin looked toward the corral, and Bethany noticed how much Taylor looked like her.

A sudden thought zinged its way through her mind. If things went well between her and Evan, this woman might one day be her sister-in-law.

Erin turned back to face Bethany. "Is Taylor around? I can't wait to see her. We've never been separated this long before. I probably should have just waited until Evan brought her home instead of driving all the way out here, but Jamie wanted to see the ranch."

"I'm sure Taylor missed you, too. She and Cheryl went riding, but they should be back soon." Bethany watched Evan and Jamie walk toward the corral. "She sure was a big help to Evan when he was sick."

Erin smiled. "That's good to know. She's a sweet girl but has had a hard time since her dad left." She looked toward the corral. "I don't know what I would have done without Evan being there to help me the past two years. We'd have never made it without him."

Bethany's heart felt as if a giant fist was squeezing it. In the past few weeks, she'd learned the value of family—of being there when your family needed you. If Evan loved her as much as she did him, it would mean he'd have to leave Laramie—have to leave his sister. How could she ask that of him when they obviously still needed him?

As if a bullet had hit her torso, a deep pain burned her heart. She couldn't. She had tried to run away from family and responsibility and couldn't ask Evan to do the same. She had to let him go.

A heaviness weighed down her spirit. Her lower lip quivered at the thought of losing him. She swallowed back a growing tightness in her throat. "It was nice to meet you, Erin, but I need to go tend to some things. Taylor should be back before too long."

Erin smiled again and waved good-bye then headed toward Evan and Jamie, who were coming back from the corral. Bethany spun and jogged up the stairs and into the lodge. She hurried around the counter and into the office, shutting and locking the door. Tears dripped down her chin and blurred her vision as she slumped to the floor.

She allowed herself time to cry, to grieve for what could have been. As the tears finally subsided, she remembered something her mother had told her: God knew what she was going through. No matter how bad the situation, the Lord was standing there with open arms to comfort her.

"Help me, heavenly Father. I'm sorry for doing things on my own for so long without leaning on You. I don't want to do that anymore."

She sniffled and rubbed her eyes.

"I don't know why You brought Evan here and let me fall in love if we can't be together. Help this pain in my heart to heal, and show me how to love Evan as a Christian brother.

"Please, Lord. Help me."

❧

Bethany opened the bathroom door and peeked both ways down the hall. She dashed toward the front foyer and peered around the corner. With the way clear, she hurried over to the registration desk and checked to see if anyone had left a message.

The loud buzz of conversation and clinking silverware echoed from the open doors of the dining hall. The spicy scent of seasoned chicken teased her senses, and her stomach complained that she'd skipped lunch, but she wasn't about to chance an encounter with Evan. If she could just stay out of his way for another fifteen hours, he'd be gone.

She jogged out the front door and to the barn. Her heart ached as if someone had yanked it out, tossed it onto the ground, and stampeded a herd of cattle over it. Unwanted tears stung her eyes and made her throat burn.

In the barn, she snatched up a curry comb and slipped into a stall. The black and white pinto turned from its feedbox to see who was there. "Hey, Patches. It's just me. How about a nice grooming?"

Pushing thoughts of Evan from her mind, she concentrated on trying to remember the words to a song she'd sung in church as a child. The tune was easy enough, but the words kept seeping from her mind like water through a colander.

She ran the curry comb over the horse's sleek hide and tried to remember the song again, but when the sentence ended in "heaven," the word reminded her of Evan. Her lip quivered and tears blurred her eyes. She rested her head against the horse's warm side. "How do I stop caring for him, Lord?"

Patches whickered, as if answering. Bethany wiped her moist eyes on her sleeve and resumed brushing the mare.

"So, there you are."

Lost in thought, she jumped at the nearness of Evan's voice. *Drat.* She'd let her guard down, and he'd found her. She ducked under Patches' chin and put the horse between herself and the man she was trying hard to forget.

"What's the matter, Bethany?"

She heard him shuffling his feet but didn't look at him. "Nothing. With Dad injured, I've just got extra work, that's all."

"There's more to it than that, isn't there?"

When she didn't answer, he moved along the stall gate as if trying to see her better.

"Come out here and talk with me. *Please.*"

She shook her head. "Can't. Got too much to do." An arrow of guilt stabbed her, but it was the truth. Her workload had doubled since her dad's injury.

Evan blew out a loud sigh. "You're going to make me come in there with that horse, aren't you?"

She ran the brush down the horse's withers. "Nobody's making you do anything."

"Fine." The latch rattled and the gate creaked as Evan swung it open then shut again.

Bethany seriously considered shinnying over the stall to get away from him, but Patches wasn't familiar with Evan, and she didn't want him or the horse getting hurt. She heard him back along the gate, no doubt never taking his eyes off the horse's hind end until he got to the side of the stall.

"The only thing worse than the front end of a horse is the back end." He uttered a nervous chuckle. He took the brush from her hand, set it down, then spun Bethany around to face him. "What's going on?"

She pursed her lips and looked up. The concern in his azure eyes stole her breath away. She had to be tough, or she just might confess her love for him. "Nothing."

His gaze clouded, then he had the audacity to grin. "You're not jealous because I'm spending time with my sister, are you?"

"What? No! Of course not."

Evan's right eyebrow lifted.

She wanted to punch that cocky look off his face, but hurting a guest was against company policy. She scowled. "Why would I be jealous of your sister? I like Erin."

Patches swished her tail, and Evan dodged it. Bethany might have laughed if her heart hadn't been torn in two.

"Can't we talk out there?"

"There's nothing to talk about." She spun around, ready to flee, but he caught her upper arm. His touch sent quivers of fire shooting down to her fingertips. He turned her around to face him again.

"Bethany, I care about you. I want to know what's wrong." Evan cocked his head and studied her. He brushed a strand of hair from her cheek. "Tell me."

She shook her head. Evan sobered and took hold of her shoulders. Her mouth went dry at the intense look on his face.

"If you won't talk, then I have something I want to say. I can't leave without knowing where things stand between us. I don't want to just be friends. I want more."

She stared into his eyes, unable to catch her breath at the intensity in them.

He took her face in his hands; his palms warmed her ears and cheeks. "I may just be a geek from the city, but I love you, Bethany. If you feel the same, one way or another we can work things out between us, even if I have to move to Denver."

Hope washed through her. "I'm not going to Denver. I'm staying here. Dad needs me, and in a strange way, I think I need this place." She held her breath. Denver was one thing, but did her city boy love her enough to leave everything he knew and live on an isolated ranch? Would he leave his sister and her children to be here with her?

"But the big question is. . .do you need *me*?"

Without taking her eyes from his, she nodded. "I love you, too."

"Thank You, Lord!" He stared up at the ceiling as if God Himself were there. Finally, Evan sighed and looked back at her.

"But I can't ask you to leave Erin and the kids. They need you too much." Tears blurred her vision and slipped down her cheeks.

He dabbed at them with his thumbs. "I don't have all the answers, honey, but God does. We just need to ask Him to guide us. Can you trust Him with our future?"

Could she? Hadn't she just done that very thing a short while ago when she thought she'd lost Evan? Bethany nodded.

Evan pulled her close and leaned down, his soft lips touching hers. All her worries disappeared in that moment, and she returned his kiss.

Patches shifted and bumped into Bethany. Evan fell back against the wall of the stall, hugging her against him. He chuckled. "Can we please leave this horse pen now?"

Bethany rested her hand against his cheek. "It's called a stall, greenhorn, and you'd better get used to it."

Epilogue

Y**ou may now kiss your bride."**
        The pastor's word *bride* spun in Evan's head. *My bride. My wife.*
        Bethany waited, her deep brown eyes alight with love—for him. He wasn't about to disappoint her. Evan ducked his head and kissed his bride with all the promise of a lifetime of love to come.

The small group of friends and family gathered in the little church cheered and clapped.

"I'm pleased to introduce Mr. and Mrs. Evan Michael Parker."

Bethany held his arm, her whole face gleaming. Her father sat on the front row next to Elsie and Margaret, wiping his eyes with a hanky. Erin and the kids sat on the opposite row. Eager to have his wife alone for a moment, Evan led her down the short aisle toward the foyer at the front of the church. Behind him the pastor invited the guests to the reception at the ranch.

"Look, it's still snowing. I hope we don't get snowed in before we can leave on our honeymoon." Bethany stared outside then turned her concerned gaze on him.

"No worries today. It's our wedding day, and I'd like another kiss, Mrs. Parker. Quickly, before everyone else gets out here."

She cocked her head, looking so beautiful in her lacy white dress. "Oh, you would, huh?"

Still smiling, he claimed her lips until a woman behind him cleared her throat.

The Groovy Grannies stood side by side, both dressed in pink. Elsie stood on her tiptoes and patted his face. "I liked you from the moment we met."

"Same here." Evan kissed her cheek.

Margaret crossed her arms. "I still don't understand why you don't want to use our RV for your honeymoon. It has all the amenities you could want."

Evan resisted shuddering visibly at the thought of going anywhere in that bright pink monstrosity, but Bethany must have felt him tremble. She pinched the inside of his arm. "That's very kind of you, but we have other plans."

Elsie grinned. "I bet you're taking that bride of yours on a wagon train trip."

Everyone laughed at the horror that transformed Bethany's face. "Not in this lifetime. We're heading someplace warm, and that's all I'm saying."

Erin and the kids crowded in beside them. She leaned toward Bethany. "Welcome to the family."

"Thank you. I'm so glad to finally have a sister." The two women hugged.

"Does that mean I can call you 'Aunt Bethany' now?" Taylor asked.

Bethany smiled. "I guess it does."

"Sweet!"

"When do we get cake?" Jamie shifted from foot to foot, looking uncomfortable in his suit. Erin cut him a look, and he glanced down.

Evan hugged his nephew. "Soon, pardner."

The ranch hands muttered their congratulations and filed out to their pickups. Polly fluttered by, waving at them and dragging Cheryl with her. "I'll hug you at the ranch, but right now I've got to get back and keep those cowpokes out of the cake."

Evan wrapped his arm around Bethany, not willing to let her get too far away. Soon he'd have her all to himself, but for now he had to share her.

"Evan, I saw a commercial on television advertising that video game you designed. You must be proud of your work."

Margaret smiled. "Isn't it exciting how God arranged things so you'd have a job that could be done anywhere?"

"Yeah, it is. I have to admit, I didn't see how things would work out, and I never imagined they'd hire me full-time, but God was always in control. I just wish Erin and the kids weren't going to be so far away." Evan hated leaving her alone, but God had made it clear that he was to move to the ranch.

Erin's bright smile made him wonder if she was keeping a secret.

Rob Schaffer handed the pastor an envelope and shook the man's hand. "Great wedding, Reverend. I hope you'll join us at the ranch for the reception."

The pastor nodded and smiled to someone waiting to talk with him. Evan's father-in-law joined the group. He smiled down at Bethany and then at Evan. "Mr. Ogden sent over a nice wedding present for you two."

"Really?" Bethany asked. "What is it?"

"Let's just say it's in the barn, and you'll probably get more enjoyment from it than your husband will."

Chuckles surrounded Evan, and he grinned.

"Whatever happened with that Ogden boy? I never got a chance to ask you." Margaret stared at Rob, who looked at Evan.

"Go on, son, you tell her."

"The judge gave Ryan and Maggie two hundred hours each of community service and sent them to a counselor. They've been helping out at the ranch every other Saturday to make restitution, and I've kind of taken Ryan under my wing, since he's a big computer fan."

Elsie clapped her hands. "That's wonderful."

"I have a surprise for you, too." Bethany's dad smiled and glanced at Erin. "Actually, *we* have a surprise. You want to tell him?"

Erin's eyes glimmered. "Mr. Schaffer offered me a job. I'm going to take Polly's place as the ranch cook. We're moving to the ranch, too!"

Evan's heart nearly burst, and he couldn't help letting out a whoop at the same time Taylor squealed and Jamie let out a "Woot!"

"That's the best news I've heard since Bethany agreed to marry me."

Suddenly Taylor sobered. "But what about the Wilkes family? They aren't leaving, are they?"

Evan knew what a blow it would be for Taylor to lose Cheryl as a friend. Without the girl's companionship, Taylor might not be so excited about moving.

Bethany grinned up at him. "Polly is pregnant. She's going to be helping with some of the new projects we're taking on and working the front desk."

"Now I don't have to mess with that crazy computer." Rob shook his head, and the group laughed.

Jingle bells sounded outside, and everyone turned their heads. The women gasped in unison as two white horses drawing a white sleigh decorated with red bows stopped outside the church.

Evan bowed at Bethany. "Your carriage awaits, milady."

Her wide smile was worth all the effort he'd gone to.

"I love it, but you can't seriously think we can ride all the way back to the ranch in that. It's freezing outside."

"How about just through town?"

Smiling, she grabbed his arm and pulled him toward the coat closet. He helped her into the long, hooded cloak Bethany had borrowed then slipped on his jacket. He was in for a big change, moving from the city to the country and getting married to the only girl he'd ever loved, but he was up for the challenge.

At the door, Evan picked up his bride and carried her to the sleigh, glad that the heavy snowfall had turned to light flurries. The sleigh's driver tipped his hat to them. Evan tucked his wife under a blanket. "Don't go anywhere."

He hugged his sister and shook his father-in-law's hand. "My SUV is parked where we agreed?"

Rob nodded and handed Evan his car keys. "See you two back at the ranch."

Jamie wadded up a snowball and tossed it at Evan. He jumped backward, right into one of the horses. The animal quivered and turned its head around, nipping at Evan. He dodged the big yellow teeth and leaped clear. His family hooted with laughter.

"C'mon, city boy. We have a reception to attend. Cake to cut. Presents to open."

Evan pressed his lips together. He was anxious to begin his life on the ranch with Bethany, but he'd be just as happy if he never saw another horse.

He climbed in beside his wife and scooted close against her, covering them both with the lap blanket.

Bethany was still giggling and shaking her head. "Whatever am I going to do with you?"

He grinned. "Kiss me, I guess."

VICKIE McDONOUGH is an award-winning author of 20 books and novellas. Vickie's books have won the Inspirational Reader's Choice Contest and the ACFW Noble Theme contest, and she has been a multi-year finalist in ACFW's BOTY/Carol Award contest. She was voted Third Favorite Author in the Heartsong Presents Annual Readers Contest in 2009. Vickie's books promise An Adventure into Romance. To learn more about Vickie's books, visit her Web site: www.vickiemcdonough.com

A Letter to Our Readers

Dear Readers:

In order that we might better contribute to your reading enjoyment, we would appreciate you taking a few minutes to respond to the following questions. When completed, please return to the following: Fiction Editor, Barbour Publishing, Inc., P.O. Box 719, Uhrichsville, OH 44683.

1. Did you enjoy reading *Wyoming Weddings* by Diane Lesire Brandmeyer, Susan Page Davis, and Vickie McDonough?
   - ❑ Very much. I would like to see more books like this.
   - ❑ Moderately—I would have enjoyed it more if _____
   _____
   _____

2. What influenced your decision to purchase this book?
   (Check those that apply.)
   - ❑ Cover ❑ Back cover copy ❑ Title ❑ Price
   - ❑ Friends ❑ Publicity ❑ Other

3. Which story was your favorite?
   - ❑ *Trail to Justice* ❑ *A Wagonload of Trouble*
   - ❑ *Hearts on the Road*

4. Please check your age range:
   - ❑ Under 18 ❑ 18–24 ❑ 25–34
   - ❑ 35–45 ❑ 46–55 ❑ Over 55

5. How many hours per week do you read? _____

Name _____

Occupation _____

Address _____

City_____ State_____ Zip_____

E-mail _____